The Time
of the
Ghosts

Gillian Polack

THE TIME OF THE GHOSTS

Published by Book View Café 2018
P.O. Box 1624
Cedar Crest, NM 87008-1624
www.bookviewcafe.com

ISBN: 978-1-61138-720-9

First published in Australia in 2015 by Satalyte Publishing

Cover design by Maya Kaathryn Bohnhoff
Cover photograph: Gillian Polack
Interior design by Marissa Doyle

This is a work of fiction. All of the characters, organizations, and events portrayed in this novel are either products of the author's imagination or are used fictitiously.

To Karen Herkes, who makes the world

a much better place.

Someone has to write this down.

Someone who has seen it all.

Seen the ghosts.

Eaten the food.

Even washed the dishes.

Prologue

Tales of Melusine #253

What does one do in Kiev in the year 1643? One yearns.

Melusine had just passed the minor trauma that is Day of Atonement. She had faced up to her Jewish soul.

Do fairies have souls? That was a minor part of the miseries of the day. Of the miseries of each and every year on that same day. Missing food and drink was another. Apologising and atonement were a third. The biggest of all was appearing publicly as Jewish and having everyone around her exclaim, "But you don't look Jewish." Three hundred years earlier she had looked Jewish, but in this place and at this time her features were slightly wrong or her eyes were too warm or her hair not sufficiently Ashkenaz.

After she faced up to her Jewish soul (whether she looked as if she had one or not) she fell into a deep depression. Every year it happened. She felt the cleansing joy of the ram's horn, ate dinner, and promptly yearned.

This year, she decided, she would rejoice instead of yearn. She never admitted to anyone how she achieved it, but within three hours of admitting that she was alone and miserable, she had picked up a good Jewish boy who was likewise alone and miserable. They shared a bed for three years, which was about the time it took for Melusine to rid herself of that deep loneliness and start yearning for solitude again.

She gifted her lover with a modicum of sight. He used this later (never knowing it was her gift, or ever realising that his erstwhile lover was anything other than human) to remove his family to Paris, just before the Cossacks, the non-Jewish Tatars, and the non-Jewish peasants decided that Jews were vermin.

Melusine discovered this exactly a century later, in another synagogue in Kiev on the Day of Atonement in 1743. She was seated next to someone who was visiting the city in search of family. She was obscurely relieved to know that her lover had survived. She was even more relieved to know that there were no adult sons present so that she could not be tempted again. It was a good-looking line, even after a hundred years. She broke her fast with the young family and added to the gift.

Her yearning was different in 1743. She missed safety and happiness.

This was when Melusine realised she must search for these things. Finding peace and safety would take her a long, long time. She still hasn't found happiness.

One

GAREMA PLACE AT LUNCHTIME has a frantic air. Random groups of public servants pushing for food and a bit of sunshine. As if Canberra never has sun. As if the day is short. Communal benches having to be shared with strangers. Strips of wall crowded with smokers and with public servants eating their sandwiches. Not a comfortable place to start a story. Kiev in 1643 was more comfortable.

Ann discovered Kat on a park bench in Garema Place. Ann contemplated behind the shelter of a book — as she did every work lunchtime (hiding from her fellow masses) — how she would handle retirement. She saw vistas of nothingness in her future and was under-impressed by them.

Ann had her friends, but the two who mattered most only visited when invited. Close friends needed formalities, Lil explained in her soft voice, when Ann had suggested they drop in on each other from time to time. Mabel didn't care. Mabel was old-fashioned and fed whoever turned up whenever they turned up. Ann wanted satellite grandchildren as Mabel had them. She wanted Mabel's home and garden. She would never have told Mabel this, so she accepted Lil's dictum. She became used to the formality.

It wasn't like her to strike up conversations with strange teenagers with enormous eyes whose arms hugged their thin bodies in protection, but somehow she did. Or Kat spoke to her. They talked comfortably about the book Ann carried, which changed from day to day. It took a week of talking before Ann realised that Kat was willing to talk about books because Kat was living on the streets and was starved for reading.

Ann had never met a teenager like Kat. Compact and self-contained.

Passionate beyond belief. Willing to do anything for other people. Not a scrap of an idea of how to take care of herself. Sharp as a razor. Emotionally whipped red raw. Full of contradictions.

Once Ann knew Kat was homeless, Kat found herself under the care of Lil and Mabel and Ann. Of the three, Ann was the baby.

None of them knew how they would give Kat the new start she had to have. None of them knew how a child so bright came to dead-end streets, but they refused to hand her over to authorities until the authorities asked. It was Lil who said it: "What that child needs is to take care of others, not to be taken care of and made subject to a system."

Mabel-the-independent couldn't see anyone who needed help. Ann said, "It occurred to me that there's us," but that was mostly trying to make sure Kat was okay.

It was Lil who had the final word. "Yes, there's us. She can aid us with our elderly lives."

Mabel snorted. "Speak for yourself. And Ann's not even elderly."

"To Kat I'm old. And she doesn't know that you are seventy-five with the body of a thirty-year-old gardening maniac," said Ann.

"And if Kat has family?"

"She will have family," said Ann. "Let's give her shelter, and she can sort herself out."

"You have faith in human beings, then," said Lil.

"Yes, I guess I do," said Ann, surprised.

"I'll be party to it, but I'm not talking her into it. The advantage of being twenty-five years past menopause is that I don't have to handle hormones anymore. You get the blast furnace, Ann."

Mabel's life needs shaking up, thought Ann. She had too many definite beliefs. At least she would come to the party. And what a party it would be. Ann wanted to see Kat undermine the quiet certainties of her friends' lives. Retirement no longer looked so dull.

In January Kat found herself installed in Lil's granny flat, trading accommodation and utilities for housework. There were still the problems of food and spending money. All three older women had an unnatural desire to see Kat have money for clothes.

"Not those horrid black depressing things," sniffed Mabel.

"If she wants to wear black, she can," said Ann. "Give her space."

"And how to we get that money to her? And how do we progress from there?"

"We can do both together." Mabel lost her brick-wall attitude. "Let's teach her what we know. We want to make her think she's helping us, after all."

"You might not require help, but I do," said Ann.

"We know, dear," Lil managed not to sound patronising. Maybe it was the soft accent. "And we know it's not the retirement."

Two days later, Mabel was disapproving again. "She won't go back to school. She won't ring her mother."

"And she hates you for asking," said Ann. "We know. Thank you for playing bad cop." Ann's heart was still breaking for Kat's hurt, maybe because it couldn't break for her own. She found it impossible to disapprove of anything Kat did. "She's only fifteen. There's time for her to find a path to learning."

"Besides," said Lil, "things are going on. We need someone young to learn from us."

"How to cook," said Mabel.

"Yes, that too."

"It's a good place to start, anyhow." Ann's brain moved from sentiment to organisation. "Remember the eighties?"

"I'd rather forget," said Mabel. "Shoulder pads," she reminded the others. "Power dressing."

"I mean, remember when we three had dinner parties every month. Themed."

"We were show-offs back then." Mabel sounded wistful.

"Let's do it again. One a month. Take it in turns."

"And how would Kat be involved?"

"Cold hard cash," said Lil. "She can serve and wash up and join us for coffee afterwards."

"And if certain matters arise during the month," Ann started to say.

"As they will," interrupted Mabel.

"As they inevitably must," said Lil.

"We talk about them where she can hear."

"We make her belong," said Ann.

"We scare her shitless," said Lil. Ann and Mabel looked across, surprised at the language. "If the word fits, use it."

5

Lil was tiny and delicate and had the whitest hair. She was also a cook. Kat looked at the kitchen and looked at the food and looked at the carefully-written instructions and wondered how anyone could think like that. Organised beyond belief.

The food was almost ready and all Kat had to do was the finishing touches and the serving and the washing up and the overhearing of gossip. A hatch next to the dining room made the last possible. Kat carefully rearranged the bench, so that she could hear without being seen.

There was something strange about her old ladies. *I will defend them to the death*, she thought, *because they are uber-cool and besides they're my old ladies, especially Ann. But I want to know what's up.*

Immediately, what was up was food. The first dish was a finished and prettified dish of cold beans. Lil had explained that the beans were in beef broth with onions and balsamic vinegar and garlic.

"Yum?" said Kat, dubiously. Lil had laughed and fed her a spoonful and it was fabulous.

"I learned this when I left home," Lil explained. "It goes well with chickpeas." And Kat tasted a spoon of the chickpea dish, made with honey and coriander. "Spanish flavours," said Lil. "Old Spanish flavours."

"Are you Spanish, then?"

"No, I was born in France."

"You don't sound French."

"I don't sound Parisian," Lil corrected. "I sound perfectly French. I'm from Aquitaine."

That meant nothing to Kat, but she nodded sagely.

She pawed a shred of chicken from the dish while Lil was carving and Lil nearly sliced a sliver off her slim finger. "Yummo," she said, to avoid a scold.

"Green stuffed roast chicken. Keep it in the warming oven until it's ready to serve." Lil covered it with aluminium foil and showed Kat the warming oven. She also showed her how to make French style coffee and Middle Eastern style coffee.

"Why do you put dried orange peel in it?" Kat asked.

"I was taught it that way. Also with spices. Modern Greeks and Turks use cardamom."

"I think I've tasted that," Kat admitted.

"You are cosmopolitan, then," Lil approved, her faint accent making each word clear and bell-like.

From there Kat was on her own in the kitchen, trying to recall all she had been shown, and to do it as if she had always been able to cook coffee on a stove, four times on and four times off the heat, and had always been able to time service and work out when the nougat-ish things got served.

She discovered all the things Lil hadn't explained and got them mostly right. And all the time her new grandmothers were sitting at the dinner table, chatting away about children and work and gardens and why the sales were so bad this year.

When the coffee was finally sitting in front of the drinkers (Lil sipping a tiny, elegant dark pool of coffee, rich with grounds and orange peel; Mabel hugging a teacup filled with espresso; Ann drinking plunged decaf with soy), everyone relaxed. Kat sat on a kitchen stool, carefully tasting the spiced drink from her own tiny cup and trying not to be surprised.

The three ladies were talking about ghosts. Not in whispery voices aimed at sending shivers down a spine, but in the practical common-sense terms one would use to agree on a shopping list.

Kat disapproved. It took the magic from the world. She switched off half her hearing on purpose, the way she had for the last year at home when she was trying to not hear the baby. Instead of practical and solid occurrences, she gleaned stray information. Her spine shivered, delectably. Misty figures wandering. Whispering shadows. Things seen, glimpsed through gaps in the veil that separates life from death. It was all good.

Kat stored it up. She was going to ask Ann for more information. Ann always told everything to everyone. She'd sounded the most excited about ghosts, too. Wouldn't strip the joy away. Kat wished Ann were her grandmother. All young and caring and open and friendly and willing to listen. She was perfect. Ghosts were perfect, too. The perfect conversation was Ann talking about ghosts. It would happen soon.

The conversation that stuck in her mind was quite different. It was of some small importance, because later on Kat would remember it as the first time she gave cheek to all her grandmothers at once.

The subject of the Inquisition came up during coffee. Kat was rather pleased she knew what it was.

"There are better topics for after dinner," Mabel sniffed, as only Mabel could.

"Yes, but are there any as juicy?"

"How, juicy?" This was Lil, looking unimpressed.

Kat shifted so she could see everyone. This looked as if it was going to be good: Mabel bored, Lil unenthused, and Ann on a rampage. Until now, everyone had been so very polite.

"Torture and evil and chasing of witches."

"Ann, my dear, do you think they could compete with old age?"

"Don't be stupid," Ann was determined to get a discussion going. "What's old age compared with torture and evil monks?"

"I should be scared of men who hate sex?" Mabel almost shifted from being bored. Not quite, but she was on the verge of engaging.

Then Lil finished the topic for good. "I have met angry monks. Menopause is worse."

"Mine wasn't," said Ann.

"My, weren't you the lucky one," said Mabel.

"But what about magic?"

"We were not talking about magic," Lil pointed out, "but about the Inquisition. The Inquisition would not recognise non-Church magic if it was bitten in the . . ."

Ann interjected, "Child present!"

"Where?" asked Kat, helpfully, and started clearing the table.

And that was Kat's first dinner party. It was more consequential than it appeared.

Two

THINGS YOU NEED TO know about my grandmothers: I should number these, so I know where they come from and where they fit. Melusine numbered her stories, and I'm copying her, therefore . . . I won't. I'm being a stubborn twenty-something. Besides, Melusine's numbering made no sense at all. And her stories always included little lies. Sometimes they included bigger lies. Sometimes they included truths that looked like lies. If I number my notes about my grandmothers then you'll know they're lies. Which they aren't. They just look like they are. Only one of Melusine's types of lies counts in my world.

Mabel told me once that the only person Ann ever lies to is herself. She'll jostle everyone else into activity and stir up their lives, but stirring lives isn't really lying, it's just pretend-lying. Call that factoid #1, except without a number. (As I write this, all those years are peeling back and my fundamental Katness is emerging like fine bones as the skin loses childish chub.)

Factoid the one after 1 (but even more without a number — laugh, dammit!) is that I still remember bits of the conversation from that first dinner party. Maybe the grandmothers sat down on purpose to let me know all sorts of things. That stinks of manipulation, though, and my grand-mothers were not that manipulative. Loving and caring and butting in all over the place (but in a good way), yes, but not manipulative.

They were convinced they were manipulative. I still pretend to believe they are sometimes, when they look fragile.

Ann was trying to loom. She casually let slip over the green chicken that she had a teensy-weensy bit of Roswell in her background. She did it so casually that Kat was impressed. Kat, unfortunately, couldn't see the looks Mabel and Lil cast at their friend. Mabel rolled her eyes when Ann said, "I was abducted. It may have been by aliens, but I prefer to think of them as fair folk."

She lost a week on a holiday as a child and had seen things ever since. That was why she squinted her left eye from time to time. One eye had much stronger sight than the other.

"I can see spirits and otherworldly things more than ghosts, though," she remarked cheerfully, still intent on communicating the normalcy of this sort of thing, to appear impressive.

"Your time away, do you have any memory of it?" Lil asked.

"Not a scrap. Mum made me get hypnotised to see if I was suppressing something important, but there wasn't a thing."

"And then you started realising that you were seeing things." Mabel was encouraging, despite the eye-rolling. "You saw shadows at first? Or fairy creatures?"

"I played with something for two years. When I went to high school we got mad at each other and I haven't seen it since."

"Where was this?" Lil's voice sharpened with curiosity. Her eyes would have betrayed to Kat that she had heard most of the story before, but not that bit. Lil was intensely curious in an all-new way.

"We were in England for a work-exchange programme."

"So you lost your little friend when you returned to Australia." The room echoed with the bursting of Ann's little balloon.

"Well, yes," she said. "But we argued first. It didn't all happen at once."

"I see," said Lil, with a faint tone of disappointment. Just a trace.

Mabel quickly spoke into the tension. "I've heard you talk about your shadow," she prompted.

"Not often," said Ann. "I think it was stolen when I was missing." Kat didn't believe this one at all, but she was still child enough to cross her fingers to remind herself she had to watch out for Ann's shadow.

"So if you and your shadow were strolling down the avenue," said Lil, "it would be hand-in-hand, old pals reunited." Everyone laughed. Old friends cosy.

❈ ◆ ❈

I must make a note about Ann's shadow. Not now, though. Now I'm dreaming of King Arthur. There was a knight's tale in Melusine's stories. Let me put it in here, for both of us. I know it's a lot of Melusine stories all at once, up here on my blog, but I'm bored to tears at work, and they're good stories. For some rather odd values of 'good.'

Tales of Melusine #2

Once upon a time, the fairy Melusine flew far, far north to visit the forest of Broceliande. She had heard that it contained her kinfolk. The news came from human tales, however, and human tales are unreliable: she wanted to find out for herself.

Her meeting with distant kin is another story and one that she refuses to tell. There is bigotry in the world of the fae, and Melusine was glad to move away from the enclosed Vale of No Return to the part of the forest that was inhabited by humans. It was kinder and far, far less wet.

Not too distant (by modern standards) from the place that became Rennes, Melusine met up with a boy-child.

He didn't know he was a boy-child: he thought he was a wolf-child. He watched her from behind a big oak tree. He was very cautious and shy, this four-legged boy who was human inside. He watched Melusine from behind an oak at first, but one thing Melusine was learning was that she had a great deal of time to dispose of, so she waited. She tempted the boy with raw meat at first, and he would dash in, snatch it, then return to his safe oak.

Gradually she persuaded him into eating meat that was heated gently, then to eat sirloin that had been seared lightly. Finally, she carefully placed a cloth on the grass. On the cloth she placed a silver plate. On the plate she placed sliced lamb, well cooked. Next to the plate on the right was a bowl with a fine cameline sauce. In front of the plate she placed a second bowl, filled with scented water. Below the plate she placed a small cloth and a sharp knife.

The child that looked like a wolf came out from behind his oak. He sniffed at the bowl of scented water. He sniffed at the cameline sauce. He sniffed at the fine roast of lamb. The wolf dipped his eating hand in the bowl of water, and looked down at it quizzically. He looked up at Melusine. All of him was still wolf, except for that one hand.

He gave a whuff and settled in front of his meal. His other hand reached for the small cloth. When he put the cloth on his neck, it fell, for he had no way to hold it. He tried again and his torso and lower body were human and clothed in garments that were too tight. He ignored them and tucked the napkin into his old, tight clothes. He reached for the knife, cut off a proper portion of meat, dipped it in the sauce, and ate it. As the meat touched his lips, he was fully human.

"My name is Raoul," he announced. "Who are you?"

Melusine avoided answering. "How did this happen to you?" Melusine asked, gently, once the child had finished and thanked her with a grave courtesy. "You are obviously well-bred."

The child shrugged, and the shrug had the feel of the wolf-huff. "Someone took me away when I was playing. They changed me to make me run faster. I ran so very fast that I lost them."

"And you didn't know how to change back? Did you like wearing wolf skin?"

The child nodded. "But I don't want to wear it forever. I want to go home."

"I shall take you there," Melusine promised. "But first I shall give you a gift. Look behind you." Behind him lay the skin that he had worn as a wolf. "Carry it with you. Hide it somewhere secret. When you wish to run on four legs, you can. When you wish to be a man again, you may. Keep your secret well."

"I shall," said the boy, his face flushed with the seriousness of the moment. "I promise."

Melusine nodded. "Then let's find your home," she said. "Let's find your parents."

Many years later she visited him again. She never developed a taste for the society of the White Ladies of the north, but she had developed a friendship for the child who had worn wolf skin. She was young and heedless, and cared not who knew of her differences. She would fly back and forth between the south and the north, once a year, once every two years, bringing gifts. The child grew strong in courtesy. He was careful to keep relations between the two of them respectful by selecting his gifts to her with great care — they never came to more than a pair of elegant gloves or a charming ring.

And thus the two were poised between the ordinary and the extraordinary for a decade or more.

The child became a man and the man married. His wife would have none of the otherworldly. Melusine visited less frequently and every time she pretended to have arrived on foot. All seemed well, except that the wife disliked the strange southern visitor. It became uncomfortable for everyone. Melusine reluctantly told her man-child that she must cease her visits.

Their connection was such, however, that she knew when his last illness would overtake him. One last time she visited. She did not tell him that he was ill, but she noticed the way his minstrel Raimbert watched and noted.

The night before she left for the last time, her man-child called both her and Raimbert to wait upon him in his chamber. There he told them the truth of his second marriage.

"I trusted my first wife the way I trust you," and he turned his long, old face to Melusine's. Melusine could still see the boy behind the beard and the lines and the failing health, and she mourned for the lack of length to a human life and for the loss of a friend. She didn't tell him of her grieving, but nodded, courteously.

"I loved her so much and I trusted her so very much that I told her of my wolf skin. Only the two of you know of it now. You, Raimbert, because I told you last week; you, my lady, because you gave it to me and saved me from running in wolf skin forever."

Raimbert's eyes open wide with shock as he looked across at Melusine. She could see that he re-evaluated her youth and re-examined her for taint of the supernatural. After a moment, the assessment turned into a leer. Oh, how she hated the changes that the men of the church were causing to the way women walked and the way women breathed. She hated even more the way the great men claimed her kin as their ancestors, leaving a tempting trail of power for anyone who seduced or raped the women of her kind.

"I can't tell stories properly, so I'll keep the rest of this very short."

"My wife stole the tokens you gave me, my lady, the ones that enable me to return to human form. She stole first the plate and then the bowl and then the cloths and finally the knife. I was a wolf in the forest and my wife's lover took my place as lord of this castle."

He spat, to get the taste of her out of his mouth.

"The duke restored me to my own body, and since then I have not used the wolf skin even once. Right until the day of his death he tried to persuade me that I should go hunting with him, me in my wolf skin and him on his horse."

"But you didn't," said Melusine, very softly.

Raoul shook his head. "I did ask him to execute my wife. Which he did. Then I married again and begat an heir and lived my life as a human."

"May I make this into a story?" Raimbert was still watching Melusine, but he directed his question at his lord. "Maybe a lai? It would make a very good lai." His patron agreed, with a faint tilt of the head.

"Change it," urged Melusine. "You should never tell the complete truth in a story."

She noticed that Raoul's wife had slipped into the room while no-one was watching. She determined then and there not to return to the forest for three generations. Raoul would be gone, anyway: there was nothing for her to return for. Nothing and no-one.

The storyteller nodded. "It demonstrates the art better to improve on the literal truth."

"I wasn't thinking that at all," she said, quietly. "I was thinking that changes make the world a safer place. Stories that mimic reality too much are capable of changing it."

"What do you mean?" asked Jeanne, Raoul's pretty and sober wife.

"Some of us carry ghosts around," Melusine waved her arms as she sought to find words. "If we tell about them too directly, they can manifest. And here, in this forest, by telling a story too precisely you can call up that which you describe. This forest is a place that carries those impressions and turns them into reality. Some places are like that. Sometimes this is very good, and sometimes it is bad."

"How can it be good?" Jeanne had been well trained in forest fears when she married Raoul.

"My love, it was telling the story of Melusine that saved me from the forest that first time," her husband said. "She was a very long way away and she heard me telling about her and she flew to my rescue." Maybe, Melusine thought, the story would reshape itself and truth wouldn't enter into it at all.

"Oh!" and Jeanne's hand flew to her mouth. She looked across at Melusine with sudden fear.

Melusine revised her estimate. Four generations, or maybe five. "I am a friend here, first and foremost. There is no enchantment binding me and no danger that should concern you." Melusine was at her gentlest. "You are not like Raoul's first wife, after all."

"But you are . . . not human," said the poet.

Melusine smiled at that, and Raoul chuckled. Jeanne's hands were nervous and Raimbert's eyes were still trying to send her entirely the wrong messages.

When Melusine next visited, a glorious castle lay where the hall had stood and the favourite story told was of the Knight Bisclavret, whose evil wife had nearly forced him to remain a wolf forever. Melusine wondered ruefully as she wandered through the beech and oak trees what the story would have said if she had slept with Raimbert. That she was beautiful beyond belief, perhaps, and had hair of gold and skin the colour of new milk. That she was an ancestress to the great lords, definitely.

She would rather, she thought, remain Melusine, with dark hair and olive skin and no children at all.

"I'm out back!" Mabel called, and Kat tried to reach her. One side of the house was blocked off by a big dump of firewood, so she tried the other. She found Mabel (eventually) past the row of citrus, weeding the raised bed that formed a hexagon around the persimmon.

Mabel didn't waste time on greetings. "Give me a hand," she said.

"What if I pull plants up by mistake?" Mabel gave her an impromptu lesson in which plants were supposed to be in that bed and the two spent a happy hour silently working their way round the big tree.

When they had finished, Mabel said, "Now you're on the way to becoming domesticated." Kat snorted and then caught herself with embarrassment. Ladies did not snort, her mother would have said. Mabel didn't seem to notice. Or if she noticed, she didn't care a fig.

"Do you have a fig tree?" Kat asked.

"Just a little one, over there," Mabel waved her arm wildly. "Why?"

"Just curious."

"Do you know how to make scones?" Mabel asked.

"Why?"

"Just curious."

"I don't," said Kat. Emboldened by the lack of formality she became brave. "Will you teach me?"

"Only if you help me eat them."

"I bet you say that to all the little children."

Mabel laughed, deeply and satisfyingly. "You haven't been a little child for years, though, have you?" Kat heard no accusation in the comment, only acceptance. "Come inside and we'll wash up."

The scones were satisfyingly messy to make and satisfyingly afternoon tea-ish to eat. Over them, however, with a pot of tea between them that was so strong a teaspoon could stand in it (or so Mabel claimed), Kat's hostess suddenly turned confiding.

"You know," Kat said, sheltered behind a huge pale green teacup full of the brownest tea Kat had ever held, "I don't know what I believe."

"I'm sorry?"

"I believe a bit in what Lil does. Maybe half believe, mostly. Not sure. It's not quite real, somehow. And I only half believe in what Ann says, ever." Kat stated her half belief with great certainty.

"Half is enough, when it's friends."

Kat found this reassuring, and nodded, then she had an afterthought. "But don't you see stuff? Don't you *do* stuff?"

"Probably. I don't believe it afterwards. Not if I want to stay sane." Mabel said this lightly, almost inconsequentially.

"I want to believe."

"I know. You're better off making scones. Ann squinting at the world is going to get her into trouble."

"Magic trouble," breathed Kat.

"No," Mabel's voice was as flat as the contradiction. "Every bloody day trouble. Watch her."

Kat didn't know whether to feel flattered or pleased that Mabel was telling such things. She'd crossed worlds. A few weeks she had been on the streets and now, now an old lady was talking to her as if she . . . belonged. It was strange. *I'll go with it,* Kat decided. *See what happens.*

"Why don't you tell her?"

Mabel snorted, inelegantly. "I have. She doesn't believe me. Belief is like that, you know. I half believe her: she believes what I say half the time."

"And you're still friends?"

"We are. We aren't as close as we used to be. She thinks you'll cement our friendship, bring the three of us closer again."

"Oh." Kat's face suggested she wasn't thrilled with this idea.

"Don't let it worry you. Decide who you like and why. Let us have our ways."

"And you don't mind if I believe in magic?"

"God, you can believe in voodoo if you like. Just remember that it's not straightforward."

"It's safe?"

"God, no."

"Then why are you letting me in at all, if you only half believe and it's not safe?"

"Because if it exists at all, then a bunch of old ladies need to pass on that knowledge. There are things that ought to be shared, and you're young enough to learn to hear. You're young enough to learn to see. And you're old enough to have a bit of common sense. Not too young: not too old. Make up your own mind."

"Ann isn't so old."

"Ann has her squinty eye, but she doesn't understand a thing. And if you repeat that to her, I won't teach you any more recipes. You don't want to die without learning how to make sponge cake my special way."

"I won't tell her."

"Don't trust me, either."

"Don't trust you. Don't trust Ann. Who can I trust? Lil?"

"If you can work out where she's coming from, yes," was Mabel's surprising answer. Kat had been fully expecting her to say 'Don't trust anyone.'

"You won't tell me?"

"Cripes, I don't know. I trust her, and she's one of my closest friends, but she's got more secrets than my garden has worms. And — as you have seen — my garden is very healthy and has many, many worms. If you dig up a small patch, they will squirm and you will scream."

"You're hinting we should go back outside?"

"There's still sunlight, isn't there?"

Kat was still thinking about the dinner party. It helped that Lil had given her the dessert. "We all put on weight so easily," she had said. "You'd better take this." And Kat took it. And Kat ate it all for breakfast, every bit. No calling herself names. How could she be Badkat when Lil wanted her to eat that dessert?

And that dessert made Kat think. The taste of it took her right back to the night of her first dinner party with the three women.

Mabel had said something in passing. She had joked at Ann, "You started it." Lil had been in the kitchen with Kat at that moment, and she had stopped. Her elegant face looked doubtful and quizzical both at once. She gave a sigh and the tableau broke.

After her strange breakfast, Kat knocked on the door of the main house. "Are you free?" she asked Lil. "I promise I won't lose it today."

Last week she had lost it gloriously and she had seen how Lil had looked at her. She had been comforted by Ann taking the emo moment in her stride and angry that Mabel gave her a 'damn teenager' look. For Lil, however, she felt a duty of care, as if this lady were fragile and needed to be surrounded by people of even temperament. It was the translucent quality of her skin, perhaps, or the softness of her voice, or her cat-like movements. Or maybe it was the feeling of coming home she sensed whenever Lil poured her a coffee. Lil moved like her real grandmother had. That was maybe it.

"Even if I slip up and call you a child?" Lil asked.

"Not even then."

"Spill, then, while I put on some coffee."

"Coffee, nom nom," said Kat, and Lil laughed.

Soon they were sitting down and nibbling on chocolate ginger biscuits. *I'm going to have such a sugar high*, thought Kat, *and I can feel my skin breaking out.* This was reassuring. The world was extracting payment for the breakfast and morning tea and, if she had paid for it, she might be allowed to have it again. After all, as her mother had said, 'The world owes you nothing, you get that?'

"I want to know more about what Ann was talking about at that dinner party the other night. It looked as if she was going to say a lot more things and it looked as if she was doing it on purpose. I need to know all about it."

"You need?" Lil lifted an eyebrow.

"Yes," Kat was defiant. Dad had done the need vs. want thing with everything except birthday presents, and they were always rushed and botched and unimportant. *Do you need this? No. You want. Want isn't enough.*

"That week is important to Ann. She truly doesn't know what happened then. All she really knows is that she emerged with a bad eye. And that out of that bad eye she sees . . . things."

"Things? Like fairies?"

"Like beings who don't want to be seen."

"Why was it important that she make a big announcement, then?"

"She was telling you."

"She could've just said." Kat was starting to get all bothered, and she'd promised Lil. She pulled herself together. "Was there a reason I had to know? Does she tell everyone?"

"I think that you and Mabel and I and her husband are the only ones who know. Mabel and I believe her, but her husband, no, he does not believe. He does not have any interest in believing."

"Why me, then?" Kat didn't sound angry anymore, but her chin jutted forward.

"Let me pour us fresh cups. I can't explain in a sentence."

When their cups were full of coffee and Kat had another biscuit, Lil began to speak. Her voice was so quiet and calm that Kat wondered whether she cared at all. Then Kat noticed Lil's left hand, resting on the table. It had a very slight shake. Lil cared too much about this. Kat filed the information for later.

"We three have known each other for thirty years."

"A long time," said Kat. "My life by two."

Lil looked into her cup, as if it held answers. "Maybe it is a long time; maybe it isn't." She took a deep breath before she continued. "Two decades ago, Ann told us about her experience and Mabel shared her own."

"What was Mabel's?"

"Ah, you should ask her. This sort of knowledge should not be shared lightly." There was a silence. Kat couldn't bring herself to ask if Lil had experiences too. Lil looked too frail.

"If you hate talking about it, I can manage," Kat said.

"I can talk." Lil's mouth twisted ruefully. "We used to joke about the creatures that Ann saw out of her bad eye. Then Ann led us into the nether-world."

The phone rang, the mood was broken, and Kat had to wait for the rest of the story.

Kat asked again. She prodded Lil into taking up where she had left off, but all Lil would say was, "Ask her about it."

Before she could ask Ann about anything, Mabel requested her help in the garden again. "The wood's gotta be shifted and it's too much for my back. I get the boys to fix it when they deliver, but this year they forgot."

"You could ask them again," suggested Kat, looking at the huge woodpile. It was an awful lot of wood for one small girl to shift.

"If you don't want the money, say so," Mabel said.

"I don't understand, though. If they pile it by the house every year, why did they just dump it this year?"

"Maybe they saw something." Mabel shrugged.

"Oh!" said Kat. "That's different."

"Thought you'd say that," grunted Mabel. "I want it stacked neatly, mind, and not too high. I want lots of air."

"You want it dry and easy to reach."

"Precisely."

"Got it," Kat said, and started work.

In the beginning there was vim and even vigour. Kat slung wood with a fine disregard for its capacity to chip at her hands and send splinters driving into her fingers. She stacked it quickly and precisely, creating the first layer of a wall that ran parallel to Mabel's house, then starting the second with care and almost architectural proportions. She saw no contrast between flinging her whole body into things and yet building with such care. Her mind was completely at one with both parts of the woodstacking. It was as if she was born to woodstack.

Gradually, though, her zen woodstacking technique faded, to be replaced by a keen awareness. Kat was aware of vague aches under the skin and of a graze on her right forefinger. Her shoulders were beginning to bow over like Mabel's ought to, if Mabel would only hold herself like a little old lady. *Which she doesn't, of course.* Mostly, though, Kat's head was hurting.

When a voice rang out from the back door, Kat was ashamed to admit relief. "Tea's up!" was all Mabel had said, and Kat went indoors like an obedient child and made polite conversation until the aches faded and then she said, "Better get back to work," in her best tradie tone. *I sound like a plumber,* she congratulated herself.

"Tomorrow'll do for the rest," said Mabel.

"Nah," said Kat, still channelling that mythical plumber. "Gotta get it done. Besides, tomorrow I'll be dying of stiffness and backache and I want it done before I feel all the pain."

Mabel nodded. "Matter of pride."

"Yep," said Kat, back to laconic tradie mode.

Kat had found a happy rhythm. Things hurt, but not as much as before. Her Great Wall of Split Wood was building up quite nicely and the pile was getting smaller and smaller. It was good. Kat felt sore but self-satisfied and each time she started a new layer, she would give herself a virtual glass of champagne. She was on her way to being well and truly virtually tiddled, when something jumped out of the woodpile. Kat shrieked.

Mabel came straight out and asked, "What is it?"

"There's something in the woodpile. It's hairy. And monkey small. And it has human eyes. And it jumped out at me then jumped right back in again."

"Oh dear," said Mabel. "I'll handle this." She walked up to the sad remnants of wood and spoke clearly into it in the slow but firm voice one uses to an errant teenager.

"Off with you. I told you that you don't belong here. D'you want me to get tough?" The creature peered out, looking up at Mabel as if she were his hope and his dream and his own deep glory. It shook its head, vehemently. "So scarper. Quick-smart!" And it did.

"It'll be back," Mabel said despondently. "Just as soon as it thinks I'm not watching. It likes to think it's protecting the woodpile. It does this every bloody year. Only this time it came early and scared the boys."

"Does everyone have critters protecting their woodpiles in Canberra?" Kat was enchanted at the thought.

"Nah, only the select few. And aren't we the lucky ones."

"You don't sound as if you think it's lucky."

"How can I maintain disbelief with a boogieman protecting my bloody woodpile," said Mabel, with as much dignity as she could muster. "Let's have a cuppa so he can come back quietly and we can all pretend that this didn't just happen."

"I ache all over," Kat said.

"Tea and cake will sort that out."

On her way out, after tea and cake, Kat looked across to admire the beautiful stack of wood she had created. At one end of it, the wood had been rearranged so that it was dense and matted, stuck with tufts of grass. Kat was certain that two pairs of bright eyes looked out of it at her; one of those two sets of eyes glared. Kat was tempted to cross herself, but she said quite sternly, "This is not Buffy and I am not Catholic," and took herself off as quickly as she could. Mabel's disbelief was obviously not hers. Let Mabel deal with the things behind the woodpile, late in winter, when the wood ran out.

Two days later, Kat broached the matter of Ann with Ann herself.

It wasn't straightforward. She didn't like how Lil had become so delicate the further they had got into the conversation. 'Further' hadn't been very far at all, either. It was obviously big stuff.

There had to be a way to get Ann to tell all. If she got all emotional, that would work. Ann responded to tears and fears. Maybe if she appealed to her generosity and shared the things she herself was scared about? That should be enough. After all, Ann wanted her to know about the week of being missing.

What scares me that I can talk about? Kat asked herself. The answer was not much. She dredged through her mind until she finally found something. She didn't know if she wanted to tell anyone, but she so much wanted to know what was up with Ann that it was worth hurting a bit.

Ann took her out for chai, every three days without fail. Kat knew Ann was keeping an eye on her, but it was a nice eye and besides Ann paid for the chai. Also, it made her feel sophisticated.

Over chai, Kat told Ann about her nightmares. "It's like I wake up, but I'm still asleep. And there's something. It sits on my chest and I tell it to get off. It doesn't. I try to scream: nothing comes out. And it sits on me heavier and heavier and heavier and I'm suffocating and I can't do anything."

"What happens next?"

"I wake up. My heart is pounding and I feel really scared. I can't go back to sleep for hours."

"I think it sounds like night fears," Ann said, sympathetically.

"There's a name for it?"

"Yes."

"Is it supernatural?"

"Sometimes it is. Mostly it's an asthma attack or a magnesium deficiency or too much dinner too close to bed."

"Oh. I wanted it to be special."

"You've got to sort out whether it's mundane first. Simple answers first. If they don't work then you try the complex answers. If they don't work then you start wondering if it could be . . . something else."

"I'm fascinated by it," Kat admitted. "I want it to be special."

Ann nodded. "I was like that with my missing week. I wanted to be special, so I wanted *it* to be special."

"And you never did find out what happened?"

"I never did. I found something special because of it though."

"Your eye?"

"Oh, more than that. After I told Lil and Mabel they told me their secrets and we started exploring hidden worlds. We've been doing that for a while now."

"I want to explore." She didn't mention what had happened in Mabel's garden.

"We shall see," half-promised Ann. "It's not always safe."

"Huh," Kat was nonplussed. *How can a group of elderly women deal with Roswell stuff,* she wondered. A moment later she wondered if Ann could read her mind. "If I didn't have this vague capacity to sense spirits and odd afterimages, I wouldn't be doing this," she cautioned. Kat was fascinated — Ann looked a bit embarrassed about it. "I'm sort of the canary and Mabel and Lil and I all work together when things go wrong. This is not something to be done alone."

"What do you actually do?"

"It depends," and Ann's hands fluttered annoyingly vaguely. "This and that. We don't ghost hunt or deal with spirits that belong here, as a rule. Lil says that the things I see all came with us Europeans. It's a palimpsest laying over Canberra and we scrape it off so Canberrans can live in the real city."

"But what does that mean?" Strange words and no real explanation. Kat wanted to beat her fist lightly on the table and engage in a little sulk, but she was being on her best behaviour. Even her best behaviour couldn't stop her voice sounding a little whiny. She hated herself.

"I don't really know what it means," said Ann. Now she was obviously embarrassed. "I just accept it and do my share of the work. More than my share of the work. Lil has all the explanations."

"Is there anything out there now? I mean, have you noticed anything special recently?"

"Recently, there's been a lot."

"What's the scariest?"

"The streets shift a little. It's as if they're restless."

"That's not scary," Kat scoffed.

Ann gave her a rueful smile. "You don't drive."

"Well, what about something that would scare me?"

"There isn't a thing."

"Tell me something that could happen then. A maybe."

"Would a death portent scare you?"

"Ooh, yeah," breathed Kat.

"I haven't seen one though, and I don't want to."

"Much better," Kat said.

"Have you heard of a barguest?"

"You mean someone who is someone else's guest at a bar?"

"No, I mean a big black dog with a coat so shaggy it can never be groomed. A dog with giant saucer eyes that sometimes shine with red fire. If you see the barguest, then someone will die."

"That's my sort of spirit," said Kat, contentedly.

Tales of Melusine #985

Once someone gave Melusine a gift. It was when she was young.

"What were your christening gifts?" a stranger had asked her.

"I had none," Melusine had said. She was about to explain that she was Jewish, but the stranger was not listening.

"I give you the gift of safety," the stranger said. "Though your path may take you through terror, that terror will not destroy you."

"That's a very generous gift," Melusine said, politely.

"Is it?" asked the stranger. "I do not give that gift to your friends, or to your children, or to any others of your kind. Only to you. Will safety seem so generous when you travel alone?"

Kat was bored and decided to drop in on Ann. Ann's husband was there and the two had obviously been arguing. Kat could smell the miasma of a household quarrel. She pretended everything was hunky-dory. She had to do the polite, now she was here.

Ann needed someone to hide behind and Kat's pretend blindness made her the person. She found herself trapped in an orgy of giving.

"I'm cleaning stuff out," Ann explained. "And I'd much rather it went to a friend than in a garage sale or to a stranger." *She'd much rather keep me round while her husband is sulking by the TV*, Kat read, *and this is her excuse*. But the stuff was good stuff and useful stuff and in nice condition and the longer she lived in Lil's place the more Kat realised how few her possessions were. And Ann was persuasive, oh so persuasive. "Take this off my hands," she would say. "Can't you see what a mess the cupboard is? Getting rid of this means that everything will fit in just so and I shall be the happier for it."

It took both of them to take everything to the car and it took Kat two loads to empty the back seat once Ann had dropped her home. She felt spoiled and special, even though she knew she really should have said no to everything.

"You spent today with Ann," Lil commented, as they passed on the way to their respective doors, Lil laden with groceries and Kat with Ann's throwaways.

"How did you know?" Kat was hoping to find some magic involved.

"She gives presents." Lil shrugged. "She has a generous spirit in that way."

"In that way?"

"Ann gives gifts of material goods. Mabel gives gifts of a subtler type. Both of them are kind women."

"And you?"

"I outgrew kindness a very long time ago." Lil was laughing, but Kat wondered. Lil was hiding stuff.

Three

SOME DAYS I JUST hate myself. I can't think of words for it. I've got this big pressure that builds up from my intestines. Or maybe my spleen. And it's me, hating me. I shouldn't be blogging this because it's so personal. I want to talk about it, though, with someone who won't give me advice. I've turned the comments off.

I know where the hate comes from. Today it came from Z. I ran into Z at the bus stop. Next time I'll hide round the corner till the bus is gone. I don't want to see Z again.

I went to school with Z, before she moved to Canberra. You wouldn't believe it, but we were once best friends. If she wanted to do something, then I would jump up bright and cheerful and say, "Yes, Z," not because it was a good idea, but because it would make her happy.

I saw her today. I said that. We were both waiting for the same bus and it was going to take ages and ages to come and we started talking.

At first it was all fine. At first we talked like we'd always talked. About food and clothes, mostly. Except she mentioned guys. And I said I didn't care about guys. Cos I don't right now. Right now I care about sorting myself out. I want to take care of my three old ladies the way they've taken care of me, I want to find some sort of future. I want to get rid of what's welling up deep inside me. I want. I want. I want.

I didn't tell Z all this. I just told her I didn't know the guys she was raving on about. She became so spiteful. She told me I was a hypocrite. She said that even when I was eleven I had watched out for boys and kept them away from her, Z. She said I wrote notes about them in my little diary.

She said. She said. She said. I don't know all the things she said. I don't want to know all the things she said. She thought I was a hypocrite. I mean, really, really thought it. That hurt so much. I believed it for a moment and then I remembered Mabel telling me, 'If someone says something bad about you, find out if it's true. If it's not true, it's their problem, not yours.'

Except it becomes your problem when your insides are all blackened from worry. I said I was sorry and I left that bus stop. I could take the slow way home.

The slow way is near a path by the lake and I got off a bit early to walk by the water. I was being followed by a drowning girl crying. I could hear her, every step I took along the water. I couldn't see her. The lake was as placid as a mill pond and everyone else was going about their thing. That was when I decided that the drowning girl was me.

I have to get rid of all the misery and stuff. I hate Z. I want to say she made me hate her, but that's becoming as bad as she is. She can rewrite the past all she likes — I'm not going to do that. I'm going to stay honest.

My first step was to blog. (Respect that this is a locked post, please. Don't go talking about it?) Next I'm going to talk to the old ladies about it. I don't want them to have to rescue me again, you see. I want to get strong so I can rescue myself. Ann was the one who said, 'The only way you can get strong is by asking for help when you need it.' Right now I really, really, really need it.

Lil and Kat laid bets on what they would find at dinner at Mabel's place and how much work Kat would actually get to do in cooking and serving.

"If she doesn't make me work, I'm going to complain, I think," Kat said. "You're all nice to me, but it's time I asserted myself."

"Win back your dignity," Lil said, smiling.

"Exactly."

Kat won the food bet and Lil the work one. Lil had bet on roast chicken, but the meat served was beef and the accompaniments were perfectly cooked, but as ordinary as accompaniments come: potatoes, roast sweet potato, mint peas, carrots and green salad. Kat didn't get to do much in the kitchen until washing up time, but she did get to peel all the root vegetables and Mabel taught her to slit the potatoes and to pour fat over them while they cooked.

"Ick," said Kat.

"Wait till you taste them before saying that, young lady," said Mabel, austerely.

When Kat sat down to her plate, after the others were served, she had to whisper to Mabel, "You were right about the potato." Mabel winked.

After pudding (chocolate mousse, with vanilla ice cream — Kat laughed at it — if Ann had made it, it would be 'mousse au chocolat' but because Mabel made it, it was 'pudding' — and the pudding was just as deliciously rich and creamy as Ann's mousse au chocolat would have been) Mabel instructed Kat to make up a tea tray and they all sat on the verandah, looking towards the garden. On their left was a big structure encased in netting where Mabel grew seedlings, on the right was more verandah and in front of them was Mabel's garden.

By now, Kat knew Mabel's garden very well. It was different at night. The big trees, each in the centre of their raised hexagonal beds, no longer looked regular. She couldn't tell the persimmon from the peach. Everything looked dark and mysterious. Kat sat herself as close to the seedlings as possible, it being the point furthest away from the creature in the woodpile. She caught it looking out at her once or twice and she glared back.

"Is there something in your eye, dear?" asked Mabel.

"Can I pour you some tea?" Kat asked, instead of giving a proper reply. Mabel gave her a 'you are sprung bad' look and Kat had to laugh. She turn-ed her chair more towards the garden so that she wouldn't be caught out again. The creature could glare as often as it liked: she simply wouldn't see.

The four of them lost sight of time there, in the gloaming. It was a perfect evening.

At the end of it, when they stood up to go indoors and collect their things, Ann quietly passed Kat a package. "Don't tell anyone," she said. "This is between us." Kat thanked her nicely and slipped it into her backpack, quietly, as Ann had suggested. It made her wonder though. Why was Ann doing this secretly? She had almost gotten used to being a charity case (because they did it so nicely) but this was different. Ann was different.

When she got it home and opened it, Kat was very surprised. It was dark anime. Black and deep and desperate. Gilgamesh. Not — Kat would have thought — Anne's thing at all.

※- ♦ -※

Kat had a notepad by her nice new computer. Lil had got her an internet connection, which she paid for with errands and housework. The notebook was to log the hours because Kat was determined to earn every minute she spent online, just as she was determined to earn her food and lodging.

She didn't have a printer, though. She wasn't going to save for one, either. First, she had to sort out basics. An internet connection was that, but a printer wasn't.

It was inevitable that the minute she and the world wide web met that the front of her notebook would show how many hours' work she'd done and the back would contain jottings of the strange things that could be found in Canberra. What her new friends couldn't tell her, her old friend would.

When she blogged, she never bothered looking back at her past posts. She seldom worried about who would read it. Kat cast the words to the world as a sacrificial offering.

One day I'll make my own Book of Shadows, she thought. *Right now is about learning so when I make it, it's a good one.*

Today she found pure gold when she delved into the web. A group of local Canberrans were swapping ghost stories.

She wrote the ones down that seemed most likely. She spent a whole page of her notebook on the story of the man who worked at an old hotel, on the night shift. The 'graveyard shift,' he called it.

He walked into one of the function rooms and heard the sound of fingers running across glass. Not just one glass, but every wine glass there. He left the room because his ears hurt, the sound was so ugly.

One time another staff member was raced to hospital to be treated for shock. She had walked into the ballroom and found herself in the middle of a big party. They were all dressed in 1920s garb. It was two in the morning. No party was booked. Nothing. She had gone out to check the function book and make sure. When she came back, there was no-one. There never had been anyone.

Ghosts. Kat loved the thought of ghosts. She especially loved the thought of ghosts having a party.

Tales of Melusine #78

Once upon a time in a nursery rhyme there were three bears.

Except it doesn't go like that. It never did. Nursery rhymes and fairy tales show the outer shell of the story, not the inner reality. Most of the time the inner reality is slower and sadder and less glamorous. It's when lovers lose each other's affection and children hurt. This sort of thing isn't pretty. Nor does it make good stories.

Melusine's tales are the tale of a fairy. They are not fairy tales.

Sometimes they are exciting. Sometimes they are dull and drear. Mostly, though, they are the stuff of daily life. Even if it spans over a half a millennium, washing the dishes is not an exciting event. Except . . . except . . .

Melusine was normally very good at advance planning. She squirreled money away and purchased property and generally handled her everyday life so that she always had resources. She knew no-one would help her in emergencies. She knew it from experience. She was too different and most people felt that difference. Or she looked independent. Or she sounded strong. Each friend gave a different reason, but none of them gave help.

Sometimes she gave herself one reason and sometimes another. The truth was that after her two hundredth birthday, she had to rely on herself. She couldn't complain about it either: many humans had to be self-sufficient from their childhood. Her first two hundred years hadn't been plain sailing, but she had family to call on and people who understood who she was. Since then, however, she had been on her own.

She had been playing careful. She had simply not been careful enough.

Melusine lost lands in the French Revolution. She had shrugged at that, worried more about the emotions and temperaments that had been stirred up than about possessions. Melusine took her money and her jewels and she left for England, as quickly as she could. She never really returned to France to live from that time, but that's another story. France changed and Melusine changed more.

Melusine had not relied on banks much. She had seen the gambling over the South Sea Bubble and noticed that too many ventured into danger. She was as careful as careful could be.

Melusine bought a nice house in London with the proceeds of some of her jewels. She hid the rest in a place that only magic could reach. She invested the gold in the one institution that had been above reproach most of the last century. The one that had avoided —

so everyone said — the lures of Bubbles and Schemes.

Alas, the Bank of England was caught up in the problems of Britain. Britain was fighting a war against France and defending its holdings in the Americas. It was sending its convicts to the other side of the world and supporting the new colonies. It had visions of greatness. Mostly, things would come right.

Melusine was French and had never understood Britain and its colonies. She had not even thought about Britain's other wars or its domestic issues when she walked into the building on Threadneedle Street and deposited all her gold with the Bank of England. In fact, she laughed at James Gilray's depiction of paper money ravishing the Lady of Threadneedle Street when it was issued.

It was Pitt's decision to pay out in banknotes rather than gold that caused her downfall, along with that of many other people.

This sounds so boring. Economic history. Duller than ditch water. It was dull to Melusine, too. She was perturbed to be holding a banknote instead of a gold sovereign, because it felt too much like a promissory note. In fact, it was a promissory note. Part hand-written, it held false wealth. She didn't realise that it meant that her gold was no longer in the Bank. The Bank of England had run its gold reserves down far too low. It had spent Melusine's money.

How she moved from having gold in the Bank of England to using her last note from the Bank, Melusine never quite sorted out. She came out of it with no cash, that was for certain. In 1800 she wasn't in debt (or bankrupt, the way many colonials were) but all she owned was the house. She couldn't access her jewels, either. That latter was her own fault — she had put them beyond her own reach three weeks before her money had run out. Her form of panic.

They would appear again in her life, sometime, when the conditions were right. Unfortunately in 1800 the conditions were wrong, and Melusine, one of the more interesting fairies of the South of France, chose to solve her immediate problems by turning her nice white three-storey home into a boarding house.

Because she spoke French, she attracted a group of émigrées.

They were single-minded women. Each and every one was single-minded, and each and every one was single-minded in her own particular way. Some were determined to embroider or sew fine seams until their eyes fell out, to earn a living and remain on just the far side of poverty. Some were just as determined to break into English court circles and redeem their pride and maybe their country. Some were determined to milk the English of all they could.

None of them thought of Melusine as anything more than a servant, the provider of cheap lodgings and food. Some stole her possessions, others treated those same possessions with almost random casualness and at least one lodger a month disappeared without paying.

She began to wonder if engaging in fortune telling in the markets might not provide a better income than letting these monsters destroy her house and devour her soul. She moved all the best furniture to her private quarters and took to demanding payment up front. Melusine hated herself and hated her fellow countrymen and cheered whenever the British won a battle or captured a ship.

And now her story really begins. Not the story of her life, but the fairy story. The memorable portion. Where the drear everyday suddenly transforms into something recountable.

To understand what happened you must remember that Melusine's magic was carefully hidden, because this was a time when most magic was hated. It was the end of the Age of Reason, and the Age of Reason was full of despite and distrust for anything that could not be explained mathematically or using Aristotelian logic. Melusine's very being defied Aristotelian logic.

She had lived through worse times, but at this moment in her life she felt disempowered. Her life seemed reduced to the ugliest of choices. If she shone, she would be killed.

She could live, or she could be herself: she could see no other choices. It was like being Jewish in Spain in 1492 all over again. Except that in 1492 she had not been in Spain.

To live meant to hide: this was her thought. She obscured her magic and dulled any beauty she might have had and layered everything distinctive about herself beneath a veneer of middle age and ordinariness. She would act as the small-brained owner of lodgings everyone thought she was.

Most people assumed she had inherited the house from some dead husband and that she was no more than chattel. Her tenants treated her as their chattel. She finally found herself accepting this, because she was alive. She was alive despite being French in England, despite having magic. Despite being Melusine. For once, it didn't matter if she were Jewish or not, for she had little interest in the new Jews who flooded London, full of superstitions and Central European notions.

Alive, but alone. Alive, but no longer Melusine.

She appeared as if she were one of those lesser nobles who had little claim to erudition or charm. The sad end of the bottom ranks of the noblesse de robe, whose ancestors had been administrators, not real nobles at all. When she went to the kitchen after the chef had left ("I want higher things from life!" he had declared.) no-one was surprised. They treated her even more condescendingly, but they accepted that she would do any task. They didn't even notice when she hired a cook to take the chef's place. She belonged in the kitchen herself, in their minds. No longer a lesser noble, she had become an upstart who had married into nobility and was finally receiving her just desserts.

Melusine realised that she was turning into Cinderella and that there was no fairy godmother to save her. She also realised that she had come too far on this journey and that she was trapped in this disguise she had invented. With no money outside the house and no security, she could not escape.

"When the war ends," she thought, "everyone will go home. Then I can become myself again and earn money teaching history and painting. I can start a school for girls here in this poor debased house and I can regain my dignity. Time is on my side, not theirs. I can reinvent myself as my long-lost daughter."

But the war continued and continued and continued, and her lodgers would not leave. Some of them could not leave. They were as trapped as she was.

Sometimes she drifted towards the alien Jewish community for a sense of fellowship, but everyone there spoke the wrong languages. The very famous Rabbi Falk practised magic secretly, calling it religious performance and mystic belief in public: he saw her for what she was. They turned their gaze away from each other and pretended not to have seen what they had each seen.

Soon after, he openly used his number magic. He stole back his silver plate from a pawnbroker and boasted quietly where only certain people could hear. He filled his coal cellar. He used his magic dishonestly and, because he was a rabbi, was given the reputation of a miracle worker instead of a cheat or an evildoer.

It wasn't fair. She couldn't openly do anything. That was Melusine's refrain for a full decade: 'It isn't fair'. What was least fair was being able to see that she had lost her ability to mock herself and move on. Melusine was trapped in another's body, and that body was humourless and middle-aged and suffering: she hated it.

One day, one of her lodgers found a pocket watch on the occasional table where Melusine left the mail, visiting cards and stray messages for upstairs. It was a fancy piece. No-one knew how it came to be on the occasional table.

When no-one claimed it, Marceline (for that was the lodger's name) said, "It's mine." Less than twenty-four hours later she was gone, with all her possessions.

"Pawned it," was the consensus. "Rent out her room, quick."

Melusine didn't. She needed the money, but her fairy self whispered that it took three by three by three days for magic to fully grow, and for its final results to be known and if Marceline had been whisked away on a quest, she would not appreciate her room being rented to a stranger.

A mere three days later, Marceline was back, with a single bag and no watch.

"It took me to Liverpool," she said. "Just whisked me away as if I were a . . . a . . . a fribble. I was on the dock, all my possessions piled up around me, the watch in my hand."

"What happened in Liverpool?"

"Nothing. I looked at the ships coming in and decided I wanted to go home. Instantly I was whisked somewhere else. I had just this one bag and no watch. I asked the way to London and I begged food and I slept on the road."

"Quite like old times, then," said Marianne, "since it's almost exactly how you escaped from the Terror. At least, it's how you tell that escape."

"Shut up," Marceline said, tiredly. The hem of her brown dress was darkened with mud and the smell from it was evident even two yards away. "I want some soup in my room and hot water for bathing. Now." This last was addressed to Melusine, of course.

Melusine did what she could. With the rule of three and the

watch, it was part of the magic that someone act as servant who shouldn't, and if she wanted to keep her limited options open that meant her. Fairy tales, she thought, have a lot to answer for. She kept portions of travel soup at the ready, so she made consommé with that, but hot water to Marceline's room? All she could bring was a pitcher. She felt as if she had failed in the care of a weary traveller, even if that traveller was sharp-nosed Marceline.

Nine days later the watch appeared again.

"This time it's mine," said Marianne.

"Will you listen to advice?" asked Melusine.

"From you? I can't see that you'd have anything to tell me."

Melusine nodded and kept the room for her when she disappeared. It took her nine days to return and she was without watch or baggage, but Marianne was radiantly happy.

"I exchanged the watch for a berth on a ship that was about to leave. I don't know why I ended back here, but I spent nine days on the way to somewhere interesting, eating at the captain's table."

"And sleeping in his bed, by the look of it," snapped Marceline.

"And why not?" Marianne was entirely unperturbed.

"What happened just before you were brought back here?"

"Nothing," Marianne was genuinely perplexed. "I threw a jug of water at the cabin boy, but he asked for it. So, nothing."

Interesting, Melusine thought, but kept her thoughts to herself. She was inside her mind: it was only when she spoke that she transformed into a housekeeper. If it's me they want, and they're transporting possessions, what will they do with my house? If it's not me they want, then maybe I can make things interesting.

Twenty-seven days later, the watch appeared again on the occasional table.

"Leave it!" said Melusine, to the group clustered round it. They turned to look at her, and on every face was astonishment. It had been too long since she had spoken to anyone using that tone of voice. She smiled at them. It felt rather nice to assert herself.

Melusine walked forward. Her tenants parted. Like Moses parting the waves. How curious. Her mind wasn't really paying attention to its own chatter. It was waiting to examine that watch.

"Well," she said, once she had picked it up and tucked it safely away, "don't you have anything better to do?" They faded faster than snow in Provence. This new Melusine was not to their taste.

She investigated the watch very thoroughly. It was extraordinarily fancy. A cover on the back that hinged in one direction and one on the front that hinged in the other, so that when it was opened fully it looked like three full moons. It was silver and ivory, with touches of blue. There was a crest etched into the back.

Melusine smiled. She knew that crest. The question was whether the owner of that crest knew who was holding the watch. He might, she thought, regret this little game on humans. Or he might not.

She prepared a little travel bag, just in case. She dressed for travel, too. She ignored her tenants and left them to talk the maid and cook into resigning. She ignored everything, in fact, except the watch and its workings.

Melusine noted that a third hand and rather suspected that she would find herself in Liverpool when it was on the twelve and the hour hand was on the nine. It was the angle that counted. Angles and relationships and planetary influences: these things were not taught to improvident French refugees. Neither, it seemed, were multiples of three.

Sure enough, the hands ticked into the correct angle, and Melusine, her watch, and her small portmanteau were all on the docks. Melusine took a deep breath of the salty air, of the rotting kelp and the thousand other scents that informed the strip of wood on which she stood. She turned half around and just caught the quaver of lines in the sky as her house tried to follow her and failed. Melusine laughed, deeply and happily, for the first time in three years.

The weight of silver in her hand brought her back to reality. Her reality. Not the human one. She smiled, still joyous.

She opened the case fully and pointed the minute hand at the late night sun of midsummer. She swivelled the watch around, took her line of sight from the mysterious middle hand and found herself seeing a particular ship. She kept the watch out, and took her bag and herself to the ship.

"I believe you are expecting me," she said to a sailor, and held out the watch.

"If you would wait just a moment, please," he said. English words in a Spanish accent. Not simply a Spanish accent. A Castilian one. Curious.

Soon the captain came down the plank, jaunty and impressive.

"Very nice," she said.

He faltered. He looked at her closely. "Dammit," he said, in a very upper class English accent, "I can't kidnap you and take you to the Caribbean."

"Why not?"

"You know why not," and he stood, arms crossed.

"You want a French émigrée," Melusine said. "Someone who is so grateful to you that they will instantly fall into your bed."

He refused to reply.

"Or perhaps you want a beautiful French émigrée? Certainly the tenants you took the first two times lacked that particular element."

"One was stupid and one was stupid and plain."

"So you didn't even try to direct them towards your ship."

"Bad bed fodder. You, on the other hand, I have lusted after for two hundred years. I still do, even with that daft disguise."

"I had no desire to hear that," Melusine said.

"I can't overpower you, and I can't persuade you."

"You have tried both before."

"And damned stupid I looked, both times."

"There is a war going on. How do you propose to get to the Caribbean?"

His rather pale grey eyes lit up. "I have discovered a way."

"How?" Melusine was obdurate.

"I refract the light and sail right past everyone. No-one sees my ship unless I choose. The sailors are petrified of me. It's all rather nice, really."

"Interesting."

"I can show you."

"Not as far as the Caribbean."

"You mean you'll travel with me?" His arms fell to his sides and he leaned forward, unable to hide his enthusiasm.

"I require some sun and some peace from all this." She waved her arm to take in the whole of Western Europe. "And if you had only stayed around for five minutes last time, you would have discovered that I'm not as indifferent as you assumed."

"You are damned formidable."

"I am myself. If you want me for twenty-seven days, you will have to accept that."

Those eyes lit up. They looked sharp, and brilliant. "Only twenty-seven days?"

"You set the ground rules by using old-fashioned counting. Besides, I have tenants, and they give me my income. I lost everything except that house in this idiotic war."

"Why don't I send one of my people to run your house? I pay her wages and she stops complaining about being seasick. For as long as you want. Until the day you dismiss her."

"Everyone is happy, in fact," said Melusine sardonically.

"It means you can stay with me forever." As he spoke he edged closer and closer to her. At 'forever' his arm slipped around her waist.

"Six months, maximum."

His laugh was resigned. "Six months, then. Sealed with a kiss?"

"Not in front of half the dockworkers of Liverpool."

"Maybe I can talk you into marriage in six months," he said, contemplatively.

"A moment ago you admitted you were terrified of me and already you want to marry me?"

"I like a challenge. D'you want to know what I'm looking into now?"

"Tell me."

As they talked, he took her bag in one hand and her arm in the other and moved her onto the ship.

"There must be ways of seeing gaps in reality. Maybe of exploring them."

"Not while I'm with you. I am the sort of person who would fall through those cracks, and I do not choose to experience that particular journey," said Melusine.

"Pity. I shall explore other things with you." He gave her a look that was a lot more private than any kiss would have been.

.

Four

KAT WAS WALKING JOYOUSLY. She was even joyous about being joyous. "It makes a change from inner doomheart," she told herself. Perhaps today her hair was dark brown instead of black and forcing her towards happiness? She had no idea why she was happy or why she was walking. She just was. She caught a bus and got off at an interesting street and simply walked.

The interesting street turned out to be a Canberra loop street. It had another loop street attached to it, so she walked that too. It was a bit of a slog, but the mystery of the curve reaching up before it faded was too tempting. What was more, a dream of people clustered at that curve. Misty figures and a whisper of talk. Where the street faded, so did the people.

"Misty," she said. "They're misty." When she had walked the full double loop, she lost that faded feel so she crossed the road and caught a bus home.

She told Lil about it over tea.

"It was almost magic," Kat said, with relish.

"Indeed," said Lil, and looked concerned. "Where did you see this?"

"I dunno. I caught a bus at random and got off it at random. Somewhere between Woden and Tuggeranong, perhaps? Or in Weston?"

"Ann saw misty figures, too."

"Oh! I forgot about them! Mine were different to hers. Mine weren't all icky. We really ought to investigate."

"Maybe we should. Maybe we should stay home. Sometimes knowing too much is its own danger," Lil said.

"Investigate! You mean Ann was serious?"

"Ann is always serious," said Mabel solemnly.

"She isn't," objected Kat. "She smiles all the time."

"So?" asked Mabel. There was no contradicting Mabel, ever.

"So tell me about one of your investigations." Kat noticed the women exchange that look, the one they always exchanged when she looked happy about something. If this had been anyone else, she would have objected to being led by the nose, but if she could hear a story from these women, then it was worth it.

This story was from Mabel: "A few years ago, we found a grindylow on Lake George. Grindylows are dangerous. You look at them and they drag you right into the water. There used to be a spirit like it 'round here, except that it was nicer. Australian water spirits can be sweet or bad. This imported grindylow was just plain bad."

"What did it do?" breathed Kat.

"Tried to drown people, of course," Mabel was irritated at having her story interrupted.

"So how did you stop it?"

"We didn't have to," Mabel's bright teeth flashed in a sudden grin. "It was stupid. It chose Lake George. Ten years ago, Lake George had water."

"I don't remember Lake George having water?"

"That's just it. It hasn't for nearly ten years. After one year of the big dry, all we had to do was encourage it to go home."

"You should have killed that grindylow!" Kat was fierce.

"Why?"

"It killed people."

"It's what it does, dearie. Anyway, we're not superheroes. Gentle encouragement is better, always."

"Almost always," said Lil. "This being could be encouraged to move on, so we assisted. Others are unhappier. When we can't do anything, we stay at a safe distance and do nothing. It's not ideal, but we are what we are: three ageing women."

"Can I tell her my Lake George joke now?" Mabel asked. "Now that I've told her the rest?"

"No, you can't," said Ann firmly. Ann who had entered the room and the conversation without anyone noticing. "I would rather you didn't tell anyone your Lake George joke. It's the most dreadful joke I have ever been forced to listen to. It hurts my brain even to think about it."

"I want to hear it," said Kat.

"Too bad," said Ann. "You're not going to."

"I can tell Ann what I saw, now?" asked Kat.

"Go ahead, kill yourself," said Mabel, cheerfully.

"Misty figures," said Kat, and the discussion had come full circle.

When the group broke up, Ann took Kat aside. "I thought you might like these," she said, and handed over a couple of books.

When Kat tried to thank her, Ann brushed it off. "I was after an excuse to talk with you. I wanted to know about those night fears of yours," she said. "If you don't mind telling. Do you still have them? Have you tried the magnesium and the deep breathing?"

"I don't mind," said Kat, a little bewildered. She just couldn't work out where Ann was coming from. "I still have them. I tried all the things you suggested. In fact," she admitted, "they're a bit worse now. Maybe a lot worse. I don't know. It's like I don't always get them at night, or I don't know when morning is."

Ann pressed her for more, but she couldn't describe it any better. "It's like day is involved," was the best she could do. She thought a bit and said, "It's like discontinuous realities. Maybe."

"It occurs to me that you've been reading too much science fiction," said Ann.

"I really don't understand Ann," Kat confessed to Lil over coffee the next day. She forgot to tell her about the presents Ann was giving her. They were making a pile in the corner of her bedroom.

She finally remembered to tell Lil about the crying girl, though. "I didn't want to tell you," she confessed.

"Why would you not want to tell something so important?"

"It's important?" Kat felt two inches taller all of a sudden.

"But of course it is."

"It's a girl who cries. It's horrible."

"Where is it?"

"I can show you on a map." They brought out a street directory and Kat found the right street.

Lil frowned. "I think I know that."

"And?"

"I don't know if we can do anything about it."

"It's like the grindylow?"

"In that it's a thing of nature, yes."

"But it's not the grindylow?"

"It is either an old ghost of a drowned girl, which is the tale I have heard tell."

"Or?"

"Or it is something older and more dangerous that was here before we came."

"Humans?"

"Europeans."

"Can't we do something? Please?"

"You wish to reform the world?"

"I wish to be not scared."

"Some things we can change outside ourselves, but for some we can only look inside. This is one of the ones where you will have to find the change. Find the ghosts inside that add to the fear and you can face a ghost."

"And if it's an ancient spirit?"

"Then best keep away from that patch of water. It is her home, and she is entitled to it."

Kat sighed, but accepted what Lil said. Part of it, anyway. *I'm not carrying any ghosts*, she told herself.

※ ◆ ※

"Where're we going?" Kat asked.

"Ghost hunting," said Ann, cheerfully. "I thought we could take a look at a couple of sites in Acton and then do something rather special this evening."

"Cool," said Kat, appreciatively. "Is the special thing haunted?"

"It's theatre. There's a play at Gorman House I've wanted to see for a while, and my husband isn't that interested."

"So you got us tickets?"

"We have to buy them tonight, but that's not a problem."

"Double cool. Triple cool." Kat settled back in the passenger seat and watched Canberra go by.

"Where are we?" she asked a few minutes later.

"Don't you know?" teased Ann.

"I don't know Canberra by car," Kat confessed cheerfully. She waited for Ann's guilty silence. It came, exactly when she expected it. Ann kept forgetting that Kat had been on the streets until that particular sunny lunchtime. Kat rather enjoyed guilt-tripping her about it. Then she realised what she was doing. Badkatbadkatbadkat. Biting the hand that was feeding her. Wrong. Wrong. Wrong. Badkatbadkatbadkat

The two of them sat in the same car, separated by their silence.

Eventually, Ann pulled up outside a big, elegant building. "This is why I took the afternoon off. It shuts in an hour."

"It's a building," Kat observed, dubiously.

"It's Art Deco. The National Film and Sound Archive. One day I'll tell you the history and show you the architecture. It's fabulous. That's not why we're here, though."

"Ghosts," Kat said, with relish.

"Lots of people claim that this is the most haunted building in Canberra. I thought if we walked round it, you could see what you could see and tell me."

"But what do you see?"

"Out of my eye?" They were approaching the front steps. "Later. Be quiet and just walk and watch."

"Okay." And they were inside, and everything was lines and sharp edges and interesting shapes and tall ceilings.

"Come back here when you have more time," said Ann, in tour guide mode. "It's free and it's fascinating."

Kat was feeling a bit overwhelmed, so she just nodded.

Ann led Kat down corridors, up halls, through exhibits. She looked at displays and pushed buttons and watched old newsreels while Kat looked around slowly and cautiously.

It was disappointing. Kat saw absolutely nothing. Not until they reached a gallery upstairs where a whole lot of stills from films were on display. The stills looked a lot more interesting than the ghosts she was hunting. Then she saw, out of the corner of her eye, a flicker of white lace.

Ann was watching her, and nodded. "We can go now," she said. "We have another place to see before dark."

"Okay," said Kat. This ghost stuff wasn't what it was cracked up to be.

As they walked back to the car, Ann said, "Well?"

"You saw when I saw something," Kat said, vaguely.

"That was the only time?"

"Yep. It was boring," she complained. "I'd rather see the films."

"That was supposed to be the most haunted building in Canberra," Ann said.

"Oh." Kat was saddened. "No ghosts for me, then."

"Actually, no. You saw the one ghost I always see there. The others are probably the very active imagination of the general public."

"Oh," said Kat again, this time more cheerfully.

"When I drive past a particular building," Ann said, starting the car, "I want you to watch for people in it. If you see anyone working, tell me."

"The person working is a ghost?"

"No," laughed Ann. "But I'm not going to break in there if there's anyone around."

"Oh!" said Kat, one more time, perfectly happy. She was going to break into a building!

The drive up Balmain Crescent was fast, even though Ann took the car as slowly as she could. When they parked round the corner and Ann said, "Anyone?" Kat had to nod.

"Maybe we can come back next week?" she asked, hopefully.

"It wasn't a curtain waving or something?"

"No. A man looked out of the top corner room. Clear as day."

"That man," said Ann, in a mock-solemn voice, "is dead."

"He was a ghost?" Kat only half-believed.

"I didn't want you to convince yourself that you were seeing him."

"Oh," and this time the word had a vast satisfaction, making it buoyant. "What now?

"We go to the theatre."

"Yay!" Kat was happy.

There was nowhere to park near Gorman House. "There are never any car parks here," muttered Ann. "Why do I always forget?"

In the end they had to park close to the shops and walk. By the time they were inside the low cream building, a queue had formed at the box office.

"Why don't you wait out of the crowd?" Ann suggested. "I can deal with this."

"Sure thing," said Kat, and found herself a quiet corner of floor. It was perfect for her, that corner, because she could watch and listen and notice all the people.

It was a long time before Ann emerged from the crowd. She was very flustered. "They didn't hold the tickets," Ann said. "They say they didn't even get reservations."

"I thought you didn't make reservations," Kat said.

"Dammit!" Ann swore, quietly but violently. "I forgot! What a mess. Sorry."

Kat gave her a moment, then shot a look across. "What really happened?"

"You saw right through me, didn't you?"

"It was the way you weren't looking at me directly. I kinda guessed."

"Well, I didn't make reservations. All the tickets were sold out. But the lady just ahead of me had gone into the theatre really early and wanted to return her tickets and get a refund. That was what took all the time. I waited behind her and was listening."

"Why didn't you take them?"

"She dragged her boyfriend out before the performance began. She had the creeps. I could feel it on her. Something foul."

"But today is ghostday, we could have done that."

"Today *was* ghostday. I don't want to give you too much too soon. Besides, I wanted to watch a play and have fun, not sit in the dark with an evil presence for two hours."

"So we go home?"

"The car is right next to the shops, right?"

"Right."

"And in the shops there is food and in the shops there is a cinema. How about dinner and a movie?"

"Is it going to cost you a lot?"

"Less than the theatre. We're getting cheap food and cheap tickets." Ann sounded much more cheerful.

"Okay, then. But I get veto rights over the movie. I don't want to see a kiddie thing. And we have to walk straight past the bookshop."

"So you don't eye off big blank books," Ann teased. Kat looked at her, wondering where Ann's mind had gone, and then she realised that she had confided in Ann, once, early on, her dream for her very own leather journal. She hadn't said that it was to be her Book of Shadows, but she guessed Ann knew. Why she would remember it now was anyone's guess. Unless Ann kept her supernatural experiences in her own volume? It was hard to visualise Ann with a Book of Shadows. Ann looked round and bright-eyed, not mystical and magic.

Kat was going to invade Ann's place and find out. *No*, she thought. *I'm not. Ann's place isn't comfortable any more. I'll let her have her secrets.*

Tales of Melusine #55

Why Melusine has never been to Japan.

Honorine was the queen of the spoken fairy tale. Others wrote better stories, but hers, told in the quietest and gentlest voice imaginable, lingered in the mind. After she was forgotten, her tales lingered. Melusine called herself Honorine fifty years later, in memory of that soft voice and its haunting tales.

This story, Honorine said, was not invented. She knew it from a traveller from the East, who had infiltrated into the city of Edo, and learned histories that Frenchmen could only dream of. Melusine wondered about that, but it was a story after all, and even if Honorine had learned it from Hasekura Rokuemon Tsunenaga himself, when he was in Saint Tropez thirty years before, it was still a story worth telling. It held the sound of truth, as good stories must.

The prince of Hizen was in love. He had many ladies, but one was special to him. This was Otoyo. She was graceful beyond imagining and gentle as a willow branch drifting in the breeze. It did not surprise him that animals followed her, for to him she was beautiful beyond measure. One night, he failed to notice a large cat that followed them from the gardens into the palace. If he had noticed it, he would have been flattered as the cat shared his taste for the lady Otoyo, but he would have put it outside, nonetheless.

Otoyo felt haunted that night. Her sleep was restless and her hands fluttered near her throat like birds, even though she was fast asleep. At midnight she woke up, for there seemed to be no air left. She woke to the darkness and a fear of it. A heavy presence made the air dense.

The lady Otoyo lit a lamp and saw, in a corner, the giant cat. She went to shoo it outside. Instead of allowing itself to be persuaded out of the door, it sprang towards her. It jumped to her face and, pushing her back on the bed, suffocated her.

When it was certain she was dead, it took her form. It buried her under the verandah and it wooed the prince, just as the real Otoyo had done.

The prince gradually became weaker and weaker. Nothing the doctors could do would restore him. Nothing his lovers and his family could suggest restored him to vigour. When he admitted to dreams of darkness and terror, of suffocating and death, his retainers agreed to keep watch. Maybe he was not ill. Maybe he was being visited at night by some foul presence? If this was not the case, then they knew they would despair, for he was losing his strength, day by day, and soon they would lose him. With love in their hearts, therefore, one hundred retainers sat at his bedside watching him sleep.

Alas for their vigilance. All the men were overcome by sleep at the same instant. The moment they slumbered, the false Otoyo brazenly walked into the bedroom and did what she would with him. Night after night this happened. Night after night the prince's health deteriorated.

He became so ill that a priest was also delegated to sit by his bedside. His name was Ruiten. He called upon a young soldier to join in the night watch. This soldier was not known at court and had been denied the honour of nursing or watching the prince. He was pure of heart and clean of body and most fervent in his prayers.

When the priest sat with him outside the prince's room, waiting for the preparations for sleep to be finished, they talked together. The soldier was not Court-trained and still knew of the superstitions of the country. He told Ruiten that the prince was bewitched and he said it so clearly and so firmly that Ruiten had to believe. "The cause of His Highness's illness," the soldier stated, "is evil, not illness."

The soldier was allowed to join the watch. On the first night his drowsiness was too great and he fell asleep with the other watchers. On the second night he jabbed his knife into his leg, and kept off sleep for a time. He still succumbed, however. On the third night, he did the same, but this time he sat on oil paper and he twisted the knife inside his muscle, so that the pain was constant. The blood dripped onto the oil paper and the solder was in great pain, but he remained awake.

He saw Otoyo slide the door open and walk towards the prince. He watched her talk and cajole. But it did nothing. An evil spirit cannot work with eyes upon it and the soldier was awake and watching, though she did not know it. All the false Otoyo knew was that her charms did not work that night.

The next morning the prince felt better. The soldier was commanded to watch again a second night, even though no-one was prepared to listen to his description of what had happened. He was too unimportant, and Edo is a city of ranks and titles. His watching kept the prince alive, however, and if that was all he could do, then it was what he must do. He sat awake and in pain for another night.

This night the false Otoyo could not come near the prince's bed, and the night after she was unable to walk more than partway through the room. After this, she could not even pass the doorway.

The councillors realised that the only factor that had changed was the presence of the soldier who had only been included in the watch at the demand of the priest, Ruiten. They asked Ruiten for advice. He produced the oil paper with blood. He said that a supernatural creature was at work.

The soldier was commanded to go to Otoyo's room and to do what must be done. He had eight armed guards to assist him. He arranged for the guards to be positioned around the apartment, so that she could not escape. He himself went to the main door of Otoyo's apartment and pretended to bear a message from the prince.

"The prince has sent me a message?" The false Otoyo was puzzled. She held out her hand for a letter.

In response, the soldier drew his faithful knife. The false Otoyo was secretly armed. The two fought quietly, the woman moving slowly towards the back of the room. When she reached a window, she turned into a cat and leapt out of the window. The cat fled to the roof and although eight men went out after her, none could catch her.

The prince became well and the soldier was rewarded. The prince of Hizen claimed that an expedition to the mountains had killed the cat, but this is a lie. She was never found. Why she wanted the life of the prince was also never discovered. What remained after the cat fled was a mystery.

<hr />

Lil and Mabel had a little excursion.

"We had to check something out," Mabel explained to the others, afterwards.

"And what was this 'something'?" Ann's voice held a dangerous edge. She was not happy about being left out.

"It happened very quickly," said Lil. "We were shopping."

"Presents," said Mabel gloomily. "I hate shopping for presents."

"So you took Lil." Ann's voice almost lost its edge.

"I always do. Otherwise my family would get nothing, ever."

"My Mum's like that," Kat offered. "Would rather give money than find something nice."

"I never give money," sniffed Mabel. "I borrow Lil and she finds appropriate garbage and then everyone's happy."

"Except something happened while you were out?"

"Yes, Ann." Lil's voice softened and she told the tale. Mabel remained silent except for tiny grunts of agreement at key words: little treat, frolic. "Something happened."

Lil and Mabel had met at Chalmers. It was no longer the best coffee shop in Manuka, but both of them were creatures of habit, and they had met there for years. When they had started it was the best coffee shop in the whole city, which, said Lil, caused her to instantly lower her expectations of Canberra coffee.

Whenever Mabel felt in a funk about shopping for family, Lil and she started with a nice cup of coffee or tea and a shared piece of cake. It turned the shopping into a ritual and gave them time-out from the more difficult side of life. The staff at the shop knew them and would recommend this cake or that chocolate. This meant they always started off these little expeditions feeling just a bit spoiled.

While they were enjoying their little treat, they couldn't help overhearing the two people at the next table. The acoustics at Chalmers are like that.

One of them was very upset.

"Calm down," her friend said. "You'll spill the coffee."

"I don't care about the damn coffee. I want to forget the last half hour. I want to wipe it from my mind. I want it never to have happened."

"You know you don't," coaxed the young man. ("He's holding her hand and stroking it," whispered Mabel.) "You know you're dying to tell me."

"You don't know a thing."

"I know that if you bottle it up, you'll hate it even more. And maybe we can take it to the police. I bet we can. I'll be there, with you, the whole way."

"Not the police," she whispered. "There's nobody, nobody can help. It's just too awful."

"Tell me then, get it out of your system, at least."

There was a long silence.

"I was walking up to St Christopher's. I nearly went in. I thought, 'Wouldn't it be a nice place to get married,' then I thought about just how set you were on the Botanic Gardens. Besides, it wasn't open. Then I saw some blokes walking out of it. Small guys. Big hair. I called out, 'Is it open? Is the cathedral open?' I thought it wouldn't hurt to check. Maybe it'd be totally awful and if I hadn't checked then I couldn't tell you that you were right and you wouldn't laugh at me and we'd miss some fun."

She paused. ("She's drinking water," whispered Mabel.)

"They all stopped at once. They turned and looked up. They were so short. And their eyes. Their eyes. Big and staring. Glassy. Horrible. One of them said to me, 'Only some parts are open, and you don't want to go to those parts, young missie.'

"'Not till we are finished our little frolic. Doin' the rounds, we are,' another one said. 'After we've checked the very last restaurant and drunk their last drop, we can have fun with you then.'

"'Our brothers are there now, and their idea of fun is different.'

"'No, don't go there now. You won't like their idea of fun'

"And they all turned away at once, like a befouled corps de ballet, and they walked down the street, to Manuka."

"That's why you wanted to come here."

"It's not a restaurant. Chalmers doesn't even serve alcohol," she said. "I never want to see those horrible things again."

"I'm taking you home," her fiancé said. "We'll order home delivery."

"Yes, please," she said. "And we're not coming to Manuka ever again, and we're getting married in the Botanic Gardens even if the mosquitoes make me blotched all over."

"I love you, you know," he said.

And they left.

"Do you know what that was about?" Mabel asked across the table, addressing her question as much at the cups and plates as at her friends. "If it was a practical joke, it was a bloody good one."

"Abbey lubbers. Drunken sots, all. It can't be anything else. That look, the way she said they moved, the drinking binge. Abbey lubbers," Lil said. "I ran into them once, in England, a long time ago. They should not be here. They should *not* be here."

"Dangerous?" Mabel's voice was sharp. "Hunt in packs?"

"Yes and no, and sometimes. They are more dangerous when they're inebriated and they will find wine almost anywhere."

"Restaurants," said Mabel.

"Indeed. The threat to the girl was probably false, however. They love drama and affect."

"But if there are a lot living in there together and they get drunk together . . ."

"That they let themselves be seen is unusual."

"In Australia, things are different. Maybe they're not quite so safe for us here."

"That is precisely what concerns me. We must fix this."

"Kat?"

"I forgot Kat." Lil frowned.

"She needs training. So far we've been all tell and no show."

"Something safe, first, to build her up."

"Yes. These creatures don't sound like a good place to start."

This is what they explained to Kat and Ann. Something had to be done, they both concurred on that, but Kat needed more training first, just in case.

"It was not good." Lil summed up. "It was bad enough to necessitate an excursion."

"It has to be dealt with," said Ann, nodding firmly. Kat thought she was like one of those anime characters, where the nod says more than the words. Ann would forgive Lil and Mabel this time, but she was going to lead the expedition. *Or she will give them what-for*, giggled Kat, to herself.

Before things could get more interesting, they were derailed entirely.

"Can I tell her my Lake George joke now?" asked Mabel plaintively.

"NO!" chorused her two friends.

"I can tell you something I found out, instead," offered Kat. "It's not a big something and it's not a joke." She was emboldened by the trio finally suggesting she do something other than sit around listening to stories or be taken on a carefully overplanned ghost trail. Not that she didn't love listening to stories or seeing bits of ghost, but she wanted more. Much more.

"Out with it," said Mabel.

"One of those misty figures — the ones that whisper and make everyone feel that the world is evil, so, someone commented on it on a Canberra gossip website."

"Interesting," said Lil. "What did they say?"

GILLIAN POLACK

"This guy saw it up close. It was a girl, about my age, and she was near a stream. He said he's seen her three times and she's always been near the stream, but that the stream moves."

"Like the streets," whispered Ann.

"Yes," said Kat. "And there's more. He's so scared of her that he turns and walks the other way whenever he sees her. He says she drowned a mate of his. He wouldn't say how and he stopped posting at all when everyone else started asking questions."

"We might have to find out more," said Ann.

"Agreed," said Mabel.

"I don't like it," whispered Lil. "It's not an old spirit and it's not a ghost. That's two incidents in a very short time. It suggests something . . . something . . ."

"I heard a story today," said Kat, trying to help. "I mean, I read a story, online. Another story."

"Tell us," said Lil, accepting the outstretched arm.

"Someone was looking for the treasure on Black Mountain. You know, the one that was supposed to have been hidden by a bushranger. He couldn't find anything, but he told a bunch of people on a website. They started talking about it. Some people talked about the treasure and some people talked about the bushranger. One bloke said that he had seen a group of figures on horseback, last Sunday, on Black Mountain, near the Telstra Tower. He was far enough away so he couldn't really make them out. They were shadowy, maybe. Anyhow, they were really loud. I mean, their voices were really loud, but he couldn't make out the words. He said that they were arguing about something. They got really mad and they were shooting at each other. He said they looked really dangerous. The guy watching stayed really quiet until they were all gone. Then he went to investigate."

"Did he find anything?" asked Ann, intently.

"He did," said Kat, triumphantly. "I wrote it all down, too. He found a pile of goods and with them a list, which he thought referred to the pile of goods. He said they looked pretty much as if they could be the same things, though he didn't know enough about these things to find out. The writing was really old-fashioned."

"Copperplate?" asked Mabel.

"He didn't say. He did write down the list though — d'you want to hear it?"

54

"Please," said Lil.

"4 gross port wine

"6 gallon hollands

"2 pieces broadcloth

"5 lbs American tobacco

"1 chest tea

"2 bags sugar

"1 set harness for a gig

"1 saddle

"1 bridle

'1 single barrelled fowling piece

"2 canisters powder

"4 bags of shot"

"Where do you find these things?" asked Lil.

"There's a website where Canberra people gossip. I keep an eye on it and follow leads and things. You weren't telling me enough stories, so I had to find more. I want to understand all this."

"Kat the detective," Mabel said, and smiled. Kat smiled back.

"Could you print it out for me?" asked Ann.

"I don't have a printer yet," said Kat, dubiously, showing Ann her sprawling handwriting.

"Let me lure you to my back room," said Mabel. "You can find the story and the list again online and print it there for all of us."

"Why do you want it, anyway?" asked Kat.

"I think that the bushrangers are ghost stories," Ann said.

"And all of you oldies have a thing about ghosts," Kat said. "Maybe it shows how near the grave you are."

"What happened to the respectful young thing I met just a few weeks ago," Ann mourned.

"She started eating properly," Kat suggested. "Green chicken."

"Admire my trees," said Mabel.

"I am admiring them," a man's voice answered.

"Each of them represents an occult property. The hexagons around them look pretty, but they're functional as well. If I had a bigger garden I would've interwoven them with the zodiac, but it was hard enough planning this one and fitting it all in gracefully."

"I don't know some of these trees."

"They don't grow in England or in this region at all normally. This section of my garden has developed a micro-climate."

"I don't understand."

"Everything's a bit warmer here, so the frost-sensitive trees flourish. Do you want a more technical explanation?"

"Not especially. I may not know a great deal, but I understand enough."

"You wanted to know how my protection worked — this is how. It's described by the garden beds and the spells are the plants. They also feed me. It's very efficient."

"That's your whole garden and your whole protection?"

"No, just the main bit. The rest is protected by another magic, not mine," she said. "I need to do the paths and entrances too, one day."

"So your power is in understanding the universe?"

"I guess."

"I admire that."

"You don't have to admire it by walking through me." Mabel's' voice was sharp.

"I cannot seem to remain corporeal today." The man's voice was rueful.

"How can what I know help? It's driving me crazy — I'm a helpless old lady. It's not like it used to be, where using my brain could get me out of most pickles."

"I don't know yet." The man's voice was tender. "When I know more, I shall tell you, I promise."

Tales of Melusine #45

Melusine found the Australian ghosts very quickly. The spirits took her a little longer. She made her peace with the spirits very quickly. The ghosts and she were less straightforward.

If ghosts are the baggage of humans, then what is the baggage of ghosts? Melusine decided, one Christmas, that the baggage of ghosts was her. She herself, Melusine. Not in a trollopish way. Ghosts did not expect her to sleep with them (although occasionally one or two would give certain hints). Ghosts expected her to support their beliefs. They expected her to understand their fear of hellfire, even though they were patently not suffering it. They expected her to go to church the way they thought they remembered they had. Most of all, they expected her to celebrate Christmas.

There was something about Christmas in Australia. Everyone was expected to celebrate it.

One recently-deceased let her know in no uncertain terms that it was her secular duty to celebrate. Another thought it was humorous to take the shape of a faded white tree in Melusine's living room. This was when Melusine found a friend of a friend of a friend and banished stray presences from her living space. It was when she protected her house against anything. Late December was bad enough without having supernatural reminders of her loneliness.

After that, mostly she left ghosts alone and they left her alone. It was when three local children found out she would be home alone at Christmas and tried to re-enact "A Christmas Carol" on her that she was forced to move house. In the end, it was harder to reconcile with the living than with the dead on 25 December. Though she did protect her new house, very carefully indeed. No more wavering Christmas trees in her front room. Ever.

Melusine refused to write down the story of how "A Christmas Carol" went dreadfully wrong. The children lived, is all she would have said, if anyone had known to ask her. She was shaken enough to move to another state, not just another house. And from then on she fiercely protected her lonely time. She also avoided ghosts and children. She developed a sense of distance from the world and hid behind a barrier of courtesy that few people had the courage to see beyond.

It wasn't that she didn't know many people from that point in her life. It was that very, very few people knew her. And of those few people, none knew her secrets.

Those children had hurt her beyond healing. What she had almost done to those children was bad: she had never ever seen herself as a possible danger to humans until now. She had changed their lives forever, and she didn't want to contemplate that, either. Fairy magic and humans had not mixed well in a very long time.

She had already thought that maybe it was time to allow herself to die. That Christmas in Sydney was the first year that she thought mortality might be a good thing. She felt old beyond reckoning and sad beyond knowing. Melusine was more alone than she had ever been before. Not even the witch craze had been this bad. It was a gentle loneliness. It was full of physical comfort. It was not like the horror that was running a boarding house in London. But it was nevertheless a desperate isolation.

Death was, she thought, a solution. Even a friend. Quiet and peace. Forever.

Five

"I DID SOME RESEARCH," said Kat to Ann.

"Good on you," said Ann, and started talking about the new shoes she was thinking of buying.

"I did some research," said Kat to Lil.

"What did it tell you?" asked Lil.

"I know a bit more about bushrangers," Kat said.

"That's very useful," approved Lil said, approvingly. "You should tell us all three together, perhaps, and we can know more about what we seek."

"I did some research," said Kat to Mabel.

"What about?" asked Mabel.

"Bushrangers," said Kat.

"Tell me some of it," said Mabel.

"How much?"

"All the best bits, of course."

Kat smiled. She told Mabel the most common bushranger ghost in the region was supposed to be Jackey-Jackey and that his treasure was buried on Black Mountain. She said that Jackey-Jackey's real name was William Westwood and that he was hanged on 13 October 1846.

"He was a real gentleman," said Kat. "Polite to almost everyone and totally awesome towards women. He didn't hurt many people either, mostly he threatened. 'Til he revolted — he killed people then."

"That's interesting," said Mabel. "The man I saw had a ring round his neck."

"You have really seen him? Truly?"

"Twice, I think. Maybe more. Do you know about the marked skin around his neck? Did your research tell you?"

"From the hanging." Kat nodded sagely. "I know more about him, if you want."

"I want," said Mabel. "I want more."

"He was educated. I mean, he could read and write. He was transported because he forged a cheque for six shillings and because he stole a coat."

"He was English?"

"Yes," said Kat. "He was from Essex."

"Ah, that explains things."

"What things?"

"Just things. Tell me more."

Kat took a moment to process Mabel's vagueness and then she continued, undaunted. "The ship he came out on had the coolest name: the *Mangles*. Jackey-Jackey kept running away once he was in Australia. He was assigned somewhere near Goulburn and he kept running away. He was punished so many times that he must've had a lot of scars."

Mabel nodded to show she understood.

"I don't know why he kept on running away," Kat said. "If he had just served his sentence, he would have been free."

"Maybe the property owner was cruel? Or maybe he hated servitude," Mabel suggested.

"Maybe," said Kat. "It wasn't the same as my running away, though. He wasn't screaming inside because he was invisible."

"Not at all," said Mabel. "Not at all. He doesn't seem the invisible type, does he?"

"Anyway, eventually, he went bush and met up with a guy called Paddy Curran. Curran was foul and horrible and raped someone. Jackey-Jackey beat him up for raping the woman and then took everything Curran had, and then Jackey-Jackey said he'd kill him if ever he saw him again. He was a real gentleman, wasn't he?"

"I'm not sure about him being a real gentleman," said Mabel. "But he sounds kinder than most. Perhaps what my father used to call one of 'nature's gentlemen'? Anyway, what happened to him after that?"

"He became like a highwayman. He bailed up coaches and things. Twice he was captured and twice he escaped. Hee, I'm getting all poetic!"

"Restrain your glee," Mabel said drily.

"A reward was posted for him. I want to see a ghostly reward poster.

That'd be cool. Only no-one claimed the reward for ages and ages. Not till 1841. At Berrima."

"So that's where he died?"

"No, he didn't die until 1846, remember?"

"All those dates confuse me," said Mabel with as much dignity as she could muster. "Dates and names and places. Buggers to remember."

"He died interestingly, too. There was a convict mutiny on Norfolk Island and he murdered three men there."

"So that's why he was hanged."

"That's why he was hanged."

"How old was he?"

"Twenty-six."

"My God," the words escaped before Mabel could contain them. "So young!"

"Do you want me to read a description of him? I've got one right here." Mabel nodded.

"Brown hair, dark grey eyes, slight build, 5'5" tall, errand boy/clerk, Protestant Religion, Able to Read and Write, slight pockmarks to face, scars on right hand and arm."

"That's him all right," Mabel said.

"Ann says we're going to look for him. Or his treasure. She thinks that should be my training excursion. To Black Mountain."

Mabel rubbed her forehead. "Can't she think of anything better than ghosts? That woman really has a one-track mind."

Black Mountain didn't look like a place that ought to have ghosts. Kat had been there once in primary school, on a big school excursion. She remembered the Tower and she thought the viewing windows shouldn't have anything except bored students walking around them, identifying morsels of Canberra. 'Look, there's a government building.' 'Look! Another government building.' Very bored students. She practised looking bored while the other three argued.

Of course they were going to argue, she realised. Mabel wanted to go to the Botanic Gardens. Forget bushrangers' ghosts. Forget fancy saving-the-world stuff. What really mattered was plants. And flowers. And trees. But mostly plants.

Ann made the mistake of saying this. "It's not about plants," she said. She actually said it. To Mabel.

Lil stifled a laugh. Mabel picked up on the laugh and that was the end of the argument. It was not precisely the best possible end to the argument.

"You go look for ghosts in the bloody Telstra Tower," she said to Ann. "And you . . ." She looked down into Lil's wide eyes with a mouth that showed she felt betrayed. "You can go look for scrapes in the earth where Jackey-Jackey hid his treasure and you attempt a bloody ghost calling and you can talk to him. I'm going to the Gardens. Alone. This is not something I'm going to waste time discussing."

And she did. Mabel being melodramatic was so rare that the others were able to do nothing, really, to make her change her mind.

Ann made Kat go with her and Kat wondered when Ann had gone from being interested in Kat to being interested in educating Kat. She got the history of Canberra at the top of the Tower and Ann sounded exactly like Kat's Grade Five teacher. The one who had to tell you things even if you knew them already. The one who made life boring without even trying. When had her favourite grandmother turned into this stranger?

Kat put on her polite face and zoned out.

Lil's search was a failure. No evidence of treasure. No evidence of ghost. No evidence of anything except tourist traps.

All Mabel said to the others was, "That fernery looks more artificial every year."

What she didn't say to the others was that she had run into a certain nineteenth century flirt in the fernery. That meeting proved to her satisfaction that ghosts can become corporeal. In fact, it proved to her that the right ghost could kiss her hand in a most elegant fashion. Her biggest worry was whether there was proof of her blushing.

Mabel was no innocent. She wondered whether he was following her. Why only she could answer his technical questions. Whether she ought to be worried about how very young he had been when he died. And about how far ghostly flirtation could extend.

Tales of Melusine #84

1843 was not a good year. The nineteenth century in general was not kind to Melusine, but 1843 was its nadir. Writing its key moment down was far more difficult than telling the tales of other years.

Maybe this moment should not be told? Or perhaps it was so crucial that she had to pin it down and find out why it terrified her so.

She knew what had led up to that moment. That evil was engraved deep, in places she would not look. One day she may tell that story. Not today. Not today. Today she is skipping most of the secular and starting with the Day of Atonement. Autumn is such a sad time. October is such a sad month.

She was breaking her fast. She remembered that much. It was Day of Atonement and she was breaking her fast. It was one of those infinitely forgettable community events, where the rabbi's wife had collected all the stray women who had appeared during the day and was taking pity on them. Melusine wondered every year what happened to the sick women, the lonely women, the women who could not brave the congregation and its inquisition about their lives. She wondered if the random men were drilled to the same degree as stray women.

It was never simply "Who are you?" or "Where do you come from?" Everyone but her was desperate to make connections, to prove that they knew her or that she knew them or that they were related in some distant way. The non-Jews of Europe and the Americas were determined to have all Jews linked and, at times like these, it seemed that her fellow religionists were all too keen to assist.

"I have no living relatives," she would say calmly. "Yes, it was tragic. No, I would rather not talk about it." And all the little women would flutter round her trying not to upset her, trying to be kind to her, trying to find out every single detail so they could tell their friends sad stories on long winter nights.

She couldn't tell these dinners apart after a while. She couldn't tell if the language was French, or German, or English, or Ladino, or Provencal, or Yiddish. The only thing that made the breaking of the fast special in 1843 was that it was the year that men moved out of her line of vision entirely. It was the year she realised that she had been so long without close company that her body had started ageing. It annoyed her that she could tell no-one.

"I don't want a confidante," she lied to herself. But she did.

When Melusine returned to her lodging she looked at herself in the mirror and decided, "This is where I age gracefully." She felt just like a human as she said it and she had human wrinkles, too. Thank

God she hadn't had human menopause. When she was grey enough she would pretend she had been through it. One more lie to add to the layers of falsity that comprised her existence.

Kat's grandmothers weren't talking about the abbey lubbers. They weren't talking about the other excursion they were planning to train her (or whatever, given the Jackey-Jackey idea had been such a dismal failure). They were fixated on the subject of bushrangers. Kat rather liked this fixation, so she was diverting them from the other topics for all she was worth. She had loved bushrangers ever since she had done a project on Ned Kelly in fifth grade.

Kat carefully snipped out a report from the Canberra Times. It described a sighting of three men on horseback. They were wearing nineteenth century clothes. One of them, it appeared, had a pair of binoculars or field glasses.

"The article said that the field glasses caught the sunlight and that between his costume and the metal and the shine, he looked like something out of a steampunk novel."

"Did the article speculate as to who they were?"

"Sorta. Said it must be some sort of student thing. Or roleplaying. Because of the steampunk look."

"Interesting," said Ann.

"I can show you the article."

"Your summary is good enough for me," said Ann.

"Put it in a scrapbook," said Lil. "Mabel can see it when she gets back from her daughter's."

Kat nodded. "And if there are other things from the paper or the web, I can collect them."

Suddenly it was dinner party time. Kat was totally mad at her three women because they talked a lot. Didn't do a thing. Kept talking and talking and talking. Not saying much either.

"How do we stop Kat from getting hurt?"

"How do we prepare her?"

"What can we tell her?"

They must have said other things, lots of other things, but they did the serious talking behind her back. She knew too much about cover-up. It nearly cost them their experiment with her. Kat packed a bag and was out the door before she could blink. Halfway down the street she decided to give them a second chance. Really, she thought, they were doing it for the right reasons. It made her smile a little that they were worried about her.

She counted. This meant she had known them two months and three weeks. Not so long. They might not be as slow as it felt they were.

Kat unpacked her bag. She would give them more time. As she did so, she felt a buzz of excitement. It was her second dinner with the old ladies. Two months of dinner parties. She was an old hand. And it was at Mabel's. She knew Mabel's place. She earned most of her pocket money there, helping in the garden.

Kat strolled nonchalantly past the lavender that bordered the front path. She tried to look as if she belonged there, walking insouciantly on the gravel. Kat stopped suddenly when she reached the front door. She wanted to turn and go back to the safety of her granny flat. Mabel's place at night meant the creature in the woodpile. Eyes glowing at her. Creature-eyes. Those eyes liked Mabel, but she was certain-sure they hated her.

Before she could run away, the door opened and Kat was safe indoors.

"You don't have any woodpile creatures inside?" she asked, anxiously. "I mean, it's night and everything."

"Not a one," Mabel said, cheerfully. "Now come and peel my potatoes. And mind you peel the skin thin — I don't want all the potato in the compost bin."

Eventually the others turned up and Lil and Ann were given sherry to placate them while the dinner was being finished. Mabel did not leave Kat alone in her kitchen for a minute. Kat was trying to work out if it was because she was not trusted, or if it because Mabel was motherly. She didn't think Mabel was terribly motherly, but one never knew.

"Does anyone here know how to unblock a drain?" Ann asked the world at large, as seated around the dinner table.

"You mean a serious blockage? Get a plumber."

"It's not serious enough for a plumber," Ann said. "It's happened before and I don't know how to handle it."

"Surely your husband can help?" Mabel was sharp. Mabel's voice was often sharp when Ann's husband came to mind. The two had sparked uncomfortable static from the first moment they met. "Even if you and he don't have the best relationship."

Ann was at her wry best. "He's always done it in the past. If he were still a husband, such things would be possible even now. Fortunately, the divorce papers came through today. I can't help him — and he can't hurt me. In fact, we're living under the same roof without even a moment of communication in any given day. It's an experience."

Immediately there was a little scuffle of attention. Lil and Mabel both stood to make her drinks and Kat leaned forward, her eyes full of questions.

"Now," said Ann, her words emerging in strong bursts, subduing the excitement, "this is why I didn't tell any of you what was going on. I don't want fuss. I want to get on with my life quietly, as always. I want to do things that matter, not worry about that man. I want . . ." her voice faltered.

"A cup of tea?" asked Mabel.

"That's right," said Ann. "I want a cup of tea."

"I'll get it," said Kat. She may have been sitting at the table with the elders, but she really didn't belong there. Not yet.

They were celebrating Ann's retirement and talking about her divorce and there had been that gaping silence when Ann dropped that her husband had been going out with a younger woman for two whole years. Kat couldn't deal with any more. She really couldn't. She was also very carefully avoiding thinking about all the presents Ann had surreptitiously slipped her: anime and books and even figurines. She suspected that Ann had stolen them from her ex-husband.

They're mine now, she thought defensively, as she put the tea things on a tray. *And anyway, he must be ick. Imagine not wanting someone as nice as Ann.* Still, she felt discomfited by the whole thing. It was as if Ann had developed a shadow and it was slightly bent and warped. It was as if she had seen that shadow all along and only just noticed it now.

"It took me an hour to get home today," Ann was saying as Kat came back into the dining room.

"You should stop chatting up handsome young shop assistants," said Mabel. "It's sure to cause trouble."

"That was not funny," said Ann.

"You saying it was not funny, was funny," said Kat.

66

"True," said Mabel.

"Why were you so long on the way home?" asked Lil, gently.

"The streets shifted more than usual," said Ann, a note of triumph in her voice. Everything she said seemed to have an added value tonight.

It's the divorce, thought Kat, *we're all focussed on her extra specially. And look how she loves it. I didn't know she wanted the whole world to zoom round her, but she does. How funny.* Then she felt guilty, for thinking evil things about someone who had done so much for her. *Badkat. Badbadbad Kat.*

Kat pulled herself together and sat up straight and listened with extra intentness to make up for her thoughts. She tried to, anyhow. All she got, really, was that the streets shifted so dramatically that three times Ann ended up on the road to Gungahlin and once she found herself in Fyshwick. And that Ann had deduced something very clever about how this linked to ghosts. She was too busy punishing herself for thinking those thoughts about Ann to listen fully. *Badbadbad Kat.*

To make up for her lapse, she tried writing notes about it later. She wrote notes for herself about it, but she forgot to identify the speakers. More *badkat*. It was as if she had taken some of the fallout from Ann's divorce. Ann was smug and the centre of the universe and Kat was full of holes.

"Reality shifts indicate humans' relationship with the environment is . . . unstable."

"So everything's unstable."

"Not everything. The rules shift, but according to our expectations."

"It's our ghosts that change things."

"Our ghosts, our haunts, our fears."

"So sending them back does no good?"

"Only if you define saving lives as no good."

"Can we stabilise things?"

"Maybe. To one reality or another — the universe can be persuaded to rest for a bit, I'm certain."

"How?"

"Try chocolate. It always helps me."

Another little snippet appeared in the paper. Kat tried to read it over the phone to Mabel.

"Just tell me," Mabel said. "I can't make sense of things people read aloud."

"Someone wrote an article about the house they just moved into. They see a young girl walking into their lounge room, but then she is gone. They see her all over the place. Once she was playing on the swing, then the swing was just going back and forwards and back and forwards by itself."

"Does the article say where the house is?"

"Duffy."

"I'll check it out, but I think we already know that one. There's a house in Duffy that's haunted by a young girl. She drowned in the lake or a stream or something around 1900."

"That was before Canberra even existed," said Kat, in awe.

"You're learning," Mabel said. "Well spotted, mate. If she's someone new I'll write her in my little book, but I think she's the old ghost."

"I didn't know you had a little book."

"Don't tell the others."

"Of course not. D'you want me round to get rid of snails tomorrow? It's going to rain this afternoon."

"Who says?"

"I'm getting a storm headache."

"If it rains, you can come over. Storm headaches are mystic stuff. Don't believe in 'em."

"How can you not . . ." Kat began, angry, when she heard the chuckle on the other end of the phone. "That was mean."

"I thought it was funny. See you tomorrow."

"Bye," and Kat was alone with her storm headache and her article about the ghost.

Hi, this is Kat. I typed up my notes and realised how many questions I should have asked. The big one was, of course, 'Are we on a hell mouth?'

I did ask Lil. It was much later and the reference went right over her head. I couldn't believe she hadn't seen Buffy. All that magic and no Vampire Slayer. Anyhow, about five minutes later she came back and said, "That's a Christian reality. You may be, but I'm certainly not."

"We need to watch Buffy," I told her. "Soon. I'll steal Z's."

"Steal?"

"Borrow without her knowing. It means seeing her, though. Maybe I'll see if the library has a copy."

She gave me a look. I borrowed Buffy anyway. Every single episode. And we watched them. Every single episode. Then she made me return them and then read all about the harrowing of Hell. A Christian friend taught her about the harrowing of Hell, she said. I liked the way she said 'A Christian friend,' as if I should be impressed.

So now we both know about different hell mouths. Neither of us believe in either of them, too, which is very cool. Which didn't help me back then, of course, but it feels good now. Mabel says I'm in danger of being educated even though she didn't know about hell mouths, at all, from Buffy or from the Gospel of Nicodemus.

We're all getting educated. In fact, I'm so busy with my education I haven't got any more time to write.

❖

Time for action.

The three had action down to a fine art. They didn't even have to think about it anymore, so often had they moved. Mostly it was for settling restless spirits (which really didn't take action at all) or for investigating something that turned out to be entirely phoney, but these things were obviously preparation for now. Because now, they knew what to do.

1. Handbags: extra big ones, containing useful stuff, including several holy books, a candle and other paraphernalia.

2. Two cars: once a mischievous creature had let all the tyres down on Mabel's car and so they always took two and parked one a good walk away.

3. Big hats: so that if their friends saw them, they would think they were someone else. "It occurs to me that Canberra's too small," Ann said, every time she put her hat on. "It's like living in a goldfish bowl."

"Stakes?" asked Lil.

"What?"

"Did you pack stakes?"

"Why would I pack stakes?" asked Mabel. "I use them in the garden, not here."

"Ask Kat."

"She wants us to become vampire slayers."

"She really doesn't understand what we do, does she?" Ann entered the

69

conversation.

"Or we really don't understand how she thinks," Mabel replied, cheerfully. "Either way, I'm not packing stakes, guns or even my stockwhip."

"Stockwhip?" Ann was confused.

"I know how to use it," said Mabel, defensively.

Lil just laughed. "Let's get on with it. The sooner this is done the sooner we can move on."

"And we have to move on," Mabel's face looked lugubrious. *More moods than a mad kitten,* she would have said to Kat, if someone else had showed all those emotions in such rapid succession. Gloom suited her long face, she thought. "More and more stuff and we just get slower and slower."

"Speak for yourself!" Ann's face wasn't nearly as indignant as her words.

"Calm down," Mabel said. "I wasn't talking about age. Just that we dither a lot right now. It's like everything's too big."

Lil nodded. "We have to make things smaller. Reduce them to our size."

"Starting here." Ann picked up her handbag, slammed the car door and walked towards the cathedral as if she meant it.

"Not that way!" called Mabel. "We want one, not a whole pack of the things."

Ann turned round and came back, glowering. "Where do we find one, then, Miss Clever?"

"You find it," Mabel said. "Spy with your little eye."

"That's right," said Lil. "One will be just out of sight. Trying to hide. They only come out in packs."

"Oh." Her relief showed on her face. "I can do that."

"Of course you can. If you've lost your special talent, we'd be stuck."

"Yeah, right," said Ann, but she looked happier.

They walked round the side streets of Manuka. Green and leafy they were. They owned all the scents of England and those scents combined to make one. *Green,* Kat thought. *This is what deep green smells like.* Old gardens by Canberra standards. New by anyone else's. The deep green fragrance mingled with the deep green trees until the three felt they were walking away from civilisation. Then they returned to where they started and shook themselves awake from their reverie.

"Try again?" asked Ann.

"Should we take it one block closer to the shops — see if we can pick up on one its way to its liquor?"

"On its way to or on its way back." Mabel shrugged. "All the same."

They tried again. The last of the daylight turned the green to black.

"The streetlights," said Lil. "They're out around here. That's a good sign."

"How?"

"It's a regular route, you mean."

"Yes."

Ann squinted ahead. "Still can't see anything. Let's keep walking."

So they did.

"Wait!" Ann stopped suddenly. "There!"

Mabel squinted into the night and saw a scuttling figure. She strode over to it and grabbed its collar. The collar came off in her hand. "Damned thing," she said. The lugger sniggered and started moving off, into a garden.

"Stop!" Lil said, real command in her voice. The big eyes suddenly looked at her, unblinking, scared. Lil couldn't help thinking of Gollum. Truly, Kat was a bad influence. "Leave Canberra," Lil said, still using that voice. "Leave Australia. Never come back." The big eyes faded into the darkness.

"He's gone," said Ann. "Entirely gone. Not just run away."

"That was easy, then." Mabel brushed her hands. "The collar's gone too, though my hands are all over muck."

"They don't wash," said Lil, absently, her eyes focussed on where the lubber had been. Then she staggered.

Mabel was beside her in an instant, supporting her. "Not so easy, I think," she said.

"No, not," said Lil. "I think coffee would help."

When they were sitting down in a nice bright coffee lounge, Mabel went to wash her hands.

"We know some things," said Ann.

Lil just nodded. She was having trouble concentrating. *Getting old is not something I'm really enjoying,* she thought.

Ann kept talking. "We know that my squinty eye is still very effective. We know that the abbey lubbers can be ordered around."

"We know that one of them can be," said Mabel, sitting down next to Lil. "And that Lil nearly fainted at the effort."

"It means we ought to bring Kat into this."

"I think so." Lil finally spoke. "If we're careful."

"Oh, we will be," said Mabel, grimly. "And if any of those buggers hurt our Kat, I'll do them."

Their drinks and cake arrived and they busied themselves with refreshments and polite comments on taste and texture. *One must observe the proprieties*, thought Lil. "I was thinking of Kat before," she said. "The eyes of the abbey lubber reminded me of Gollum. That same stare."

"She's been making you watch her favourite TV too, then." Mabel sniffed.

"Movie, in this case."

"Same difference."

"She's determined to bring the two of you into the twenty-first century," Ann observed. "It's entertaining."

"Teenagers are so difficult." Mabel sniffed again.

"That's why you spend so much time with her." Lil sniffed back. *We're fighting over Kat's favours*, she thought. *This ought to be amusing, but somehow, it's rather sad.*

"I meant to say," said Ann, "I wanted to thank you for all the help you are giving her. I didn't realise my life would be so very troubled and I haven't been able to give her the odd jobs I expected."

"She could have cleared your sink the other day," said Mabel.

The two glared at each other. Lil let them.

On their way home, Lil and Ann and Mabel encountered a ghost. They had entered a twilight zone. In fact, they encountered several ghosts. Twice. That was how Mabel explained it to Kat (for her scrapbook): "Several ghosts. Twice." She made Twilight Zone noises, so that Kat had the benefit of the joke as well as the summary of the experience.

"Now I know why the others don't think your jokes are funny," Kat said.

"My jokes are *very* funny," said Mabel. "Let me tell you my Lake George joke."

"Let me get this all down first," replied Kat, tactfully.

The first encounter was supernatural. Ann saw it first. "Look," she said.

Lil and Mabel's eyes followed the line of Ann's finger. There, about fifty metres away, was a horse and rider. The horse looked as if it was sketched in charcoal. The lines were beautiful. They moved gracefully, but through them the women could see the street and the grass and, as it passed a house, a letterbox. Mabel shuddered.

"Horses should not contain letterboxes," she said.

"Look at the rider," Lil said.

He was drawn in oils. Not quite real, but with that semblance. He had dark hair and was wearing black and white clothes. Boots.

"Nineteenth century," said Mabel.

"I think so," said Lil. "Maybe 1870s?"

"But who is he?" asked Ann.

"I have no idea," said Mabel, definitively. The others looked at her for a moment. She had said it so very firmly.

"You sound as if you think you ought to have an idea," said Ann.

"Maybe I ought," said Mabel, calmly. "But in this case, I don't. Oh! Look!"

The women turned their eyes back and the horse looked like a real horse and the man looked like a real man. No more see-through; no more sense of clever artistry. Behind him loped a giant dog. It was black and bushy and its eyes shone baleful red.

"We must leave," said Lil. "Now."

"Why?" asked Ann.

"That dog, he worries me."

"That gun, it worries *me*," said Mabel.

"Fine, let's go then." Ann didn't bother hiding her annoyance.

When they were nearly at the car, they heard another horse clopping closer and closer.

"Oh dear," said Mabel. "Here's trouble."

"We couldn't hear the horse before." Ann's voice was full of worry.

"It's a different horse," said Mabel. "It's not even coming from the same direction."

"There is no barguest with this one," said Lil.

"Barguest? What's that?" asked Ann.

"Later," said Lil. "Let us deal with one problem at a time."

The three walked faster, hoping to beat the horse to the car, but it was faster, and very shortly they found it blocking their way. They were close enough to smell the grassy and earthy horse scent. It was so real.

"Hard to believe it's a ghost," Mabel said.

A young man with a head too large for his body slid off its tall back. He held the reins and walked right up to them.

"Hard to believe you're a ghost, too," Mabel said.

A charming smile lit up the man's pock-marked face. He only stopped walking when he was right next to Mabel. His arm went round her and he gave her a resounding kiss. "I've been waiting for that," he said.

Ann turned bright red and looked at the horse. The horse looked back, curiously, so Ann turned her gaze on the ground.

Lil laughed. "One of you," she said, "is perhaps a little young for the other."

"Haven't you heard of the kiss of friendship?" asked the young man, in a pleasant tenor.

"I have. I know of the kiss of friendship and I know the kiss of peace, but neither is quite so . . . carnal . . . as that."

It was Mabel's turn to blush red. "This is William," she said, nevertheless. "He's promised to help us."

"You can call me Jackey-Jackey," said the dead bushranger. "Everyone else does." He then proceeded to kiss Lil's hand and then Ann's hand. He was very nineteenth century in his attitudes and his dress was also very nineteenth century. There could be no doubt, despite his modern-sounding language, that he was a ghost.

"You don't have to look so amused," scolded Mabel.

"How can I not look amused," Lil said, "when the situation is so very amusing?"

Six

KAT REPORTED SOME MORE news from her useful gossip website. Sightings — many sightings — of a Cobb and Co. stagecoach. It was the same coach every time, the gossips had determined. They worked out, in fact, that it was the same scene every single time, from the rumbling of the coach along the road to the moment when a shout hung over it in the still air.

"Stand and deliver!" the call rang out, and then the scene faded.

One thing she had been able to ascertain: three bushrangers were involved, and none of them was Mabel's William.

Lil was trying to explain Jackey-Jackey to Kat. She felt it was essential to let Kat know about Mabel's interesting relationship with the ghost, because she rather suspected that Kat would easily become fascinated by him. Not bad looking, flirtatious, polite to a fault and very, very dead: just the first love for teenage Kat. And it would not do. It simply would not do. It was bad enough that Mabel knew the man far too well, but if Kat fell in with him, there could be trouble.

She failed at the explanation.

Kat wove the makings of a rich beef stew and rice for that night's dinner party in with the idea that Mabel was falling in love with a ghost. She just couldn't take it seriously, not while she was making stew with very strange spices. Lil was joking. Obviously.

Mabel's version of the story had reached her first and she trusted Mabel more than anyone. Ever.

Lil understood that Kat was less than interested in Lil's version of the story. Lil hoped it would be enough. Time would tell. Maybe it was simply that Kat was young. Maybe Kat had no interest in pretty young men yet. Maybe Kat was dealing with so much else that romance was something she was avoiding. Or maybe she really did think Lil was joking. Lil sighed.

"I like this salad," Kat said, nibbling some. She couldn't see what the fuss was about.

"It's not salad," said Lil. "It's greens."

"Why is it greens?"

"Because of where the recipe comes from, and who it reminds me of."

"Not because we're rabbits?"

"Certainly not that. Although I admit you have a small resemblance to one, with your mouth full of green."

Kat tried to smile, but found she had to finish eating the leaf in question first. It wasn't the type of lettuce she was familiar with. It was longer and flatter and prettier and tasted more complex. "Can you tell me what's in the greens?"

"You helped make them, surely you can work it out?"

"I can't." Kat was defiant. "I don't know the names of anything. Even the lettuce is strange."

"Iceberg lettuce is modern. That is an older variety. Cos lettuce. With it we have put mustard greens, marjoram, fennel and nasturtium."

"I know the nasturtium."

"Considering you picked it from the garden a half hour ago, I should hope you recognise it."

Kat laughed.

"It's dressed with balsamic vinegar and sea salt."

"I don't care how it's dressed."

"You should always care how your greens are dressed. You care enough about how you are dressed."

"It's nice, though, isn't it?" Kat smoothed her new skirt. It was a chocolate-brown, with traceries of red and purple and bronze near the hem.

"Very nice. Like my greens."

"Like your greens," Kat repeated, dutifully. "Only my skirt doesn't taste odd."

"I used to eat that on Saturdays, every Saturday for a while. After I left home."

"Where was this?"

"Andalusia."

"Andalusia?"

"Spain."

"Spain was home?"

"Cordoba was the exotic place I escaped to when I left home. Just as Canberra is your exotic place. Everyone I knew there is gone — I thought it would be good to remember them. All I have is the memory of salad."

Kat was bursting to ask what sort of tragedy meant that they were all gone, but she remembered that Lil was Jewish and that tied her tongue in knots. They did a class on the Holocaust once: she had cried for two days. Before she could untie the knots in her tongue and find a way out of the sadness, Lil's mood had changed.

"I ought to admit, that was an exaggeration. I have many recipes. I'll cook them for you this year, perhaps, when it's my turn to host these dinner parties. You can share my salad memories." She smiled such a beautiful smile that Kat could do nothing except nod and smile right back.

Everyone was very polite to each other over dinner.

Kat worried for her grannies. It was unnatural for them to be so very nice. Mabel didn't snark and Ann didn't dig and Lil didn't gently intimate that she had known many things. They talked about the weather and the state of shopping and they wondered about the idiocies of local government.

It wasn't until dessert was served and Kat was sitting down at the table with them, nibbling cautiously at a small pastry filled with nuts and sweet things, that everyone settled.

Mabel started by asking, in her pragmatic way, if anyone had heard more stories of children.

"Children?" asked Lil.

"I've heard of them too," offered Ann. "Whispering shadows with child voices, saying evil things."

"That's the one," said Mabel. "Scares the hell out of everyone."

"They don't do anything though," said Ann.

"They scare people," said Lil, slowly. "Maybe that is already too much."

"Do we know where they are?" asked Kat. All eyes turned to look at her. "You know," she said defensively, "even if they don't have bodies, the people who hear them do."

"I'll get a map," said Lil.

They spent the next fifteen minutes trying to pin down the sound of nasty voices. When they had done the best they could and were looking at the map in a kind of shocked contemplation, Mabel said, "Why don't we map everything?" *Slow. All of you are slow*, Kat thought. She loved them very much though, and kept her thoughts to herself.

"How does this help?" asked Ann.

"Place makes a difference," said Mabel. "The configuration of the landscape might encourage activity."

"Your garden," said Lil.

"I beg your pardon," said Mabel.

Kat giggled at the rhyme, but subdued herself when Ann threw her a quelling look.

"You have configured your garden."

"Mostly for safety," Mabel said.

"What system did you use?"

"The elements, the humours — you know," Mabel said, vaguely.

"Good," said Lil, surprisingly. "Very good. We should work on our map a little, each of us alone. Then we can return to it and discover if there is a system there as well."

"It's not my fault," Mabel said, defensively.

"It can't be your fault," said Lil. "But your garden shows how receptive this land is to what we carry with us. This means that land may be a factor."

"We have infested the land with our filth," said Ann, disgustedly.

"Perhaps," said Lil. "Perhaps not. Let us discover the shape of things before we judge."

She used coffee as an excuse to divert the conversation. Ann remained stubbornly silent: if she couldn't state her opinion, she thought, she wouldn't participate.

Kat noted this from Ann's expressive face and body language. She also noticed that Ann refused to make eye contact. She didn't praise the food. She didn't say anything she wasn't forced to say. And her lips were slightly compressed whenever she thought no-one was noticing.

Kat also noted that Lil was extra careful to keep discussion away from the supernatural. In fact, Lil led the conversation, which was a rarity. She wondered what internal visions those evil children and the map had conjured up. Kat listened for all she was worth, trying to work out where Lil was coming from.

It was interesting to see exactly when Lil became fed up with Ann's silence. Lil was going to do something fascinating any minute, Kat was certain. She positioned herself so she could pay close attention to both women.

The closer she watched, the jumpier she became. When Ann dropped a teaspoon Kat nearly leapt out of her skin. All three women turn to stare at her, which made it worse. Lil filled the gap by springing her surprise. Kat subsided into her quietest self and listened intently.

"I think the silliest play I ever went to was during World War II." A startled silence met this. Brains were calculating how old Lil must have been during World War II. Old enough to see a play? "It was in Yiddish. I've never been much for Yiddish theatre. I didn't learn the language young enough, perhaps. Anyhow, I still don't enjoy it." As if there had been any in Canberra in the last thirty years — Mabel and Ann gave each other significant looks.

They obviously weren't sure they even knew what Yiddish theatre was, either. Kat held off on the coffee and just watched.

"Tell us about the play," Mabel coaxed in her softest voice. It wasn't particularly soft, nor particularly coaxing, but Lil obliged anyway.

"Sidney Cohen," she said, then stopped again.

"I think we're supposed to recognise the name," Ann observed sagely.

"Jewish," said Kat, then abruptly tried to fade into the furniture.

"Oh, sit down," said Mabel. "We're not going to eat you." And so Kat sat, carefully half-hidden behind the coffee pot.

"Cohen and his men made a forced landing on Lampedusa during the war and the whole island surrendered to them, probably by mistake."

"Cohen was Polish resistance? What was the Polish resistance doing on Lampedusa?" Ann was trying to link the unlinkable.

"That would have been funny. No, he was RAF. A Brit. Captain. Two crew. They were called the Kings of Lampedusa when they handed the surrender papers in at Malta. They were instantly heroes."

"Sounds fine," said Kat.

"The play was silly, is all I can say," observed Lil. "Dancing and bad jokes about the local butcher."

"And how old did you say you were at the time?" Mabel was determined to get to the bottom of it. "Did your mother know you were out?"

Lil laughed. "I'm not going to sate your sudden curiosity about my age. I am the age that I am and I was born the year that I was born. May I have some more of that coffee, please?"

And Kat was pressed back into service. She wished Mabel had been less determined to discover Lil's age. The Kings of Lampedusa sounded like an amazing story, even if the stage version had included dancing and bad jokes.

"We gotta do it," Kat said to herself.

She was happy she was along for the ride, but she was scared as all get out. She was going to brave this down and she was going to stand by her grandmothers. She listened to what she had just told herself. Kat giggled. One day she would not think so tangled, too.

She hopped into the back of the car and watched everything. *Everything. Gonna commit it to memory,* she thought. *Gonna learn every secret of the trade. Kat, Vampire Hunter!* Or something. One day she'd find out what.

She felt she was changing inside. Big time. The thing she had to hang onto was this learning, this finding out, this watching.

What she couldn't work out is why they drove so far to travel so close. Then she realised she wasn't watching properly. Stupidkat. They were driving round and round in circles, staying in the car until they saw something. What they saw, eventually, were two streetlights that had blinked out. Darkness where light should have been.

"Here," said Ann. "I can see them." Squinty eyes. Good stuff. Kat was impressed. "There's a whole gang, lurking underneath the big tree, just ahead, on the right." The big tree was deciduous and the moon shone very clear through its skeleton.

Suddenly, Kat didn't like what she saw. Not at all.

Ann seemed to know what she was doing. She walked right up to them and towered over them and said, "Get out of here. Get out of Canberra. Get out of Australia." Her voice was very firm. She was very brave.

A moment later she was surrounded by short jeering manlike creatures with big eyes and bigger mouths. "Git outta here, yersel'," one said. "Gunna make us?" The crowd laughed and chattered and pressed in. The abbey lubbers were short, but they were threatening. Kat took a step back.

Mabel took two steps back. A couple of the little men noticed her. Instantly half the swarm was around Mabel as well, poking and prodding and pushing. Mabel stepped back and back, until she was pressed into a big letterbox.

The jabbering and the hollering and the calling got louder and more vile until even the air sounded crowded. Some of the lubbers started making obscene gestures and calling to their mates what they wanted to do to the women. One or two started doing more than gesturing. Kat stood there, stunned. Her grannies were being attacked by little manlike things. It was indecent. It was wrong. It froze Kat to the spot. Silent. Hurting.

Then, just behind her, to her right, she heard a quiet sob. Lil was crying.

Kat lost her temper. "You there." She strode in and poked at one of the lubbers crowded against Mabel. "You think you're so bloody big. Look at you. Tiny. Takes a really small man to say those things to an old woman. Takes an idiot. A real twerp."

Big eyes looked up at her in shock.

"You think you're an abbey lubber? You're not a lubber. You're just a lub. Something small and stupid." Kat kept talking. She didn't even notice that everyone and everything was watching her and that every single mouth was agape. She was so focussed on that one creature and his Gollum-eyes that she couldn't stop herself. At the back of her mind she heard Lil crying, always, she saw Mabel scared, she saw Ann trapped. "You hurt my grannies, I hurt you."

"Do you know how many teenagers there are in this city?" Kat flung the words at the crowd of creatures like a challenge. "Ten times your number. A hundred times. A thousand times. Every single human age thirteen to nineteen, every single teenager in this town, will stand outside every pub and every bar and every restaurant and they will watch for you. I won't tell them what to do, either. They will know what to do. Teenagers know stuff. Some of them will just stand and look. That night you'll all be grateful. Just a bunch of teenagers, standing and looking, standing and looking, standing and looking. Have you ever seen how a teenager can stand and look? It's the ugliest thing you've ever seen. It shrinks you inside. It makes you tinier than tiny."

"But that's not the worst thing that will happen to you. Oh, no."

"Some of us are old enough to go into bars. Some teenagers drink. And those friends of mine, those drinking age friends, they'll notice you. In every bar. In every restaurant. Wherever you get your drinks. They'll notice you."

"They'll look at you and laugh at you and point at you. You won't be able to hide in the darkness, finishing up everyone's leftovers. Everyone will see your dirt and your eyes and your strange mouths. Everyone will know you don't belong here. Everyone will watch and watch and watch until you can never be invisible again."

"Look at me looking at you. I'm memorising you. I'm going to go on the internet and tell everyone. Everyone. Not just in Canberra. Everywhere. Every teenager in the world. And you know what? We don't even have to hate you. We don't need to poke you the way you're poking my oldies. We don't need to say rude things and threaten. We don't need to be obscene.

"All we have to do is look. Thousands of us. Millions of us. Tens of millions of teenagers. No church will hide you anymore because everyone wants teens to come and volunteer in churches. We will come and clean up every corner and we will stare and stare and stare until everyone can see you.

"If you want to be safe, you'd better avoid all of us. Not just here. Everywhere. Run. Now. Because I'm not giving you a second chance. You hurt the people I love: there's no second chance from that."

The lubbers started to back off when Kat got going and by now they were just a fringe of big eyes in the darkness. When Kat stopped for a breath the one she was looking at joined the eyes in the darkness. There was stillness.

Then Mabel spoke up. "She's right. We can do that too. Stare for all we're worth."

The lubbers backed off faster.

"You know all teenagers are like Kat," Ann shouted after them.

Kat took a look at Lil. She was still very worried. She saw Lil biting her lip. "Are you still crying?" Kat asked, softly.

"Oh no," said Lil, and burst into uncontrollable giggles. "That was so well done of you," she managed to say. "So very well done."

The crowd of abbey lubbers turned, each movement echoed by the others. One said, "You can keep your fat mouths. We don't like that much lip. We're gone. You keep away from us and we'll keep away from this damned place."

The women were very silent on the way back to Lil's place. If they had gone anywhere else, there might have been chatter, but they were silent for the few minutes it took to get to Lil's. Kat wondered why. She wanted to know if they were shocked or scared or . . .

The matter was settled the moment they walked into Lil's front hall. Mabel just stood there, looked across at all her friends and said, "Oh boy! We did it."

"We did," said Ann. "They're going. Every last one of them."

"We were lucky," Lil said, quietly. "We had Kat."

So well done, Kat replayed it in her mind. *So very well done.* "I wonder why they find teenagers so terrifying?" Kat asked.

"It's not teenagers," Lil said. "It was you. You saw their soft underbelly."

"That was luck," said Kat. "I just got so mad."

"Oh, stop analysing it," said Ann. "They're gone, aren't they?"

"At the very least, they're in hiding," Lil said.

"Cheerful sod, aren't you?" Mabel responded.

"I'm going to make some coffee," was Lil's answer.

"Can I help?" asked Kat.

Each time Mabel met with Jackey-Jackey, he become more solid, more easily. He was very enthusiastic about taking advantage of this. Mabel wasn't quite of the same mind.

"I'm old," she said.

"Not to me," he said.

"That sounds like a line out of a movie."

"What's a movie?" he asked, with just a hint of a regional English accent.

"Your accent," Mabel said, making it clear she was changing the subject. Better he remained ignorant. She wouldn't trust this ghost to behave in the darkness of a cinema.

She had trusted her husband and it got her tied to him for life. It was a charming wedding, but it had been organised in a great hurry. Not that this had really been a problem after the first few rushed years of childbearing — they had enjoyed their life together — but she still hadn't forgiven him for upping and dying ten years ago. She cast everything against his memory. She still missed him.

"Is charming?" prompted Jackey-Jackey.

"No. I mean. You confuse me," she grumbled. "I just wanted to know where it's from."

"England."

"Oh. I knew that."

"I am from Essex."

"That's right. I remember. You were a highwayman there. And a forger. I read about you. Kat told me about you. I just forgot."

"I am a man of many talents."

"Your hands," scolded Mabel.

"What of them?"

"It's where they are. They're not behaving particularly well."

"They are very talented, too," teased Jackey-Jackey.

"Move them."

Jackey-Jackey sighed. "If you don't want me, what do you want?"

"Answers."

"Admit that you are interested in me and maybe I'll give you them."

Mabel snorted. "Of course I'm interested in you. It's wrong, though. You're younger than my youngest child. A lot younger."

"Or I'm older than your mother. A lot older."

"Answers?"

"You're a stubborn woman." Jackey-Jackey smiled. "Shall we sit down demurely on this bench and I shall give you any answers I have."

'Demurely' turned out to include his hand around her waist. Mabel slapped it down when it explored too far, and they both dealt.

"People have seen four bushrangers. You're the only one who doesn't repeat events."

"There are four of us. I came here first. My ghost never left, in fact, so becoming solid comes easiest to me. I have not run with the others in a very long while. I love the Monaro. It's my district. It's more home to me than England ever was. I've enjoyed it ever since the day I died. I roam free. I have an affinity with life — my companions have only affinities with death."

"They're more dangerous than you, then?"

"Oh, yes. They didn't hesitate to rape or kill when they lived. I doubt they will hesitate now."

"But they keep repeating events."

"They began as shadows. When they are fully of this reality, they will be able to move beyond their lives, as I do now. They will carry all their violence with them. The Clarkes will probably try to form a gang. They could join one that already exists. Either way, they will try to dominate whoever they're with: they like being able to extend their violence. The stealing is — for them — something extra. Their joy comes from control and from causing pain and from the suffering of others."

"Damn," said Mabel.

Jackey-Jackey looked at her admiringly. "Ladies didn't use bad language in front of me when I lived. I preferred it that way. Bad language was for the gutter or the prison. But in you, with your modern accent and your modern way, with your education and your bare ankles, I find it erotic."

"I'm enriching your afterlife, then," snapped Mabel. "Tell me more about your three companions."

"Paddy Curran. I stockwhipped him for raping a woman, near Goulburn, and I told him never to darken this region again. Then there are the Clarke brothers. I've already told you. They murdered for pleasure. I understand how they haunt, but I don't understand why. They have no unfinished business, and they left many ghosts behind them. They are dangerous."

Mabel noticed that his hand was . . . less noticeable.

"You're fading," she said.

"When I have more control, we have other business to discuss."

"When you grow up," Mabel said, sarcastically. The bushranger just laughed, and spent the last of his corporeal energy kissing her, very thoroughly.

"That was about the most unsatisfying question and answer I've ever been in," Mabel announced to thin air.

"Admit it — you want me," came a fading voice, out of that thin air.

Mabel laughed.

She gave the names of the three to her friends and explained about them starting with echoing their lives. "They can move on. They can become real. They can hurt people."

"How did you find out? How did you get all this stuff?" asked Ann.

"You really don't want to know," advised Lil.

Mabel acted annoyed. "I asked, is all. Stop making drama."

"D'you want me to look them up some more?" Kat asked.

"Good idea," said Mabel. "We already know they're dangerous, though."

"We don't know nearly enough," said Lil.

"An excursion," said Ann. "We can find out for ourselves. Kat can come along. This one will be much safer than the last."

"Yeehah!" shouted Kat. "Looking for bushrangers!"

"No," said Lil. "There are many things we have to look for. The bushrangers can wait."

"But why?" Kat didn't hide her disappointment.

Lil was patient. "Mabel has already given us warning that those bushrangers are very bad indeed. We shall start with something less dangerous, I think. Let us not tempt fate. Last time was a concern. Last time we were lucky, too. I do not want to rely on luck. I also do not want Kat to have to save us every time, simply because we don't think things through."

"No to the bushrangers? I don't get to meet Jackey-Jackey?" Kat was bewildered when the three women said "No!" as one. "I'm back on training wheels," she sulked.

"I was thinking. With these things," said Ann, with the long-suffering tone of the experienced, "you choose the safe path to build up information. It's standard operating procedure."

"That's right," said Mabel. "No danger until we know how to face it."

"But you talked to Jackey-Jackey," pouted Kat. "And I did those abbey luggers good."

"Answer that one for her, Mabel," said Ann. "Explain you and Jackey-Jackey. I want to hear what you two talked about, too. How you get to see him and we don't."

"He has given us his best information."

"So that's where it came from," said Ann, smug. "I thought so. What else do you talk about? What else don't we know?"

Mabel ignored her and kept talking. "We need other sources. We can choose anything from our list, from all the safe things." Then she corrected herself. "Safer. Nothing's really safe, after all, not even crossing the road."

"Or driving home," said Ann.

"Our list?" Kat was determined to keep the conversation on track.

"We were supposed to write down events, like you do with your newspaper clippings and website. When the time is right we said we'd look for patterns. In this case we can simply compile our lists and choose something. We can investigate. This is an investigation."

"Because we don't understand enough," said Mabel.

"Not nearly enough," added Lil.

"So what are we doing on this excursion?"

"It's a choice between water spirits, haunted houses, werewolves and whispering children, I think." The others nodded agreement at Lil's summary. Obviously they were used to doing things this way. It didn't matter that they had just defined a way of saving Canberra from its haunts that would include Kat and then proceeded to ignore her scrapbook and all the information she could offer. Obviously they talked new talk and then walked the path they always had. *Oldies*, Kat thought, *and their ways.* Annoying ways. Frustrating ways. Staid ways.

Kat wanted to scream that the path had changed, that they should do the research. That they should look at her research. They weren't going to listen, though. They were going to think they were listening. Then they were going to do whatever it is they had done before, when things hadn't been so evil. Kat decided the only way through the thicket of the minds of older women was to ignore the contradiction and its implications and let herself get excited anyway.

"Ooh, that's almost as good as bushrangers." *Whispering children*, Kat thought very strongly. *Choose the whispering children.* She hated the thought of water spirits and didn't believe in werewolves. The whispering children though, they sounded good.

"What do you choose?" said Ann.

"Werewolves. Of course I choose werewolves." She couldn't believe she said that. They gave her a choice and she said 'werewolves.' Stupid Kat. Stupidstupidstupidkat.

"Of course you do," said Mabel. "You would choose vampires if we had them, wouldn't you?"

"Of course. It's my inner Goth." Suddenly it all made sense. She made sense. Life was good.

❀ ♦ ❀

"What I really want to say is . . ."

"Don't go there," Ann warned.

"What?" Kat pretended bewilderment.

"You know what I mean. Every time you start 'What I really want to say is' you end up complaining about your mother and stepfather."

"They're important. It's important. I have to talk about it. You said."

"Not as important as the rest of your life. And I said — past tense."

"If it wasn't for the baby I wouldn't've been on the streets." Kat's observation was almost unctuous.

"You say this, you know, every single time." Lil was baiting her, and they exchanged slight evil smiles.

It was a source of great satisfaction to Lil that Kat could be unctuous and self-righteous now. Even a few weeks ago, she was still defensive and angry and volatile. Also, it was surprisingly good to hear how she and Ann argued. Lil admitted to herself that Ann was too proper and too generous and too loving and entirely too nice. It was beginning to annoy her, the way her friend assumed that she was the centrifugal force and that the world revolved around her. For years Lil had just accepted it. Kat's presence had meant that Ann was no longer the treasured youngest child: Lil found that she was expecting Ann to act like an adult.

"I need tea," announced Mabel.

"Peacemaker," Lil teased.

"I'll make tea," Kat announced. "Since none of you want to hear my utterly amazing insights."

"You forgot to call us 'old birds,' you know," said Lil. "None of you old birds want to hear . . ."

"If I called you 'old birds' you'd tell me I couldn't come on the excursion, and look, I'm all packed." She held up her carefully personalised backpack. Kat was particularly proud of the black rose she'd painted. She was going to annoy her grandmothers every moment she got. Besides, it looked good.

"Too right," said Mabel. "I still need tea, though."

Kat escaped to the kitchen. Mabel settled into the big chair. Lil watched, eyes bright, as Ann stood up and wandered the room until her long fingers rested in a bowl of potpourri. The air was filled with the scent of old tea rose and lavender by the time Kat came back, carrying a big brown teapot.

"I'll just get the milk and mugs," she said.

"Cups, I think, for today," Ann said, her hands momentarily distracted. "After all, we're not going in search of bushrangers." Kat wondered why cups were inappropriate for bushrangers. *Sometimes Ann just says things*, she realised. *They just come out of her mouth and make no sense.*

Their search took them south. Out of Canberra. Not very far out of Canberra. Just as far as Tharwa.

"Why Tharwa?" asked Kat.

"Because it's the last town in New South Wales where a werewolf was killed." Ann said this as if she didn't believe it.

"Werewolves in Oz — wow," breathed Kat.

"Don't get overexcited," advised Mabel. "All there is now is a shrine. And Tharwa isn't in New South Wales, anyhow. The town we really want is Brewarrina, but Ann and Lil don't like long trips. They're both lazy buggers."

"I know that shrine." Kat burbled with excitement. "The Tharwa one. We saw it on a school excursion. Our teacher said it was because of road accidents."

"Well, it isn't," said Mabel. "There's a candle there and it's always kept burning. If the candle goes out, the wolf will return."

"So says the story," said Lil.

"So says the story," said Ann.

"And so do I," said Mabel. After a moment she said, "Say it. Say what you're all thinking. Say 'Mabel's a stubborn git.'"

"Why should we bother saying it," said Ann, "when you say it for us. Every time."

When they finally reached Tharwa, it took them about fifteen minutes to locate the shrine. It had been moved from near the highway to back a bit, right next to a four-metre high security fence.

"I wonder why someone put this thing up?" Ann said, as they drove up to it.

"At least it still exists," said Mabel. "Even if it's here, it'll do the job."

Kat was learning to look across at Lil for her reaction, and Lil wore a frown. Kat was the first out of the car and the first to see the shrine right up close. "I thought you found a light?"

"There should be," said Ann, and joined her. "A nice, safe, electric candle."

"There has to be," said Mabel, and took two big steps towards the shrine. She stopped so quickly that Lil walked into her. "It's gone out," she whispered. "Someone has cut the wires."

"We'd better relight it," Ann said.

"Too late," said Lil, and pointed to the right. About twenty metres away was an animal. It was wolf-like, but big, a foot or so longer than a human was tall. It looked at them for a long moment, then turned. It took three giant bounds then jumped straight over the security fence.

"What do we do?" asked Kat.

"We leave, quickly." Mabel fitted her actions to her words and got into the car quickly.

"Can't we do something?"

"Yes," said Lil. "Just not today. We would have to make preparations for something like this."

"And even then we might not be able to help. We've never, ever dealt with a werewolf. Not a real one. Not one big enough and strong enough to jump over a massive fence."

Kat didn't know whether to interpret the odd look on Lil's face as "We'll do this anyway," or "We will do this without Kat," or even "Speak for yourself." She wanted to work it out rather desperately. But she could see the wolf, over the other side of the fence, its head turned back and watching them intently. She felt extraordinarily exposed. Kat got into the car, quickly.

The four didn't come together again until the next monthly dinner party. The excursion for Kat had turned out to be something quite different, and they all needed time to think.

Mabel and Ann did research into werewolves, and so did Kat. They put off telling the others that this was what they were doing. None of them had expected to actually see a werewolf that day: they had all thought that Kat would see the shrine and then they'd go to the Brindabellas and spend the afternoon communing with nature. All three women were busy finding solutions.

Everything they searched said that the only way of dealing with a werewolf was with a shotgun and silver to fire from it. None of them had a gun license and none wanted one.

Lil was in a different position. She already knew one way of handling a werewolf. What she was worried about were the consequences to her.

None of the four was surprised when the subject didn't come up during the dinner party. They all pretended that the burning topic was Ann's retirement and they all made play of the fact that this was her retirement dinner. It was at Mabel's place, but it was Ann's turn to cook dinner and she insisted on doing so.

"Cooking your own retirement dinner. That's ugly. You should be treated tonight," said Mabel. "I should have done it."

"I wanted to eat this food," was Ann's reply, "and I can't see you cooking it."

Nor could Kat. Three different types of kebabs (one vegetarian), yellow Greek flat bread (from a packet — slightly splodgy), sliced Spanish onions, sliced tomato, side salad of iceberg lettuce, rocket, pine nut, grated parmesan, ancient balsamic vinegar. It was rather delicious, but too lazy to be made by Lil and not old-fashioned enough for Mabel's kitchen.

The dessert could have been described in exactly the same way: delicious, lazy and a trifle exotic. It was a fruit salad, made with everything tropical from the local greengrocer. Ann had given Kat the honour of opening a tin of translucent palm somethings and one of lychees and tipping them in. They turned the fruit salad into an edible stained-glass window. Kat said this to Ann as she brought the big bowl to the table: Ann laughed.

Ann was humming absently as she spooned out the fruit salad. "Da-dum-dum-dum da-da-da dum dum," she hummed. Kat thought, *Sometimes my old ladies are strange.*

"The King's Outlaw," said Mabel, triumphantly, after a little.

"You win $1,000 and you may advance to the next round," said Lil.

Ann looked up, puzzled.

"You were humming," said Lil. "A TV theme. Mabel identified it."

"The King's Outlaw. Nineteen sixties."

Ann blushed. "Sorry, I didn't realise. I don't know what I was thinking of."

"Handsome young men?" and Lil raised an eyebrow. "Outlaws? French bushrangers?"

Kat decided it was time to sort them out. Before things got really out of hand. Old ladies should not be talking about handsome young men. "What TV show was that?"

"Programme. It's a TV programme. 'Show' is American."

"I don't know it, but."

"You wouldn't. Before your time," said Mabel. "My kids used to watch it. Every Saturday morning."

"Along with Kimba the White Lion — I visited my cousins and pretended to baby-sit them."

"And that samurai thing."

"With the really bad dubbing."

They both laughed.

"What was your first memory of television, Lil?" asked Ann.

"Bob Dyer, Pick a Box."

"Oh God," said Mabel. "That must have been the first game show ever."

"In Australia, anyhow," smiled Lil. "I didn't like it much, but a friend didn't have a television and she used to come over to watch it. My house was the only one in the street that had a TV, at first."

"And you were too polite to say you didn't like Bob Dyer?" asked Ann.

"She didn't give me any choice. She used to bring gingernut biscuits with her and I would make a pot of tea. The coffee was so bad back then, even I drank tea."

"I used to watch Graham Kennedy and IMT," said Mabel, her bony face softening at the memory. "That man was so funny. About as vulgar as they came, but there's never been anyone that funny. Never. And Mr Squiggle."

"I watched Mr Squiggle," said Kat, with interest, "when I was little. He's not funny, or vulgar. He was cute. I think that's the only TV I can remember from when I was little."

"I watched it with the kids," said Mabel.

"It's been around forever," said Ann, dismissively. Kat so wanted to ask her if she had seen Mr Squiggle, but didn't quite have the courage. When Ann exuded lack of interest it was hard to ask even the obvious.

"It was around in the 1950s," said Mabel. "I remember so many good things about the 1950s."

"We can tell you love the fifties — you still cook the food," said Ann. Kat looked at her with surprise — so much snark.

She braved the silence. "Ann, what did you watch when you were young?"

"Dr Who?" Ann said. "I can't remember. I know I watched the ABC. ABC3, it was, back then, it said so when I visited the Film and Sound Archive."

"But you don't remember what TV programmes you watched?"

"Maybe. Yes. I don't know. It's not important."

Kat was determined to break the mood. "I'm going to so download all your memories. I bet somewhere on the Net they are all hidden, just waiting for me to find. I already have *Boom Boom Baby*," she said confidingly to Ann.

"What is that?" asked Lil.

"Crash Craddock," Ann said, snark magically in abeyance and smugness emerging. "I am introducing Kat to fine music."

"Crash Craddock? *Boom Boom Baby*?" asked Mabel. "Sometimes, Ann, you worry me."

"Other things worry me more than the fact that you don't understand fine music." *Oh*, thought Kat, *she was snarky because something's wrong. She's still a nice person. That makes me ick*. She started feeling all kinds of badkatbadkat for thinking bad thoughts and practising snark diversion.

"Tell us, Ann," instructed Lil, looking her friend straight in the eyes.

"It's those children," Ann began. "I was taking a walk because I just couldn't stand being in the house with that man any longer and I heard them. They whispered and slithered around me and I couldn't see them and they said evil things."

"What sort of evil things?" asked Mabel.

"I would rather not say," said Ann, stiffly.

"They were bad?" Lil's voice was infused with sympathy.

"They were awful. And there were shadows. Whispering children give me the creeps. And I'm scared to walk that street, but it shifts and I get drifting dark wherever I walk. I have to take the car to buy milk."

"This is why I didn't see you in your usual seat the other night?"

"That's right," she whispered. "Shade at night and shifting streets and everyone who knew what was happening at home: it was all too much. I know what causes it," Ann said. "I know why all that evil is following me." There was a silence. "It's my shadow — it's a dead giveaway. I'm vulnerable."

"I always linked shifting streets to menopause," Lil said. "It's not that they never happen, it's that we're only aware of them for a small part of our lives."

"I really hate that thought," Kat said.

"Why?" asked Mabel, always practical. "You've a long time to go before you get to menopause."

"What's the use of solving the shifts now, though, if I have to go through them all over again later on?"

"I see your point," said Mabel.

"Not everyone gets lost at menopause," Ann said, back to sounding snitchy. "Don't dramatise. Maybe make some tea, instead."

"I'll give you a hand," said Mabel.

Kat didn't blame Mabel. It was her kitchen, after all, and Ann had just done the unthinkable in ordering Kat around on Mabel's night. Even if she was retiring and had commandeered Mabel's place because her ex-husband was still haunting her own, even if she had every excuse in the world to be a pain in the neck, Ann didn't have to be so very, very . . . Kat gave up on thinking and went to make the tea.

Kat was having those dreams again. An animal sitting on her chest, pressing the air out of her. A mouth pressed to her mouth sucking the air from her. An oppression surrounding her, slowly dragging the life from her. She accepted it passively at first, as one does in dreams. As the nature of it flowed and changed and drained and drained and drained, she found a spark of anger.

I always get angry, she thought. *Badkatbadkatbadkat* and she settled back into the dream and the slow leaching of her self. She was being drowned by darkness.

A pinprick of light caught her. It reminded her that she didn't have to drown. She let her anger catch fire again. The light grew and grew and grew. Soon it was large enough to make out.

Eyes. It was those eyes. They hurt her.

Kat woke up and felt a cool breeze against her face. She put her hand to her cheek. Her cheek was wet with tears. She blinked her eyes and the room was clear.

I feel strange, she thought. *Like those eyes were piercing my soul. Like a hurt lay inside. I don't know if they made it worse or were investigating to see what it was that hurt. They were clinical, though. Those eyes didn't care. They may have been human, once. They may have cared, once. But when they were looking at me they were cold and clinical. Yucky. Very, very yuck.*

Kat looked up. She saw the eyes again. This time she knew she was awake. Those eyes were real, looking at her, the wall visible behind them. Those eyes pierced her soul, just the way they had in her dream. She sat there, trying not to look, failing miserably.

Then her brain kicked into gear. *It's about time*, she thought. *I'm gonna write this down*, Kat finally decided. She spent two hours documenting the whole thing, from the first breathlessness at night to the moment this morning when she was so very clearly awake and was returning the gaze of those brilliant eyes.

"So very sharp," she wrote. "Those eyes are incredibly sharp. Like they can see through reality."

The process of writing made her feel better. *It's not finished yet, though. I don't want to know what comes next.* She didn't write that down. She was worried that she even thought it.

Seven

"I'VE DONE SOME RESEARCH," announced Mabel, her resolute look carefully arranged to impress the others. "It was about time someone did something useful around here."

"What sort of research?" asked Kat. She loved it that Mabel needled her. Sometimes she was the teenager; sometimes Mabel needed to be one. It helped her remember that adulthood was not without hope.

"Child-like beings. Not the same as the girl by the lake. Not the same as the ghosts. That's why we can't sort them out in our minds. They're something new. Like those abbey lubbers. They come from somewhere in Europe. Never been reported in Oz before. Ever."

"What do we do?" whispered Lil.

"Nothing fits," said Mabel. "We can only handle the ones we understand until we find out what has caused all of this."

"You think there's a single cause?" Ann's quick voice was unaccustomedly slow and thoughtful.

"I think that something has stirred up what was here and brought what was hidden into the light, and more besides. If we don't discover the heart of it . . ." Lil's voice dragged the sentence to an unwieldy stop.

"Then we're like those fool doctors who treat symptoms and let the patient die."

"Something like that, Mabel," said Lil.

"I don't like it," sad Ann. "I don't like the thought that there's something bigger. I want my shadow back and I want to move back into the daylight world. My life is too dark all round. I don't need to be haunted either by children or by streets. I need time out from insanity."

"All we can do at this point is add the notion of a cause to our list of things we want to do. We can think about it, but we can't instantly restore things, Ann. You know better," Mabel said. "Unless one of us has maybe an inkling of how to regain shadows."

Everyone knew she meant Lil. Lil said nothing.

After a moment, Mabel said, "I wonder . . . what if I ask Jackey-Jackey?"

"If you're still flirting with that bushranger, that's really stupid."

"I'm old enough to be allowed some small stupidities in my life," Mabel said, mildly.

"Just don't ask him about my shadow. I'd rather find out about it by myself."

"Have it your way."

Kat wondered if Ann had a shadow or not, in reality. Whenever they were outside, there was no sunshine. It was as if Ann had planned cloud and shade to hide beneath. Ann claimed that the shadow cast by artificial light wasn't the same thing. Then Kat wondered if shadows cast by moonlight were different, too. Her mind floated away from the conversation and she thought that moonlight shadows might be evil, and the moonlight shadows of children must be terribly awful. That would have to mean that Ann really had lost her shadow, though. Or maybe that her own mind was just drifting. She drifted herself right back into the conversation and pretended she had been with it all along.

"Perhaps we could discuss something else," suggested Lil.

"I know what I want to hear about," said Kat.

"Go for it," encouraged Mabel.

"Werewolves."

"Why on earth would you want to hear about werewolves? Haven't you had enough of them?"

"Nup. Besides, I've been thinking. I don't even know that there's only one kind. What sort of thing was the one we saw? Was it like werewolves in romance novels, or in films? Or in books? And which sort? I mean, how can I understand what's happening if I don't know more?"

"More than one kind of being can be called a werewolf," Lil admitted. "In fact, there is a European tradition that anyone can transform into a werewolf. It's not the way the horror movies suggest, or the way the books say. It's simpler and more dangerous. All a person needs is a wolf strap."

Kat started at those last words and leaned forward to listen very closely.

"What's a wolf strap?" Ann asked. Kat thought a quiet thought about one of the Melusine stories, but she stayed silent.

"I don't really know. Maybe just a piece of leather? Maybe a bridle? I've not come across one."

Kat wondered why Lil looked uncomfortable saying that. Was she hiding something? Not telling the whole truth? Or maybe she wasn't telling the truth at all? Time to sound Lil out, perhaps, to see if she was willing to talk about her secrets yet.

"How about werewolves?" asked Kat. "Have you talked to one of them? Asked them?" Her tone was surprisingly strong, almost suspicious. She felt guilty about her tone, but she had asked, and it was too late to sound nice and trusting.

"Not ever," Lil said, comfortably. Kat started stabbing her dessert with her spoon, looking down at the mess she made but not actually noticing it.

When she was alone, she hauled the Melusine stories out from under her mattress and turned to the story labelled 89. When she finished, she looked at the page as if it were as unsatisfying as that frothy dessert. Just how fictional were the Melusine tales? And who was Melusine? They were Lil's stories and she knew what was in them, but had she written them? And were any of them true?

She felt that she had no choice. Kat had to find out.

Tales of Melusine #89

Once upon a time, in the lands and towns that we think of as Germany, there was a small village. It was a pleasant enough place. It was a comfortable distance from a charming town, which was itself a comfortable distance from Mainz. It was far enough from the town so that it kept its closeness and its friendships. It was near enough to Mainz so that it welcomed strangers. It dripped with icicles and sweeping snow in midwinter and it glowed green in summer.

Every village has a fairy tale moment. This moment might be precipitated by a stranger passing through or an old friend revisiting. It might be caused by the wind blowing from invisible lands, or by a strange pedlar selling magic trinkets. It might be brought on by a bard or a poet. This village's fairy tale moment was brought on by a strap that old Gust brought back from the fair.

Old Gust only told one person about the strap, but that one person was Bertha-who-lived-by-the-smithy, and she was worried by what she heard. She visited Freda in the big house. Freda could write. Bertha went and asked her to send for Melusine.

Melusine had once visited the village and three women carried the memory of that visit: Bertha-who-lived-by-the-smithy, Freda from the big house, and Freda's mother. Freda's mother was ill, but she would have agreed to sending for Melusine if she had known, for the strap was a wolf strap and that only ill could come of it. She had heard that of wolf straps, that they brought out the evil in a person.

"Should we tell the village?" asked Bertha.

"Better not," said Freda. "Let them think Melusine is a friend of mine if she comes. We can ask for her, but we cannot depend upon her."

"But why?"

"Because they burned a cousin of hers, two valleys over, claiming she was a witch."

"I hadn't heard that."

"It happened a long time ago."

"We need to protect the fairy if she comes." Bertha was now worried.

"She shall be a distant cousin of my family, paying us a visit. That's all. You know nothing of her."

"As you know nothing of the wolf strap."

"That's right."

The letter was sent through the fireplace (as was the custom in those days) and after the sparks had carried the message into the night sky, Bertha went back to the house by the smithy and Freda went back to nursing her sick mother and the rest of the village was none the wiser.

Nothing much happened for the while (small villages live in their own small village time, even when they encounter their fairy tale moments) but eventually, Gust became too proud of his wolf strap.

When he first obtained it, he realised that it was evil and he hid it away. It was in the chest that held his books and other precious possessions. It lay there, wrapped in a piece of fine cloth.

The wolf strap preyed on his mind. He thought about it: what would it be like to touch it, to feel it, to stroke it, to wear it. He was strong, and he refused to give in to temptation. He didn't give the strap away, however, or try to destroy it. He was rather proud that he had a bit of sorcery within him, and he enjoyed having such a treasure hidden safely in his oaken chest.

After a while, he started taking the strap out from its hiding place to stroke it and pet it and wonder if it really had the power he thought. He wondered if his knowledge of magic would make a difference. Whether it would give him control over the strap. He would smile and tell it, "I'm stronger than you are," and put it safely away.

One day, he was tempted beyond his capacity to resist. The leather shone so warmly and the strap was so inviting: he put it on.

At first, his life was not much changed. Initially, he simply became a wolf for a little and then shucked the strap to return to normal. It wasn't too long before he started to wonder what it felt like to eat raw meat and to run wild in the forest. He would look anxiously at the woodcutters and think: "Soon the forest will be gone. I must act now."

For two weeks more he only put the wolf strap on in the privacy of his home, not wanting to cross the Rubicon. He carried it with him everywhere, though, stroking it when it lay safe and snug in his sleeve. Even then, with his growing besottedness, he was not beyond redemption.

It was not the fading forest that changed his mind. Nor was it the smell of meat or the thought of running wild in the wind. Instead it was Ernst, the smith's son.

Ernst was not a nice child. Everyone in the village knew it and everyone in the village kept a watch out for his mischief.

One day, Old Gust caught him teasing a puppy. The puppy was frightened and hurt, and Gust lost his temper. He whipped the wolf strap out of his pocket, donned it and chased Ernst down the street until fat little Ernst was puffed and even more terrified than the animal he had been torturing. Gust felt a quiet satisfaction, and it warmed him so much that he said not a word of his action to anyone. The wolf strap was still his secret.

Good deeds are seldom rewarded. The strap was like a drug. Every time Gust used it, he desired it more and his need for it was doubled and tripled. The natural powers he was so proud of counted for nothing. The lure of the strap caught him without him even realising how profoundly he had been caught. He would wrap it around his arm without thinking and then the beast in him would out.

He roamed through the woods and the fields. He stared in open windows and trampled flower beds and crops. He savaged dogs and children and cattle.

The whole village was terrified of this strange beast. No-one knew that the wolf terrorising the village was Gust. No-one except Freda and Bertha. The two women would not even look at each other as they passed in the street; they tried very hard not to show each other that they were losing hope.

Bertha and Freda were silenced by Gust himself. He knew that Bertha knew, you see. If Freda had named him, Bertha would be in dire trouble. So the two friends continued to give each other worried looks in the street and to bar their doors at night.

Two things happened then. Two things on the same day. First, Melusine arrived in town with a child who had run from the village a while back. She returned the child to her parents then she spent the afternoon and most of the evening in private talk with Freda and her mother. The next morning, the household learned of the other thing that had happened.

Someone knocked at the big front door. The maid let Bertha in.

"You're shaking," said Freda.

"Protect me!" said Bertha.

"You told someone?"

"No, not I. Gust must think so. He came round last night and said he would kill me."

"Come in! We'll get you a hot drink and then you can tell us the full story."

While Freda was sorting out refreshments with the help of Melusine's new young friend, Sarah, she whispered to Melusine. Melusine carefully sat within hearing, but out of Bertha's sight. "I don't know the solution to this yet. She is in no position to deal with half-hopes."

It appeared that the farmer whose land adjoined Gust had been suspicious for a while. He knew that Gust had a book on magic. While he did not know of the wolf strap precisely, he had seen the wolf cross his land once too often, perhaps. Or he knew that Gust's fascination with the supernatural was rather greater than one old book suggested. Either way, he had deduced that Gust had a wolf strap.

Everyone knows the way to handle someone with a wolf strap. The farmer mounted his horse, brought it to Gust's front door and held out a big piece of dripping red meat on a stick. Eventually, the smell of the meat reached Gust as he sat by the fire. Immediately, Gust reacted to the smell and strapped himself and changed into wolf form. He came out the side door. As he got closer and closer to the horse, he went wild for the smell of the blood. His neighbour's horse reared, but the farmer remained calm. He cried out Gust's name three times.

As Gust's name faded for the third time, his wolf form faded with it, leaving a human man with wild and glowing eyes. Gust fell to the ground, exhausted.

His neighbour quickly thrust the wolf strap into a sturdy bag and closed that bag tightly. He then trussed Gust up so that he couldn't move. He secured his horse and calmed the beast. He was a strong man and it was a matter of moments to load Gust onto the horse's back and tie him securely.

He took Gust to the village square for justice.

Something had to be done. Something permanent. Everyone knew it. No-one was happy about facing this nightmare. Gust may have dabbled in magic, but before the wolf strap he had been a good member of the community. Addiction is a terrible thing.

The village slowly assembled and discussed the subject around and around and around.

Melusine spent most of the day recalling possible solutions. All of the permanent ones would kill the owner of the wolf strap. Gust may well have been a sorcerer and he may well have been a very stupid sorcerer, but he was not evil. She could not countenance killing him. She also could not countenance demonstrating her secret knowledge.

This was a hard land for Jews and a hard time to be Jewish. These people might share a religion, but they shared their fears with each other as well. Showing her magic would cause far more trouble than a real cure would do.

While Melusine was thinking, the small town was in a ferment. Word had spread, and every rumour grew and grew.

Melusine's little friend Sarah came to see if Melusine had any messages to run. While Melusine was finding her money, Sarah reported what she had heard. "You know Gust, who turned into a wolf? You know what they're saying about him?"

"No, I don't know," said Melusine, resigned to a bunch of nonsense. She brought out some biscuits, so that Sarah at least got a rest while she gossiped. Her family was so poor and Sarah had worked so hard — it was why she had run away. Now she was back, they would work her even harder. Melusine worried about her.

"They say Gust's eyes aren't the eyes of a wolf: they're the eyes of a demon," Sarah said. "I want to see his eyes. Red and glowing, like two lumps of coal." She munched on a biscuit and Melusine waited patiently. "Oh! And they say he has cloven hoofs. Like the devil! Just like the devil!"

When Sarah was gone, Melusine wondered how this little Jewish community that had been here God knows how many hundreds of years had taken on the trappings of Christianity. When had it started to believe in the Christian Devil and to sacrifice its own beliefs and knowledge?

Why it had done so was simple. It was to survive. Believing in the Devil, and granting it cloven hoofs and burning eyes, was saying to the Christian neighbours "Look, I'm like you. Don't kill me."

Melusine remembered her thought twenty years later, when everyone Jewish in the town was murdered under Nazi rule. Sarah and her husband and her children and her parents and their strange half-breed folklore were all consumed by the hatred of those very Christian neighbours. That was twenty years later, though, and Melusine never had the gift of prophecy. She could give it to someone else from time to time, but she herself never possessed it.

When Sarah returned that day, she had a new announcement. "They're going to burn the wolf strap. They've built a fire in the marketplace. Come and watch with me?" She would not go alone and she so desperately wanted to be part of the excitement. Melusine couldn't say no.

Sarah dragged Melusine by the hand to the marketplace. Everyone was there, and they all stood back a bit from the biting flames, because the fire was so hot and because it snapped so very fiercely. This meant that the circle was big and Melusine could see everything.

The mayor was the one who the town chose to throw the wolf strap into the flames. Melusine noticed that the priest was as absent as the rabbi. The mayor wove the strap around the tines of a pitchfork.

"Careful," someone joked. "The pitchfork might turn into a wolf."

When the fire was hot enough, the mayor thrust the pitchfork deep into the flames. The crowd raised a cheer.

A moment later, Sarah was huddling in Melusine's skirts for comfort. The strip of leather had leapt right out of the fire and was squirming about a foot away. It looked alive. Melusine drew the worst of the life out of it with a gesture made underneath her warm shawl.

Sarah turned big eyes up to her and said, "You're scared too."

Melusine nodded.

The mayor was a brave fellow: he tried again. The same thing happened. He tied the strap more and more tightly to the pitchfork and tried again. And again. And again. Each time the wolf strap drove the crowd back a little way. Each time Melusine drew as much of the life out of it as she could without being noticed. Each time the pitchfork became hotter and hotter.

The last time, the strap stayed on the pitchfork and it was the pitchfork that flew towards the crowd. This time the crowd screamed and ran away. The pitchfork was left on the ground, red-hot and twitching. The wolf strap appeared completely undamaged.

Melusine packed her bags that evening and moved on. Old Gust had summoned a larger power than he knew. If it noticed other powers in town then the townsfolk would be in trouble. It almost killed her to leave little Sarah behind.

Twenty years later, though, was worse. Much worse. Twenty years later she swore never to live in Europe again.

I've been re-reading Melusine's tales. Time to blog!

The werewolf story was important to me. Remember, I was fifteen. Remember also, that I had started to hope.

First up, I wanted to tell Melusine how stupid she was. I mean, she ran away. In stories people stand up and kick ass and save everyone. She should have kicked ass and saved Sarah. Not just from the werewolf, but from the gas ovens, too. Fairies are magic. Magic folk can do anything. They can save the world.

Then I realised, Melusine was a fairy, but she was like a human. Humans do things differently. I remembered, *I ran away. In the real world.* I was being very strong that day. I remember this clearly. I remember that my mind went badkatbadkatbadkat and I pulled myself back from it. Strong.

Partly I was strong because I had stuff to think about. I had to think about this. What if Melusine's stories were pretend (because stories are) but set in a real world, where real people run away rather than kicking ass. What if Melusine was scared? Scared and lying to herself about it.

I bet she was scared. I bet she wasn't kick-ass. The werewolf story was all dislocated: it had a hole in the middle. There wasn't a kid and then there was a kid. Melusine hadn't been in the village for years and years, and still the kid knew her. She brought the kid back and gave no reason for that. I bet she was trying to remember and then found she didn't want to. I bet there were two stories, or maybe three, and she just ran them all together because it was easier than remembering. I wonder what really happened?

It must have been bad.

I thought all this, but I couldn't find any answers without asking Lil. I wasn't brave enough to tell Lil I had taken her stories and read them.

The solution I found was to read more and more. It also started me thinking about things. Before that I was all into stuff like vampires and werewolves because they were romantic. Teen novel vampires and teen novel werewolves. After that I didn't know what I was into. Reality, I guess.

"Fear reduction," said Ann, rubbing her hands enthusiastically. Kat couldn't see that it needed enthusiasm. She just wanted to get in and do something. If Ann was involved, though, she would bet on it being ghosts. Not any of the things they needed to do, just ghosts. Ann, Kat was beginning to suspect, had a thing about ghosts. Maybe she was kidnapped by spectres and given that squinty eye? Maybe a phantom was what had her shadow? "That's our aim, fear reduction."

"And our method?" Lil was not bringing any emotion. She offered this question, in fact, without any indication that she might have private feelings on the matter.

"Ghosts," said Ann. *I knew it,* thought Kat. "We can deal with ghosts.

We know we can. Sending them on will help Canberrans be less scared."

"Which will help in what way with werewolves?"

"One step at a time, Mabel. One step at a time."

The trouble was, when Ann said something, the others did it. Always. So ghosts it was. They made a list of targets and went after them in an orderly manner. Kat wanted the women's handbags to contain stakes, but she peeked inside Mabel's and the most interesting thing she found was a small pack of tissues. Not even any holy water.

I've got to stop laughing at them behind their backs, Kat decided. *This is serious, even if they're stupid in how they do things sometimes. I don't want to, but.* What she wanted to do was to sneak stakes and holy water and maybe a crucifix or two into each handbag and then say, "What about vampire hunting instead?"

Except that there were no vampires. She could hope that vampires were not real. Or she could hope that they could never come to Canberra. Besides, she just could not see Lil with a crucifix. Actually, she could. Lil would extract it from her handbag very delicately, hold it between her thumb and her forefinger as if it were something a little uncomfortable, and then say, "I do wonder how this came to be here." Fun to contemplate, but not worth the doing.

"What's wrong, Kat?" asked the lady in question. They were both in the back seat of the car by this time. Kat hoped that Lil didn't notice the pink flush. Even more, she hoped Lil couldn't read minds.

"I was just fretting," Kat said.

"We can't banish the ghosts, you know," Lil said.

"I thought we could. I thought it was one of the things we *could* do?"

"It's a special talent, persuading them to move on, and none of us have it. All we can do is reduce fear."

"How?"

"We're nearly there." Mabel turned her head to say, "You'll see." It sounded to Kat as if they really didn't know. Not even Mabel was giving a straight answer.

They parked the car and walked a short way to a school. To Kat's surprise they knocked on the door and were let in.

"If you can do your thing again, it'd be a great help," the principal said as they all walked down school corridors. Kat scuttled behind to catch up. No introductions. Just work. Maybe she was wrong, then. That'd be nice.

They reached some stairs. "Look up," Lil's soft voice whispered in Kat's ear. They saw a student, dead. "That's our ghost."

"Is it doing anything new?" Ann's voice was all business.

"Nothing. It's appearing more frequently, but that's all."

"Whose turn is it?" Ann turned to her friends.

"Mabel's, I think," said Lil.

Mabel heaved a huge sigh. "Waste of bloody time," she muttered. She walked up the stairs until she was very near the ghost. She turned her head up and looked firmly at it and proceeded to give it a scolding. As she told it off for scaring people, it faded.

"It's always so commonplace when she does it," the principal said. "Next time I might ring you a bit sooner."

"It's up to you." Ann shrugged.

They all filed out again.

"That was all?" asked Kat.

"Half our afternoon's work, all done," Ann rubbed her hands again.

"But you didn't do anything."

"The ghost has its rights too, you know." That was Mabel. "But I hate that kind of work. I don't like going up close. It's cold and just a bit gruesome."

"If you did it from a distance, would it work?"

"Probably, but would it be fair on everyone?"

"It sounded," Kat said, "as if you were the ghost's grandmother."

"That's right," said Mabel, cheerful again. "That's what it's supposed to sound like."

By the time they reached their next destination, it was later. Late enough so that Kat was shivering.

"Didn't you bring a jacket?" asked Ann.

"You said it would be quick."

"It will be, but it still takes us out after dark."

"Here," and Mabel handed Kat a jumper from the boot. "I always bring extra. Never know when you get the chills from this stuff."

"Thanks."

"Listen," said Ann.

A voice was crying out into the night, full of despair, "Give me my blue cardigan. Give me my blue cardigan. Giiiiive meeee my blue cardigan."

"I don't believe it," said Mabel.

"That's the ghost?" Kat wasn't sure she believed it either. A blue cardigan. How stupid could it get?

"The question is," asked Lil, "whether we have a blue cardigan. Or rather, the correct blue cardigan."

"We do," said Ann. "I checked with the police and found out who died here and I discovered that all her possessions went to the Smith Family. I bought that blue cardigan for three dollars, this afternoon."

"Good," Mabel said. "Let's get this over with."

Blue cardigan, snorted Kat, purely to herself, as she watched Ann, in her turn, rummage through the boot. She looked down at the jumper Mabel had loaned her to make sure it wasn't blue, just in case. *Sometimes this is silly. Really, really, really silly.*

"Three pieces, Ann," reminded Lil, as Ann came back.

"Give me my blue cardigan."

"But we've got the right garment," argued Ann. "Let's get it over with."

"Three." Lil was adamant. Ann sighed and went back to the car.

"There's only this," and she held up a rather sad raincoat.

"Take my jumper." Kat shrugged off the borrowed garment.

"Giiive me my blue cardigan."

"Oh, put a sock in it," said Mabel. "We're coming."

"Giiiive me my blue cardigan."

"It's upped the pace," observed Kat.

"Giiiive meeee my blue cardigan."

"It's noticed us," said Lil.

"Giiiiive meeeee my blue cardigan."

"It's a bloody drama queen," grumbled Mabel, and strode out with the first garment.

"Here is your bloody blue cardigan. Take it." Except it wasn't a blue cardigan. It was the sleazy raincoat.

There was a moment's silence, then "Giiiive me my blue cardigan."

"Right, your turn." Mabel handed the jumper to Ann.

"Thanks a bunch, Mabel." Ann walked into the gloaming, arm outstretched, saying, "Here, here is your blue cardigan."

The ghost didn't even deign to wait a moment this time. "Giiiive meee my blue cardigan."

Lil's turn. By now it was so dark that Lil faded into the gloom. Or was it that Kat was so cold she couldn't see for shivering? She could hear Lil asking politely, "Is this your blue cardigan?"

The ghost didn't reply, but Lil came back without the offending garment.

"Thank God that's over," said Mabel. "Let's go get warm."

They took the direct route home, but instead of taking just a few minutes, it took nearly an hour.

"It's the streets," said Ann, gloomily. "They're shifting again."

"How do we get out of it?" Lil was worried.

"We just keep driving."

Mabel said, "I'm going to park the car, get out and walk."

"Don't do that." Ann was genuinely horrified. "If you do that, the whispers will come. The whispers are worse than the streets."

Three intrepid ladies and one intrepid girl, out to scare a werewolf. It sounded good from the safety of Mabel's kitchen. It didn't sound nearly as much fun now they were next to that huge wire fence at Tharwa, looking down on the wreckage that once had been protection.

Mabel took a quick look around. "Can't see anything. Let's put this to rights."

"Good idea. Kat, give me a hand with this." The two of them hoisted and pushed and pulled until the stand was upright. Immediately, Lil and Mabel stepped forward with the bits of shrine they had collected, to put them in place.

"Mabel," Lil said, "I have replacements for the electric light and replacement wires and a new battery in the boot."

"Good. I'll go get them." Mabel turned and there, between her and the car, stood the giant wolf.

"I don't think so," it said.

Mabel ducked to the side and the wolf, lunging out, held her arm in his big jaws. He looked her straight in the eyes for a full ten seconds, then gently let her go.

"Next full moon." The deep male voice coming out of the wolven jaws was all kinds of wrong. "You might find yourself in a spot of bother. If any of you were a decent age, I'd suggest you join me, but you're either too young or too old. I don't want to see you lot again." He loped off, as if he had not a care in the world.

Mabel, on the other hand, was staring at her arm in horror. "He broke my skin. He did. He broke my skin."

"In the car," said Lil, businesslike. "Let's get you some first aid and then let's get you home and get a cup of strong tea into you. Right now."

It took nearly twenty minutes to reach Mabel's place and things were very quiet the whole way. Underneath the surface no-one was even close to calm.

"What if she turns into a werewolf?" Kat worried.

"She won't," snapped Ann.

"But what if she does?"

Before Ann could get angrier, Mabel said "Can't you see the kid's scared?"

"She didn't get bitten, you did."

Lil sighed. "I can ensure that she won't turn into a werewolf," she said, directly to Kat.

"You can?"

"I most certainly can."

"Oh, a new talent," Ann said.

"Shut up, Ann," Mabel said, the tiredness and hurt making her voice fade," Can't you see you're not helping."

"I can help then?"

"Go make us a cuppa."

"Your answer to everything."

"Yep. Now just go. I can't deal with your bad mood. Not right now."

Ann looked embarrassed. "Sorry. I'll go make some extra-strong tea."

"Just the way I like it." Mabel managed a grin.

"Kat, do you have any materials on werewolves?"

"Some," admitted Kat.

"If you wouldn't mind sitting in my study and reading it to see if it tells us anything new, that would help us for the next encounter."

"We have to try again, don't we?" said Kat.

"We do," said Mabel.

"And I shall cure Mabel of any tendency to transform into a wolf."

"While I'm gone."

"I cannot have witnesses." Lil was firm.

"Call me when you're ready?"

"Of course," promised Lil.

When Kat was out of the room and the sound of cups and clatter could be heard from the kitchen, Lil took off the bandage that hid Mabel's arm. The bite was clear and nasty and the first aid had only disinfected it.

She sighed. "Mabel, I trust you will tell no-one about this."

"I thought you were pretending, for Kat."

"Because it's for Kat, I shall not pretend. She needs honesty. "

"So you will cure me of lycanthropy." Mabel managed a smile.

"At least it will tell us if lycanthropy it was. Maybe we will have more possibility of a less disastrous outcome next time."

"Next time." Mabel's voice was almost nothing. Then she rallied. "Well, get on with it."

Lil carefully smoothed her hand over the wound. Mabel nearly snatched her arm away from the pain.

"Shh. Rest. It will be easier at the next pass."

Mabel held out her arm, stoically. Lil smiled at her. "I knew I admired you for a particular reason," she said, and gently smoothed the wound again. This time Mabel winced, but that was all. The third time, she didn't even wince. Lil nodded. As she took her hand away, Mabel's arm glowed slightly. There was just the trace of an old bite. Not an open wound. Faint tooth marks.

"I did not expect this," Mabel said, looking closely at her own skin.

"And I did not expect Kat to be right. She has an instinct. We need to listen to her more."

"You mean . . ."

"You would have changed at the full moon."

"I was a real old-fashioned werewolf. Who'd have guessed?"

"You sound very pleased about that."

"It's a surprise. I like surprises."

"As long as they're safe."

"You really cured me?"

"I really did."

"Then I'm safe. And we can cure that bloke what bit me."

"It may not be so easy with him. The process has gone a great deal further. Also, he appears happy in wolf skin. It's hard to cure someone who believes they're not ill."

"Mm," said Mabel. "Let's think about it."

"Let's tell Kat she was right. Then we shall drink Ann's tea and celebrate the fact that you can admire the next full moon through human eyes."

❖

Kat was reading stories about ghosts. It was one a.m. and Lil would have told her to sleep if Lil had been the sort of person to issue instructions. But she wasn't, and Kat was rejoicing in smugness. And reading about Australian ghosts.

"Frederick Baker," she said, and decided she liked him. "If ever I go to Melbourne, I'm gonna go to the opera at his theatre. And there will be an empty seat beside me and we'll sit and talk." Like Mabel and that bushranger. A bit flirty. She smiled.

The smile was wiped off her face as she moved to the list of schools and asylums that were haunted. "Much more yuck," Kat decided. "We don't deal with that sort of . . . of . . ."

The door opened quietly and Kat jumped and gave a small scream.

"I saw your light on," Lil said in her most polite sorry-voice, "and I was wondering if you would join me for supper."

"It's late," Kat said, with the accusatory tone of a twelve year old caught doing something forbidden. She tried to act like a cool fifteen year old. *Which I am*, she reminded herself. "Supper?"

"I made some pastries, and they are best eaten very fresh."

"You knew I was reading about ghosts." Kat's voice was flat. She didn't need humouring.

"I did, and you may read whatever you like, whenever you like. I have said this before. Pastries and maybe a little hot chocolate will make reading a little . . . happier, that's all."

"Nice pastries?" Kat said, suspiciously.

"Delectable ones."

Kat gave in and laughed. "You get me every time," she said, and swung her computer chair round exuberantly. "The computer will wait till I get back."

"No doubt."

And it did. The screen showed her blog when Kat returned, but Kat thought she had closed the tab, and she wasn't worried. She always kept her blog up there, somewhere, even though she didn't use it much. It made her feel as she belonged to a bigger world. She wasn't worried by the feeling of cold that stole over her as she slept, because she had learned to switch off from sudden cold when she was on the streets.

So Kat slept.

The cold intensified. Inside it, a pair of eyes peered out. They were bright, but the body was hidden by a luminous haze. As they stared, Kat turned in her sleep and muttered. The presence withdrew a little. After a bit it grew more confident and moved close to Kat. A hand reached out of the haze and rested on Kat's brow for a moment. Kat turned over violently and threw out her arms wildly. The eyes watched for a while longer, then gradually faded away.

Kat woke up from a comfortable dream. In the dream she had decided she had to move house, so she picked up her doona, put on her slippers and dragged the doona after her, moving to her new house.

A few minutes later she was blinking and almost awake. This room was so warm. Lil's lounge room. She must've walked there in her sleep. That was the moment when she realised her granny flat had been cold. The realisation didn't mean anything, because her mind was quite a bit more asleep than her body and she just stood there, her doona puddling about her feet.

"I sleepwalked again." This was her next thought. "I haven't done that since the baby came." She said it aloud.

"Then come sit down," Lil's gentle voice whispered behind her.

Kat started shivering. Within moments the shivers had turned to shudders.

With an expertise borne of experience, Lil whisked the doona from Kat's feet and wrapped it around her. She sat next to the girl, rocking her gently.

"It's a panic attack," said Lil. "Nothing more. In a few moments, I shall make you some hot chocolate and we will eat chocolate biscuits and maybe the rest of the pastries and you will feel better."

"I had two dreams," Kat forced out. It was hard to speak. Her teeth wanted to chatter.

"Do you want to tell me them?"

"The first only. I think I scared myself with the ghost stories."

"But you want to tell me anyway?"

"Please?"

"Then tell." Lil stopped rocking Kat. Her voice was soft in Kat's ear. They sat together on the couch, huddled closely and comfortingly.

"I was looking down from the ceiling at myself asleep. I looked funny. I remember myself thinking, 'I want to laugh at how I look, like a baby bunny all curled up.'"

"Or maybe like a kitten?" suggested Lil.

Kat turned her head and looked Lil in the eyes, all her shaking suddenly over. "Yes, a kitten." She gave a little smile. With a small part of her brain she noticed that Lil's hold of her had suddenly softened, as if she needed reassurance more than protection. She missed that protection, but drew a deep breath and kept the room from getting quiet. Quiet was too like her dream. No sounds in her dream. There had been no noises at all.

"I saw a man. He had the sharpest eyes I have ever seen. I tried to memorise his face, but all I can remember are his eyes. He was looking up at me as if he could see right through me." She shuddered.

"Were his eyes warm or cold? Did you get any sense of him?"

"No," Kat said slowly. "The room was cold, but I just remember the eyes were really sharp. Like a sailor's eyes, maybe. Or like an archer's." She waited to see if Lil had more questions, then she continued. "He turned and watched me on the bed for a bit and for a moment it was as if there were two Kats, one on the ceiling and one on the bed. I didn't like that, so I went back to the ceiling. A bit later he walked to the bed and he put his hand on my forehead and then I was in my bed."

"Did he do anything else?"

"He wasn't there. Not when I was in my bed."

"And after that?"

"I had my second dream, and it was all about moving house, so you don't need to know that."

"I don't think you had that dream by chance, ma p'tite. I think you wanted to feel safe."

"And your lounge room is safe?"

"All the rooms are safe in this house. Why don't you sleep on the couch for the rest of the night and then we'll move you into the spare room tomorrow."

"But what about your privacy?" Kat's voice was shaky and lacked resonance.

"When this is all settled, I will send you out to the granny flat again. Until then, we will both sleep better if we know the only dreams you battle are imaginary."

Kat's shocked eyes looked suddenly into Lil's. "He was real!"

"I believe so. I do not know who he is, nor what he is doing in Canberra."

"But you can keep me safe."

"I can."

"Then, yes please. And can I help you make the chocolate?"

"You need to be useful."

Kat nodded.

"Then let us make sublime hot chocolate, since we are to share a home. We must celebrate."

Eight

"I KNOW ALL ABOUT sleepwalking now," announced Kat to Mabel and Ann. "I've finished moving my stuff," she informed Lil. "I've got a lot more stuff than I had a few months ago."

"We can have a garage sale, if you want," suggested Mabel.

"I'd rather keep it. I'm working on being a capitalist."

"What on earth have you been reading?" asked Ann.

"Everything. I'm working through Lil's bookshelf. My aim and intent is to develop an impressive vocabulary."

"I thought you were working on lists of otherworldly beings," Lil said.

"Oops, I've been sprung." Kat sounded inordinately pleased at being sprung.

"Why were you moving your worldly goods?" asked Ann into the miniature silence that welcomed Kat's grin.

"The sleepwalking," said Kat. "Except it wasn't just sleepwalking. Someone was stealing my breath. And, and . . ."

"It appears someone is moving into the granny flat. Someone who belongs on one of our lists."

"It means we can start our map with here," said Kat. "I forgot to say," and it was patently obvious to everyone that she hadn't forgotten at all, that she had taken this time to pluck up courage to mention it, "I sprang the new occupant twice today as I was moving my things. He's like that bushranger: he gets more and more corporeal. There's a haze in the granny flat. I had to keep dodging it."

"Corporeal is such a lovely word," said Mabel.

"It is," agreed Kat. "I just wish I didn't have to use it so often. It's a bit yuck when it's where I lived and when it's someone who tried to hurt me."

"If he was more visible, can you tell us more about his looks?"

"Yes, Lil. I don't want to, but I can. I saw him sort of clearly, just the once. I think he's got some muscle and he looks like one of those people who used to have a suntan and it's faded. Sorta like the memory of a suntan. His eyes are still the big thing, but he's not quite human-looking also. Elflike, but without the ears. Not pretty. But he could be pretty. Except he's beautiful. I kept forgetting that, and looking at his eyes. His eyes scare me."

"What sort of clothes is he wearing?"

"Historical ones. Same as the bushrangers. Maybe a bit smarter. Black and white and boring."

"Ring any bells?" Mabel addressed the room at large.

"Too many," said Lil. "That description could be anyone, and the way he manifests, no-one."

"I'm interested in seeing him," said Ann. "Male beauty is to be admired."

"He's not safe," said Kat, sharply. "That's why I moved my things. He's the reason I had all those night fears."

"There is a small possibility he was protecting you against something else," Lil said, determined that Kat not be scared.

"But what about the breathlessness and the weight on my chest? And why did I leave my body in the first place?"

"That's a mystery," said Lil. "Another one. Let us start our map and see if it helps us towards any solutions."

"Before we start on the map," said Mabel, slowly, "I have a confession to make." Everyone in the room was instantly riveted. Even their bodies leaned slightly towards Mabel. This was when they would find out the truth of her and Jackey-Jackey. "Last night I sleepwalked, too. I found myself in the middle of my hexagon, at midnight."

"Exactly at midnight?" asked Ann.

"Near as I could tell."

"Why the middle of the garden?" asked Kat. "And do you remember your dreams?"

"I remember I had a nightmare. It was awful. I can't remember the details."

"But you walked to somewhere safe."

"I did."

"Why is the garden safe?" Kat was determined to get to the bottom of everything.

"Because she built all sort of esoteric protections into it: each tree represents different qualities, each garden bed symbolises stuff. It's supposed to be amazing." Ann managed to sound both supportive and a trifle condescending.

"It *is* amazing," said Lil. "Her dreams took her to a very secure place."

"What can I do?" asked Mabel. "I'm certainly not coming over here and sleeping in your study."

"I can't see you doing that," said Lil. "Why don't we take all our papers and finish our task at your house? I can check it out and maybe put some protection on."

"If you can make it safe, then that's a good solution."

"She can't make it safe," said Ann. "None of us have that sort of ability."

"You used to know more," said Lil, sadly.

"I used to believe more," said Ann. "The other day I walked down the street and saw my shadow. If I have a shadow, how can I trust my squinty eye? Anyhow, these days everyone sees what I used to see. I'm nothing special."

"But you are," said Mabel.

"You are," said Lil. "What is happening in Canberra is an aberration. The invisible is becoming visible. We don't know the paths yet, but there's ghosts who are new visitors and were properly at rest before, and some of those beings should simply not be there. Your eye is a little confused by it all: you still have that talent."

"Well, I feel useless."

"Can we deal with that later?" asked Mabel, plaintively. "I feel scared, and that's easier to handle."

"Only if you believe Lil can do magic. Which I've never seen. Not even out of my squinty eye. She is human and mundane and can't help."

"You can believe that if you like," said Mabel, "though I'd rather you phrased it less rudely. I trust Lil's magic, and I'm the one who was walking in the garden after midnight, for all the wrong reasons."

"Maybe it's the Clarke Brothers, using you to get at Jackey-Jackey?"

"We won't know until we see," said Lil. "Should we take separate cars?"

Two cars and twenty minute later they were in Mabel's place in Weston Creek. Lil let herself in first, while the others went round to the back verandah to wait until Lil announced the all clear. Ann strode straight towards the woodpile, while Mabel walked slowly, like an old lady, towards the woodpile side of the house. Kat followed, but then veered off to the other side when she heard Mabel mutter to the protector of her wood, "It's all right, mate, the cavalry is coming. Lil is inside now, checking on things."

She raced back to the far side when she heard Ann scream. "It's just the thing from the back of the woodpile," Kat said crossly, before she could see anything. The first thing the teenager saw was Mabel, shocked and white and staring.

She went up to Mabel and put an arm around her. "What is it?"

Mabel raised her arm and pointed down. There on the ground was the woodpile creature, eviscerated. Ann was quietly retching in a corner. "It never did anyone any harm," Mabel said.

"I bet it protected you 'til you got to cover. I bet you were in real danger and I bet it saved your life." Kat invented as she went, but it had the ring of truth. That creature had loved Mabel.

"I'll bet it did. God, I'll miss the damn thing."

"Let's go round the other way, and wait for Lil."

Mabel nodded and allowed herself to be guided to a seat next to her seedling stand. Ann took a while to come, and Kat could do nothing about it. She couldn't be there for both of them and Mabel needed her more. Mabel showed every inch of her age. Her worry lines stood out and she looked as if she would blow over in a small breeze. Kat desperately wanted to make her a cup of tea, but couldn't do a thing until Lil had spoken.

When Ann finally came, she said, "I've cleaned up everything. My mess as well. I buried that poor thing under one of the trees. I hope that's okay."

Kat wanted to put an arm around her, too. Ann seemed much more likeable now she wasn't hiding her vulnerability. And she wished she had thought of cleaning up. Except she wasn't sure she could've done it.

Finally, and eventually, Lil emerged. She was as white as the others. She looked as vulnerable. "It's all safe now. It wasn't easy, though. I'll tell you about it when we're indoors."

"I can make tea," suggested Kat.

"A cuppa sounds very, very good," said Mabel.

Kat supported Mabel to the kitchen table and Ann came along a bit later, carrying all the papers. "We forgot these," she said.

"Later," said Mabel.

"Today though," said Ann. "After we sort out what happened here."

Kat wanted to say, 'Look at Mabel, she can't take any more today.' Before she could say words that wouldn't make Mabel feel even frailer, Lil spoke.

"I know how I feel. I can only imagine how you all feel, but this is part of a bigger pattern. We've been acting like dilettantes, as if we've all the time in the world. We don't have that luxury any more."

"We can take our time," said Ann, changing her mind. "In fact, we should. We're hurt. We need to heal."

"We are under attack," Lil said, bluntly. "Ann, you through your fears, Kat and myself through a different type of fear and Mabel, Mabel my dear, last night something tried to kill you. We can't pretend it didn't."

"It killed the little creature that protected my woodpile," said Mabel, her voice drained of energy.

"That was the death I felt." Lil nodded. "It was a very brave little creature. It saw you to safety then took the full brunt of whatever it was that had been planned to kill you."

"We have witchcraft here?" asked Ann.

"Nothing like that. We have yet another being that should not be here. Or perhaps one of the ones we already know. Except that this being is cleverer than most and has access to a different range of power. It's looking for threats. Mabel, your garden protected you, but I also think it drew its attention."

"It knew that I knew stuff."

"I'm afraid so."

"I'm not getting rid of it!" For a moment her usual self shone through.

"That would be the worst thing you could do. Your house is safe now, and most of the back garden always was safe. I'll work on the verandah and the odd unplanned bits of garden when I've had a rest."

"And me?" asked Ann. "Am I under threat?"

"We all are," said Kat. "That's what Lil was saying."

"And will I be attacked in my sleep?"

Lil suddenly looked hundreds of years old. "I can give you protection too. Tomorrow. I am old. There are limits to what I can do in one single night and day."

"You can stay here tonight, Ann," said Mabel.

"I'll think about it," said Ann, stiffly.

They played around desultorily with a one-page map of Canberra for a while. Mabel was still in shock and found it hard to focus; Ann wanted her house protected immediately and kept diverging from working on a map; Kat wanted to make everything far more detailed; and Lil just wanted to get the basics over so that they could start working. She also wanted a good night's sleep, but, as she said to her friends, "I'm not going to get any rest until you are all less upset. This map should settle us."

"We'll know more about what's out there, perhaps," Mabel said, dubiously.

"Or maybe we can pinpoint one supereviloverlord who is our nemesis and only have to deal with him," said Kat. The older women didn't laugh at that, but they looked amused. It was something.

Eventually they discovered that almost all the things they could think of, with their brains in such odd states, boiled down to two regions: around Yarralumla and Manuka, where Ann and Lil and Kat lived, and Weston Creek, where Mabel lived. There were a few exceptions: water spirits and Jackey-Jackey were the obvious ones.

"There are some things that were here before the current rise of paranormal," Kat said.

"Impressive language," Ann replied.

"Comes from the very good fiction I read." No laugh this time round, either, but they were getting closer to one. "What we need," said Kat, still thinking of what paranormal romances had taught her about the world of magic, "is a mega good spirit on our side. Like a good fairy, who likes humans. Someone to fight big time."

"And if we had that," Lil still sounded old, "what would we do with it?"

"Alien vs. predator. Godzilla vs. whoever he fought. Mega battles! Stomp! Stomp! Gnash! Gnash! World saved!" After all, life had more facets than paranormal romance.

"Half the city destroyed under their feet, you mean?" said Mabel, her sense of irony fully restored.

"Yes! No. Not really. I just want something simpler than all this murk. We've got our maps, now. Just no simple answers."

"Maybe we don't have our good fairy because such a being would have no idea what she could do."

"A stupid good fairy," said Ann.

"Ann, you always find the dark side of things. Why is that?" Kat immediately put her hand over her mouth and bowed her head. Her voice was muffled, but the words were clear. "Sorrysorrysorrysorry, badkat badkat, badbadbadkat."

Lil and Mabel look very worried.

"I thought we cured you of that," said Ann.

"Ann, stop it," said Lil. "You are not helping."

"If you will excuse us," Ann said to the others, "I need to talk to Lil. We'll go to the next room."

"Ann, is this the time?" Mabel sounded tired again. Kat agreed with Mabel. She couldn't say it, though, because she'd already got Lil into trouble. Maybe they should have stopped the conversation when they worked out the main problem areas? She couldn't say that either. In fact, she didn't want to say a thing in case badkat came out by mistake. So she didn't. She kept her hand over her mouth and her head bowed. That was safest.

"This is important," Ann said to Lil. The minute she thought the others were out of earshot, she said, "I want to clear the decks. You have been, quite regularly, interfering with my relationship with Kat. I've reached the stage where I can't tolerate it any longer — you have offended me once too often."

"Ann," said Lil, wearily, "with all that has happened to us today, is this really the right time to discuss it? Aren't we all just a bit too emotional?"

"This is the perfect moment. It's a time for honesty."

"No, really, we should wait."

"All year I have waited. All year. My life has dissolved and I have been patient. I have put all the group feelings first when my husband had his fling then wanted a divorce, when I was made to retire early, when I couldn't even sleep in my own bed. All year, I have said yes and no and three bags full and put you ahead of me. It's stopping here.

"I said we would help Kat." Ann's emotions rasped through her voice. "And so I am responsible for her. I am, not you. Lil, you are old. You have nothing in common with an emo teen. Hell, you don't even know what emo is. You pretending you understand is going to give her a false sense of security. You have taken over her life and it's bad for her. Wrong.

"Lil, you're holding her back. She reverts to that scary badkatbadkat self-immolation and she hurts. You hold her back." Ann concluded, "She hasn't even rung her parents yet."

Lil sat patiently through the diatribe. When Ann ran out of words, she asked, "First, isn't it up to Kat when she feels she is ready to ring her parents? And isn't it up to Kat how much of her child descriptions she needs to cling to when life is difficult? I thought she handled today and tonight extremely well. I also thought that it was up to her and each single one of us on how our relationship goes. If you're unhappy with the way Kat is talking with you, changing the way she talks to me won't help."

"I don't agree with you," Ann said, strongly.

"I doubted you would. However, you have said your piece and I have said mine and now we can leave it until we are less emotional and unhappy. This is not a good night for this type of discussion."

"I think you're wrong. This is the perfect night. We are all open, because of those experiences. I have discovered this through experience: pretending that the experiences haven't happened doesn't help. We are more open now than we usually are, and so we should talk things through."

"If open means red-raw, I'd agree, but in this case we need time to recover."

"You said there was something else?"

"I did?"

"You said 'First,' and you never reached the second thing."

Lil was not amused. "So I did. I think we shall not speak about the second thing. It might not be good for our friendship. At the very least, it might entail an apology."

"Apology," said Ann.

"To clear the air, perhaps?" Lil's voice was sweet acid. "You might want to apologise for rummaging in my private things, last dinner party, when I was in the kitchen. I did not want to mention it at all, however, much less on a night when we're all . . . what did I say? . . . rubbed red raw."

"There's no humiliation in it. I was helping. Both then and now." Ann's excuse sounded feeble even to Ann herself.

"There would have been even if the others were not just around the corner, listening. Don't try that again. If I have done something wrong, tell me — don't manipulate my emotions to make yourself feel superior. Ask me questions when you need answers. And never, ever go through my private things. We shall pretend this conversation did not take place, I think, in the interest of continuing our friendship." She walked back to the dinner table where Mabel and Kat were very, very quiet and their faces very, very red. Ann followed. Her face was a different red.

She announced, "I shall stay at a hotel until Lil deigns to protect my house as well." Then she left.

Kat sat quietly. Eventually, she spoke up. "Can I ask something?"

"You look so very timid," Lil chided, gently.

"Please don't laugh," Kat's voice sounded tiny and small and maybe a bit frightened, even in her own ears.

"I promise. Ask, and I shall try to answer."

"Why were you so very angry with Ann? I know it's the wrong time and everything. You don't have to tell me. We can wait a few days or something."

Lil was quiet a moment, then she shrugged. "I promised," she said, half to herself. "Ann and I had a discussion many years ago, about my privacy. She has always been more curious about me than is sensible. I warned her off once. Now I have warned her off twice. The next time will not be so civilised."

"She wanted you to stay away from me. And she wanted to know more about you."

"Yes." Lil paused to find her thoughts. "If she had just asked, there would have been no offence. If I had wronged her over you then it is right I should apologise."

"Those things don't belong together," Kat thought aloud.

"No, ma p'tite," Lil answered. "They don't. Nor do they belong with that stoked self-righteousness she displayed tonight. And apologies should never be demanded or driven out of one."

"Or emotionally blackmailed." Kat suddenly felt old.

"That was where the perversion lay. Someone else asking the same thing would not have asked it in such a way or with so many nearby ears, and would not been offensive," Lil said. "It hurt me when she tried to compel me to feel sorry, but it hurt her when I reacted to what she was doing. She needed me to accept it, passively. If I were more sensitive, I would feel pangs of remorse for scolding her."

"And as it is you're just mad as hell."

"She demeaned both of us."

"You know what you told me about your New Year? With all the apologies and stuff? Are you going to apologise to her, then, on your New Year?"

"After my New Year," said Lil, a glint in her eye. "Before the Day of Atonement. One does not sully days of joy with this sort of thing; one saves them for the days when one is soul-searching and seeking improvement."

"But you are, aren't you?"

"Of course I am. I shall feel due remorse by then for I shall have considered my sin. I shall have wronged her in thinking she wanted words from me tonight to assuage her ego rather than to clear the air."

"Oh," said Kat. "I need to think about that. You're being very complicated tonight." There was one bit of it she didn't want to think about. She had read those Melusine stories. They hadn't been in Lil's bedroom chest of drawers — they had been sitting under the TV, with some books, but they were still private. Kat was as bad as Ann. Maybe worse.

"Think away."

"In the meantime, can I ask another question?"

"Of course."

"It's about the personthingiebeingwhatever who's in the granny flat. I've noticed stuff about him: I thought maybe you might be able to work out who he is from that stuff. Will you?"

"I shall try. Not, perhaps, tonight. And I suggest you stop peering in the window for a little. We are all red raw — you need to heal as much as we do."

"And you were trying to make me feel good before, weren't you?"

"I was."

"He could have been attacking me. He could have attacked Mabel."

"Yes."

"Can I say 'damn'?"

"I think so." Lil was weary beyond reckoning. "I really think this is the right moment to use strong language."

"Damn," said Kat, but it didn't make her feel any better.

Kat and Lil's conversation, once started, continued for days. Even on the way to the fourth dinner party, in fact. They had all been healing and gearing themselves up for the battles they knew would come. They had to explore Weston Creek and Yarralumla. They had to banish what they could and maybe even do worse than banish.

Kat was petrified, but determined. She had got herself into this, she would see it through. She loved having Lil to talk with. She wanted to tell Lil everything, but one thing Ann had inadvertently taught her was that some things required the right time and place. And maybe she was wrong anyway. Maybe Ann's special vision was right and she was wrong.

That was something she could find out about: Ann's special vision. Lil gave her the lead-in she needed, when they were cooking together for that fourth dinner. The healing one. The one that would bring them all four closer again and help them face the impossible.

"It's curious that Ann's sight has been so unreliable recently," Lil commented to Kat, adult to adult.

"Maybe it's because she's already awake to the things she needs to see — Mabel and I are half asleep by comparison."

"She sees more, you think?"

"Oh, I do!"

Tales of Melusine #1

Telling a fairy tale is very difficult when the fairy refuses to keep to form.

Fairies may be wizened and full of grumbles, or beautiful and full of poetry. They can't be snarky. Snarky is so out-of-canon it's inconceivable. Yet Melusine was snarky. And she lied. She still is. She still does. Five hundred and seventy three years (if she tells the truth about her age) of pure, unadulterated evil comments on the world. Funny as hell. Annoying as hell. Too literate for anyone's good. And so un-fairy-like that it's impossible to tell her tale.

This is the first in a series of attempts at impossible tales. Full of truths and untruths. Melusine's stories, written down by her in a series of fits of pique or misery. She wrote this tale last. Or maybe first.

One time, somewhere in the twentieth century, Melusine visited Spain. She wanted to see how the place she knew had changed.

Last time she had been there she was very young. This time, she was returning a visit to a friend. They went to synagogue together and snuck looks through the little grille upstairs at any potential husbands. Not that she was in the market for a husband just then. She had buried her third, and was not particularly impressed with the keeping qualities of human men. She was not impressed with the character of fairy men, either. Good hybrids were rare.

"Why do you look, if you think it's such a waste of energy?" asked the friend, who was human but had what Melusine thought of as a fairy brain. Her friend had already worked out exactly who she would approach when the service was over.

"Looking is fine. Touching is very fine. It's just marriage that's out."

The lady standing next to them looked daggers and moved a little away. Melusine sighed. Jewish law said nothing about sleeping with someone single and she wasn't planning on seducing a married man. The mores of humans didn't match their laws, and that could be annoying. If only human men weren't so pretty.

Usually when she was annoyed with halacha she sought out a rabbi and involved him in deep argument, turning his brain inside out. The advantage of age was that she had time to read the law from several directions and interpret it to fit. Usually snarkily. The bigger advantage of her particular age was that she had studied with the most educated women in Europe: Rashi's daughters. She'd gone into Rouen young and impressionable and had come out educated and thoughtful. It was not hard for her to turn a rabbi's brain inside out, back when she had visited Spain last.

It had been two hundred years since she had talked Talmud with anyone anywhere. She was still Jewish. How could she be otherwise? But she had not liked the way Jewish law was tending since the time her friends moved east, and so she stayed clear of legal discussions, of rabbis, and of anything that might make her look magic. Magic in the eighteenth century was not a good thing.

Now was different. Rabbis lived in Spain again, though not many. Magic was sexy, even when people didn't believe in it. Melusine was beginning to unwind. To celebrate, she had paid that visit to Spain.

Spain in the twentieth century was not familiar. It was so proud of its heritage, but the only thing that she recognised were the streets. Oh, that little synagogue was there in Cordoba still. White and sparkling on the outside. A tourist attraction now, the upstairs area where she had once gossiped used for storage.

It was all wrong. Pretty, but wrong. There was no heart left in the region where once she had friends.

Melusine returned to her homeland and hid herself in the shadow of Carcassonne for six months, letting the sun of Provence warm her ancient bones. She didn't live there: even Provence couldn't warm her old heart. She gave up seeking stories in Spain and simply complained about it to anyone who would listen.

Maybe this isn't a tale. Maybe there never were any stories in Melusine's life. Perhaps tales about Melusine are still impossible. Or maybe the tales are still to come. Life is no less rich after one turns fifty, after all, and Melusine turned fifty a very, very long time ago.

The only predictable quantity in the stories is Melusine herself and the only certainty is the level of snark she brings to the world. Even to tourist Cordoba in the 1980s. Especially to Provence. You really don't want to know why the owner of 'Poterie Judaica' in Cordoba hid her face in her hands and couldn't stop laughing, or why her husband turned bright red and stormed out of his own shop. You absolutely never want to know why three American tourists in Aix eyed her askance and started backing off.

Maybe you do want to know. Snark is infectious. Once it appears somewhere it creeps everywhere. Like here, where the proper and correct snarky response to your query about what Melusine said in both places is, "Work it out yourself."

Ann knew she was being difficult right now. It was like being a teenager all over again. She could see what she did and she could deplore it, but she couldn't stop herself. When she fell into that numbness she had started feeling when she had no work to escape to, and had to face the fact that her marriage had died ten years before, she felt the underworld creeping through her. Shifting streets and evil, whispering children were just symptoms of a disease that was peculiarly hers.

She felt tired of being afraid. Tired of snapping. Tired of trying to run the world so it marched to her tune again.

Before this year it had marched to her tune so very naturally, it seemed. Now, whatever she did, she was on the edge. Undesired. Unwanted. Uninteresting. She had never been uninteresting in her whole life. She wasn't sure how it happened or what she could do to become the centre again.

"I can do something about other things, at least," she said to herself, as she walked out the door. "I can go to one of the places I ran from and I can deal with things. I can."

And so she did.

She found the place where Jackey-Jackey had hugged Mabel and she hung around for a bit. Nothing was happening, so she went to the nearest café and bought herself some takeaway coffee. As she came back, she saw a horse coming up the road. On it was a rider. *Tall,* she thought. *Maybe not Jackey-Jackey. We only have it from him that other ghosts are dangerous. How reliable can he be?* Ann was determined to find out.

She nearly went straight back to her car two seconds later, when it looked as if a dark shadow was loping along behind the horse. *The barguest,* she thought. *Dangerous.* But it wasn't. That dark shadow faded as the horse clip-clopped closer and closer.

This means it's safe. Besides, they are wrong, thought Ann. *I can see through the bushranger, even though I can hear the horse. It's not the rider that's the problem. Besides, look what Mabel did. I think she may have even slept with one. It's disgusting.* And, filled with righteous indignation and a touch of competition, Ann refused to run. She stood her ground as the man rode up to her on his big red horse.

He swung off the horse. He was a bigger man than William Westwood. Bigger and burlier. A Clarke, perhaps. Or Paddy Curran. She was positive that the stories about them were exaggerated. History is all like that, after all. Lurid tales classroom teachers use to keep their charges pacified. Look at Jackey-Jackey, all let-me-kiss-your-hand, and he was hanged for murder. Ann stood her ground.

He walked right up to her and asked, "Who are you?"

"My name is Ann."

"You want me?"

"Not particularly. I just didn't feel like running."

"You should," he said, and, raising his arm, slammed her hard across the head. He stood looking down at her when she fell to the ground.

"Eh," he said, "you'll know better next time. Me and my brother, we don't want the likes of you round. We thought we made it clear, with that other woman. We got help now. We got friends. Better watch out."

Ann couldn't stand up. She tried, but everything swam and her head hurt. She did what every twenty-first-century woman is told to do in an emergency: she rang 000. Twenty minutes later she was in hospital.

She knew she should ring her friends, but she didn't. She didn't even ring them when she was home again. She didn't feel guilty that she was suppressing evidence that would help the four understand what was happening. She felt hurt that she could be beaten up so very easily. One big slap to the head had been all it took. And look what Mabel got from the same situation. Life was unfair and she was not going to ring her friends. They could ring her.

Except that they didn't know she had been hurt.

Three days later, Kat found out about it. She didn't know it was Ann at first. Her little website with Canberra gossip had a report from the ambulance driver.

"I saw a man on a horse, watching," he said. "He wasn't doing a thing, just watching. The woman said he hit her and she might be a bit concussed. She said he was dangerous and I should stay clear. I said I'd ring the cops. She said no. She didn't think they could do anything. She was right about the concussion.

"I rang the cops when she was in the back, but when they came there wasn't anyone. It's criminal. The bloke's going to bash up someone else. If you see him hurt anyone, lay charges. This is the fifth incident and it's not going to go away unless we get some evidence. And no-one's speaking. Not that woman, not any of the others."

In the answers section, things looked even worse. Kat went over to Mabel's to print it out. Mabel read the page over her shoulder.

"This is the bit," Kat said, and pointed.

"When the men have a dog with them, they fire guns. Three people have been admitted to hospital with gunshot wounds. One had been in a critical condition, but stable at the time of the report," Mabel said.

"Yep. What gets me is that there are guns only when there's a dog."

"Or that the guns are real only when there's a dog."

"Think the dog's the barguest? Like we guessed?"

"I bet it is," said Mabel, grimly. "I'll call the others." She began with Ann, which is when she discovered Ann's little adventure. She came back to the computer room spitting mad.

"Ann saw one of the men and got herself hurt," she told Kat. "I've rung Lil. We're all going round there, pronto."

"Should I finish printing this?"

Mabel looked at the computer screen as if she had entirely forgotten it. "Oh. Oh yes. We may need that. Bloody Ann. We'll get her some flowers on the way. What an idiot she can be." That last was said affectionately.

They went to Ann's house via Lil's and picked up their friend and flowers and chocolate, and Kat learned some very interesting language as she sat quietly in the back of the car and heard Mabel give her unvarnished opinion of her friend's actions.

Once they arrived at Ann's, their hostess was care personified. It was left to Lil to give Ann a very polite dressing down. Mabel dragged Kat into the kitchen to help her make teas and coffees. "You don't mind, do you?"

Mabel asked Ann, not giving Ann a chance to object. This was Mabel's idea of a dressing-down.

"You know," said Kat, "I think the hierarchy you three have is very funny."

"Nonsense," said Mabel. "We don't have a hierarchy."

"Yes, you do. Lil's senior and you're second and Ann get mad because she thinks she's more important and you're both senior."

Mabel's hand froze above the plate she was filling with biscuits. "I never thought of it that way." She shrugged and finished filling the plate. "It can't be right, though. She's never done anything alone before."

"She's never been retired and divorced before, either. She hasn't got status at work because she's not in the workplace, or at home because her husband is a prat."

"Ex-husband," corrected Mabel, absently.

"Ex-husband, then."

"How did you work all this out?"

"Been there, done that," said Kat bitterly. "Except I ran away instead of getting bashed up by a ghost. Except it was a baby and not a husband or a job."

"Very sensible of you," and Mabel stifled a grin.

"I think so too."

Then they were all sitting in Ann's leather lounge chairs ("Which I'm keeping, by the way, no matter what his late majesty says.") and talking about bushrangers in a very artificial way. It was as if Ann had never had her encounter, nor Mabel her romance.

"Do we know which bushranger is which?" Lil asked. "Can we identify them easily and from a safe distance?"

"William Westwood is short," said Ann, "very short. And slim. The Clarke brothers are big and muscular. One of them has a red horse."

"Is red the technically correct name?"

"I have no idea. All I know is red horse with a black tail."

"Fair enough," said Mabel. "We just need to find out about Paddy Curran."

"Tall, too," said Kat, and showed them page three of her new printout. They passed it round and pondered it for a bit.

"So the bad guys are tall and the good guy is short."

"Doesn't work so well when they're on horseback."

"Still, better than nothing at all, and Jackey-Jackey's horse is more grey than red."

"And those three are dangerous whenever they materialise."

"But extra dangerous when the barguest is there," Kat said. Ann shifted in her seat. Kat wondered if the barguest had been there during her encounter. If it had, then maybe Ann got off lightly.

"Never forget," said Lil, "that the barguest has always portended death."

"No-one's died yet," said Ann, slightly defensively.

"Maybe the barguest has yet to fully materialise. Maybe," said Lil, "the worst is yet to come."

Nine

"EVERYTHING'S GOING TO BE very calming and old-fashioned tonight," Mabel said to Kat, her muscles at work making her arms look less stringy and aged. "All our nerves are frayed, and old-fashioned is soothing." As part of her attempt to make May more comfortable than the April dinner had been, Mabel explained all the food to Kat in vast detail. "April was wet — now it's beginning to get cold at night. We need comfort food. Things are unhappy and we know winter is coming. The dark nights are starting to scare us."

"So we eat comfort food," said Kat, slowly. "That makes sense. What is comfort food, though? I always think of hot chips as comfort food."

"It's gourmet comfort food, by modern standards, but everything tonight my grandmother taught me. I may have modified it a little," she warned, "but not much. We're going to make a sage stuffing for the duck, and roast it nicely. There are two ducks, just in case we're hungry."

"That's a lot of bird," said Kat.

"Not as much as it looks. Duck is all bone and fat. I'm going to make stock from that bone tomorrow."

"Ann's going to hate the fat."

"She won't tell me. I shut up about that horrible flat yellow bread last time, after all." Mabel gave a wicked grin. "While you stuff the birds, I'm going to make a butter to rub on."

"First, shake your cow muchly, then milk it," said Kat.

"Very funny. It's just butter. I bought it from the supermarket. I'm going to mix it with thyme and forest berry herb. Duck and thyme are even better than duck and orange. Don't tell the others about the forest berry herb. They think I'm a stuffy cook, and I want them to continue thinking that."

The roast vegetables were both different to last time, and a little the same. Mabel took her tin of dripping, which she kept, old-fashioned, on a shelf near the stove. She had Kat cut the potato the same as last time, but also chop up swede and pumpkin. Kat got to take the trays out from time to time and to spoon the melted butter on the duck over and over, and dripping onto the veggies, until everything was crispy and fragrant.

As the scents permeated the kitchen and made it smell warm and wholesome, Kat said to Mabel, "I like your way of cooking. You're right. It's comfort food. Even the process of cooking is like that. Happy-making."

"That's why I do it this way. Most people think it's because I'm an old fuddy-duddy."

Kat thought of Jackey-Jackey and thought that Mabel was the least fuddy-duddy person in the whole universe. Okay, so the other vegetables were peas and cauliflower, but they grounded the conversation and brought a sense of peace to the four women. Even Ann was more like her old self. *Comfort food*, thought Kat, *is a type of magic. Comfort food can chase ghosts away.*

Mabel switched off the lights before she let Kat bring dessert in. It was a hot fruit salad made with macerated apricots and peaches and pears, dowsed in brandy and set alight. Ann made ghost noises as the blue flames danced into the room. Everyone laughed. It was as if they had been given a giant release and all their problems were suddenly less important. Mabel looked smug in the eerie light.

Kat put the round tureen down as quickly as she could. It might look impressive, but it was hot and heavy and she did wonder what the flames would do if she dropped it.

Mabel asked, as she was serving the fruit salad, "Can I tell my Lake George joke now?"

"Mabel, my sweet," Lil said, "it is time to tell you a sad truth."

"What?"

"We are never going to let you tell your Lake George joke to Kat. It is a bad joke and she is not in need of bad jokes in her life."

"Yes I am," said Kat.

"You are most certainly not," said Ann.

"I'll tell you when they're not around," Mabel reassured her.

"No," said Lil. "If you do that, then I shall take revenge."

"Oo-er." Mabel laughed. "I'm quaking in my boots."

"You ought to," said Lil. "But you lack wisdom. It only comes, you see, with age."

They all laughed at that, for Mabel would be seventy-six very soon. Even Mabel laughed.

⁓ ◆ ⁓

Blogpost time. So much to tell, and even in these locked posts you're only getting a small bit. It's like Melusine's stories, isn't it? Snippets of lives.

The laughter turned a switch on in Ann's mind.

It took me a long while to realise that no-one was sure how Ann's mind worked that year, not even Ann. Anyhow, Ann, at that very instant, switched off from me and switched on to Mabel. Frail elderly, you know. Needs taking care of. Hah! Mabel won't even need taking care of on her deathbed. If you try it she'll haunt you for ever and ever. I know this because she told me so.

I loved every one of my three grandmothers, but just at that moment I loved Mabel most. She was always pretending to be serious. All grumpy and down to earth when really she was funny and romantic. I adored that.

I miss her.

I missed her that night, too. Once Ann focuses on you, no-one else had a chance. I was left with Lil. Or Lil was left with me. One or the other. Not just from that night. On that night. From the moment Mabel dolloped cream onto the hot fruit, Ann zoomed in and tried to trap her in a honeyed web. It was like she had been competing, and had decided that bringing Mabel onside was the best solution. It was terribly, horrifyingly obvious.

Lil and I, we looked at each other across the dinner table and we kinda shrugged our shoulders when Mabel, won over, let Ann help carry the empty dishes into the kitchen.

"Ann," I said.

"Ann," Lil said, though in a really sad way. We bonded over Ann's miseries.

That was when I finally felt relaxed with Lil the way I was with Mabel. I never unwound with Ann. I was zingy and happy with her, but there was a tight little place inside me, the whole time. Maybe she was too kind. Kindness scares me a bit, still.

I was thinking about that sad voice and wondering. It made me say something strange. I still wonder why I said it. That's the reason I remember

135

that night. Look how many other nights I've skipped, but that night, that night is one of those engraved on my memory. I'm getting pompous. Or I'm channelling someone. Probably Ann. Ann's the sort of person who other people channel.

"I've got ghosts," I said. Just like that.

She looked at me with those big, big eyes. "So do I," Lil said.

"What sort?"

"Friends who have died. Memories that won't be forgotten. Sorrow and joy and lives unfinished."

"That's my sort, too. Do you know that by the time I was ten, three of my friends were dead?"

"How did this happen?"

"Two were in car accidents and one was a botched hospital thingie."

"You miss them."

I told her the truth. "I think they're ghosts because I don't know. Five years is a long time and I might be inventing them, rather than remembering them. That's what my parents said."

"When did your parents say that?"

"I was thirteen. Just. It was the week after my birthday."

"I think you were remembering and missing. Maybe inventing a little, because we do that. But mostly missing."

"When they were alive, life was better."

"Because of them."

"My parents. They were real parents then. They set me a place at the dinner table and everything."

"My dear, it sounds to me as if your parents had their own ghosts."

"And I was one of them." That was a stupid thing to say. It left us both uncomfortable. I tried breaking the silence. "Those whispering children, I'm hearing them now."

It wasn't the right thing to say. Or maybe it was. I still don't know, even today. I don't know much, these days. I knew less, then. I just thought I knew more.

"We will do something about them," Lil said very definitely.

"You didn't when Ann complained. And Ann had more shifting streets than me, too."

"Ann is an unreliable witness. We love her despite that."

"But the children are real. And they're awful."

"But I could not be sure of that until I heard it from someone else.

Someone who was suffering similar problems."

"How are my problems similar to Ann's?"

"You have a void in your life right now. It leaves you open to certain things."

"Yay. I've always wanted to be a canary," I made my voice as dark and dire as I dared.

Lil just laughed. She has the best laugh I have heard anywhere, ever. If I were a man or a lesbian, I would fall in love with Lil, just because of her laugh.

Lil didn't try to get Mabel and Ann together to talk about the shadows. She knew that if she did that, Ann's game-playing would influence things. Ann would get over the game-playing, but some things couldn't wait. A teenager under threat could never wait. What disturbed Ann and made her preen with her knowledge of specialness could do much worse things to Kat.

Lil rang Ann. "I was wondering," Lil said, after about five minutes of chitchat, "if there are any true priorities in dealing with all that we see."

"True priorities?"

"Do we tackle the bushrangers first? Or the streets?"

"Those children," said Ann, definitively. "We do something about them."

"That sounds very sensible," Lil said, and Ann was sorted. Simple. She didn't even know she had been sorted.

"Mabel," said Lil, on the phone again, twenty minutes later, "I am worried about Kat."

"Kat's good," said Mabel. "She's turned out surprisingly reliable."

"Not from that point of view," said Lil. "I think she's developing some of the sensitivities. I've said this before."

"This is good, isn't it, if we want her to work with us?"

"It is in that way, but it concerns me that she's hearing those evil and whispering children. It seems to me they could be targeting her before she has the strength to fight back."

"We need to do something about that," Mabel said, definitely and instantly. "She's too impressionable. Those whispers could be dangerous. I'll organise a get-together."

"My place?"

"Why your place?"

"I can't imagine Kat being happy at being excluded. I also suspect she is concerned about us 'helping' her after Ann's recent behaviour. If it's at my place then she can pretend not to know we're doing it for her. The decencies are observed."

"Fine. What time is good for you?" Mabel asked this with the prosaic tone of one who assumes that everything will operate, unchanged.

"And can we find something convincing to say to Kat?"

"What do you mean?"

"She's not stupid, you know."

"You come up with a reason for us to act, and I'll sort out where we go so that we find those children."

"Sounds good."

The room was elegant in creams and golds. Lil's skirt and top were likewise elegant. Mabel was as close to elegant as she got, which was very respectable, but not quite shiny. Ann was dressed in practical slacks and a top. Kat had turned all Goth again and flitted around, offering a small cup to Lil and a big one to Mabel and a medium one to Ann. The air was all coffee and faint spices, which fitted the tableau the women made. Kat didn't see the room quite like that, however. She was too busy calling Mabel "Daddy bear" and Ann "Mummy bear" and Lil "Baby bear" in her mind, and wondering if she should go blonde just to make herself Goldilocks.

Lil was entirely wrong as baby bear. She was small enough, but too cat-like and elegant. Mabel was big, but too bony to be a bear. That left Ann. *Ann wanted to be Mummy bear*, thought Kat, not entirely happily. She put extra sugar in Ann's medium cup before she handed it to her. If Ann was going to be a bear she needed to be much fatter.

When everyone was settled, her mind settled too, so she never did tell anyone which bear they were. She knew this was a good thing, but she regretted it, as well.

"We've decided so many times that we have to act, then we do nothing," said Mabel.

"Something comes up. Like Kat's man or like your poor creature."

"Something's out to get us," Kat said.

"Don't be stupid," said Ann. "We just have to learn how to deal."

"Well, we're going to," said Lil. "We are going to Weston Park. We are going to buy a cup of the best coffee in Canberra, and we are going to start looking."

"Why Weston Park?" asked Ann. Kat wanted to know too, but her mind hadn't quite caught up with talking.

"Those maps. Weston Park is in an important position on them, if my theory is correct. There are two regions where almost all the incidents have occurred, and I drew a Ptolemaic map over them last night. The part of the two regions that has most water and parkland and has the sphere of Mercury running through it is Weston Park. It's the most likely place to find at least one of our phenomena."

"You're making this up," said Mabel. *No*, Kat wanted to say. *I've been waiting for Lil to say something like this for ages. Don't discourage her*. But she still felt silenced. She worked hard at getting herself back to where she had been recently, able to speak and even give cheek. Somehow, though, today was a difficult day for being herself. Even hiding in her dark clothes and with gorgeous makeup, even that didn't give her that inner confidence. She leaned back. *It will come. Be patient*.

"A bit," admitted Lil. "Ptolemaic constructs predate modern secular science. They carry the burden of our emotional reality for us, even if we're not aware of it. A friend showed me this in operation. He taught me that if you use deep cultural constructs, reality can change around you. He used those constructs to sail his ship safely through a war. No-one could see the ship: not a single splinter of a single plank was damaged from all that fire around us. We were perfectly safe."

"I don't believe you," said Ann, bluntly and with perhaps a touch of scorn.

That scorn gave Kat the boost she needed. "Why not?" asked Kat. "I mean, you must have a reason."

"Because she's talking about a wooden ship. Why would she be sailing on a wooden ship?"

"Because she's . . ." and Kat bit her tongue. She wasn't sure. She didn't want to say anything unless she was sure. Besides, what she had been about to say was improbable. More improbable than bushranger ghosts and abbey lubbers and barguests.

Lil looked over at her and raised an eyebrow.

"I believe Lil," said Kat, thinking fast. "And surely we can have this conversation another time. It's all deep and meaningful, but it's not going to solve problems right now, is it?"

"Bossy," said Mabel. That word made Kat happy, for some reason.

"No," she answered, emboldened by that small happiness. "Just wondering why we can't go to Weston Creek and test Lil's theory. Why we have to argue all the time. I want all the icky stuff to go, and arguing isn't going to make that happen."

"That works for me," said Mabel. Ann had slumped into one of her 'You have overruled me, but I'll fix things later' silences, and the other three took that as consent. They all piled into Ann's car, bought their coffees at a little tacky tourist place that ought to have served instant coffee, but instead had an old espresso machine with a gold eagle on top.

Ann sniffed at her latte. "This is really good," she said.

"You think I would recommend bad coffee?" Lil asked. "Especially when we just had some of my very own rather good coffee?"

"Of course not," said Ann. "But I've been avoiding that place for years because it looks so rundown."

They found a bench and table to sit and drink their coffee companionably, then they walked down to the lake.

"Nothing," said Ann, looking at the slope of green leading to the lake and scrutinising the structures that impeded the flow of green. "Just the playgrounds and lots of grass."

"Not here," said Lil. "Maybe down a bit."

They walked uphill again and came down a bit further on, where an artificial set of bridges were set over an artificial watercourse. It looked surprisingly ordinary.

"Why have that here?" asked Kat.

"To help keep the water fresh," said Mabel. "Look, there's a pump making it move, just there."

"It's still dank, despite that. Let's go just a bit further. I think we're getting there."

So they climbed over little wooden bridges and crossed that slow, green water. Behind them everything was bright and cheerful. The lake was a silvery blue and twinkled at them whenever they looked back.

Ahead of them lay a place where the lake was a darker colour and didn't twinkle. It was shaded by willows and behind the willows were pines. Underneath the pines nothing grew. Underneath the pines not even the swans ventured. Underneath the pines the hollows were dark and half-hidden and held a feeling of danger. All of them stopped and just looked.

"I think we've found our place," Mabel said.

Kat suddenly wanted to go home. It was as if the darkness underneath the pines held all the fears she had carried earlier in the day. She wanted to be as far from that darkness as she could. Except she had to stay. She was here with her grandmothers.

Kat walked into that deep hollow without any real thought of what might be there. Preying on her mind was the fact that she really owed it to Lil and Mabel and Ann to do what needed to be done. To not let them down.

Her gaze was on her feet. Every step she took, she liberated a little more of the smell of old pine and every step she took she slid a little further than she meant. And every step she took she felt as if someone was watching her. Not one pair of eyes. Many. Little ones. Prying ones. Dusty, shuffling ones, rustling in her ear like dry leaves.

Kat decided she could not go any further just yet. In a moment, perhaps. When she was used to the dry coolness of the hollow. In a little.

She stood there, hesitant. It was hard to think. Kat leaned against the rough trunk of one of the pines, and listened to the tree. It whispered. A little, evil voice; a child's voice. Badkat, it said. Badkatbadkatbadkat. Tears rolled down her cheeks. She nodded in time to the whispers. Badkatbadkatbadkat.

She felt a hand in her hand. Softy, it pulled her away from the tree. Gently, it pulled her away from the clearing. Kat saw the sunlight on her arm and then on the rest of her and she came to life again. "Thank you, Lil."

"Some of us are more vulnerable to whispers than others," Lil said.

"I thought it was how many ghosts we carried," said Kat. "But that's not what they were telling me."

"What were they telling you?"

"Me," Kat said. "What I tell myself. Badkat." She said the last word bravely, without self-condemnation.

"Ah," said Lil. "That explains a great deal. Shall we sit in the sunlight a little? I can tell you something about goodkat."

Kat smiled wanly. "You know all about badkat."

"I don't really know badkat at all. She's only a hollow shell."

"I don't understand." Kat was twisting her hands in the straps of her backpack. She tried to stop herself, but she couldn't.

"You need sunlight for this," Lil said. "On your skin and on your spirit."

"Will it hurt?"

"Not at all."

They found seats and a picnic bench and sunlight and the two of them talked. They forgot the whispers and they forgot the other two. This was only fair, as the other two forgot them.

Mabel didn't like the darkened glade, but she looked anyway. It was like an investigation. "Nothing," she muttered. "Nothing out of place. Plants are all as they should be." She rested her hand lovingly against a tree trunk and stood under a pine and watched. It was very peaceful, there, in the silence.

When Kat fell to pieces she started to move, but saw Lil stepping in and leaned back against her tree again. *No whispering,* she thought. *Odd. Kat heard something though. Curious.*

She turned to look for Ann, to see what she was up to. If anyone could hear something in this quiet place, it would probably be Ann. *Though really, maybe we give her too much credit,* Mabel thought.

Ann's little world was drenched in the smell of decaying pine. The willow prevented her reaching the grass and the park and the safety of everyday. No sounds floated up from the lake or the playground. Only whispers, whispers, whispers. It was as if the whole universe had shrunk until it contained nothing but that dark hollow beneath the trees.

We warned you, warned you, warned you.

You are ours, ours, ours.

The whispers floated among the trees. They filled the hollow. Children's voices, not quite in unison; not quite individuals.

We saw you, you, you.

You walked our streets, streets, streets.

We know you, you, you.

Safe, safe, safe.

You are safe with us.

To Mabel, Ann was just standing there, listening. Ann felt trapped. Unable to tear herself away. It was as if the voices owned her.

Ours, ours, ours.

You are safe with us.

Mabel walked closer.

Old, old, old. Ugly, ugly, ugly. Hurt her, her, her.

Send her away.

"She's my friend," said Ann, bravely. She had not spoken to the voices before, only listened.

Don't like her, her, her. Be safe with us, us, us. Bad man won't hurt you. Safe with us.

"Get me out of here!" Ann called urgently to Mabel. Mabel took her by the arm and dragged her out of the hollow.

When she was in the sunshine, she fell to her knees. "Thank God, they're gone," she said.

"I think know your secret," Kat said to Lil that night. "I'm not sure, though, and it's no use telling the others if I'm not sure. I wouldn't tell the others if I was sure. I mean, I wouldn't tell them just for the sake of telling them. It's your secret, after all. It's private."

Lil remained silent. Very silent. She wasn't sure what Kat knew, or how she knew it.

"The thing is," said Kat, "that we need more firepower and right now you're it. Or you're the only it I can think of. Unless Ann suddenly puts on a cape and turns into Super-Ann, that is. I guess she could. Turn the shadow into a cape and then become Super-Ann. Or is that confusing?"

Lil decided to gamble. "I want solutions that don't leave me in a difficult position," she said.

"Are there any?"

"Maybe, maybe not. Maybe I should teach you how I knew where the children were? Share my knowledge?"

"Show me your secret map?"

"My map need not be so secret. The others simply were not interested."

"They're like that with maps and information." Kat shrugged. "They like everything to be touchy-feely. Could you show me your map and teach me why you think it's important?" She paused a moment and then added, "Please?"

"Its importance is simple. I explained it earlier. It's a matter of cultural transfer. We bring our ghosts and fears with us into new lands. We carry them deep within us. We don't even know they're there, most of the time. Sometimes, though, life gets difficult. We call on them and they emerge. Sometimes they emerge just for us. Sometimes they emerge for others."

"So you map where they come out? That's not so different from my map, then."

"Ah, but that's only the first part of it. These ghosts and fears aren't

143

carried loosely. We carry them tightly. In patterns. It's how we can carry them without seeing. They conform with the deep cultural constructs."

Lil took a sip of her drink and paused to reflect. "Some of those deep constructs lend themselves particularly well to mapping. I laid one set of those deep constructs over a map of Canberra and they led us to the children. This means my principles are correct — we can find any of the beings we need to find, whenever we choose."

"This could be important, yeah?"

"It might mean we begin to have some power over our reality again."

"I think I need to understand it better. I still can't make sense of it. What's a deep cultural construct?"

"Something we carry with us, everywhere. Something we use to shape our universe. Something we use to explain our reality, while never really understanding that it's there."

"Racism is a deep cultural construct then," said Kat. "We can find racists using your map."

"It's a product of them, certainly: it's not the same. Deep constructs govern how we understand space, time, infinity, existence. They rule our sense of what the universe is and what paths we can take to interpret it. The ones we're looking at now fit on the map because the map is cosmological in nature — it shows the way the universe was conceived to have worked. It doesn't show how human prejudices work. Both of them are about how we shape our universe and use it to carry fears with us."

"And turn them into reality."

"And turn them into reality."

Tales of Melusine #21

It was the New Year. It was England. It was the year 1591. Melusine had just been given a handsel and she was totally at sea.

She wanted to say to the young man who had given it to her, "I don't know your customs. Do you give New Year presents to all the women you know, or only to the ones you have interest in?" She couldn't.

She had been in London along with a group of people who were trying to play Court games. Influence and power and jockeying for position.

The Queen would die soon. Elizabeth had been old forever and she had ruled forever and she would die soon. The last of the Tudors. Every year courtiers debated the date of her death and every year potential courtiers flocked to London and to Westminster and to wherever the Queen happened to have taken herself to play the game of influence. Most of them were away from London now, because it was less salubrious than they had expected. Also, because Elizabeth wasn't there. She was busy touring the provinces, like a player. She was busy controlling her nobility, also like a player.

Melusine had found London changed. She noted the changes as if they were pieces on an accounting table. It wasn't just the surprising absence of the court and its entourages. Most of London was still lovely and Southwark was still a place that was not suitable for ladies, but the city had become tired around the edges. It had grown too quickly and its water supply was not going to grow with it and its sewerage already had not grown with it and its public baths had been shut down so long before that its poorer citizens had one hundred and fifty years of makeshift washing behind them. Just the thought made Melusine feel a little tired and unclean.

At the same time it was prosperous. As long as the residents of the big city mixed in the right circles, life was full of luxuries.

The problem with being French, however, was that some of the right circles were less than welcoming. Too much politics. The air of London was all about politics. So when her party split up for Christmas (in the absence of a welcome at Court) to go where they could, Melusine found herself invited to a house party near St Albans.

She handled Christmas with dignity and was able to say, honestly, that she was not a Roman Catholic, despite her nationality. "I have always been an outsider in my own land," she explained, over and over again.

Only one of the twelve days of Christmas was a problem then, and that was New Year, with its presents and small romances.

Melusine was being wooed by two men. Both were named Henry. One was young and gave her a handsel. One was starting to turn grey and gave her a book. She wanted to shake them both off, but the quarters were too close and gossip too rampant. All she could do was smile sweetly, accept the gifts, and promise nothing.

On New Year's Day, no-one stirred. The staff were able to do what they must to keep the household comfortable and Melu-sine was able to sit down with her book and find out what it was. A little book. Printed. Just within the confines of a respectable gift. A bit more sumptuous and her options would have been easier — she would have had to return it.

Under a tree in the orchard, wrapped up against the frosty morning, she opened the volume. When she looked at the front page, her nice country Christmas seemed suddenly rather fraught: it was by Paracelsus.

She knew that book. She knew all the books by those who considered themselves learned magicians. Some were very good at what they did. Some were less so. Most were frauds.

The problem was, how could Henry Smith, who gave her the book, know that she would know? Or that she could even read it? It was a very dangerous little volume in far too many ways.

With a sigh, she rose from her seat under an apple tree, and went to find out what she could.

Henry the elder had not yet risen, but Henry the younger smiled at her and asked if she cared to walk for a little. There is more than one way to skin a rabbit, Melusine thought, and nodded her agreement. They walked in one of the embroidered gardens, where everything was Frenchified and elegant. Melusine persuaded him to talk about everything from the delights of London to whether the Queen really was going to die one day soon. Along the way he let it slip that he was courting her only partly for her beauty and charm and wit. Mostly, he was seeking his own safety.

"I have heard that there are abbey lubbers in the town," he said.

"Surely they are no great concern? One or two of them at most, and always sotted?"

"I am not so much worried about them, than about what comes with them," Henry the younger said. "There are very few in our party who can handle a dark child."

"I don't even know these dark children."

"I suspected you might not. You have such knowledge, but you also know yourself and trust yourself. You are a woman of the sunlight and around you everything is clear and joyous. The dark children whisper to the doubts within us. They grow and fester."

"Until people take their own lives?"

"Yes."

"Why have I not heard of them?" Melusine's voice was hushed.

"You have the reputation of one they will avoid. Around you it's safe."

"Safer to leave, I should think."

"And ruin my prospects?" Henry the younger was bitter. "Damned either way."

"So you do not love me," Melusine mocked, to take the sting out of his unhappiness.

Henry laughed. "I was terrified of you when we first met. Your reputation preceded you and your gaze is very clear. You are, however, easy to love."

Melusine looked up into his eyes and said, very carefully, "If being near you protects you, then I am happy to be near you. I feel nothing for you, except charm from your companionship and wit."

"There has to be return for the protection." Henry was visibly distressed.

"Why?"

"It's something my mother taught me." Now he was stiff and uncomfortable. "Never receive without also giving."

"That is very good advice. The return does not have to be something unwelcome to either party, however."

"What would be welcome to you?"

"Companionship. Information. Even friendship, if it comes naturally."

Henry looked relieved. "What sort of information can I give?" Not companionship or friendship — she was right to have doubted his sincerity. Still, information was the essential.

"Anything about the other Henry and magic. There is something about him . . ."

"Indeed there is." Suddenly the two were relaxed together. It was as if they had never negotiated love for protection. "As I heard it, he has no ability with magic. He has, however, a very great interest in it and thinks that the knowledge denotes the ability. So he has all the knowledge, but no power. He discovered this at Court, in public, where John Dee made a mockery of him. I don't know the details, but he was a laughing-stock for a season or two.

"Now, the gossips say," continued Henry, "the man seeks more and more knowledge, in hopes that it will give him what he lacks. He has spent most of his fortune on books and paraphernalia." Melusine thought of the volume by Paracelsus and nodded. "He has been seeking power as long as I have known him. The gossipmongers say that he found a dark fairy and nearly signed a contract with him."

"That would have been a dreadful thing. I am relieved he thought better of it."

"He changed his mind at the last minute, and fled for his life. He left his shadow behind. That's why you never see him outside on bright days like this."

"So he wants his shadow back," Melusine said, thoughtfully.

"I think he is still fascinated by power."

"He is stupid, then."

"Aren't we all, when it comes to seeking power?" Henry smiled self-disparagingly.

They spent the rest of Christmastide in each other's company. When Melusine was late rising, Henry would gossip and when she appeared, he would bring her information. Everyone assumed that they were more than friends, which suited both of them.

The abbey lubbers caused many small upsets and a few larger ones. One girl was molested; one man was knifed.

"See," whispered Henry. "They are bolder than usual."

"I do not like it," said Melusine. "There is nothing I can do, however, since they belong here."

"Then I shall remain at your side and let everyone think I am protecting you."

"That's a very noble deed, Henry," mocked Melusine.

"I am a very noble person."

One afternoon there was a little performance. Just a small piece of theatre to entertain. It showed sprites and other beings cavorting in an England that was markedly unlike the one they knew.

"Blue grass." Henry poked Melusine.

"I see it. I also see a green sun."

"Do you think claiming that magic can only exist if the world is different to the one we know, will make it so?"

"It is possible." Melusine shrugged her slender shoulders. "But very unlikely. It is more likely that magic will be hidden and secret."

"You won't suffer." Henry was suddenly anxious.

"I am already hidden and secret."

"Except to your friends."

"Of course. And to others, of course. John Dee has changed the environment for such as I. I wish they would stop prancing: those strange beings are making me seasick."

The play, it appeared, had a story. It was about travels in the New World, to West India, and a shipwreck and a fanciful island where all the fairies of all the ages now lived.

"Those things are supposed to be fairies. Note it well," Henry said.

"I have noted it." Melusine smiled up at him.

After much leg shaking and strange posturing the fairies began crying and moaning. With some trouble, Henry deciphered that they were mourning that their queen is in England and not with them. They send a message to her to come.

A male voice shouted from the audience, "Those fairies aren't fairies, they're angels."

Another voice answered, "The playwright wants the Queen dead!"

There was a momentary silence, then two or three people rose from their seats. One hit the man who mentioned the Queen. The others jumped in and started fighting with the performers.

"Who wrote this extraordinary piece?" asked Melusine, unperturbed.

"Your friend and my namesake."

"I think I shall cease my inquiries. I think I shall stay as far away from him as possible."

"Does that mean leaving here?" The violence was spreading from the small group, although it was still well away from the two friends.

"I promised you. I shall remain here as long as you do."

"Thank you," said Henry, his voice no less heartfelt for his gaze being on the incipient riot.

"I think the rose garden might be a pleasant place to visit just now. What do you think?"

"That perhaps the play on twelfth night will be less perilous than the one we have just seen?" Henry the younger gently led her away from the violence.

Out of the blue, Kat said to Lil, "It was you who gave Ann back her shadow, wasn't it?"

"Without it she could never leave us. She would be wedded to magic forever."

"So she has had two divorces in the one year." Kat shuddered.

"Worse, her shadow came back dark. Different, somehow. I think that is why the streets shift and the voices whisper."

"We need to tell her!"

"I have tried. Ann won't listen."

I wanted to know what was happening in the granny flat. I wanted my space back. That's what I kept telling myself.

What I really wanted was to be bold and brave and daring. I still want that, now, ten years on. I am better at pretending I have it now. I couldn't pretend anything then.

I was angry enough to be bold and brave and daring, too. Little things had just turned me past twisting point: Ann's latest claim on my soul, Lil's latest gentle evasion, Mabel's latest slightly bossy joke. Ann annoyed me the most because I kept on wanting to be sympathetic. I knew what it was like, what she was going through. She never understood that I knew, though. To her I was still a little girl who needed someone to look after her. That really got my goat.

What made me extra angry was that I knew what the real problem was. *I could just ring Mum and get it over with*, I thought. That was the truth of it.

At first I felt rather good about myself. Totally miserable, but smug inside. They knew I was alive, after all, which is more than they deserved. They knew I was alive because I had sent one postcard, aeons ago, when I hopped off the train on my way to Sydney.

I was going to go to Sydney and remain there forever and ever and ever. Sydney is big enough to hide from anything.

Anyhow, I got off the train at Cootamundra because they had a kiosk thing and I was hungry and I was scared of train food. I have no idea why I was scared of train food. Something Daddy had said to me once, perhaps. Daddy is the most frightened person I have ever met. I found a postcard and sent it. The train had gone by the time I was finished. I found a bus, though, a connecting bus, going to Canberra. I did a lost child act and they let me on for free.

For all my parents knew, that angry morning, I was still in Cootamundra, or I was in Sydney. They had the postcard, at least. And until that morning that had suited me just fine. Really. I kept on telling myself. Just fine.

Except this spark in me flamed at little things. And then it got mad at that guy with the eyes. I don't know why I thought it was a man who owned those piercing eyes. It was. I knew it. And he had thrown me out of my little granny flat. And boy, was I going to get him for that.

Something triggered it, though. I need to remember what.

It was something quite small.

My three grandmothers had all annoyed me in little ways. I used to go to one of them when another one made me mad. I'd get on the phone to talk to Mabel when Lil was too French and put everything away and looked perfect and acted perfect and all. I'd have coffee and feel kinda civilised with Lil when Mabel or Ann made me feel ragged. I'd ring Ann when I felt all little and small, because she was good at making me feel someone was paying me attention. The others just sometimes acted as if I was ordinary there. Mostly it was cool. Sometimes I wanted someone to be worried about me getting high or whatever. I wasn't going to do that, but Ann never realised that. I rang her heaps.

That's it. That's the trigger. I rang Ann and she was upset and wouldn't tell me why and I got mad but couldn't act mad because she was upset and . . . excuse me, but I think I'm just going to move on from here.

Kat was in a ratbag mood. None of her grandmothers would have a thing to do with her. Each of them had given her the brush-off in their own way. Each of them was quite old enough to know that a fifteen-year-old ratbag is sometimes best left alone.

Unfortunately for Kat, she wasn't old enough to know this. She was more and more annoyed with each kind 'Come back later,' phrased in all sorts of ways and hiding all sorts of sentiments. Finally, she lost it.

She went to the granny flat and stared pointedly through the window. If Mr Smart-Eyes could do it to her, she could do it right back at him.

At first, there was nothing to look at. Things were pretty much as she had left them. Her possessions were mostly gone, except for a few books, but the clutter she and Lil had decided against cleaning was still there. In fact, things were the way she had left them that last day, exactly so. Nothing moved. That was a bit odd in itself. She looked more closely.

They had left the window open in that last race to get out before Mr Eyes came back and stifled the life out of her. And yet everything was as she had left it. Despite the big blowy wind and everything. Lil had gone back and shut that window and had said that everything had blown everywhere. That was right. Everything had blown everywhere and she had taken the opportunity to tidy it up. She had.

This was like a bad movie. The continuity was stuffed.

"I have to go inside," she said to herself. "Except I shouldn't, because if this was a horror flick the first thing the evil guy would do is separate the teen chick from her wise friends and then lure her inside."

She dithered at the window, wondering and watching.

As she kept looking, the crumpled papers on the table were replaced by something. That something made Kat absolutely mad. It was the last good present her parents gave her, before everything went wrong. It was her little leather notebook, with the silver Celtic cross she had stuck on herself, when she was thirteen, with all her private thoughts and inner self from her twelfth year, lying there in plain sight, on the table.

For four days she'd thought she had lost it. For four days she'd been totally miserable. It was her most important connection with her parents. She had nearly rung them, too, just because it wasn't there, under her pillow, where it belonged. What the hell was it doing on the table?

She didn't have a key any more, but she tried the door anyway. It was unlocked. Which it shouldn't have been, of course. Lil kept all her possessions safe and locked everything, carefully. She even checked doors twice as she left the house, to make sure that everything was sealed up, tight as a drum. Lil was a careful old lady.

The handle turned and Kat nearly walked right in. She was spitting fire, she was so mad. How dare he leave the flat unlocked? It was Lil's. It had her possessions. And Kat's own diary.

She saw Mr Eyes sitting at the little table she used to keep her computer on, his back to her. She glared at him and said, "Get out! This isn't your place. Get out!"

He turned round. It was then she realised that he was for real. That it was him. Those eyes were unmistakable.

"I hate you," she said, as she stood in that doorway, her hands on her hips. "I want my place back and I want my book back and I want everything back." She had the corner of her eye set on the table and the rest watching the man. He just stood, arms akimbo, and watched Kat advance. A slight smile adorned his face.

She found it very difficult to walk through that door. It was almost as if there was a barrier.

"Invisible barriers, huh," Kat said. "This is real life, not some TV show. You don't belong here and I do." And she pushed and pushed. Nothing happened. She pushed some more. Her book was in that room. She was going to get it back. She was going to make him so sorry.

Suddenly, the resistance broke. Kat staggered into the empty space.

Inside, everything was different. Her book was not on the table. There was no table. There was a faint shadow of a table only, an echo of furniture. It showed up, barely, through a golden haze.

The only clear element in the whole room, apart from the haze and from Kat herself, were the man's eyes. Sharp and brilliant, they looked as if they would eat Kat's soul alive. She took a step back. Their force pushed her harder. Another step back. Harder. She took one last step, and was caught against the barrier.

In front of her was nothing but a universe of gold. Then the eyes returned. Slowly, like a shadow, a man's body shaped around the eyes. As the echo of life formed, the power pushing Kat against the barrier intensified.

With a start, she found herself on the other side of the doorway, looking in at a perfectly ordinary room. Her book was clearly visible. So was the man.

"Come back later, perhaps," he said, mockingly. "When you feel a little stronger."

I was angry as anything at first. I don't think I've ever been so angry my whole life. I liked being angry. It was such a clean emotion compared to the sick feeling I had when I left home. I treasured my anger and I held it close.

When I was in bed that night, I thought through the episode over and over and over again. I didn't sleep. Not one bit. That's one of those long nights that one always remembers. Always, always, always.

After a few hours of being angry I suddenly crumpled. Badkatbadkatbadkatbadkat. There was no other way of seeing it. I had made things worse. I thought I had stopped making things worse. I thought I had stopped ruining everything around me. Being an excrescence on reality. But I hadn't. Badkatbadkatbadkatbadkat. Badkatbadkatbadkatbadkat. Badkatbadkatbadkatbadkat.

I got out of bed and sat on the computer, playing silly games. I had to. I had to be quiet so that Lil wouldn't hear me. I couldn't tell her what I'd done. I couldn't tell anyone.

After a while I was calmer inside. Maybe I hadn't been as bad as I thought. I'd been stupid, for sure. Very stupid. But stupid isn't the same as badkat.

Maybe if I could work it out from another direction, I could turn it into something a little bit useful. Then I could tell the oldies without feeling badkat. Then I could redeem myself a little. Then I could stop sliding back into badkat. I immediately played more computer games. I needed to let my back brain think. Or maybe it was needing time to let that water stuff stop flowing down my face.

After a while my back brain worked out what was wrong. My front brain works through my leather notebook and still had to find a way of retrieving that, somehow. What was wrong was that all the fury had been from me. Mr Eyes actually did no harm. Not a jot. He knew me, because he had my diary and he hadn't done anything. I had tried to hurt him, and he had defended himself, but my pride was bruised, not me.

Maybe he hadn't been trying to kill me in my bed? Maybe he had been trying to save me? Lil had suggested that, after all. Maybe she hadn't just been trying to cheer me up?

I just assumed, at first, that he was a bad guy. But what if he was potentially an ally for us? No, that was taking it too far. He hadn't hurt me, that was for certain. But he had driven me out and stolen my private possessions. There was no reason for either of them. None.

I needed more information. Much more. I needed to go back again, and try to find out. Once I had worked out how. It wasn't going to be easy. It could be quite hard. Because at that moment he must've been pretty angry at me.

❖

The horse bucked briefly. Its neck arched gracefully and its legs stuck out at odd angles. The rider brought it under control very quickly and its body was in harmony again. This is more than could be said about the women who watched. Just out of sight of the rider was another man, and another horse.

"This is going to be complicated," Mabel said.

"I don't like it at all," was Lil's response.

In the end, it wasn't. Jackey-Jackey was on one horse and Paddy Curran the other.

"It's about time for some truth," said Jackey-Jackey to the women. He rode off after Curran. A little while later, he came back with Curran's collar in one hand and his whip in the other. Neither horse was in sight. "Tell me what he says, will you?"

"I warned you," Jackey-Jackey growled to Curran. "I told you to stay away. Just because you're dead doesn't change what I said." He reached for his whip, shoved Curran down to the ground and laid into him, angrily. He held him down with one hand and hit with the other, his blows creating a kind of awful rhythm. The women hated this. They watched anyway, with a kind of dogged fascination, wincing every time a blow hit.

When he was finished, the wiry bushranger said, "Now tell us what you know. About the Clarkes, who they're travelling with, what they're up to."

"They're in league with those children. Whispering. I hate them. They forced me to join them. Honest. I know this is your place. I wouldn't've come back if those evil whispers hadn't told me to. Over and over and over they told me. Over and over and over. And the Clarkes with them. I had no choice. Honest."

"Anyone else?"

"Just one. Just one more. Don't make me talk about it, please. Don't make me talk." Paddy Curran burst into tears.

"Tell me!" Westwood threatened him with the whip again.

"I can't. I can't. It can change the streams. It can change the streets. It scares the Clarkes. It scares everyone. I can't." And that was all Jackey-Jackey could get out of Curran.

"This is worrying," said Lil. "Very worrying."

"Just as well Kat isn't here," Mabel said, grimly.

"She'd start hunting the superevilvillain."

"Then we'd be in a pickle."

Lil was silent.

Don't laugh at this blogpost, please. I've been reading Strasinki's stuff online. I can't spell his name. He's the guy who did B5. I didn't see *Babylon 5* back when because Mum said I was too young. I saw it all at once when Mabel wanted to watch the whole series. She did ironing the whole time, which was so . . . I dunno.

Anyway, because I was at her place after each episode I came here and blogged. Yesterday I didn't blog. You probably didn't even notice I wasn't here, right? I was reading.

Someone took all the answers he — the writer bloke — gave when the series was being made and put it all together. Some of it didn't make sense — I need to see more episodes. Some was boring. Some of it was really, really important. Bits made me cry.

There's one bit I'll always remember.

He listed five kinds of truth:

Truth one: you tell to strangers.

Truth two: you tell to friends (if you trust them — you gotta be careful with friends).

Truth three: you tell to very special people who you do trust.

Truth four: you tell yourself.

Truth five: you don't tell anyone, not even yourself.

I keep wondering what truths belong to everyone I know. I told Ann the truths I tell to strangers. I tell Mabel the truths I tell to friends. I tell Lil truth three.

I'm telling truth four now.

I wish there was a way of finding out what truth five is. I really, really want to know. I think some of it is what Lil taught me about deep cultural constructs. I need to understand them better, too. They're not everything though. Truth five is the one I need.

Kat decided it was time to solve one big problem. She wanted her diary back before her oldies did anything exciting. If things weren't going to be safe then she wanted to have her diary with her. It was that simple.

No, it wasn't. She just wanted it to be that simple.

What she really had to do as well was say she was sorry and get Mr

Impossible Eyes on their side. He had magic power and none of the rest of them really did.

Ann talked big but had got lost inside herself.

Mabel knew some strange stuff, but was like one of the witches from Pratchett and used headology. She might be able to do things, strange things, magic things, but the longer Kat knew her the less useful it seemed. Kat loved Mabel, but Mabel wasn't going to save Canberra from its ghosts. She couldn't even save her woodpile creature.

Lil was . . . Lil. It might be bad for her if she did stuff. She was so old that everything tore her body to pieces. And she was scared. And did she know how to do stuff or did she just know weird things?

Then there were the Melusine stories. Which Kat couldn't even ask about because Lil needed support, not someone picking on her. She was the oldest of the grannies and it was showing. Kat loved her so very dearly. She didn't want her to go all rumpled and translucent. She wanted Lil round for a long time. If finding someone else magic would help, then she would do it.

Kat's diary was just an excuse. It was a very good excuse, too.

This time, she didn't peer in the window and let herself work up a steam. This time, she knocked, very politely, on the door. After a bit of a wait, she knocked again. Still polite. She kept her good face on, just in case he could see through doors. She had seen his eyes in the wall near her bed too often to believe he couldn't. In fact, she was scared. Scared, but still polite.

When the door opened, very gently, her fear turned to terror. Her face, though, was still polite. Her good face. She made it smile. Nicely.

She looked at Mr Eyes properly, for the first time. He had muscles. For some reason this made her a bit less fearful. Not enough so that she wouldn't bolt at the first chance, though.

"I came to say I was sorry," Kat said. "I thought you tried to kill me and I thought you took my book and you're here, in my granny flat. I just got really mad. I thought I should ask if you did any of it."

"And then get really mad again?"

"Maybe. I don't think you tried to kill me, though. I've been thinking about it. I think you tried to save me."

"You'd better come in. I can keep the room solid for a time," he said. "I'm sorry I took your place, but I don't know where I am, and until I know where I am, I don't know where I can go."

"I can tell you where you are."

"In relation to where I was?"

"I don't know where you were."

"I think I am from another reality. Very different to this one."

"You're speaking the same language as me, but."

"Not like you. Your accent is odd."

"It's still the same language."

"I could read your diary," he said.

Kat held out her hand. "Give," she said peremptorily. "Now. Or I won't help."

"You're a proper piece of work, aren't you," he said and laughed. The only person she knew who laughed that well was Lil and there was such a big difference between them. Lil was so very old and so very frail and this bloke filled the room they were in. He wasn't that big, but he took up a lot of space.

"My parents gave it to me. I need it back." His eyes seemed to penetrate her skin. "And I don't like it when you look at me like that."

"You are human, then, though with a touch of something else. This is a human world."

"Yes. This is a human world. I coulda told you that," she said, grumpily, "Give." He pulled the diary out of a drawer and carefully presented it to her. "Thank you."

"You are welcome. Please, take a seat. I have not resolved the food and drink situation yet, so I cannot offer you anything, though it pains me to say that. I was better brought up than that."

"You live without food and drink?"

"I have water," he said, helpfully. "I miss tastes and textures."

"How long for?"

"I'm sorry?"

"How long can you last without food and drink?"

He shrugged. "No-one has ever tested it. I don't even know how long I was between realities."

"So what are you?"

"I have not found the words for that yet. I think you might call me a fairy, or maybe a demon, because I have been called those in my own place and time. Spawn of Satan is my favourite description." He smiled.

"So you're evil? I was wrong and you did try to kill me."

"No!" his face scrunched. He was genuinely revolted by the thought. "Something . . . detestable . . . was trying to steal you. To take your life and cut your soul loose. One of your souls."

"Thank you again, I think. I can't think why anything would. I mean, look at me."

He looked at her, sombrely. "Maybe you do not know yourself."

"What don't I know that I need to know?"

"That you are part fairy or demon."

"I am a spawn of Satan?" Kat was entirely delighted with this thought. "How much? Do I have super powers?"

He laughed again. "You remind me of someone. Just a little bit. Someone I love very much." He looked again. "You have a slight look of her, about the eyes." He looked deeper and deeper, until . . .

"That hurts!" said Kat indignantly.

"Sorry," he said, very unrepentant. "One of your great-grandparents was fairy."

"So not much fairy in me," Kat was disappointed.

"Enough. I may be able to teach you."

"Cool." *I can be the supermegapower that saves the day! Except . . ."*We have a real problem. I mean, it isn't just someone hurting me. That's why I was so mad. I'm still so mad.

"Just not at me."

"A bit at you. You read my private diary."

"I was trying to discover this reality. To find out where I am. What can I do to redeem myself?" He was amused at her, but Kat didn't care. He had saved her life and she had mucked up really badly, and she didn't feel a bit like badkat. She ought to, but she was comfortable with him. It was surprising.

"I'll help you if you help us," she said.

"Help me, how?"

"I still think it's suss that you speak English, even with a funny accent."

"English? It's English we're speaking?" He sounded surprised.

"You thought it was whatever babelfish do?"

"I don't understand."

"Instantaneous translation."

"Something like that. I can feel it happening."

"So maybe you speak a different English. Your accent is funny enough."

"That . . . may be right. Some words and meanings have shifted, perhaps. I had assumed an entire language." He shook himself to clear his head. "So you would help me find out if this is my reality, and why you speak so oddly."

"Yep."

"That sounds good. Very good."

Yay! Supermegapowers! From him! Lil might get through this yet. And Kat suddenly realised how very much she was worried about Lil. How very, very much. When did she start caring about Lil so hugely?

"Where do we start?" he asked.

"This year is 2009. That's the best place to start."

"Goddam it!"

"What?"

"I walked out on my own true love, showing off like an idiot, and came back over two hundred years later. Over two hundred years."

"Australia was only just settled then."

"Australia?"

"You're in Canberra."

"Not England. I had expected that. I hoped perhaps Ireland or the New World."

"The other side of the world."

"Van Diemen's Land? New South Wales?"

"It's a country now. We have our own Prime Minister and everything. And this is our national capital. We don't even have convicts anymore. We're all grown up."

"And one of the great mysteries of the world has been solved."

"What do you mean?"

"Terra Australis, the Great Southern Land. How big is it?"

"Big," said Kat.

"Does it reach down to the ice cap? Does it encircle the globe?" His voice was vast with excitement.

"Not that big. You know, when all this mess is over, you could explore it."

"I landed myself here, in the Great Southern Land, because I tried to explore. I think I shall stay still for a little."

"So help us?" Kat hated it that she sounded wistful.

"It will be my great pleasure."

"I need to introduce you to Lil, then," Kat said.

"Lil?"

"My grandmother. She owns the granny flat — I just lived here."

"I need her permission to stay?"

"It would be the polite thing to do."

"I . . ." he sounded suddenly nervous. He didn't seem the sort of person to get nervous. "I don't know if I'm ready to meet anyone else yet. Two hundred years is such a long time. I was certain this was a different universe. I need time to get used to the idea. And to stabilise. I don't think I'm fully here yet."

Kat nodded. "Sometimes even two days is such a long time. How about I tell her about you?"

"Not who I am, not where I come from. It's too much for a human to understand."

"I get that. Lil's good with strangers and with strange things. She's very cool. But you need time."

"If you please."

Kat shrugged. It was as if they'd known each other forever. She loved the way his English was sometimes normal and sometimes all odd and formal. His babelfish didn't always work so well. "Fine with me. I'll bring my maps and things in and update you."

"Knock twice, first, the way you did just then. It will give me time to make this room solid."

"You know," Kat said, "I can't wait till you sort out that haze thing and it's solid all the time."

"You're in good company with that," the man said. "When that day arrives, I want a good meat pie. I miss meat pies." He looked suddenly worried. "You do still eat them?"

"We still eat meat pies. I'll buy you one, when you're properly here."

"Thank you." He dipped his head, courteously.

It was only when Kat was in her own room that it all sank in. The magnitude of what she had just done. And that she didn't even know his name. And that she was too shy to ask. Blasting a door down was different, somehow, to asking a grownup his name.

It was finally June. Cold, but sunny. Not a sad month. Except for Ann. Ann was frantic to fill June. June was a busy month for the public sector in Canberra and she was missing her job. June — for Ann — was empty.

"Why did I retire?" she asked Kat, rhetorically, as Kat prepared cut bread for bruschetta and mixed the topping. "It was the start of everything going wrong."

This would be the last dinner at Ann's house. Next time it was her turn, Ann would have a unit somewhere.

"It's going to be very hard to cram all my life into a unit," Ann confided, as she dipped her chicken schnitzel cuts in ground almond, ready for frying.

"Less housework, but," said Kat. "What do I do with this?"

"It's sour cherry sauce. You empty the bottle into one of my little Chinese bowls and put a spoon in. We'll help ourselves to it."

"What do we eat it with?"

"The schnitzel."

"Yum," said Kat dutifully. Ann needed to hear that 'yum.' She was so miserable. "I vote you get all the good kitchen stuff."

"I vote that too," said Ann, without cheer.

They had eaten their way through the bruschetta then the schnitzel and a big bowl of mixed greens with balsamic vinegar. They were half way through the tiramisu when Mabel asked Lil the impossible question. The question everyone had been avoiding, these last three months.

"What can you do? I mean. That we can't?"

"Like Ann's squinty eye," Kat said, helpfully.

"It's hard to say," said Lil. "I'm not happy to use any special ability I might have."

"But why?" asked Mabel. "People are hurting here."

"I know," Lil said. It's just that . . ." she trailed off. When she began again her voice was low and reluctant. "There's a part of me that's a little . . . difficult. It doesn't come out very often, but when it comes out, it will not go away until it's finished. It was not a part of my childhood. It came upon me later. Maybe in adolescence. Maybe it's the result of much unhappiness."

"Bad temper? Ann asked "We all have them."

"No," said Lil. "I have that too."

"Never seen you lose it," said Mabel.

"My temper is rare and I can usually hide it. This is something else."

"Can you get counselling?"

Lil looked at Ann with faint disdain. "I should tell someone my past so they can tell me I must live with something I already know I have to live with? This is your counselling. I will have none of it." She sounded far more French than usual. This, then, was her temper. Kat was quiet as a mouse, then Lil swung round and looked at her. "Do you think I need counselling?"

"I don't want help," Kat said. "And you found me on the streets. Why should I make you get help?"

Lil smiled at her, a rather dangerous smile. "We shall treasure our flaws together, is that what you were thinking?"

"No," said Kat.

"Then what?"

"I was thinking," Kat mumbled a moment. *It's about time*, she thought. *But do I dare?* "And you're not going to like this. I was thinking that if I was writing a fan fiction I'd put you in it with a dark secret. Your difficult bit would be turning into a vampire or something."

"You think I would make a good vampire." Lil's voice was suddenly soft.

"Oh, yes!" Kat's was vigorous with enthusiasm. "Your voice is gorgeous and your age is unknowable and you've got a dark secret and you don't always sound Australian."

"I think we should change the subject," said Mabel, firmly.

"Always so practical, Mabel mine," said Lil. "Let's talk about the menu for dinner next week."

"I can't remember whose turn it is," confessed Ann. "Except it's not mine, because mine is tonight, here. I can't even remember why it's next week and not next month. I have Mad Old Cow's Disease."

Ann was put out and was trying to refocus the conversation on herself. It was she who had found Kat on the streets, not Lil. She wanted to say so, but she looked at the serpent glitter in Lil's eyes and she bit her tongue.

Mabel had dragged Kat with her, screaming. Only metaphorically screaming, of course. "Real screaming can wait until we face the horror," said Mabel, as she pointed her car towards Duffy.

"Aren't you going to look at a map?" asked Kat.

"I know where we're going. We're going to a creek. This spot is supposed to be haunted by the ghost of a young girl."

"You're going to teach me to banish ghosts, at long last?"

"We don't banish ghosts. No-one banishes ghosts. They persuade them, politely, to move on."

"Oh." There was a pause. "Move on where?"

"How would I know? Do I look dead to you?"

"So why are just the two of us going?"

"I want to find out if this ghost is the source of your drowning girl screams."

"Sounds good," said Kat, with forced cheer. "Only now I know why you said you were dragging me screaming. I don't want to hear her again."

"You have to, just this once."

"I know. I'm screaming inside about the screaming outside, but."

"I know," said Mabel.

Soon they pulled up in a little suburban strip. It had big nature strips, but no footpath.

"It squelches," said Kat.

Mabel nodded. "We're close to the stream."

They walked and they listened. Mabel heard nothing. Kat heard a faint whisper. She tilted her head to hear it better and tried to follow it. Mabel stopped trying to listen and started watching.

As the whispering became closer and more insistent, Kat started walking more quickly. Her eyes emptied and the light within them was replaced by shadows. Mabel saw this, but did nothing except watch and remain close.

Very soon, Kat was skipping and tripping in her haste to catch the voices. Mabel caught her arm just as she was about to tumble headlong down a slope and into the creek.

"How did I get here?" Kat's eyes cleared and she looked around her in astonishment.

"Did you hear the screaming?"

"No, I didn't hear anything." She stopped and thought. "Or maybe I heard whispers. Just whispers. I couldn't make out what they were saying. I kept trying to hear them."

"You followed them," said Mabel. "And they were leading you to this spot."

Kat looked at her feet at the edge of that sharp slope, and she shuddered.

"I would of broken something," she said.

"Yep," said Mabel. "They were warning you. One thing's for certain: there's no ghost here. Now let's get out of here."

"I thought it was me. Something wrong with me," Kat said, as they walked back to the car.

"I think something's after you. You know, like . . ." She trailed off.

Kat knew exactly what she meant, though. The suffocation at night she herself had suffered, the poor woodpile creature.

"Why is it after us?"

"Because we're dangerous to it."

"Okay, I get that. What I don't get is how I'm dangerous."

"There's something different about you. We've all noticed it."

"Even Ann?"

"Ann doesn't normally pick up waifs on the street, you know."

"I thought it was to do with her retiring and stuff. She wants to nurture me."

"I think it's her eye."

"I don't believe in her eye anymore," Kat was defensive. She didn't want to be strange, right now.

"She doesn't either. Are you finished worrying? We two have got work to do."

Kat's laugh was a little shaky, but she managed to say, "I've finished worrying."

"If my weeping girl isn't an old ghost and if it isn't that native spirit, either, then what is it?"

"Why do you say it isn't the native spirit?"

"She hasn't been seen since her log burned up, in the bushfires. I have notes about her."

"Well, there you are then."

"So what is it?"

"Dunno." Mabel was thoughtful. "Time to talk to Lil, perhaps."

Once Mabel had finished with Kat, she had another errand. She drove herself to Red Hill and stood in the big, flat parking lot, looking out over the whole of Canberra.

"It's a pretty place," Mabel said, just in case anyone was listening. On her right, she heard a noise. She turned, smiling. She saw a tall horse striding out of the darkness, all its lines stretched and elegant. That darkness was new, Mabel noted. Maybe Jackey-Jackey had sorted out the see-through body problem?

It appeared he had.

"We should have met at my place," Mabel scolded.

Jackey-Jackey smiled and changed the subject. "Do you want my treasure, my love?"

"Not really."

"So many people have looked for it."

"Dug holes on Black Mountain — I know. Let them look."

"They will find nothing."

"Because you don't have any treasure. You spent it all on nice clothes."

"And beautiful women. I have very fine taste in women."

"You like them seasoned with age."

"Age does not hide beauty."

"For most people it does."

"Come here." The highwayman's voice went soft. Mabel couldn't resist him when he sounded like this, so she didn't.

The next day, when she and her friends had coffee, she didn't say a word when Kat asked, "Did we find out just how corporeal ghosts can get? Is it something we know?"

"I know it," Lil said, "but not for Canberra. Rules are not always universal and Canberra is a little odd."

"What are the rules?"

"Ghosts can become solid under certain circumstances, like great emotion or strong magic," said Lil, prosaically.

"We should get your map and see if there's a pattern to the oddness. See how the ghosts' physicalness fits into the circles thingie and the deep cultural construct thingie."

"Why? What are you talking about?" asked Ann.

"Because if ghosts can be corporeal and the man in my granny flat has a body and a bad temper and shouldn't even be here, then it might help us stop things getting worse."

"Out of the mouths of babes," said Mabel. "Make us a map, Kat."

"I have one that has ghost sightings," said Ann. "I started it years ago."

"Except it's not whether they can become corporeal, it's when they started to become corporeal."

"How do you know that, Mabel?" asked Lil.

"I found a ghost and asked him, of course."

"Can you give me your sightings for my map?" asked Ann.

"Maybe." Mabel shifted restlessly. "If I can remember."

Kat hesitated, then blurted out her own question. "Could you all give me your details and I can put it on my map?"

"Why?" asked Ann.

"Because I already have Lil's circles and all my information from the internet on it. It'd save time." *And because I want to ask Mr Whoeveritis in the granny flat. I bet he has answers. But I'm not going to tell my grannies that. Except maybe Lil. If she really wants to know.*

"Is there anything new you found on your internet searches?" asked Mabel. "Anything that could help?"

"Something very new," admitted Kat. "Icky, too."

"Icky?" All the women looked surprised.

"Some of it's from the werewolf, I think. Four things on the map. People reported sightings of a big dog, and reports of tooth marks and savaging."

"That sounds ick," said Mabel.

"It isn't though. I mean, it is, but compared with the other, it's only horrible."

"One thing at a time," said Mabel, brusquely.

"Yes," said Ann. "I need to get home."

And so Kat and Lil were left alone, some time later, in the quiet of Lil's house.

"Something's still very wrong, isn't it? Tell me, then," said Lil, gently. "Start where you want to."

"Not where I left off before, I mean, with the yuck things."

"Where you want to start. It's the best place."

Kat was very still for a moment. She had to compose herself. This was something that she was very uncomfortable talking about. How often had she wished it on her baby sister, in the months before she ran away from home? "I wanted my sister to die," she said. "I dreamed of it."

"This is where badkat began?"

"Mum called me Kitty, when I was little. She said I was her own little kitten." A very long silence followed this statement. Lil let Kat explore it.

"Daddy died and Mum replaced him. Then she got pregnant again. I was nine. She was so sick. No-one told me what was happening. I got my-self up in the morning and I got myself breakfast and I did everything I had to do. I was so good. I was so very good. I went to school and I played with my friends and I was happy-happy because I didn't know what was happening."

"Were you happy?"

"I dunno. Everyone told me I was. They told me primary school was wonderful. They told me my family was lovely. I tried to believe them for ages and ages. I was so very good, for ages and ages."

"I was pinkgirl then. Pretty fairy princess. Me and my friends, we all were. I took my play to their houses and Mummy said Good Kitty, because she was so tired all the time."

More silence.

"Then the baby came and cried and cried and Mummy got better, but didn't want me back. I wasn't good kitty anymore, I was bad. Everything I did was bad."

"Everything?"

"No, not really. Mummy gave me a cool book for my eleventh birthday. It wasn't the book I want now — now I want a big empty book that I can turn into a Book of Shadows. When I was little, though, I dreamed of having a diary. And they gave me one. Real leather. I brought it with me, here. I filled it with everything that was happening that year. It kept me safe, inside." Lil nodded.

"But then my friends changed, too. They said I wasn't Kitty — I was badkat. They were nice, but didn't want me at their places, because I dressed in the wrong clothes and didn't do the right things anymore. Because I got angry. Because I wrote poetry. Because I was real. When I got to high school, they weren't there. Or I wasn't there. And Mummy and Dad and Leila were family, and I didn't belong. So I left."

"And your dream?"

"That's why I left. I thought that I would stop dreaming about stealing Leila's breath when she grew up, but she was crawling and then she was walking and then she was talking and no-one wanted me and she was cute and everyone loved her and wanted to make her happy all the time. I used to dream of her not waking up in the morning."

"What can I do?"

"You've done it," Kat said, surprised. "I don't want it to happen anymore. Leila can have all the air she needs. She can sleep safe."

"You can go back home one day."

"Maybe." Kat was dubious. "I will ring them, though, tonight, after dinner. I've been saving up for the phone call. I was scared to make it. I'm not scared of Dad any more. I'm not scared of being alone."

"I can pay for the call."

Kat shook her head. "I have to."

"Can you tell me why you're telling me this now? Or is that too difficult?"

"I've been hating myself for it. Forever and ever. I hate myself for thinking those thoughts. Today I thought, at least I'm not like those monsters. I haven't suffocated a baby or a child or a mother or a father. I wanted to. I ran away instead, though. I didn't hurt anyone."

Lil drew in a sharp breath. "Who has been doing this? Who has been suffocated?"

"It's on the map. It's what I was going to talk about after the werewolf thing. Near here. Cot deaths, the website called them, then they started calling them other names. Seven grownups and five children and three babies. It's so awful. At first I thought it was me. I was sleepwalking or something. Then I realised that I was being really stupid and it couldn't be. You lock everything so carefully. I love it so much that you lock everything so carefully. Then I thought it was the thing who took the granny flat. Then I realised that my nightmare was someone else's daydream. A real monster."

Lil nodded, sharply. "I need to look at that map." Kat went to her room to bring it out, and the moment was broken. Both of them had a great deal to think about.

Immediately, however, there was something far more urgent. Kat had been entirely right. There was a rash of a very particular type of illness. Lil looked at the map and her face paled. Kat immediately worried.

"I need to get you something."

"No, we need to do something. We keep saying we should pay you attention and we never ask you the right questions. People have died because of us. Because of me."

"You know about this? You know what the monster is?"

"Oh, yes." Lil sounded bitter. "It's quite possible that this is a monster I know."

"Don't badkat yourself," said the teenager. "I'm learning not to, so you can't start. You would be a bad role model, you know."

Lil smiled, wanly. "What do I do, then, when I know I've had the answer and I know I could have stopped these people dying?"

Kat looked very reflective. "Does hurting yourself help?"

"No."

"Then don't. If you've got the answer, then tell me. And then tell the others. And then we do something. Before anyone else dies."

Lil played around with the map, to give herself time. "Look," she said.

"Your little blue stickers are all around Melbourne Avenue. The Embassy district. If I were to draw a line like this and like that and going here, what is it?"

"A spiral, from that building."

"The Japanese Chancellery. You see," said Lil, "Europeans aren't the only new arrivals to Canberra. Other people have brought baggage, too."

"Is there anything else it could be? I mean, just in case it's, say, a circle, and it starts somewhere else?"

"It could be lilin," said Lil, dubiously. "It's improbable. They ought not be here. I suppose, however, if other beings aren't playing by old rules, then maybe it could be lilin."

"What are they?"

"Little devils that steal breath at night."

"Oh. It could be that. Where do they come from?"

"Western Europe," said Lil. "And Central Europe. And North Africa."

"Does Western Europe include France?"

"Yes." Lil was puzzled.

"Then it can't be lilin," said Kat, positively.

"Why?"

"It can't be you." Kat looked worried.

"Why would you even think it was me?"

"Lil — lilin — Jewishness — magic: it all fits."

"Not nearly as closely as you think," Lil was genuinely amused. "The little creatures are creations of an angry woman. I am the creation of two loving parents."

"So you've never stolen anyone's breath?"

"Maybe a man's on occasion, when I dress up."

"Oh," said Kat. She did not find the joke funny. "Then what are you?"

She watched Lil go all kinds of still, then realised what she had done. Kat covered her mouth. "Oh, I'm so sorry."

"It's about time I said this," Lil replied. "I, my dear," she proclaimed, "I am a fairy."

"That was supposed to stop me in my tracks," Kat said, wryly.

"I have come to believe that nothing can stop you in your tracks."

"You *are* Melusine, aren't you? And the stories are your life."

"I am a melusine and I should have hidden my stories," Lil commented. If she was surprised that Kat had found them and read them, she wasn't showing it. "Folk tales talk about one fairy called 'Melusine.' Tales are not always right. I have many names. The one I use now is 'Lilith.'"

"After the lilin?"

"No, we were both named after Adam's first wife. She divorced him and married King Ashmodai. I am one of their descendants."

"So you are sort of human?"

"I am like humans. I am the nearest to a human you will find of fairy kind."

"But you are really and truly a fairy."

"I am really and truly a fairy." Lil smiled, sadly.

"Oh wow," breathed Kat.

"It does not make me all-powerful," Lil warned.

"No, of course not. But it makes you unbelievably cool."

Lil laughed. Her laughter echoed right through the house. A pair of brilliant eyes could be seen at the window, but neither of the women were looking. Those eyes were lonely.

Ten

MABEL WAS WANDERING HER garden. It helped settle her mind, and it helped her keep track of everything in it. She needed to walk and touch and feel: life was just a bit too much right now. She was over by the fence. 'Unprotected area,' Lil had called it, but it still needed the same care as the rest of the garden.

Behind her, something scuttled. The woodpile was there. Without turning, she said, "I have to admit, I'm glad you're there. I miss your mate something dreadful."

There was a silence, then a low chuckle. Mabel turned quickly. The laugh wasn't that of a woodpile creature. It was something much darker.

There was nothing there.

"Not safe," said a child's voice. "You should be careful about being not safe. I don't like you, you see."

Hah, Mabel thought. *Safety is just two steps away. Lil did more than you think. She did everything she could, short of ending up in hospital.* Mabel strode across that thin divide between safe and not safe, and smiled triumphantly.

"Not safe," said the child's voice. "I told you. You should be careful."

Mabel realised that she had not moved at all. Or maybe the ground had shifted and brought her back to where she started. Three times she walked bravely to the protected area and three times she found herself back where she started.

"Not safe," said the child.

"This is getting boring," said Mabel.

"Wait. I'm getting my body. Last time I got my body your creature got in the way. I've been waiting. Nearly there. Nearly there." There was no malice in the voice. That was the most terrifying thing of all. Mabel remembered the way her poor little friend's guts had been strewn over the ground.

"I don't want you to have your body back," she said.

"Too bad. Not long now. Keep trying to leave. It stops me getting bored."

This is when I need a mobile phone. But she didn't carry her phone with her into the garden. She heard more noises. *I don't believe it.* She peered down the path, past the terrified creature peeking out of the woodpile. *The cavalry is coming.*

The ghost horse and rider managed what Mabel's good strong feet had not. Mabel was swept into the safe portion of the garden.

"Sorry I took so long," said Jackey-Jackey. "It was hard to become solid tonight."

"It was me," the dark voice gloated. "I took your body to come here. I'll be back, too. I can wait."

"Doesn't it feel better all of a sudden?"

"It does," said the bushranger. "That's one wicked creature."

"I need a cuppa."

"Me too."

"You can drink now?" Mabel was teasing, but there was an undertone of seriousness.

"I believe so."

He tied his horse and the two went inside. A bit later, Mabel was winding down by talking it all out, and Jackey-Jackey was humouring her.

"If I had died, wouldn't I have joined you?"

"If I knew that, maybe I would have acted differently."

"Besides, we don't know how temporary all this is. You may become see-through and the others may go entirely." Mabel felt she was sounding like Kat. Or Ann. Or anyone but herself. She felt miserable beyond belief.

"If it weren't for you, I would not object to that," came the answer. "Canberra is better without my rivals. I felt no pain in being a ghost. But here, now, holding your hand — why would I want to give up that?"

"We can't let this continue, though. I don't mean hand-holding. I mean the other stuff."

"And if it means we can't hold hands . . ." His eyes twinkled down at her. "Well, we are mature."

"Grin and bear it?"

"Survive."

"Then we'd better go see the others. Pronto."

"Which others?"

"Lil and Kat."

"They were looking for vampires, I believe."

"Mobile phones are a wonderful invention," said Mabel, still channelling Kat. She rang Lil and was promptly answered. "They're in trouble, too. We have to go. How long can you stay stable?"

"They have transport? They can get you to your car?"

"Yes."

"Then let me get you to them."

"It's further than Red Hill and Red Hill to here was enough of a problem for your horse."

"So I take you to Red Hill and we drive the rest of the way."

"You'll get in my car?"

"You think I am too old to be excited by the wonders of the modern world," he answered, sarcastically.

"You're older than you look, anyhow," replied Mabel, holding up her car keys. "Got everything. Let's go."

In an ideal world, the worst would have been over by the time they found the others. It would have been especially ideal given that, the minute Mabel got in the car, it didn't go where she wanted it to. Eventually she stopped and called Jackey-Jackey until he came.

"It's the streets," Mabel explained. "I go somewhere and find myself coming back the other way."

"It's not happening to me," said the bushranger.

"Maybe being a ghost helps."

Mabel was being sarcastic, but Jackey-Jackey was serious. "I shall walk the horse in front of your car. Watch my horse, and not the road signs."

"Will do," said Mabel, and turned the key in the ignition. It was very slow, but it worked.

They found Lil a block away from Melbourne Avenue. "I can't make the last distance," she fretted. "The streets keep shifting. The Clarke brothers were there, too."

"Were?" Mabel asked.

"They passed me one way then came back the other. They were laughing."

"This sounds bad."

Lil nodded. "I can't get to Ann and Kat. I can't do anything."

"Ann's there too?"

"Oh, yes," Lil said. "Just try walking down that street to reach them, and see what happens."

Mabel tried. "I feel like the Red Queen," she said. "It doesn't matter how hard I walk, I stay the same place."

"Interesting," said Jackey-Jackey. "Let me try. Here, Mabel, hold my horse." He walked down the street half a block and then back again. "No problems." He was very cheerful. "Whoever set that up didn't allow for friendly ghosts."

"Over-friendly ghosts," muttered Lil.

"What did you say, Lil?"

"That our hands are tied — we can't help."

"William Westwood to the rescue!" The man suited his action to his words, twitched his reins back from Mabel, mounted his horse, and rode off down the road.

He found Ann and Kat outside the Japanese Chancellery. They were standing at the iron fence, looking in. Looking out at them was a big cat. It was taunting them from the elegance of a Japanese ornate garden.

Jackey-Jackey didn't waste time. "You girls can't get out of here, right?"

"No, we can't," said Ann.

Kat added, "The Clarkes came along and saw we were stuck. We thought they were going to kill us. They brought out guns and everything. Except they didn't. They worked out we were stuck and they laughed at us and rode away."

"We think something's waiting to get us," said Ann, gloomily.

"Probably is," said Jackey-Jackey cheerfully. "Mabel met it earlier. I can't take you on the horse — it's ridden too far already — but I think I can get you out of this." He slid from his mount's back again and, holding the reins in one hand, stretched the other out to Kat. "Now, you hold this hand and Ann can hold your hand."

"How will it help?" asked Ann, suspiciously.

"I can walk in and out."

"But why?"

"Don't just stand there." Jackey-Jackey was getting impatient. They linked up and talked as they walked. "Whoever is after you is friends with the Clarkes — wasn't going to stop them moving."

"So all bushranger ghosts can get through?"

"That'd be the way I see it. Now, what happened back there?"

"We got trapped by whispers and the streets keeping moving, so we couldn't leave."

"Yes, I saw that. Why were you there at all?"

"We were trying to stop more deaths. We were hunting the soul-vampire." Ann spoke loudly, as if to encompass the giant difference of a person in between. *Either that, or she isn't happy about talking to him at all,* Kat thought. *That'd be nice. Two of us who go 'ew.'*

"Did you find it?"

"There was this tall Japanese woman with big long eyes, but she went behind one of the buildings in the Japanese place," Kat said.

"All we were left with was that bloody cat, laughing at us."

"You're sure the cat was just a cat?"

"No, it's big, but it's just a cat. No lightning in its eyes or bloody footprints or anything." Ann sounded disappointed.

"But it was taunting us," Kat said.

"Cats do that," said Ann, gloomily.

Two days later, Kat was helping Lil prepare dinner. It wasn't just any dinner party: it was the monthly one.

She wanted to throw the casserole dish on to the floor and hear it smash. She wanted to sweep the row of wineglasses off the bench and hear them tinkle into sharp fragments. She wanted to dance among the shards until her feet bled.

"What's wrong?" asked Lil.

"We're not doing anything!"

"It does feel like that, doesn't it?"

"What are we doing, if it only feels like we're doing nothing?"

"Tonight we're restoring our confidence and gathering strength and reminding ourselves that we will not be beaten."

"That sounds good," admitted Kat. "How are we doing this?"

"We're eating patsas."

"Patsas?"

"Lamb casserole. But there's more."

"More?"

"You are making dessert."

"Me?" Kat was terrified. "What am I making?"

"I found you a cookbook and bought ingredients for six dishes. Choose one."

Kat chose a baked orange dish. She found it soothing to peel the oranges and satisfying to know she could cook. Lil was right — dinner helped. Kat couldn't see that it should have helped, but it did.

Tales of Melusine #43

This is how Melusine told it to her new friends of Liverpool. She said it defiantly. As if it were real. She lived in a small place and taught anything she could to keep life, body and soul together and she always, always went down to the docks. The ship would come in from time to time and the men would say, "Not yet. We haven't seen him yet."

This is how Melusine told it.

"I dressed up," she said. "I took his breath away. He was so struck by me that he married me at once."

Her new friends would admire the baby boy and girl, and they would be reassured when, from time to time, they would meet one of the crew (when they were in Liverpool) and that sailor (or even the captain) would ask respectfully how she was and give her the latest news on their search. They had no money, and they themselves kept ends meeting by taking on odd jobs. The ship still had the uncanny skill and kept itself out of trouble. As time passed, though, and Melusine made no demands, the captain and sailors assumed the ship was theirs, and they faded gradually from her life. If they kept an eye open for Melusine's husband, she didn't know. It didn't matter as much as it should have, which would have surprised her if she had stopped to think.

Melusine was not happy, but she was content. Those infants were the centre of her life. They had a magic all their own. She could wait for her lover. She could watch for him. And she could be there for her little ones. Her girl she called Gwendolyn and her boy, Owen. He would have liked that.

Until they were three, they were everything children should be. When they turned three, everything changed.

One night, Melusine heard a commotion in the children's bedroom. The nursemaid was standing over them, screaming. Above their little beds, Melusine saw swarms of lilin, fluttering their little wings above both beds.

"Get out, now," she told the nursemaid. The nursemaid fled.

Melusine used her superior stature and power and got rid of the pests at once. "Go," was all she had to say. Then she raced to Gwen's bed. She was fine. A bit pale, but breathing peacefully. Melusine ran a hand over her head to check for any change or damage. None. Melusine sighed in relief.

Then she went to Owen. Owen was pale. Pale and still. He wasn't breathing. Melusine tried to revive him. No good. Not all her powers could bring him back to life. She picked him up and held him and rocked him all through the night and well into the day. No-one dared disturb them.

The nursemaid came and took Gwen in the morning and fed her and bathed her.

"What's Mummy doing?" Gwen would ask, over and over. "Where's Owen? I can't see Owen."

"Hush," said the nursemaid. "I'll tell you later."

Gwen was a good child. She waited. Gwen was also a sensitive child. She didn't show the hurt, but it was there, buried deep. She didn't know she blamed her mother, because she buried that deeply as well.

Eventually her mother came back to see her and they both said goodbye to Owen.

Quietly, very quietly, Melusine went away for three days. Just three days. She went because she did not want to do what she must do anywhere near her daughter. Her daughter was no longer simply loved. Her daughter was life and love itself. A big burden for any child, but especially for one who has lost a twin.

Melusine went somewhere just outside the normal world. In that place, she sought out every one of the lilin. She used up the reserves of power that she had kept untapped for hundreds of years. She flung her anger into punishing them. She flung her hate into constraining them. She forced them into a deep and irrevocable promise that none of them would ever hurt her or hers again. She trapped their life force into the promise, to ensure that nothing they could do would break it. They were not even able to come within a hundred miles of anyone related to her. Gwen and her children and her children's children were all safe.

And then life went back to normal. Or as normal as life can be with the gaping void of a lost child.

Melusine pretended to age at human pace. Gwen grew up into an elegant young lady. They lived in Liverpool still, and still Melusine hoped for news of Gwen's father.

One day, Gwen questioned that dream of a father and she had words to her mother about it. It had taken years to come, but finally, Gwendolyn had started unburying her unhappiness. It was a miserable day for both mother and daughter. If that had been an end of it, Melusine would have endured.

Not long after Gwendolyn brought her new fiancé home and apologised charmingly for not introducing him sooner. "I was in a bind," she said, still charming, but hurting Melusine with every word. "For father is dead and it is wrong to ask one's mother."

"Where I am from, one asks both parents," Melusine said.

"And where are you from?" her to-be son asked, politely.

"The south of France," she said. "A very old family."

Things were not good from then. Gwen didn't believe her mother for she would not accept what her mother was. She wanted to live in a human world. She wanted to marry someone 'with prospects' and she wanted to have children and a home free of oddness.

In 1843 Gwen gave birth to her first child. She showed Melusine her grandchild and let her hold the baby, then she said, very bluntly, "I never want to see you again. I don't want magic near me or mine. I never want to lose a child the way you lost yours."

And that is where the story of Melusine's family ends. The melusine was alone again. This time, it hurt beyond bearing.

Kat was terrified. She could feel her chest being pressed and she could feel her breath going.

"Stop that!" Lil's voice rang out, soft but clear.

"She is mine." Another woman's voice confronted Lil's, but the feeling of being overwhelmed abated. "You are mine, too. Your heart and her breath."

Kat opened her eyes and looked up. An elegant Japanese woman stood on one side of her and Lil stood angrily opposite. Around them were the trees of Yarralumla. The familiar sight helped Kat take her next breath and the one after.

The Japanese woman had long and beautiful eyes and Lil's were as round and angry as a cat's. Everything was not quite real. She thought, *If I close my eyes again, maybe this will go away. All I wanted to do was buy more milk.* But the milk she had just bought was spilt all over the ground and home was three blocks away.

"I have been very patient," said the Japanese woman, as Kat scrunched her eyes and pretended she wasn't there, couldn't see. "Your little one has given me only tastes. Now I need all of her."

"You can't have her and you can't have me." Lil's voice was steady. "While I have life within me I shall defend her from you."

"I shall take your heart first, then," said the lady. "Her breath is but bread and butter. Your heart will be something extraordinary."

"You know, then," said Lil, heavily, "that I am not human."

"You pass for human better than most," said the lady. "But I am not stupid. I can see the flying one underneath the skin." She leaned over Kat, to reach for Lil's heart. Lil did not move.

"Can you see my heart?" Lil asked. "The reason I ask is that you should not be able to."

The woman paused in mid-movement. Her left hand hovered directly over Kat's supine body. Kat breathed very low. She didn't want to attract attention. She couldn't see how Lil would get them out of this one, either. She remembered the night terrors and looked up at the beautiful white face, with its powder and its glamour, and she recognised that this was the being who had given her those fears and burdens after dark. Kat remembered and she trembled.

Lil said, "How unfortunate for you that I have left my heart somewhere safe."

"You have what?" The hand whipped back like a snake and the woman's whole body leaned over Kat, angry and spitting.

"These are dangerous times," Lil said, calmly. "I am old and frail. What else was there for me to do?"

"Give it to me," the woman said.

"Find it first."

Kat wanted to believe Lil was lying. She so wanted to believe it. Except . . . the catvampirething believed her. And it was better if she believed Lil. Even if it made Lil scary. Kat lay perfectly still.

"You are different," it said. "I cannot see why. Next time, bring your heart." Her tail flicked disdainfully in the air and she flounced off. Obviously, without Lil's heart, Kat's breath was not nearly as interesting.

Kat and Lil looked at each other.

"We still have to pick Ann up!" Lil said.

There was a knock on Kat's door. "Yes?"

It was Lil. Who else could it be? "I'm going out for a little. Ann needs to see me urgently. I thought I should warn you because I'm not locking the door. If you go out, would you mind?"

"Sure," said Kat. "Only I'm not going out. I ran out of money big time and I'm confined to home entertainment until I can afford things again."

Lil laughed. "Good, then. See you later."

So Kat was in her bedroom. She got suddenly hungry. It didn't happen often, but when it did happen *Gotta have something* was all she could think. She went to the kitchen, to see what yummies Lil had stashed away. On the way to the kitchen, of course, was the lounge room. And in the lounge room was Ann. Why wasn't she at her house, talking to Lil? What was particularly odd was that she appeared to be opening every drawer in the dresser.

"Are you looking for something?" Kat asked politely.

Ann jumped. "I forgot something." Ann was obviously lying. "I just came round to collect it."

Kat was troubled. Ann had rescued her from the streets. She owed her. At the same time, Ann had no right to be looking through Lil's things. And, also at the same time, Kat had done exactly the same thing, probably for exactly the same reason. Kat had read the Melusine papers. *Wrong things always catch up with me*, she thought, bitterly.

"Okay," she said, then she had a thought. "I can help."

"It's fine," said Ann, "I found it."

"Cool. Can I get you a cuppa?"

"That's okay. I had coffee with a friend. I was just on the way home." Then came the sticking point. The unforgivable. "No need to tell Lil I was here, okay?"

"Okay," said Kat, again. This was not a good agreement, but she had led herself into it. She didn't like Ann for making her say it. She liked herself even less for having read the Melusine stories. About the only good thing in the universe right now was that Kat had not done badkat. Except not doing badkat ought to have been a thing for great celebration and this, this was ick. Yucky. Foul.

She pretended to smile and she let Ann out the door. *Growing up sucks,* she thought.

Kat was having a busy afternoon. Her brain was busy, too. She posted to her blog.

"I keep wondering," she wrote, "about being human. Walking down the street I look at people and I think — how do we know they're human? They could be human outside and strange inside. Or human outside and special inside. People can be hiding all sorts of magic as long as they look human.

"We think it's only about TV and films. That supernatural looking like us can only happen there. Or in books, maybe. In fiction. But how do we know for sure?"

Her brain turned this over, and turned it over some more. She thought about what Ann could be looking for, since she didn't actually know about the stories. Maybe a magic book? But Lil didn't have a magic book. If she did, it was hidden somewhere. Besides, Lil herself was magic, she didn't need a magic book. Or maybe she used to have it and then got rid of it.

Her brain turned again and thought different things. She started thinking about the Melusine stories and their content. Several magic books were described in them. She found one with Queen Elizabeth and one that was not nice and . . . and there was storytelling. Kat caught her breath. In France. Someone told a Japanese story. About a vampire cat. It was killing a prince by taking its breath or its life or something.

She wondered. Just how big could cats get? And just how many cats were there who were so very impudent and who haunted the Japanese Chancellery? The Japanese Chancellery: that same building complex where Lil had thought the vampire stuff started.

"It's not my fault!" Kat typed hard at the keyboard and watched the words display on the screen. "All I wanted was a bit of a chat. Just because she's way older than me doesn't mean I can't talk to her." *Does typing this hard break the keyboard? Does it make me feel any better?*

"I won't tell you who it is because it's ugh-making. Really ugh-making. Impossibly ugh-making. Pure and utter ugh." *Maybe I should just come out with it? Who reads my blog, anyhow?*

"She is old. Grandmother-old. I drop in on her all the time. Hell, I do her gardening and wash her dishes. I help her." Kat knew she was self-justifying and trying to recover her pride. But honestly.

"Honestly, we're really close. Can talk about anything, almost. 'Cept . . ." Maybe she shouldn't've used the key. Maybe she should have knocked.

"She was having sex. In the kitchen. With a younger bloke." *Can't do this any more.* Kat kept hitting backspace until all the text was gone and went for a long, long walk.

Ew ick, thought Kat. She was in a curious state. She knew grown-ups had sex. She wasn't exactly an innocent herself in that regard. It was just that she really hadn't thought it happened with people she knew. She especially hadn't thought it happened with old people she knew. And Jackey-Jackey might be old, but he didn't look it. *Ick. Ick. Ick.*

Mabel looked at Kat. Kat looked at Mabel. Kat said 'sorry,' and almost ran out the door. Her mind had suddenly started badkatbadkatbadkat and running was the only solution.

An hour later, the two women were arguing on the phone. An hour after that, Kat rang Mabel back.

Kat realised that if she wanted to keep Mabel in her life, she was just going to have to accept that seventy-six year olds might have sex lives. *I don't have to like it, but*, she thought furiously. *And I am not badkat.*

"Mabel," she said, tentatively. "I'm sorry."

"So am I," said Mabel, stiffly.

"No, I mean, really sorry."

"I supposed you're going to tell me some story about your childhood."

"No. I'm just going to say 'sorry.'"

"I suppose we're all under stress right now," said Mabel. Kat remained silent. "I suppose we just have to deal with our differences until all this is worked out."

"'Sorry' doesn't work then?"

Mabel sounded her age for an instant. "It's your tone, Kat. It doesn't matter how often you apologise when the way you talk says 'ew yuck, that old woman's just had sex.'"

"That's something I have to sort out, but. It doesn't stop me from meaning the apology."

"Are we still friends?"

"Maybe. You're still my grandmother. You being strange doesn't stop you being my grandmother."

"You adopted me and now I'm stuck with you, eh?"

"We adopted each other. And we have to be adult about it."

"Lil would say that there is no place for childishness or sulks when things are at crisis point."

"I was trying not to."

"So, my dear, was I."

"Bags you tell the others what they need to know."

"That's fine with me. The others do not need to know a thing. This is between us."

Mabel and Kat decided to redeem themselves with each other.

"I've been thinking about that getting solid thing," Mabel had said.

Kat almost said 'Don't', but caught Mabel's steel-grey eyes and bit her tongue. She just nodded, instead.

"I think that if we can trick Paddy Curran into becoming incorporeal, he won't be able to come back."

"Why?"

"Because he's hopeless. Jack told me some stories about him. He's a lazy, selfish bugger."

"You mean he kinda got dragged into this."

"Yeah, and went along with it."

"Will it help us with the others?"

"Nup." Mabel sounded resigned rather than cheerful. "The Clarke Brothers are bastards."

"But if he's not there, then it'll be two, not three."

"That's the idea."

"What do we do?"

"Surprise me."

First, they had to surprise Paddy Curran. This wasn't as hard as it should have been. Curran really wasn't very bright. Every sighting of him had been in the same street in Weston. Wittenoom Crescent. Every sighting had followed the same pattern: clop-clop of hooves, then the transparent horse, then the horse became flesh, then Paddy bailed up whoever-it-was, bashed them around a bit and faded with his loot. He hadn't seriously hurt anyone since Jackey-Jackey had given him what-for, Kat pointed out.

"I see what you're getting at," said Mabel. "I think we can do this, just the two of us."

"Bags I play the innocent," Kat said.

"It's risky," warned Mabel.

"That's why it has to be me. If it's you and you get hurt, your boyfriend will make my life a mess, so I'm not safe either way. You're safe if I play the innocent, but."

"I'll pay that," said Mabel slowly. And this is how Kat found herself alone on Wittenoom Crescent, just before dusk.

Clop-clop went the hooves. Kat looked up and saw the letterbox through the transparent animal. She tried not to smile. She tried not to be scared. She didn't quite succeed with either.

A moment later everything was solid, and Paddy Curran was hauling himself off his horse. He tied it to the self-same letterbox that had shown through its stomach and he lumbered over to Kat. Kat found it surprisingly easy to pretend to look terrified. Her eyes were made up big and vulnerable and she kept them as wide as she could. She was dressed in pink and white and she'd made her hair five shades paler. *Vampire bait,* she thought. Goth was better. Scary was always better than scared.

Curran loomed over her. "How old are you, little girl?"

"Fifteen," Kat said, tilting her head very slightly as she looked up at him.

He chucked her under the chin. "Enough of a woman, then." Smug, that's what his voice was. She took a step back. It was in character, after all. And besides, this man was a rapist and she, Kat, was vampire bait. How could she not have seen that before? Vampire bait was not a safe thing to be. She took another step back.

He grabbed her shoulder. "Don't you run, girlie. I'm going to have some fun with you."

Hurry up, Mabel. He's not going to get more solid than this. He's not going to get more confident than this. Hurry up, Mabel. Before it all goes wrong. Hurry!

Clop-clop sounded again. Kat wasn't expecting that. Her head went up, alert as a sparrow. So did Paddy Curran's. He frowned.

Mabel's voice came ringing out. "William Westwood, where the hell have you been? I've been looking for you everywhere! Come here at once. That Paddy Curran's here. He's messing with a friend of mine."

Curran's hands were off Kat in an instant. A moment later he was untying his horse and swinging himself onto his back. Then he was gone. His horse was still there, unperturbed, but Curran had simply disappeared.

Mabel came round the corner, carrying two halves of a coconut. "Well?" she asked.

"I don't know," said Kat dubiously, squinting at the horse. "It was sudden, and he went, but he might come back."

They waited and let the horse wander down the road at its own slow pace. They didn't try to tie it up or hold it. They just stood there, watching, with Mabel occasionally clopping the coconuts together randomly.

After a few minutes, their patience was rewarded. Paddy Curran appeared again, half on the horse. He half fell off it, too, but faded before he could hit the ground. A few minutes later he was on the ground, half-visible. His face snarled up at them and he reached out towards Kat. Then he was gone.

"Well, that was entertaining," said Mabel. "Who'd have guessed?"

Around dusk Mabel and Kat found themselves carefully not talking about what they'd done.

"It can wait," Mabel whispered to Kat.

"It can wait," Kat whispered back to Mabel. Neither of them wanted to face a tongue lashing from Ann, or one of Lil's considered looks.

Tonight was the big night. They needed all their attention on it. The four of them were going to get rid of those whispers, for good. "The way we dealt with Curran," Mabel said to Kat, out of earshot of the rest. Kat nodded, but in her mind she was replaying the fear she had felt when Curran had chucked her under the chin. She shuddered.

It was a strange excursion. Kat was already inside her own head, scared. Ann was the person she always was, outwardly determined but with something awry. And these two led the trek down dark streets in search of whispers.

Ann didn't mean to lead the others astray. Kat didn't believe in the shifting streets, deep inside her. The two of them led the quartet down one street and back into the same one. No-one noticed. They were all intent on finding those whispers and getting rid of them for good. That was the mantra: "rid of them for good." Then they could all move on and deal with the nastier stuff.

When the women reached the end of that same street the second time, the houses dissolved around them. This, they noticed.

"Out!" said Lil, from behind. "We have to get out!"

"How?" asked Ann, reaching into the strange dissolved landscape, as if touching it would tell her something.

"Backtrack," said Mabel. The street they came from still looked perfectly normal.

They tried. They tried very hard. Each step they took, however, left them inside that strange dissolved landscape.

Whispers invaded their souls. Each of them was caught in a dark dream, their own fears spiralling them down into despair.

"Sebastian would know what to do," said Kat. "We shoulda brought him."

Lil looked at her, assessing. "Who is Sebastian?"

"You know, guy from the granny flat. I don't know his real name, but I call him Sebastian and he mostly comes when I call."

Lil's face was inscrutable. "We can try calling him, at least."

"Seb!"

"Sebastian."

It didn't work. They were so deep inside their despair that their cries could not reach out beyond the small strange streetscape.

"I can do this," Lil said, almost to herself. "I can." She pulled her tiny self very tall and reached somewhere deep inside. From her elegant mouth came a shriek so loud it pierced the sky. The other women covered their ears. Ann started to cry. Lil slumped a little, then collapsed onto the pavement. Kat went straight to her and sat on the pavement, rubbing her hand. She didn't know what to do. She couldn't imagine her life without Lil. Not now. Not ever.

A moment later Sebastian was with them. He appeared from nowhere, it seemed. He drew figures on the pavement with chalk and muttered strange words. A moment later still the street was normal. He picked Lil up as if he had known her forever and knew to an ounce how light her fragile bones were. Lil was unconscious. She didn't see the loving care with which he held her. She didn't see how he looked down at her. She had overextended herself.

Ann took her car home, and Mabel took everyone else to Emergency.

The next day felt strangely normal.

"Have some of my grapes," Lil offered.

"But they're your grapes," Kat objected.

"You look hungry. Besides, I'll be home tomorrow and then you would eat the grapes anyway, one day later."

"Humour her," said Mabel. And so Kat did.

"Where's Ann?" asked Lil.

"Goodness knows," said Mabel. "Being a selfish bitch, perhaps."

"Mabel!"

"She's haunted, but she thinks she's the only one. God, if my life had been as easy as that woman's . . ."

"It's not easy, but," said Kat. "She's had a tough year."

"We all have. Ann's the only one who thinks it's all about her."

"What has she said, Mabel mine?" Lil sounded weary.

"She wants to know things about you. She was sounding me out. I told her to ask you. Yourself. Directly. Like an old friend."

"Yet you yourself don't ask me."

"I know enough. I know enough to trust you with my life, in fact, which is a damn good thing, given what's going on. The rest of it — I know you're you. That's all that matters."

"I thought you were going to say 'You'll tell me when you're good and ready,'" said Kat.

"If she'd wanted to do that, she would have done that sometime in the last thirty years, don't you think? We all have secrets that aren't for sharing. A good friend respects that."

"And so the trio is broken." Lil's voice was soft and bitter.

"It happens," Mabel was casual about it, but it was obvious she was just as cut up as Lil.

"You know what it is," blurted Kat. "It's not secrets. It's ghosts. Ann can't handle her ghosts and you two can. So she thinks you haven't got them. She thinks everything's fine with you."

"So her ghosts get worse and worse."

"And they let the dark children in." Lil's voice was as soft as ever, but piercing.

"And, then," Kat added a piece to the puzzle, "they saw you two. I mean, early, when she let them in."

"And we were dangers."

"And I was something in between. I mean, Ann mothered me."

"But something didn't like you," Mabel said. "Breath stealer?"

"Not the cat. It can't be the cat."

"Why, Lil?"

"If the cat had been so close to my house I would have known."

"Or the granny flat man would have known. He said it was something without a body."

"When did he say this?" Lil's voice had just a note of inquisition.

"We've been talking."

"I think I should speak with you later about that."

"No problems." Kat was cheerful as possible. *It's about time they stopped avoiding each other. Or her avoiding him, anyway.*

"You're very relaxed," said Mabel, "considering how bad everything is."

"How can it be that bad?" said Kat simply. "When I've got you two?"

"So we all have our own ghosts and we all have each other. I like that," said Lil.

"I don't like to say this," started Mabel.

"But you're gonna anyway," finished Kat. The two exchanged a smile.

"Cheeky brat. What I was about to say, but am now reconsidering, is that we three are closer than you and I." She nodded to Lil. "And Ann."

"In all my life I have never experienced this," Lil said.

"And the stuff that's happening to Canberra, have you experienced that?"

"No, Kat, never before."

"That's good, then, right?" Mabel sounded almost hopeful.

Mabel had decided that they all needed more comfort. She also decided that it needed to be all four of them. They could not let Ann go that quickly. They had to help her — if they could — get through her dark patch.

"Shored up against what must follow," she said, with a gesture.

"How long did it take you to find those words?" asked Kat, admiringly.

"Too long," grunted Mabel, as she tried to shape her crown roast.

"It was worth it," said Kat. "It was a very fine phrase."

"Sometimes you sound like an American."

"It's the very fine TV I watch. What do you want me to do next?"

"Veggies," said Mabel. "I've got the veal under control, so we need spuds and parsnips, peeled and cut. Unless you want to do dessert?"

"Do I know how to cook it?"

"I can tell you. It's bread and butter pud, with whipped cream."

"Do I get to put raisins in the bread and butter pudding?"

"Maybe," said Mabel.

"Then I want to learn. I like stealing raisins."

Mabel gave her a look. "It's not about stealing raisins at all. You want to put other things in it, too, don't you? You want to devastate my dried fruits."

"Maybe." Kat made her voice sound cagey.

"Do the veggies and then we'll do the pudding together. After you finish the root vegetables, there are beans to slice."

After the beans she prepared cabbage and spinach, but eventually they got to dessert and eventually Kat put raisins in her pudding and she was happier than she'd been in weeks.

She was less content five minutes later. The phone had rung. It was not much use feeding Ann comfort food when Ann wasn't going to be there to eat it. She wanted to cry, but she decided that this would not be good for Mabel, so she hid in the bustle.

"Don't break my plates," Mabel told her, as Kat put the small pile of big plates down with a thump. She stopped Kat with an unexpected arm around her shoulders. "It's Ann's choice. We have to respect that."

"But what about her ghosts? What about whatever it is that wants to eat her up? It's hurting her!"

"We can deal with the eating up bit. It's part of what we have to do for ourselves as well. We can't deal with the ghosts Ann carries inside. Only she can. She doesn't want to deal with ghosts. Doesn't even want to admit she has them."

"It's so awful!"

"It is. She's a small person right now. Can't face her fears. Can't even face herself. When she's ready, she will. We can't force that on her."

"But what if she's never ready," whispered Kat.

"We can't change that, either. Some people are small for bits of their lives and some find it safer to be small forever. You and I can't make that decision for anyone but ourselves."

"What can we do?"

"Worry about Ann. Do what we can at our end to make things better. And eat comfort food. Lots of it. We need this dinner tonight, don't we? Put the emotions on hold, turn the front right jet on and put the saucepan for the cabbage on it. Spinach goes on the next one along in a few minutes."

"You're going to boil them to smithereens."

"That's the comfort way of doing it. Over-boiled greens take me back to my childhood."

"Limp cabbage is comfort food." Kat gave a half-hearted giggle.

"It will give Lil something small to worry about. Take her minds off the big things. And the small people."

"Oh," said Kat. "I never thought of it from that angle."

"Think about it from that angle, then, and start putting the damn saucepans on."

Then Lil came and they all settled down. It wasn't as bad as Kat had thought, but they all missed Ann. *We're too nice to each other without her. Not enough sarcasm. When Ann is around Lil gets snarky and funny and Mabel tries to tell bad jokes and everyone shuts her up.* Kat nearly asked for the Lake George joke.

"I wish it wasn't so cold," said Mabel, suddenly.

"Why? I like the cold," said Kat.

"I want to sit outside, on the verandah."

"You still have a creature in your woodpile then? It didn't run away when the other one was killed?"

"I think it's lonely."

Lil looked thoughtful. "We can walk outside for a little, and then have a hot drink to warm ourselves up after, surely."

"We can." Mabel sounded robust again. "I have jumpers if either of you need."

"Let's need them. Mabel's jumpers are all big and squidgy. It would be fun to all look big and squidgy."

"Thank you, Kat, for that compliment."

"I have more, if you need them. I have a vast store of most excellent compliments. And they all contain the word 'squidgy'."

"Preserve me."

Lil gave her big laugh and suddenly all was right with the world.

"My jumpers are not squidgy," said Mabel to Kat, as they followed Lil down the verandah stairs.

"No, they are—"

"Sh," came Lil's voice out of the dark. "Quick!"

Two steps into the darkness. Three steps. Just around the corner, where the woodpile was just a small, messy portion of the grandeur Kat had stacked last summer, two creatures were having a standoff. One was the second woodpile creature and the other was the same oversized, graceful cat that they had met at the Japanese Chancellery complex.

The cat was fluffed up enormously. The wood sprite was standing between it and the path to the door.

"Lil," cried Kat, softly and plaintively. "What can we do?"

The cat was losing its fluffiness. It was taking on a predator look. It suddenly became very obvious what had killed the woodpile creature's mate.

Behind them, Mabel had been busy. She had with her now a big bucket of water. She threw it at the cat.

The cat snarled. Wet and bedraggled, it looked much smaller. Its glance fell on Mabel, and it turned to advance towards her. The little woodpile creature jumped on the cat's wet back and sank its claws in. The cat yowled.

Mabel had some more water ready and threw it again.

"Sorry, woodpile creature," called Kat.

Lil said something rapidly in a strange language.

The cat fled, the creature jumped off its back and took refuge in the dregs of wood, and it was over as suddenly as it had begun.

"What did you say?" Kat asked Lil excitedly.

"A spell."

"I thought you didn't do spells."

"Desperate times call for desperate measures," said Mabel. "I don't usually pull muscles throwing water about, either."

"Let's get you inside and treated," said Lil.

As they retraced their steps, Kat called out again, "Thanks, woodpile creature. I'm worshipping at your feet. Just so's you know."

Tales of Melusine #31

In a quiet moment, life moved on without her.

A month before there had been four women, leaning close to gossip. Four women bound tightly in their corsets, bound tightly by their society. One day, one of them was going to grow right out of the group. Melusine never thought that it would be her. Nor that the fault would lie with a man.

For twenty years Melusine had pretended to be Christian. It was easy enough in this tiny English society. Neither small town nor big city. Attendance at church and enough servants meant she was accepted.

She made her friends at church. Louisa, of warm heart and forgetful mind; Caroline, whose laughter and relaxed manner made you forget her self-opinion; and May, who needed attention, always more attention. The four together laughed always and enjoyed life. The men in their lives came and went, as men did. The children in their lives were relegated to the care of nursemaids and governesses when the four met. And so they all grew a little, talking and sharing lives.

Louisa's headaches and her capacity to fling herself into anything led to the group's downfall. She took laudanum. Alcohol would have been better, Melusine thought, for she knew the poppy of old and avoided it carefully.

The other three listened to their sermons too carefully. They hated alcohol and they hated Catholics about equally, which reflected the private life of their minister (though they weren't aware of that). He preached against alcohol when he was hung-over, against Catholics when he was angry, and against miscellaneous sins the rest of the time. He had a very useful book he used to inspire the sermons and when he was particularly hung-over he would read from that book of sample sermons word for word.

Melusine would have given up on church long before if it wasn't for the possibility of catching him out (since she had a copy of the book as part of the two dozen she bought to turn her into a convincing member of the congregation) and if it weren't for friends.

She needed friends. She found the prosperous English of this period smelled too much of meat and not enough of soap. And she hated, hated, hated her corsets and constrictive clothing with a vehemence. Small annoyances would pass. Friends would help them pass. The joy of the company of others made every pain a worthwhile one. Almost Christian, she felt, was the suffering.

Until it passed she could use these devices to become accepted. To have friends.

They were bright and perceptive and interesting women, Caroline, Louisa and May. They thought themselves free thinkers, but they fitted charmingly into the lower echelons of the upper middle class. If they had been born a generation earlier, they would have read Byron. As it was, they occasionally talked social reform but more often talked literature. Fine conversation with fine women.

Maybe it wasn't the laudanum? Maybe the literature was a stage the three were going through and when they came out of it, Melusine was left behind?

Melusine didn't know, and she couldn't ask. All she knew was that — after one impassioned moment where she spoke out against opium — the three banded together in patriotism and the right to drug oneself. It should have passed. It ought to have passed. In a group of friends, losing oneself and showing one's less social side ought to be possible, occasionally.

Except that maybe there were three friends in the group, right from the beginning, and Melusine was tolerated because of her money and her books and her ability to mock the minister. Maybe it was nothing to do with anyone growing. Maybe it was just that the three had never seen Melusine for herself and when she grew a little inconvenient, it was easier to meet for tea without her.

At church they were friendly. The four of them helped decorate the altar with harvest fruits just as they did every year. Louisa made jokes that included all four and May worked with all four. Only Caroline stood a little stiffly from time to time and a little aside. Only Caroline cast looks at Melusine, suggesting that she had somehow not fulfilled her part of an important bargain. Only Caroline tried to limit what Melusine could do and took her aside and explained carefully that she talked too much: "For this is a church, and you need to be respectful." Louisa's jokes turned a little daring and she wasn't pulled aside. Only Melusine, for laughing in a manner that might not quite have been English.

Melusine gave a thousand reasons. She couldn't know which of them was true. All she knew was that when she sent notes out asking her friends to visit, they gave excuses. When she was ill, they did not inquire after her or send her baskets. And every few days she could see the members of the trio walk down the streets on their way to one house or the other.

It had happened so often in her life. Every time it happened, she hurt as if it were the first time. She wondered if other fairies suffered from losing human friends. They had made a difference to her life, but she wasn't even a whisper in theirs. Sometimes she wondered if this was why there were so few fairies. Maybe her kin had died of heartbreak.

This was the last time she would let it happen. From now on, she would be distant with humans. She would watch them rather than befriend them. Solitude was safe.

⋯✦⋯

Mabel and Lil were comparing notes.

"What is it?" Kat slouched in, not quite awake.

"Someone's not happy we keep getting away," Mabel said.

"Someone writes an appalling hand," was Lil's contribution.

"It's pretty."

"It's copperplate, Kat, even appalling handwriting is prettier in copperplate than modern writing," said Mabel.

"Why are there two notes? Why not one for all of us? Or three: one for each of us?"

"They're not addressed. If you look," said Lil, "there are no names at all."

"We found them in the letterboxes."

Kat was curious. "Can I read?"

"Are you literate?" mocked Mabel.

"Only sometimes."

Mabel shoved both letters across the table.

"They just want to scare us," Kat said. "I mean, all they say is things like 'We're coming to get you' and 'We shot a man on the highway yesterday.' Why do they want to scare us?"

"Because they intend to kill us next time they manifest with the barguest?"

"Well, yes, but we kinda guessed that anyway. And this makes it pretty obvious that they're with the whispering children and that cat. But we coulda guessed that anyway too. Why do they want us to know for certain?"

"That's a very good question," Lil said slowly. The three passed the notes around in silence and read and re-read them.

"They think we've been doing all this on purpose," said Kat, suddenly.

"All what?"

Kat turned to Mabel. "Getting away."

"Ah," said Lil. "You're referring to the bit that says 'So you think you're clever.'"

"Yes. But why the notes?"

"Psychological warfare," said Lil. "They want to terrify us into making stupid errors."

"I don't feel scared," Mabel admitted. "How about you two?"

"I ought to," said Kat. "But those notes just make me laugh. It's so wrong. I ought to be squeaking with fear. Except . . . they can't spell."

"They're real now, though," said Mabel. "They can manifest and cause damage to the world now."

"And they know where we live."

"We ought to be terrified."

"They misread the situation," said Lil. "We've been on edge for so long that they can't push us further. We've already been in the position they want us, and now we've moved beyond that. It's a bad mistake on their part."

"What position did they want us in? I still don't quite get it." Kat's voice showed her frustration.

"They want us frozen with fear: unable to move."

Ann was on the phone for Kat. Both Kat and Lil were surprised and both of them were unsuccessful in hiding their surprise from the other. Thus they were exchanging conspiratorial grins when Kat said into the phone, dubiously, "Hello."

"Hi, Kat. I'm just checking up on you. Making sure you're okay."

"I'm fine, thanks."

"And those night fears?"

And those night fears?" It was as if a whole sequence of events in Kat's life hadn't happened. Kat gave a mental shrug and played along with Ann's game.

"Haven't had them since I moved into Lil's spare bedroom."

"Do you think you're long enough past them to talk about them?"

"I guess."

Kat and Ann arranged to meet in Garema Place, for coffee. They talked in a desultory fashion for a bit. It was as if they were feeling their way with each other; that they were on uncertain ground. Eventually, they found themselves talking about Kat's nights.

"We never did find out what caused them," Kat said. "We only found out what didn't."

"I was thinking." Ann was oddly hesitant. "I was wondering if you could tell me the sort of feeling you had."

Kat shuddered. It was not intentional. She started to speak, but Ann cut her off.

"No. Let's do this another way. One that makes you less uncomfortable. Let me tell you some things and you tell me which ones match your experience."

Kat nodded.

"You felt you were walking along streets that felt familiar, but you didn't know where you were?"

Kat shook her head.

"There was a voice, whispering. Or maybe more than one?"

"Just one. It was the drowning girl's voice. I just thought it was me. My unhappiness."

"I've heard that voice, too. It took me a while, to hear the single voice underneath the many."

"And then you remembered my dreams."

"Yes. I also remembered that I didn't like to press you too hard about them, because they made you so unhappy."

"It starts to make sense, you know."

"Yes," said Ann unhappily. "But I don't want to talk to the others about it. It's my life. I don't want them to interfere."

"Do you mind if I talk to someone?"

"Who?"

"Lil."

Ann thought for a long, long while. "OK. Talk to her."

Kat caught the bus back home and spent her time in diligent thought. It should have been about the night voices and that Ann shared them. It should have been the most amazing moment of breakthrough and the world's problems should have been solved. Kat solved some of her own problems on that bus ride, however, and that was equally important.

When she had told Lil about Ann's dreams, she found she couldn't stop talking. "I feel less impossible about the three of you being human and fallible. Or fallible, at any rate. Ann doesn't have to be perfect, because I'm not perfect."

"That's good," said Lil. "That's a good way of spending a bus ride."

"I did more, though," said Kat, triumphantly. "I'm going to ring the education people and find out about getting back into school."

"What prompted this?"

"Ann stopped learning. That's her big problem. Today I found out she faces her fears, just like you do. She doesn't do it directly and she's incredibly slow, but she gets there. She just has trouble learning and taking on new things and dealing with the big stuff from that direction. I want to learn how to learn."

"School may not teach you that," Lil felt impelled to warn.

"Oh, I know it doesn't. University might, but. And there's more. Other stuff. It fits with what you taught me." Kat couldn't seem to stop explaining. "Canberra is kinda a centre for Australia. Everyone hates it, but that doesn't make government go away or stop it from being a place lots of people visit and leave."

"I'm not sure that's it," said Lil.

"That's cool." Kat smiled. "It wasn't the most important bit of my theory, anyhow. It was just my lead-in. Do you want to hear the most important bit of my theory?"

"I'd love to."

"What I was thinking was that we don't have all the stories here. I mean, some stories and folktales are coming to life and others aren't."

"True. And interesting."

"What I see it as is some taking root on those deep cultural constructs you talk about and they grow if they have the right conditions. Somehow Canberra has the right conditions for the ones we keep seeing. And then there are others that stay buried because they've taken root, but the conditions are all wrong. And then there are some that didn't get to take root at all and have died away."

"I would agree with all that," Lil said.

"Yay! Now we can go and do the four musketeerettes thing."

"Very kind of you," Lil said graciously. "Although I wish you would find a better description than 'four musketeerettes'."

"Hey, it has style, don't knock it!"

The four musketeerettes thing was surprisingly easy and just a little dull. They found a place through the maps and their discussion and sent Ann in just ahead, to spot the whateveritwas. She walked gently and kept stopping and waiting and listening and looking. Eventually she beckoned them forward and pointed. Kat could see a girl walking nonchalantly down the centre of the street. They four fanned out, surrounded the girl and held her by her arms, firmly.

"It's not a young girl," said Kat, to whoever would listen. "It's older than any of us. And its skin feels funny." A glare from a pair of angry dark eyes was the only response.

"All together again," whispered Mabel to Lil. "Why doesn't this feel more like the Four Musketeers?"

"Give me my freedom," the old and wizened whateveritis demanded. "I am not she whom you seek."

Kat said, "She isn't, you know. Her voice is wrong."

"We have her, though," said Ann. "We can't just let her go."

Three of the four women didn't know what to do. The one thing they had not allowed for was catching the wrong creature. This had looked like a small girl and it was dark. It was old, however, and not evil. It was patently not evil. It was, however, angry.

"Give me my freedom. I have done nothing to hurt you."

Lil sighed and said, "Let me handle this." She stepped close in and looked the girl directly in the face. "I want a promise and three pieces of information and in return, I shall give you your freedom."

The creature eyed off Lil scornfully and laughed. "What can the likes of me give the likes of you?"

"Safety from retribution for us and ours from you and yours, plus three pieces of information."

"You know too much already."

"People have said that before. No doubt they will say it again. Right now, however, I need information that you possess. For I know who you are and I can name you."

"I can name you, too, and fat lot of good it does me."

Lil spoke softly, but so threateningly that Kat had to look to see if it was still her grandmother speaking. "I can name you and I can make that name stick. Where would you be without your shape changing? Where would you be if Death could see you clearly?"

"Dead," the creature said. "Fine. It's a bargain. Let's make it quick so I can get out of here."

"You promise all the safeties I require?"

"Only from me and mine. I can't promise for anyone else."

"For everyone here and for all they care for?"

"Yes, yes. Get on with it."

"Tell us the three things we most need to hear."

"Isn't that a bit broad?" asked Ann.

"Shush," said Mabel "Lil knows what she's doing."

"Fine then. First, you need to diminish the dark child. Do that and the voices and shadow will fade. Me, I'll be getting out of here, just in case you fail. Old birds, you know, and old cats, and old guivres — not worth a thing."

"Second is for you." She swivelled and stared at Ann. "Leave our world soon. It will hurt you if you stay. The others belong here. You do not and never will."

"And the third? Ah, the third. It's for you, my ancient friend. Your future is in your past: follow your heart."

"I have no future," said Lil. "I am dying."

"Your kind gets more stupid the older they become, I've always thought that." With no more ado, she was not there.

"Yoda she wasn't," said Kat. "She looked a bit like him, but."

"Can we trust her?" asked Mabel.

"Absolutely," said Lil, absently. Then she heard what she had just said. "That applies to me as well."

"Then we need to think," said Mabel. "Our problem is this dark girl. How do we diminish her?"

"I have no idea," said Lil.

Ann moved like a woman who knew everything. Her brown eyes and pink skin and her suppressed and pinned curls all pushed forward, as if she was going to bulldoze through all difficulties. It was not a friend standing at Lil's door: it was a force of nature.

"Come in," said Lil, mildly, and, "What can I do for you?" when they were comfortably seated at the kitchen table. Mabel was already there. She looked across at Ann and moved her chair a little closer to Lil's, protectively.

"I have something for you," said Ann. Her voice was as pushy as her body language had been at the door.

"How nice of you," said Lil, her voice sounding like an ancient piece of porcelain, so frail the light shone through and breathing would shatter it. A beauty that brought forth only tears.

"Lil," Ann warned, "you can't fool me that way."

"I'm sorry?"

"Sounding old."

Lil's voice became gentle, douce, as if she were talking to a small child. "I am old, Ann. In fact, I am dying. There is no simple solution to death when one is as old as I am."

"You have a few years left," Ann said, robustly. "And I can prove it."

Lil was very amused. "You have been talking to a doctor on my behalf."

"Don't be silly. I've been doing research. I found you this." Her declamation was spoiled by her not being able to find whatever it was in her handbag. Eventually she hauled out a little white paper bag and handed it across the table.

"Thank you," said Lil, gravely, and opened the bag. She pulled out a tiny figurine. "It's lovely," she said. "A tiny mermaid, if I mistake not. And old. Where did you find it?"

Ann was bewildered. "At the trash and treasure. There's a guy that sells —"

"Mostly erotic snuff bottles, as I understand it. Mabel was exploring them one day. I suddenly realise that Mabel's recent behaviour is not inconsistent with her earlier behaviour." Mabel spared her a glare, but was otherwise silent. "How odd that I had not considered this earlier. I am getting old, I think. Now, did you give me this very pretty figurine for any particular purpose?"

"Don't you feel different?" Ann's puzzlement burst out of her in a rush.

"Not at all,' answered Lil, calmly examining the figurine.

"The stories say that if you give a mermaid wife an image of herself, she becomes that image and she loses her age. She returns to her fairy state."

"That would have worked if I were a mermaid wife," said Lil, apparently calm. "But I'm not."

"You're not human. And I know there are scales involved. I know it!"

"What I am is none of your business. It is even less your business than a few weeks ago. No friend would put someone to that test. If I had been what you thought I was, you might have killed me."

"She meant well," said Mabel.

"And would good intentions have saved my life if I had been a sea creature, stranded in air? Dead is dead. Mind you, all you would have done is hasten the inevitable."

Ann gave a funny wail and fled.

Eleven

TALES OF MELUSINE #6

Melusine once had a close encounter with two books. They were bound in one volume, but they were two. They were called the final books of Moses and the rather mystical rabbi in the town she lived in claimed that they were holy, but she doubted it. They had a stink to them.

Once Melusine had come across the actual Sixth and Seventh books of Moses. She could not read them, but her mother could. They were her mother's most treasured possessions.

Each was a single scroll. Once her mother laid the Sixth Book on the table to introduce her properly. Melusine, age nine, started walking at the beginning of the scroll and walked ten paces to reach the end. Her mother showed her how it was made, with sewing and fine handwriting. Melusine could not yet read any language very well, so she simply admired the old Hebrew script and the neatness of the shapes it made.

When the sun shone on it, light reached out from the ancient manuscript and met the sunbeam. Melusine's mother smiled. "Let me roll this up," she said. "I want to show you something very special."

She took her daughter and the book outside and sat down with them under a beautiful mulberry tree. Sunlight stippled their skin and made Melusine wriggle in happiness.

"Now you have to be very quiet," her mother said. She carefully unrolled just the very beginning of the scroll and started reading aloud. Melusine couldn't understand what she was saying, but the words sounded lovely, because her mother's voice was dulcet and soft. As soon as the reading began, animals gently came up and lay down to listen. There was a hare and there were two doves and a deer. The cat and the dog — who never talked to each other in normal life — rested beside in other in perfect contentment. Another hare came and sat on Melusine's lap for petting.

The moment the scroll was closed, the animals went away. They made no fuss about it.

"What was it about?" Melusine asked.

"When you're older, dear, I'll teach you."

Melusine's mother was killed by a bigot, five years later. Melusine had only been half a column into learning the manuscript at that time and it disappeared. It became a treasured memory, like her mother. Something almost mythical. A sunbeam of happiness. A fragment of joy.

This other book, three hundred years later, was a bound codex, page upon page of crowded text. The Hebrew was badly written.

"This is not a holy book," Melusine said.

"I believe it is," said the rabbi. "I have tried burning it and it does not burn."

"I do not deny that it's magic. It's a bad book. I have read the first page and it promotes cruelty and unhappiness. I want none of it."

"I shall keep it, then."

"I cannot stay in the same town as the book."

"I admire you," said the rabbi, "for your learning and for your great ancestry, but I cannot give up this book. I am sorry."

"So am I," murmured Melusine, and moved on.

Melusine resolved to learn the arts of destroying such things. Evil should not be allowed to win, simply because of ignorance of combat.

Tales of Melusine — unnumbered (Text crossed out)

Melusine woke up in the middle of the night and longed for a man's arms around her, to comfort her. She longed for the sound of her daughter in the next room. She longed for the sound of her baby son, murdered by lilin. For years she had done this and for years her imagination had been enough. Tonight though, she found she could imagine nothing. She was alone in her bed. She got out of bed and made some hot chocolate, only to find she was alone in her kitchen as well.

Was it time to move on? Finally, was it time?

The calendar page was turned to July. They had entered the darkness of the year. The days were longer, but the nights were fouler. July in Canberra is the month of no hope.

The three women had a dinner party. They set a place for Ann and they invited Ann, but they really thought that she was unlikely to come. What they never said to each other was that they hoped that she would not come. For if she came, she was still entangled in business that would only hurt her. What the creature had said was true, and every one of the three women knew it.

It was not a comfortable evening. They held it in Mabel's front room, overlooking the street. It was a pot-luck dinner, for no-one had the heart for a formal affair. Kat insisted on serving, because both of her grandmothers looked as if a breath of air would blow them over. Everyone was twitchy.

Throughout the evening one woman or another would see things through the gaps in the front curtain. Mabel would get up every now and again and check on her woodpile creature, even though Lil reassured her that the protection now covered that whole area. The only thing settling in was fear.

Mabel was dogged. "We're going to put this together and we're going to deal with it."

"How do you eat an elephant?" asked Kat.

"Tell me. How do I eat an elephant?"

"One bite at a time."

"So what bite do we take first?" Lil asked.

"The cat? At least we know where it lives. I don't know how we deal with it, though. Or we could try the werewolf."

"Not the werewolf." Mabel shuddered. "The cat. The cat at the Chancellery."

"We don't know anything about it. We can't do anything unless we know what to do, and that requires knowledge of the creature. How about the children?" said Lil. "I think the children are small enough to deal with, now that Ann's not round to be sucked into their vortex."

"Vortex?" asked Kat.

"What did you say the other day, that I needed to learn science fiction and fantasy words to describe things so they made sense?"

"I really didn't mean vortex. It's good, but." She hastened to reassure the elderly lady. "Just unexpected."

"I take it we're officially undecided," said Mabel, scathingly.

"Maybe we need a good night's sleep," suggested Lil.

"We should have gone to your place. You're too tired to drive."

"Give me a cup of tea and I'll be able to manage." Lil smiled. This didn't deceive anyone. Lil never drank tea for comfort or restoration.

The next day, Kat dropped in to talk to Lil, who was still looking exhausted. She made them both coffee and they sat down to chat. "What are you thinking?" Kat asked.

"It saps and drains you," Lil said.

"Bloodsucking vampire." Kat's voice was full of gloom and gusto.

"Nothing like that. It just draws on energy, I suppose."

"If you knew it was here, why did you buy the place?"

"I liked it, I suppose." Lil waved her hands vaguely. "I didn't really know it was here. I guessed it, after a while. And I got rid of it. What you're seeing is old age."

Kat ignored the comment about age. "I thought you knew these things?"

"I know about these things. My actual abilities lie elsewhere. It's Mabel who can talk to ghosts when they don't manifest, and sometimes Ann. My abilities lie," and her hands fluttered again, "elsewhere."

"But you realised eventually, and you didn't ask them."

"I didn't. I was too tired."

"See, it sucked your blood."

"Neither my blood nor my breath, little one. Remind me to tell you of the Japanese vampire cat one time. This presence was not that."

"What is it then?"

"I don't know. Someone who loved and lingered, perhaps? A visitor, my friend calls them."

"You have a friend who is a ghost whisperer?"

"I doubt that she would call herself that." Lil smiled, but her voice sounded very French, very suddenly.

"Can you ask her to help?"

"Do we need help?" Lil's eyes bore down on Kat, forcing her to learn backwards, suddenly. Kat survived the gimlet gaze.

"We do. You do. You need to have more energy. Even if it's only your echoes that get fixed, or whatever. I don't think any of us see you properly or appreciate you. And big stuff is going down. You lot said so, last night. And besides, I need to know."

Lil sighed. "You want to know everything, ma p'tite."

"What's wrong with that?"

"Nothing. As long as you are willing to face consequences."

What consequences could there be to getting rid of the after-effect of death? Kat wondered, but said nothing. She nodded to herself as she heard Lil on the telephone a few minutes later, talking rapidly in French. She put the kettle on and by the time Lil came into the kitchen to say, "It is done. In three days' time my friend will see to it," Kat had a cup of coffee all ready for her third grandmother.

"The rewards of good behaviour?" Lil asked.

After a while she told Kat the truth. Again. This time, Kat heard what she was saying. "There is no life-sucker here. I protected myself against such things. All there is, is me, myself. I chose to age and it seems I have chosen to die."

"Can't you change your mind?"

"In theory, it is possible. At this moment, however, I lack the will. I linger because there are some pleasures in life: your company, Mabel, sunlight on my pillow. I am fading. I am dying. Not even you and Mabel and sunlight are enough to prevent that."

"Is it old age? Or is it an illness? Is there any fairy doctor?"

"Not really old age. Not really an illness. You have read my stories. Things went so far awry in the nineteenth century that I decided it was time. It has taken this long for my body to reach this stage, that is all."

"I don't want you to die."

"I would rather live and watch you grow. You are a great joy to me. But it is not enough."

"What would be enough?"

"What would cure me of age?"

"Yes." Kat stuck out her jaw, obdurately.

"Something special. Something uplifting. Something so very wonderful that it would force my transformation."

"Into someone young?"

"No, ma p'tite, into my other form. I am a melusine. When I fly, I gain back everything I have lost."

"When did you last fly?"

"Two hundred years ago." The room felt desolate. "You see it has taken me a long time to reach this stage. I should be accepting of it. I should welcome my death."

"I have no idea what we're doing." Kat declared this calmly, as if it was unimportant.

"My dear, none of us do."

"We're walking in hope," Mabel said, her chin a little lifted.

"Without Ann."

"But with the men," said Lil. "Your Sebastian as well as Mabel's Jackey-Jackey."

"Not that they're much use," Mabel added.

"You're in a mood."

"I don't like the Clarke Brothers. I don't want to do this. I want to be in my garden making the world beautiful."

"I want to be on the computer, playing games," said Kat

"Why aren't you?" Mabel was in a real mood.

"Because bloody Seb chucked me off."

"That would be why he is late," observed Lil.

"Yep," said Kat, with relish. "He's on my computer, playing games."

Lil's voice took on a slightly harsh undertone. "Seb," she said softly. Two minutes later he walked out the door. For once he was not nonchalant.

"Don't do that," he said, as if he had known Lil forever. "You know it leaves you drained."

"Don't play games on Kat's computer, then, when we have arranged to meet her."

Sebastian had the grace to look abashed.

Kat poked Mabel in the side. "Call him," she said.

Mabel sighed. "You're so uppity these days. He can't come."

"Why not?"

"We talked about this last night?"

"Was I there at the time? Because I don't remember talking about it at all."

"You were getting us drinks."

"So, what did you say to each other? Is it top secret? Did you wait till the room was a teen-free zone?"

"If Westwood is here," interrupted Sebastian, "then the Clarke Brothers will be more solid. He has to stay away."

"Pity," said Kat. "He's handy to have round."

"Thank you for that affirmation," said Mabel, acerbically.

"You know," Kat decided to say it, after all, "you sound exactly like Ann. I guess this means she's here in spirit." Mabel glared and Kat grinned back and Mabel's glare dissolved into a reluctant smile.

"Perhaps," Lil's voice was very small and had lost its customary purr, "perhaps we should leave this until we are in a better frame of mind." She kept looking sideways at Sebastian and rubbing her eyes. It looked to Kat very much as if she were trying to clear cobwebs from her sight.

"Nonsense." Mabel's voice got back its usual tone. "No time like the present."

"Kat?" Lil's voice held an appeal.

Kat didn't like to say it, but, "We're not going to have a really good chance at this anytime. No way to trick the Clarkes and we know they're monsters. What we need is State Troopers, not us."

"But we are all we have," said Sebastian.

"And that's why we should do it now. Because if we get any more scared, we won't be able to do it at all."

No-one answered immediately. Eventually, Mabel spoke up. "I forgot to tell you my message from Jack, didn't I?"

"What message?" Sebastian's voice held reproof. *He so likes to know everything*, thought Kat, *and tell everyone everything*.

"He's going to steal their guns."

"So they can't just fire at us once and kill us and then it's all over."

"That's about it."

"I like this better," said Kat. "I still think we're being idiots, but there's a chance we won't end up dead idiots."

Lil looked at her a long time and everyone else watched that look. In the end, she nodded. "I like the way you are growing up, ma p'tite."

"See," Kat said, "the day is redeemed. You think I'm growing up."

Lil sighed.

"Can we get on with this?" Kat's Sebastian was getting irritable and so they all moved.

They went to Weston Park. Not by the lake or near the willows. They settled themselves on the broad slopes of grass near the road, and waited.

"Come out, come out, wherever you are," called Mabel, quietly.

"Don't, Mabel. That's creepy."

"This whole thing's creepy."

"Should we go in a bit further, away from the road?" Sebastian wondered out loud, but it was obvious from his tone of voice there was no purpose in his wondering.

"I think we should go closer to the road, actually." Kat started thinking it through. "Close to our getaway vehicle."

They not only did this, they moved themselves to the entrance to the park and hoped that the coming and going from the main road wouldn't attract too much trouble. Far, far too soon, two horses were within sight. All eyes were fixed on them. All faces were white.

No-one could quite agree what happened next. There was shouting, for certain. Kat swore that Mabel was hit by one of the brothers and Mabel swore that Kat was. Sebastian hid an enormous bruise for weeks. But no-one could agree on what happened or what was said or how it happened. All they knew was that, at a certain stage, all of them had been grouped together by the Clarkes and their whips and those flickering bits of hide had pushed them back and back and back and back . . .

Until they found themselves on the main road. A bus came along, all orange and green. The friends saw the bus and scuttled to the other side of the road. The Clarkes had no idea what a bus was, and crossed that road, whips at the ready.

"Boys met bus, bus didn't see boys — oops, boys gone," was Kat's summary to Ann, later. And that was the most any of them could say.

Tales of Melusine #32

Melusine hated long voyages. She hated them with a vengeance. The only comfort of a ship was the water. She stared at it as if it could swallow up the travelling time.

Once, though, she had to take one. A cousin was caught up in the Civil War (another story entirely) and she had to get there. She had no-one to leave behind at that moment, so her time was her family's.

Reluctantly, she took a ship from Liverpool, which was and still is an English port. It was not through love of the English, but through greater trust of their capacity than that of any other country's to get her to the United States safely. There's another story in how she found that ship and how it made her revise her view of the English, but again, that's a story for another day.

In port at the same time as her ship was one called the Agincourt, a dangerous-looking battleship. Melusine hoped this was not an omen.

She didn't want to arrive in North America in an American port. She wanted to come close and then cross the border quietly: she knew too well the risks of war. Her plan was to take the ship to Montreal, where her accent would be less obvious, and then travel to her friend's aid.

The liner she boarded that first day of travel had two funnels and was called Canada. This is what Melusine claims. She can't be right, though, because the screw steamer Canada was wrecked in June 1857 just south of Quebec. Never trust the stories a fairy tells you.

I hope that her story about the voyage is just as unreliable as her memory of the ship she took. The day she told me this one I looked at the person sitting opposite me on the bus and I wondered, 'Would they have done this to the person sitting next to them?' Then 'Would they have done this to me?'

It all started off very innocuously. A group of people banded together for company on the voyage. Melusine didn't join them, but they were often near her and she paid attention to them. One always pays attention to humans.

One had a club foot. She was a nice girl. Pale skin with freckles, a cheeky smile, a sense of style in the way she wore her clothes (though the clothes themselves were rather ordinary) and a garrulous charm. There was intellect there, albeit untrained, and Melusine focused on the group initially because of Aline's caustic comments and her way with words.

It was her foot and lack of arm muscle that brought the group together. She was unable to carry her baggage and no-one was willing to help her for either a penny or a smile. Four people independently came back. Four people decided that this situation could not be borne. In the end they all took a corner of her trunk, men and women alike, and got it on board. This was what caught Melusine's attention properly.

Melusine gave Aline a hand with her other baggage, despite all her resolutions to stay adrift from humans, and Aline was unpacking when the ship sailed.

"I thought they had people to help with everything," Aline confided, "but it's a question of money, isn't it? I spent my inheritance on my passage and luggage, but I'm on board now, so it doesn't matter, and it won't matter until I reach the other side. This is my time. Without pain and without poverty. And without tips."

"What are you travelling for?"

"The usual." She shrugged. "New life. New country. It took the death of a near relative to find a fare. Montreal may need seamstresses, but if it doesn't then there's always America."

"Better than England?" Melusine asked.

"There's no happiness in England for the poor."

It's hard to hold a conversation after a line like that, so Melusine drifted off and watched the water. It was not her water, but it was beautiful for all that.

As the days passed she sometimes watched the water and sometimes watched the progress of the little group Aline had fallen into. A preacher and his wife were returning to America, but visiting cousins in Canada on the way. The wife was obviously happy to be travelling, but the preacher was nervous-footed and missing his work.

He set out to reform Aline. He would talk with her intently about religion and about duty and seemed quite disappointed she was a regular church goer. Melusine wondered at his attitude at first, because there is a wealth of worlds between an Englishwoman who attends church and a deeply religious soul, but the preacher was not of the Church of England and maybe didn't understand this. Also, Aline was educated, or at least enough educated to garner the preacher's respect.

Memory tugged at Melusine. She could never remember his name. Neither him nor his wife. All she could remember was that he was from the South and that his wife had insisted on a sabbatical to visit relatives.

His wife was a commanding woman. She was the one who had

determined that the trunk would be carried and that Aline was a respectable girl and should be included in their party. She was the one who had recruited another lonely woman (she called all women alone, lonely) to their midst. "Women must stand together against the perils of this world," she proclaimed, joyously.

The other woman had a name. She was large and a widow. A loud widow. A widow whose husband had owned a factory. One with not quite enough money to rejoice in her status; and not quite enough background to rejoice in her station; and no-where near enough money to rejoice in the Lord. The preacher should have been looking to her salvation, not to Aline's.

Jane (the name suddenly returned to Melusine's mind, along with the loud voice and a merry manner) was not in the business of being saved: she was in the business of command-ing attention.

She commanded attention by helping Aline. Aline's needs were first in her mind, she declared, and she forced the minister and his wife to attend to Aline's needs also. They weren't reluctant about it, once they had begun.

They attended to those needs so very thoroughly that Melusine would find Aline alone, late at night, staring at the ocean as if it were her saviour. "Don't look at it like that," she suggested, and Aline looked up, startled. "There's no solution there."

"I don't know if I can endure this until Montreal," the young girl admitted.

"Endure?"

"I am expected to think like them, worship with them, fetch their cups of tea and be their poor cousin."

"This is what you were escaping, in England?"

"I had escaped it. I had escaped it so far that I had no income. Maybe it's my life." Aline didn't sound confident about her statement, and for this, Melusine was glad. "Maybe I'm doomed to be everyone's shadow."

"You can say that. If you were truly anyone's shadow, you would have no voice."

"You've been there too." Aline's whisper held a wisp of wonder.

"Been there and come out the other end."

"How long did it take to come out the other end?"

"It took until the day I realised that it was my life, not theirs. It took until the day I packed my bags and walked away from them."

"It's not long until Quebec." Aline was trying to comfort herself. Melusine found she had run of out things to say. She quietly slipped a fresh daisy into Aline's pocket as the girl passed her. She would find it later. Maybe it would give some joy.

It did not. It gave Jane something to wonder about. Whether Aline had met a young man. Where she could have found it, a bright new daisy in the middle of the Atlantic. Jane made it sound as if Aline had reached into the ocean to pluck it. No-one believed she had found it in her pocket. Who could believe such a thing?

Not the minister and his wife. For them the world was full of predators and Aline was in danger from that daisy. It reminded them how alone she was and how vulnerable with her sweet voice and damaged leg.

Melusine came across Aline on deck late that night, staring at the ocean.

"They're talking about me," she said to Melusine, as if the two had been friends forever. This is only the fourth time we've spoken, Melusine realised. "They want to save me from the sewers of Montreal and New York. They think that I'm in danger."

"In danger?"

"They won't say more than that. When I argue, they shush me and tell me I'm fine. When I say that my soul is my business, the minister tells me that all souls are his. When I point out that my morals are perfectly respectable, they tell me of course, of course, who could think otherwise. Yet still they watch me and hound me and the only time I'm let be is late at night."

"Sleep is a great blessing, when it silences the stupid."

"It is," and Aline herself fell silent. Melusine remained with her a little while, companionably, then she slipped away. This time she didn't do the trick with the daisy. She didn't want Aline's soul to be endangered through a small and friendly act. She felt an unwonted anger at the three busybodies. The voyage will soon be over, she reassured herself. Very, very soon.

The next day she watched from a distance and what she saw worried her. The three older people loomed over Aline, then diminished her. Their voices boomed over Aline, also diminishing her. Aline's sense of style and of self were wilting, visibly. Melusine tried to bring herself to intervene, but she could not. Human business. She could not get caught up in human business when her cousin needed her. She had to remain free and unfettered.

When she saw Aline at dinner that night, silenced and small amidst the bustling busy souls, she wished that she were free. There must be something I can do, she thought. Something. Maybe tonight, something will come. A solution, simple and elegant. If not tonight, then tomorrow.

Late that night Aline was in her usual place, her eyes turned towards the ocean. She contained no energy in her anymore. She simply stood there. "They're taking charge of me when we land," she said, without turning her head. "They think I can find a simple job, not too taxing. I need no money, they say, just enough to keep the wolf from the door."

"And books?" Melusine prompted.

"Oh, I don't need books." Aline was bitter. "Apparently girls with no prospects also have no intelligence to speak of."

"You have prospects," Melusine said. "You told me so yourself. You can sew."

"Not if they don't let me." The two stood in silence. It was not a comfortable silence. Aline still did not turn her head. "If you don't mind," she said, "I think I would rather be alone."

The next day the ship was in a flurry. Aline could not be found. In the end, the captain determined that she must have fallen overboard. Her friends looked suitably shocked and sad and said the right prayers and took charge of her possessions.

Melusine watched. Melusine should have acted, but she had watched. Aline's last wish rested like a ghost on Melusine's shoulders.

Lil was leafing through an old copy of *The Strand Magazine*. Kat came in to start dinner preparations. "I was going through the cupboard," Lil said, "and I found these." A whole pile sat on the chair next to her. "Do I throw them out?"

"Did you buy them new?" Kat asked.

"Yes."

"Then keep them until you're ready to get rid of your past. Maybe. We ought to look at them first. Over coffee."

"That sounds like a very good idea," said Lil and they spent a happy half hour reading out snippets and showing each other the pictures.

"Perhaps I'll keep them," Lil said. "For a little."

"Can I borrow them, but? Just for a week."

"What do you want to do with them?"

"I want to read them and," the next words came out in a rush, "I want him next door to read them. He needs updating."

"You have been talking to him."

"For ages."

"He's safe, then."

"Not safe, but safe for me. He treats me like a daughter or a baby sister or something. Patronising sometimes, but nice."

"Should I meet him properly?"

"You met him. The other day."

"He was not fully corporeal. I could not see him."

Kat was surprised. "He says he's almost got things under control. I think he's scared of you, but."

"And you think he's safe for you?"

"If you didn't, you would have done something, ages ago."

"True. I have no idea what he is. That golden light is foreign to me and he hides beneath it, but I can't see any evil. So, yes, you may borrow the magazines."

"Cool! I'll give them to him now."

"Tomorrow, if you don't mind. We have dinner to prepare."

"Okay. What do you want me to do?"

What Lil wanted her to do was almost everything. She was tired and she wanted just a little strength to enjoy the dinner with. She gave instructions to Kat on how to make her favourite white bean dish with herbs and meat and eggplant.

"What meat is this?" asked Kat, dubiously.

"Young organic goat."

"Oh. Sounds like something Ann would enjoy."

"I know," said Lil, softly. "I thought it would remind us of her in a far better way than an empty place at the table. Besides, the beef didn't look as good."

Kat made a salad with romaine lettuce and fennel and then a rice dish with onion and pine nuts. The dessert Lil had already made. "It looks fabulous," said Kat, as she looked at the dish of quinces in the refrigerator. "But you shouldn't've."

"I didn't realise that until too late, I'm afraid. It's why I'm having you do everything else."

It was too late at night to be civilised. Lil knew she ought to be in bed, but her feet were restless. Kat had also been wired-up by the dinner party. She was watching a DVD as if her life depended on it. Lil pottered around gently. Kat's gaze was intense, as if the film was all about her.

"I went shopping with my stepfather the day before I left home," Kat said, without any warning. Her eyes were still fixed on the screen. "There was a school excursion and I needed stuff. I needed three things for home, and I really wanted some stickers to put on my diary."

She paused to let the dialogue filter through and the on-screen argument to fill the air. Her voice interrupted the drama. "I had so many things on my list and he was in a hurry. He was always in a hurry. He said, 'You can have one thing from the list. Everything else can wait.' I tried to tell him about the excursion. He didn't listen. One thing. I got the stickers." There was a profound silence. Kat had turned off the TV and turned her pale face to Lil. "I couldn't go on camp without half the things the teacher asked for. I took my rucksack and I ran away instead."

"You took the stickers with you?"

"Yes."

"You didn't want to run away."

"No, I didn't. But every time I went to school I was laughed at because I didn't have the things I was supposed to have. They called me names. I had to run."

"What did your parents say when you rang them?"

"They wanted me back. I didn't tell them where I was. I hung up."

"And now you've had time?"

"I keep remembering the stickers. I keep remembering not being listened to. I keep getting scared."

217

Twelve

Tales of Melusine #72 (perhaps, or perhaps not)

Sometimes stories start with loneliness. They can be the most interesting tales of all.

Once upon a time in Spain, Melusine had a friend who had the largest heart in the world. Alas, for Melusine, friends with such large hearts can be bad friends. Hilda had swept Melusine into her world and they had bonded as only women can bond. When Melusine had to leave, she wanted to say a proper fare-well. This was a woman with whom she would like to stay in touch, even if it had to be done by letter, to combat the ageing issue.

"Sorry, she's busy. Can't come," said the maid.

Melusine listened to the sounds of the house. Sometimes they helped to interpret why a servant was brusque. The inner courtyard echoed with the sounds of women's laughter.

Do I leave her a message? Melusine wondered. She shrugged. "Then I shall leave without seeing her," she told the maid. "Please convey my regrets that I was unable to say farewell." Melusine returned through the iron gates and found the street again. For a moment she leaned against the white wall of the house, feeling its warmth for the last time.

She never wrote. It was not safe to write, after all, in those times of trouble.

All Melusine could do was retreat into a tiny, tiny world and hope that the religious wars would pass soon. In that tiny, tiny world she became young again, as her kind will. Even as she looked at her unlined face in the mirror she wondered — for a hundred years she wondered — if her friend had ever missed her. Had their friendship been so much more to Melusine than to herself that Melusine could go without a farewell? Had Hilda secretly been scared of those religious differences? Or had her heart simply carried her onto her next friendship, leaving Melusine behind as debris? Or had the maid lied?

This is not a story. This is the ghost of a story. Melusine's friend is still a ghost of a friend. Melusine warms herself in the memory of that large heart from time to time, then shivers at the cold of being thrust away from the hearth without even a farewell.

Melusine needs to learn how to tell real stories. She has real stories in her past, too. Derring-do and bravery and feats of fear and courage. All she can find in her to write right now are the ghosts of tales and the ghosts of friends. For this is the time of the ghosts.

The woodpile was full of creatures. Mabel wanted to show them off. She carefully asked the young mother's permission and said, as a by the by, that she had finished with wood for the year and she was too tired to clean the driveway and the pile would just have to stay a while longer. She heard no protest and she hoped that was agreement, because the little creatures were cute as could be, and one of them had climbed into her hand that morning and she really wanted to show Jackey-Jackey.

Babbling like an idiot, she castigated herself, with a smile.

Jackey-Jackey was as taken with the babies as Mabel was. He took a pendant out of his waistcoat pocket. He gave it to the little mother, with a polite bow.

The woodpile creature looked at it, shook her head and handed it straight to Mabel. She then gave Mabel a meaningful nod.

So many nods and so little sense, thought Mabel. The pendant was a locket. Mabel opened it. The face was very, very familiar. Like Lil as a young woman.

"Have you looked at this locket?"

"It's just a trinket."

"You stole it?"

"No. No." Jackey-Jackey had to find words to explain. "I have a hoard because popular opinion says I do. I have no idea where it comes from."

"I think I know. Take a look at this. And hang onto it while I go get something."

She was back out in a very short time with a pretty necklace. "My daughter gave me this, years ago. It needs a good home." She gave it to Jackey-Jackey and took the locket back.

He carefully presented the new trinket to the new mother. This time she approved, and she went back to her place in the woodpile with the pretty around her neck.

"Can this be Lil?" Mabel asked. "It's a very old picture. Maybe it's her grandmother."

"Shall we ask her?"

"I think so."

"Let me just call my horse." He whistled and the horse came down the drive.

"I didn't realise you had a stockwhip as well as a normal whip," Mabel said, eyeing his equipment.

"Do you want a demonstration?"

"Do *you* want one? I can use a stockwhip perfectly effectively, you know."

"That's my girl."

"Jack?"

"Yes?"

"Do you think that a man and a woman, bearing stockwhips, could scare a werewolf?"

"Where is this werewolf?"

"Tharwa way."

"I bet I get there before you do!" and he faded.

They met next to the tall wire fence. Mabel arrived first, and cracked her six-foot whip, startling the horse.

"Damn you," the bushranger said, amiably, and tied the horse up a fair distance away. He unloaded his own whip and cracked it on his way to Mabel. He was showing off: his whip was twenty feet long and cracked as he whipped forward as well as when he whipped back. It was a bravura performance and Mabel clapped.

"Not here," Jackey-Jackey said, briefly, referring to the lack of werewolf. If he had been there, the noise would have brought him.

"Good," said Mabel. "Gives us time to get things together."

"Think he'll come?"

"Oh, he'll come all right." Mabel's voice was savage. "He left his mark on me. He'll feel me."

"Let's get enough space then," and they moved apart, both whips curled and at the ready.

Soon enough, the werewolf came a-loping, his jaw slightly dropped, grinning. "You again!" his voice rumbled cheerfully. "Got a taste for my life?"

"Not at all," Mabel replied, coldly. "I'm cured. Smell."

The wolf nose raised slightly to sniff the air. "Well, well," he said. "Seems as if I'd better do it all again. You and your boyfriend, too."

"Never knew wolves ate ghosts," said Jackey-Jackey, his tone full of mateship. His whip snaked out softly and hit the wolf on the flank. The wolf's head whipped back a little, following the line of hurt, and he snarled.

Mabel's whip then lashed out and flicked above the animal, cracking annoyingly. "Do you have a name?" she asked, her face calm and completely oblivious to the twist the wolf's head took as it snapped at the whip.

"Adam," he growled. "I'm Adam."

"If you said 'Madam, I'm Adam', that would be a palindrome," said Mabel.

"Mabel," warned Westwood, "that doesn't help."

"He bit me. He deserves bad jokes," and the whip flashed out again this time soft and targeted, forcing Adam to back up. A moment later and he had his back to the big wire fence. His hackles were up and he was snarling, all wolf and no man.

"Now we can talk," said Mabel, curling her whip up and having it ready.

"I don't want to talk," growled Adam.

"Then you want a taste of the whip," said Jackey-Jackey, and hit him hard on the muzzle. Adam whined and Mabel gave Jackey-Jackey a look. She did not like this aspect of her man.

"I'm going to get my friend to cure you, the way she cured me," Mabel said.

There was a moment's silence as the wolf changed into a man. It took less than a flicker of an eye. Naked, he leaned against the fence with no apparent embarrassment. He was a big man, brown, comfortable in his own skin.

"I don't want to be cured." Adam-the-werewolf was adamant. Mabel simply could not take him seriously. He was such a hefty bloke, and so direct, and so blokey. But he was Adam. And he wanted a female werewolf to breed with. Adam and Eve. The names had so much bad joke potential.

Fortunately Jackey-Jackey kept his mind on things. He always did. "We don't want you here," he said to Adam.

Mabel smiled. Then she put on her serious face. "Not on a farm, either, eating other people's livestock."

Adam was exasperated. "What am I supposed to do, then?"

"Become human?" suggested Mabel.

"Die?" suggested Jackey-Jackey. "It's not always the end of everything."

"That wasn't helpful," said Mabel, giving him one of her looks. Jackey-Jackey just smiled at her and she shook her head back. This annoyed Adam. Everything, it appeared, annoyed Adam.

"I know," he said. His voice had the wolfish growl again. "Why don't I buy my own bloody property and eat my own bloody sheep."

"That'd work," said Mabel.

"Sounds fair to me," said Jackey-Jackey.

"It's a deal," Adam said.

"I'll be checking up on you," Mabel warned.

"Oh yeah," Adam scoffed. "How're you going to do that?"

"Ever heard of the telephone?"

Adam laughed. "You'll be my parole officer."

"Me or one of my friends."

"You're going to teach them how to use that damn whip, too, aren't you?"

"You bet. Eat your own sheep and you can be a wolf whenever you like. The minute you get up to mischief —" and the whip lashed out . . . CRACK.

Tales of Melusine #582¼

Melusine was ignoring her own past for all she was worth. She did not want to think of the planes of her recent past, for instance. She shuddered at the thought of the creaky fights of the 1950s or the excited crowds that had clustered around the biplanes of a few years earlier. All she wanted was a giant cup of coffee and a place to sit and for the flight to be boarded and then over.

She felt old. She felt grey inside. She felt wilted and sad and her bones ached. There was no solace in the thought of her ancient homeland. There was no solace anywhere. All the beings the French once called fairies or fata or a thousand other things (mostly polite) reached a stage when they didn't want the world anymore. Melusine knew, deep within herself, that this was that time.

She would go gently into that good night. Raging against the dying of the light was for the young, and she had not been young for far too many years.

She looked as if she was just leaving middle age. As if she should see a doctor and be checked for the illnesses of incipient old age and lightness of bone. Without renewal, she would age gently and slowly and die. Not soon by fairy standards, but soon enough. She would have time to say goodbye.

Except she had already said all the farewells she was going to. That was what this plane flight was for. What remained of her life had already been sent, just as her house had already been bought. This was her last false birth certificate and her final false passport. No more running. No more magic. No more thrilling flights on the morning breeze. No more Melusine.

"I am already half gone," she said to herself. "I am a faded fairy."

Australia was a good place to finish fading. It was a good place to die. It was unfamiliar. She had visited, but never lived there. It held no ghosts. When she left, it would be peacefully.

Melusine held her airport coffee in both hands, treasuring the warmth. Realisation had chilled her. She was scared of her own ghosts. Of her pasts. Of any future. And there was nothing to be scared of. She remembered the poem that had lured her to Australia. The past was gone. It was safe. Her human cousins had murdered the original inhabitants and there were no ghosts. Not hers. Not anyone's. Terra Nullius. Vast. Old. Empty. Safe.

We are going, we are going, we are gone. Kath Walker said so and it felt true. An empty continent with the shell of civilisation. That's what everyone said about Australia. They thought of it as a promised land, but for her the promise was different. Safety and rest. Sleep and sweet dreams. Then gone forever. The world didn't need magic. Melusine didn't need the world. All would be well.

She boarded the last plane she would ever take. Sydney to Canberra. Then she would be done.

1967: the end of hope.

───※ ◆ ※───

"Why is all this happening? Look at the news and look at our hearts. We brought the fear with us, in our dreams, and now our fear has awakened them."

"We keep saying this," said Kat, "but it really doesn't help."

She and Lil were hunkered down over coffee, trying to keep misery at bay. It must be the caffeine, Kat thought, because we're getting sadder and more deep and meaningful by the minute.

"What are words that mean 'sadder' and 'more deep and meaningful' — ones that sound impressive?"

"Maudlin and philosophical?"

"That's good," Kat said. "That's us. Maudlin and philosophical."

Lil laughed. "The next step is for you to ask me if you can ask a question."

"I am that predictable." Kat mourned, making a funny face.

"Do you?"

"You know I do. I always do. That's because there are so many questions to ask, but, not because I'm boring."

Lil raised her hands in a warding gesture. "God forbid you should ever be boring! So, which question is it today?"

"It's a difficult one."

"In what way?"

"It's personal."

"I reserve the right not to answer it if I don't want to."

"That's fair." Kat smiled, gamely. She wanted to ask and she wanted an answer, but this one had haunted her so long she wasn't sure she could ask it. "What I want to know is why you wrote everything down. You know, your tales of Melusine. And when."

"That's a good question. I need to think about it for a moment." She paused and the two sipped at coffee to fill in the emptiness. "Death doesn't come quickly to one of my kind. I gave up on life over 150 years ago, and still I'm alive. It must be fifty years ago, that age started to show. I felt as if I was leaving middle age.

"So much of my life has been hidden. Almost all of it, in fact." She sighed. "Most of the time, I like it that way. There's a safety when one is invisible, after all, and invisible people can still have friends. But about fifty years ago I wanted to leave a legacy. I didn't know what I would do with it, just that I wanted to put a few of my tales in writing, so that the stories of my life would continue even after I was gone."

"I like that," said Kat, with a shy smile. "It's a good reason to write. Though it would be much better if you had decided to live, you know. Much, much better."

"I don't write now," Lil said sadly. Kat was all twisted inside. "I stopped a few years ago. My stories started off as stories. They were interesting. But as I walk more intimately with death I find I have lost the ability to tell stories. Look at my notes. The younger the tale is, the less it is a tale."

"But the numbering -" Kat said.

"The numbering is me playing with the mind of anyone who happens to chance across the tales. I didn't write them in that order. Some I have edited and some are just my thoughts. On the whole, though, the closer I get to the present, the less I can say."

"I don't want you to die."

"I don't want to die. I chose not to grow and change in 1843. When I did that, I chose not to let my body and mind repair itself. I am more human than fairy now. And very, very old. You know this — I have already said it. I don't want to die. I want to watch you grow. And I have left it too late."

"Have you?" Kat asked wistfully. "I mean, really?"

"I can't do anything. Oh, Kat, I have tried and tried. These last months I have done everything I can do to push myself into change. I can't."

"You can't. How about the man in the granny flat? He must be powerful."

"The one you call Sebastian? How far did you get with your talks?"

"Quite a way in some ways and not very far in others. He's only just worked out how to be here properly. He says that all of us will be able to see him, now, all the time, if we want. He said to wait if we wanted a cuppa. The stuff he did with us as a group really took it out of him. He says it's not becoming corporeal — he says the problem is of his own making and he'd rather not talk about it. What this means is we get to talk about life in the twenty-first century in general and I get to show him things and explain him things. He was going to solve everything, but he can't until he is here. He says he's close. When I knock it's to warn him to make himself solid. Now there's almost no time between me knocking and him telling me to come in."

"You believe him."

Kat thought. "Yeah. I do. Actually. Because it hurts him when he comes and goes. He's not doing it on purpose. His skin is kinda pale when he has just got his body back. But I do think he's almost got it sorted. He's not just claiming it. Though he is starting to get really solid, more of the time. He says something a bit like you — he needs an emotional pull. But he knows stuff. I bet he can help more."

"Shall we ask his advice about the life-stealer first? And the children?"

"I want you to live." Kat's jaw showed her stubbornness.

"Cherie, I'm not certain it's possible at this stage."

"I wish you could find out if it was."

Lil looked thoughtful. "Maybe I can. Just perhaps. Let me try an old test."

"Old test?"

"It's called the flourishing staff. If I plant it and it flowers, then there's hope for me."

"Why haven't you tried it before?"

"I didn't want hope before."

"Do we get some wood from Mabel?"

"I have something special. Wait here."

She emerged five minutes later looking flustered. "I am sorry it took me so long. It was buried." She was carrying an old walking stick.

Kat refrained from saying that Lil should have asked for help. It was enough that Lil was doing this whateveritwas.

They went outside. Lil stuck the stick in the ground.

"What next?"

"We watch. If anything is going to happen, it should happen soon."

They watched. They stood there and watched a piece of wood stand upright in a bed of lobelias. Nothing. Just being a piece of wood.

Kat went closer. "Come and look!" she cried.

Lil went closer. "It's budding!"

And it was. Ten minutes later the staff was showing a green layer all over and ten minutes after that, it bore many small white flowers.

"Daphne," Lil said. "I love the scent of daphne." She filled her lungs with the fragrance, then stepped back to let Kat near. "Well," she said, with a big smile, "it does look as if I need to meet your Sebastian again. Meet him properly. We shall ask him for help with the breath-stealing first, remember that, Kat."

"Yeah, yeah," said Kat impatiently. She was going to make sure Lil

GILLIAN POLACK

lived, somehow. She wanted it to happen quickly, though. All this waiting was idiotic. Kat knocked on the door of the granny flat.

"Come in," the man's voice said.

"Are you decent?"

"I am solid and clothed, will that do?" He opened the door and his eyes sparkled down at her.

"I need to tell you a story," Kat said.

"Then come in and sit down."

At the end of the tale he looked unexpectedly happy. "I think I should see your Lil soon," he said. "I was wondering, you know."

"Now would be nice. If you're sure you're stable."

"Indeed. Shall we go?" He offered her his arm and they walked to the back door in fine style.

Kat let them in through the laundry door and called out, "Lil."

"I'm in the kitchen."

They went through to that pleasant room. Kat wondered a bit, herself. Her companion seemed very nervous. Maybe he was scared of Lil? Maybe that was why he had refused to meet her earlier? He had helped, but he had never actually stopped and talked to Lil. He'd carried her as if she were precious, but avoided her after that. It was odd, now Kat reflected on it.

When Sebastian saw Lil this time, he stopped dead in his tracks. Kat heard him draw a deep breath. "I kept thinking it wasn't you, but it is. I kept seeing you everywhere. But it is you. Kat said so."

Lil looked up inquiringly. Her eyes narrowed. She looked at him more closely.

Kat had to step back as Lil ran right up to Sebastian and started beating him with small fists. He just stood there and took it. After a moment, she burst into tears, and that was when he enfolded her in his arms and held her as if she were infinitely dear to him.

Kat felt bad, watching. She knew who he was, though. She couldn't breathe, she was so awed. This was the fairy sailor who had disappeared between realities, all those years ago.

Finally, Lil was out of anger and out of tears. That is when he spoke. "When did you let yourself get old? Mind you, you make a charming and delicate old lady."

"Thank you so much," she said, backing to a safe distance. "For saying that. And for walking out and leaving me pregnant."

"Pregnant?"

"He didn't walk out," said Kat, quickly. "He got lost."

"I knew that," said Lil, sadly. "It didn't leave me less alone." She burst into tears again and, walking quickly, wrapped her arms around him and held him tight. They looked like mother and grandson. It was so sad. *No, it's tragic.* Kat blinked to clear her tears.

Kat wondered if she should let them have some time alone. She wondered if she should say something. She wanted to ask so many questions.

He spoke, though, and asked the most important one. "Pregnant?" he asked softly and gently.

"Twins. A boy and a girl. The boy died young." She paused a moment to recall him and his loss. "And the girl grew up just fine."

"What happened to her?"

"She threw me out. Said she wanted nothing of magic. Not then. Not ever. She told me never to see her or her children again."

"When was this?"

"Eighteen forty-three. It was the worst year of my life."

"I did wonder why Kat reminded me of you."

"*That's* why you were nice to me," Kat said.

"How could I be anything but nice to someone who reminded me of the most beautiful woman in the universe?"

"You haven't changed," Lil said, and moved away from him again. She took the four steps to bring her to Kat's side. Looking deeply into Kat's face, she then said, "Why didn't I see this?"

"See what? You're being all confusing again," said Kat.

"I'm not your grandmother," Lil said, but her sentence was finished for her.

"Great-grandmother, as I reckon it," her man said.

"Not quite. Great-great-grandmother. And you would be her great-great-grandfather. It's no chance that brought you to Canberra, ma p'tite."

"Oh my God! Can I faint or something?" Kat decided not to take them seriously.

"You wanted more fire power," said Lil, with a broad smile. "Let's go inside and use it."

"Can't you do the romantic reunion thing first?"

"It's too late," said Lil. "Nothing has changed in this body I inhabit. I'm still dying."

"Oh," Kat's voice became very small and full of tears. She had thought . . . had thought . . .

"One thing at a time, my dear," said the man. "Let us take a look at the papers Kat told me of."

Kat brought out all the papers. While she was doing that, Lil and her man stood there and looked at each other. *Why can't they be more romantic?* Kat wondered. *An impassioned kiss or two?* She knew why not. It didn't matter how often Lil said it, Kat didn't want to admit that Lil was dying. It maybe also mattered that she looked so old and felt so old and that for her true love, no time had passed. He had told her so himself. "It was either no time at all, or it was eternity. I measure how close I am to being able to remain forever in our reality by how much sense of time I get when the mist takes me."

Yep. Still standing there, staring. Kat pulled herself together. She turned practical. First she spread everything out on the kitchen table, then she put on a pot of coffee. "I hate to break you two up, but I can't think of anything else to do," said Kat. Guiltily.

They came to the table and sat each near a corner. They kept looking. Kat betted they were holding hands under the table.

All three were completely silent as they pored over different pieces of paper.

"I need a name for you," said Kat, breaking the silence. "A real one. Not the one I called you because you sounded funny."

"Names are dangerous," murmured the man.

"She means a use-name," said Lil. "If you don't choose, I shall choose one for you."

"Go ahead, then." There was challenge in his eyes.

"Sebastian," said Kat.

"Why Sebastian? Last time it was because I sounded funny — why this time?"

"I gate crashed a picnic of a writing class and they told me that they used Sebastian when they couldn't think up a name. That's the real reason I called you it, anyhow."

"That's an appalling reason," said Sebastian.

"You should've thought up your own name, then," Kat retorted. "It's too late now."

"Now that I am Sebastian, can someone tell me about this map?"

"It's Canberra, and Lil drew all over it." Kat was being very helpful.

"Lil? You know, I hate calling you Lil."

"It's what I'm known as here, *Sebastian.*"

"Suffer big time," said Kat, with relish.

"I can see some of you in her," Lil informed Sebastian.

"So can I," and he sighed. "The map . . . Lil."

Lil gave her wonderful laugh and Sebastian looked as if all was right with the world. "It's based loosely on what you taught me, and also what I know from my own studies. I've imposed a Ptolemaic cosmological system on . . ."

"Ah," Sebastian interrupted. "So the circles are the spheres. Whose system did you use?"

"Mostly Paracelsus. It's the one that conforms to the mixed views here with least adaptation."

"Fine," Sebastian said. "That should work. Let's see what it produces." He bowed his head and looked at the circles emanating from Commonwealth Bridge. "A compass," he said and snapped his fingers.

"That is not a compass, my love," said Lil. "That is a map."

"No, I want . . . oh damn . . . can someone please find me a compass."

Lil nodded to Kat. "It's in the top drawer in the study. Make him ask. Every time. He thinks he owns the world, otherwise." Sebastian grinned and looked like a chubby-cheeked boy, caught out in mischief.

"What's a compass? Tell me what to look for." When the two adults looked at her in horror, she grinned and said, "Just kidding."

Soon Sebastian was bent over the map like an antique geographer, drawing more circles, drawing lines, muttering and murmuring. "Paper," he said. "Need more paper." Then he looked up at Lil and added, "Please."

Kat got him the paper and poured everyone coffee. She had completely forgotten about the coffee. It was very stewed. No-one noticed. Lil was happy looking at Sebastian and Kat was content watching them both. It was so very funny, and yes, it was romantic, in a sad way.

"Dark of moon," said Sebastian, out of nowhere. "Cold/wet transition — that's how that happened." And he rummaged through Kat's notes about incidents and scribbled something against one. "You didn't calculate the correspondences," he accused Lil.

"I did, but I lost the paper. They didn't seem to do anything," she said mildly, "so I didn't recalculate."

"They're key," he informed her. He wrote letters on one of the secondary maps.

"What're those letters?" Kat asked.

"Correspondences."

"Yes," Kat prompted. "And what are . . ."

"Too complicated."

"You like it when you know more than everyone else," she accused.

"He always has," said Lil, fondly.

"Except you, you're allowed to know," said Sebastian.

"Thank you so much for that honour," said Lil.

"Because otherwise you would leave me."

"Even old, you want me round?"

"You were old when we met —"

"Correspondences," said Kat. "Before she strangles you."

"Things that belong together," said Lil. "Correlations of various sorts. The simplest are wet with children corresponding with the season of spring with the moon in its first quarter. Where different parts of the natural order have affinities and can influence each other in quite specific ways."

"Do the children match with water?" asked Kat.

Sebastian held up his hand. "That's just what I'm checking."

"Not only water," he said triumphantly, "but they are at their strongest in the first quarter."

"What about spring?"

Lil looked around, as if trying to remember something. "That's when they started to whisper, I think. I can't quite recall."

"We don't have dated notes for it," said Kat, regretfully. "Are there any other correspondences that are really important? I mean, have you found any?"

"Yes, I think so," said Sebastian, stretching. "It's winter now. Old age, cold and water. Things will be at their most dangerous when the moon is in its fourth quarter."

"And the children will deal well with winter, won't they?"

"Yes. I need to do more calculations."

"But we know stuff."

"You know the simple explanation of a small part of what your grandmother and I have been doing. I need to think some more."

"Can we beat them?"

"Only if we don't let them come to terror time."

"What on earth is terror time?"

"It's the unmarked time between years," said Lil.

"So we have until 31 December?"

"No," said Sebastian. "This map shows an imposed reality. It's not the influence of the real sun we need to worry about, but the cycles that the children have imposed on this region."

"So they came during our year, but they now have their own?"

"Precisely." Sebastian smiled as if at a good pupil. Around him was a haze. He frowned and focused and became solid again.

"So you're going to calculate the best time to fight them, just like Feng Shui."

"I don't know that term, but yes, I am going to calculate time and place and see what will work against them. Can I use this table?" Sebastian addressed Lil.

"Of course," Lil said. Kat felt that Lil would agree to anything Sebastian asked, as long as it kept him in the house.

After two hours of numbers and lines and circles and much scribbling, Sebastian emerged from his thought-cloud. He said, "I don't know all the monsters and some of your reckoning is different to mine, but if your society has had them and brought them then they would create . . ."

"A palimpsest world," said Lil.

"Yes."

"Please explain," demanded Kat.

"Careful, youngster, I can hurt you if you become obstreperous."

"Huh," said Kat. "You won't. You can't. You tried and failed. Besides, you're related to me. You'll explain palimpsest and how it all works."

"Bossy, isn't she?"

"She gets it from you," Lil informed him.

"So what do we do?" demanded Kat. "I mean, is there anything we can do that's simple."

"Take the fertiliser out of the field," said Sebastian.

"You can't do that. Once a field has crap in, it will always have crap in."

"Not if the field is the human mind."

Lil said wearily, "Sebastian, just explain."

"People here have created a fertile field for all of these changes. Through their fears, through their hates, through their distrust."

"So we have to change all of Canberra? That sounds very big."

"No," said Lil. "I think he's saying that we have to find our own fears and deal with them."

"The only ones of us who have had problems with streets and whispers are Ann and me. Ann's running away."

"That leaves you."

"Couldn't you just have said that?" she said to Sebastian. "I've already been thinking about my stuff."

"And?" Sebastian prompted.

"I'll ring my Mum right now, if you like." She wouldn't talk to her father, but she'd face him, when she was ready. She'd already worked out that she couldn't just run. Ann taught her.

Kat made the phone call. She and her mother talked for two hours and came to an understanding. When she came back to the other two, she found them deep in conversation. They didn't even see her. She smiled to herself and backed out of the room very softly.

The next morning she woke up very early. She had dreamed of her childhood all night. It was as if a memory stream had been unblocked. She lay in bed for a while, just thinking things through. Kat felt more at peace inside herself than she ever had. She wasn't ready to go home yet, but she was ready to belong to her family again. The words she treasured most of all were the ones she had wanted to hear for the longest time: 'I love you.' She had also heard 'I missed you,' 'I'm glad you're well,' and 'You've already rung a school — that's wonderful.' It was as if she had fallen into a dream family.

She knew it was just the wonder of her having rung twice. She knew that the gloss would fade. But she'd learned a lot recently, and she knew that even if things weren't going to be perfect, her mother had been telling the truth about loving her and missing her and being worried about her.

When she finally emerged, tousled, and entered the kitchen, she found Sebastian at the table and Lil making coffee. Lil looked younger, she was sure of it. She was also pretty sure Sebastian had spent the night.

Kat wanted to say 'ew' and 'yuck' but Mabel had been really angry when she did and her inner feelings weren't right, anyhow. They loved each other, after all. And maybe if Lil kept on looking younger, it wouldn't be so yuck. And it was really, really nice that her hand had lost that faint shake. Kat decided to be all grown up and just went to the cupboard and got out her cereal.

"Morning all," she said.

"Good morning, Kat," answered Lil. "Did you sleep well?"

"Not really," Kat said cheerfully. She loved the guilty look the two gave each other. "I had strange dreams the whole way. They were good dreams, but. They sorted me out."

"That's good," said Sebastian. "We've solved a problem, too."

"I bet," said Kat.

Sebastian looked shocked and Lil just had to laugh. "You will just have to become used to the twenty-first century," she scolded Sebastian.

"Some things are more difficult than others," Sebastian replied. "The knowingness of young ladies is one of them."

"I bet kids my age were just as knowing back then. I bet they just hid it from you."

"That's exactly right," agreed Lil. "They did."

"So what was the thing you sorted out, if it wasn't embarrassment-making."

"It was, perhaps, a little embarrassment-making," said Lil, calmly, while Sebastian turned bright red. "In the process, however, we managed to make Sebastian's transition to this reality full and complete."

"No more stupid golden mist?"

"No more stupid golden mist."

"Then we're getting there. That's us protected way more against the streets and the whispers and the dark child since yesterday."

"Did you say dark child?" asked Sebastian.

"Yes," Kat said, dubiously. "That what we got told. Dark child."

"I didn't see that in the notes. I need to think about it."

"Anyway, there is one more gap sealed," said Lil, pragmatically. "I hope you don't mind it."

"As long as you are around, I think I can manage."

"That might be a problem."

"Where there is a problem, there is a solution."

"You never change." She kissed him.

After breakfast, Sebastian and Kat went back to the papers, while Lil got on the phone to Mabel to update her. She took the phone to her bedroom. Kat would have loved to hear what they said to each other.

"Can you show me the difference between things that were happening before the changes and things after?" Sebastian asked.

"I thought you'd already sorted all that out."

He shook his head. "All I sorted out yesterday were the details of the framework — basically I refined Be . . . Lil's drafting. Now I need to see how it all fits. For that I need a sense of what changes have happened."

"I've got some notes on that."

"Directly on that?" Sebastian was curious.

"No. Just ghost stories dated a couple of years ago."

"Very nice." Sebastian approved. Kat found she had to smile at him.

Kat found him the story of someone who drove past Lake George and saw someone standing by the road. When the driver turned again to look, the bloke wasn't there. He had seen a picture in the paper, afterwards, showing that he had been killed in a car accident on that very spot.

"I do not understand everything modern yet," Sebastian worried. "This car — it had horses?"

"Mechanical," said Lil, coming to sit down. "You've surely seen mine. I park it just next to the granny flat."

"That vehicle is a car?"

"Yes."

"Good. Ghosts from accidents fit very well into an ordinary pattern of events in the city."

"All too well," Lil said. "I would rather we had fewer of those ordinary ghosts."

"I have a story of a car on fire," Kat said. "Is that less icky?"

"A ghost car?" Lil was intrigued.

"Yep. On the road from Uriarra Crossing. I have heaps of sightings for it. Apparently people call the cops all the time to report it, but it isn't really there. I've got some really good detail on this one." Kat enthusiastically rummaged through the papers on the table. "It was a 1976 electric blue Toyota Celica."

"That's ordinary, too? Good. Someone must have been killed and the memory plays and replays. Now," said Sebastian, "find me something that is borderline."

"I have one," said Lil, unexpectedly. "A water maiden story started doing the rounds a few months ago. I'm afraid I tried to suppress it."

"Why? What was it about?" Kat couldn't suppress her excitement. She was trying to imagine Lil trying to hide a story. Lil was all about stories. Mind you, she was also about hiding them.

"Several people have seen water maidens. Young girls near the water, moaning and wailing."

"Like my girl who was drowning?"

"Like that, but not as terrifying. Someone told me that they decided to have a picnic by Lake Burley Griffin. The wind was bad that day. It had a particular sound to it, almost like a human voice. A girl came by and she heard the wind wailing and she said, 'My sister Melusine cries for her children.' Then she put on a cloak of feathers and flew away."

"These people saw the girl themselves?" Sebastian sounded suspicious.

"It was a friend of a friend."

"Then my guess is that they have changed a real experience into a folk tale."

"And you have a super-duper conclusion," said Kat.

"I have, but it's something you already know."

"All that work." Lil shook her head in mock despair.

"Will help us find a way to send her home. It's impossible to drive her out." His tone was sombre.

"Her who?" asked Kat. "And we tried driving her out and it didn't work."

"The dark child. If you've tried one thing then all that remains is persuasion. The whole city is lost, if she does not leave."

"You make her sound very bad indeed," Lil said sombrely.

"She is. She should never have come here. The longer she is in this city, the more imperilled the place becomes. She is a child like no other."

"The dark child," repeated Kat.

Thirteen

EVERYONE KNOCKED COURTEOUSLY ON Lil's door. It was something about the lady. The doorbell was ignored. Always.

This knock was insistent.

Kat opened it. She didn't waste time with pleasantries. "You could've walked straight through and saved me the trouble," she said to the bushranger on the far side.

"And you could grow up," he retorted.

"Come in," called Lil from the lounge room, and Kat stood aside. He walked in and behind him was Mabel. Mabel gave her just-because you-don't-like-him-doesn't-mean-you-should-be-rude look, but Kat just grinned.

Jackey-Jackey didn't sit down, even when he was invited. "I have something of yours," he said, "and I want to get this over with."

Kat realised that he didn't know how to be polite. Or he didn't know how to treat Lil. He was so chummy with Mabel that she thought he was one of those blokes who got on with everyone. But he was hopping from foot to foot as if . . . as if he had been called to the Principal's office. He held out a brown cloth bag. Lil immediately came over and he gave it to her, as if relinquishing a burden. "I didn't mean to steal them, honest," he said.

Mabel said, "He's a bushranger, it just came natural." He gave her a very exasperated look. "Well, you apologised for taking them and you know they just sort of appeared. You didn't mean to do it and you still had to say sorry. I think it's funny."

So did Kat. She bit the inside of her mouth until it hurt, just to avoid another of Mabel's looks.

"You don't understand," said Westwood, stiffly. "There are those in the half-realms who you do not take from, not even by accident."

"Because they're terrifying."

"Because they are special."

"You would've stolen from her when she was alive, I bet," said Kat, cheerfully.

"When I was alive I couldn't see as far," said William Westwood, much deceased.

Lil interrupted gently, having looked inside the bag. "Jackey-Jackey?'

"Yes, ma'am?"

"Why this and why now?"

"I feel . . ." He stopped, searching for words. "I feel as if it cannot wait much longer. That I am trespassing on mortal ground and that the time is nearly gone for such trespasses."

"I thought so." Lil sounded smug. "You feel as if a gate is closing."

"Yes."

"Sebastian and I were discussing this. It may close very quickly, or it may close slowly, but he thinks we have dismantled some of the props that kept it open."

"So if we remove the chocks, the door will shut." Mabel's tone was mixed.

"For good and for ill . . ."

"Yes, Kat, for all of us and with all kinds of results."

"If Jack has to leave, what about Seb?" Mabel was fierce.

"Sebastian is of this world. He thinks it is chance that he found the door open and came back, but he belongs here."

"He even has descendants," Kat pointed out. "It's not fair, but."

"Life isn't fair," said Mabel. "Lil, put your baubles away and let's go find Ann so we can start this thing."

"I shall say farewell before I leave," Jackey-Jackey promised.

"You'd better," said fierce Mabel. "And it better be a bloody good farewell, too."

Mabel was angry at the universe. She was going to lose her lover and her best friend was dying and everything was going wrong. She had very little tolerance for things that kept going wrong. She couldn't tackle Lil's frailty and she couldn't talk Jackey-Jackey into staying, but she could fix other things. She could also permit herself the luxury of real anger.

The other thing she decided to fix was Ann. What she wanted to do with Ann was give her a piece of her mind. What she actually did was find out about Ann's shadow.

She borrowed Kat's papers and sorted through them. She didn't say she was looking for Ann's shadow. How she explained herself was, "Bugger off. I've got a lifetime's worth of arcane knowledge, and I'm using it. Go play with your own secrets."

Kat wanted to say that she didn't have any secrets, not any more. Mabel wasn't going to budge, though, so Kat left her computer and all her papers in her friend's hands and went window shopping.

After a while, Mabel left Kat's possessions to their own devices. Kat swore when she discovered the mess Mabel had made of her computer files. Mabel had managed to delete a whole bunch of them. Kat went into retrieval mode and didn't even notice that Mabel had gone somewhere, by herself.

Lil didn't notice, either. Lil was too ill to notice. The youthfulness Kat had noticed had only been a flourish: Lil was very frail. Seb was sitting by her, making a fuss of her, trying to persuade her that she really should not be giving up on life, not now that he was back. Even his abundant ego was struggling with the task.

Mabel picked up Ann on her way out. Ann was given no choice. "Into the car. Now," was how her friend phrased it.

"Where are we going?" asked Ann.

"We're getting your shadow back."

"I thought I had my shadow back?" Ann was confused.

"False shadow. Dragging you into foulness. Cause of half of our troubles, that one is. We're sorting you out and getting rid of it at the same time."

"Oh good," said Ann, vaguely.

Mabel drove them to the place where they had given a spirit a cardigan.

"Why here?"

"We were misled," said Mabel, grimly.

The moment their feet touched the ground, a familiar voice started up. "Give me my blue cardigan," it said, over and over again. "Giiive me my blue cardigan." It was plaintive and it hurt their ears.

"Don't start," Mabel warned the voice, and the shadow of a girl appeared, about six steps away. "We gave it to you before. It wasn't your cardigan and that shadow you're hiding in is someone else's."

The spirit laughed. It was an echoing, mocking, hollow laugh. "The dark child told me to do it," she said.

"The dark child can bugger off," said Mabel. "And so can you. The minute you've swapped shadows with young Ann here."

"Make me," the shadow girls' voice taunted.

"You really want me to?" asked Mabel. "You really want me to call on the four quarters of the wind and on the twelve signs and maybe even on the summer goddess? I can, you know."

There was a stillness.

Ann gave a startled cry. Her false shadow was ripping itself from her. Soundlessly, jaggedly. It crept and crawled slowly towards the spirit. "Creepy," said Ann.

"Shush," said Mabel.

Both of them watched as the shadow slipped up to the spirit. When it reached her, another shadow flitted away. There was no ripping this time. No creeping and crawling. Ann's shadow danced back to Ann and attached itself as if it had never been gone.

"Now bugger off," said Mabel to the spirit. "I don't want to see you in Canberra again. If you hurry, maybe the dark child won't know what you've done."

"If I hurry, she won't catch me at all." The girl's voice laughed. And the shadow-spirit was gone, leaving only sunlight.

Ann stood still. Far too still.

"You're in shock," Mabel said. "We need to get some tea into you."

As she drove back she talked non-stop. Ann's mental state prevented her from seeing that it was from fear, and there was no-one else to notice.

"That dark child was the whispers. It can't be anything else. That's why you kept being drawn into them. There was a plot against you, because they had your shadow. Didn't matter how clever you were, they had your shadow. Nothing to be ashamed of in that. Just as well we moved now, though. You would've been dragged in eventually. Sooner, maybe. That world of hushed shadows. Don't like that thought at all. Better you're here, even if it's difficult for a bit. Now let's get you that tea. Very strong. Lots of sugar. Some biscuits. You'll be right as rain."

Ann wasn't right as rain, but she was well enough to face down the others with Mabel and listen to the scolding they were both given. She still didn't react. It was as if something deep inside her had paused for reflection.

When Lil asked her what she was thinking, she said, "Of moving on. Of leaving Canberra. I have a shadow and no husband and no job. I can go anywhere. Rural Tassie near my daughter, or Melbourne with my son. Anywhere I like." Then she was silent again.

Everyone spoke over her and around her. It was as if she was already gone.

They were planning to take on the dark child.

Fourteen

"IT'S SIMPLE." SEBASTIAN WAS in his element. "Ann and Kat and Lil are the most vulnerable to the cat and the dark child, so they will serve as a focus. They draw their attention and I use Mabel as a conduit to take their energy and put it on Mr Westwood here. He fades forever and takes them with him."

Mabel had a look on her face Kat had never seen before. She looked as if all the goodness of the world has fading. She looked her age.

Before they could do this (and Kat really couldn't see how it would be accomplished — Sebastian used lots of words and big promises but didn't make things real, as far as she could see) there was the problem of the vampire cat.

"Mine," said Kat.

"Just because your name is Kat doesn't mean you get to deal with it." Mabel was obdurate.

"It's not that. It tried to eat me. Besides," and she paused for effect, "I bet I know its weakness."

"Okay," said Ann. "Tell us." Her arms were folded in front of her, protecting her from anything Kat could say.

"It doesn't want just anyone. It wants special beings. It wants to eat something of us."

"You are suggesting we act as a lure for it?"

"No," said Kat. "I'm suggesting we make a fake person and it tries to eat it and it starves."

"We can do better than that," said Lil. "We can feed it Ann's old false shadow."

"But the shadow girl is gone."

"No, she's still here. I can feel her," and Lil laid her right arm on her left shoulder, as if the girl was touching her there. "She's a ghost and more hollow than a ghost. It will work."

"I thought we'd got rid of her." Mabel was despondent.

"This time, for sure," said Kat.

"Indeed," said Sebastian. "This time Mr Westwood has agreed to help us. He will cut the ties that keep her attached to this world. If we are very lucky, he will take both her and that dark child creature with him when he goes."

There was no hope to be found in Mabel's face. None. This matched the look in Sebastian's face. Kat knew what Seb wasn't saying: Lil was also a lynchpin. And Lil was near the end of her resources.

It was like old times, hearing those words: "Give me my blue cardigan." Except that this time, it was different. This time they knew the danger.

The luring of the vampire cat had worked like a dream. They had managed to make her follow them from the Japanese Chancellery buildings down street after street, first chasing Kat and then Lil and then Sebastian and then Kat again.

Mabel picked up Lil in the car and refused to let her take another stint. "They can manage without you. They're big and strong," she scolded. Lil was pale as a feather.

"It wasn't just the cat," she said. "We thought it was. The cat is in league with the shadow child. And the shadow child commands the whispers."

"She was lying to us?" Mabel's voice was sharp. "She's the dark child."

Lil nodded. "I can feel it. She's no longer hiding."

"All the more reason for you to keep your strength. We're going to need all of us. Kat said to give you this, by the way." 'This' turned out to be a bar of chocolate. The two women shared it as they waited for their friends to appear. Sebastian came along soon and helped them and so did Jackey-Jackey. "Eating while you can, I see," said Mabel acerbically. Westwood smiled and reached across her for another piece.

Kat finally caught up with them. "Ann's got it," she said. "She thinks she can do the last leg. The vampire cat thing is hooked — will chase anyone now. Just as well, given."

"Given?" Sebastian's voice demanded an answer.

"The whispers. They're chasing us up the street."

"You can still walk?"

"No problems — they want us to go in that direction. They're herding us."

"So we want to be where the dark child wants us," said the bushranger.

"God, I'm scared," said Mabel.

"When in doubt, eat chocolate," said Kat, bravely.

"We've run out," said Sebastian.

"Then it's just as well I got more," and she hauled a second bar out of her bag. They had hardly started on it, though, when Ann appeared at the end of the street. Not far after her stalked the cat. Large, elegant, very dangerous, it matched her step for step. Ann looked ragged and tired and kept looking round.

Kat moved to open the car door. "Not yet," whispered Jackey-Jackey. "We follow them into the park."

"But she looks so alone."

"Yet still, she must do it."

And so they waited and watched and waited and watched, huddled in Mabel's car.

"Now!" said Jack, as Ann stepped onto the green grass.

They followed the cat that followed Ann. The cat didn't notice them. This was fortunate, because the moment their feet hit the grass, everything became whispers. Dark whispers. Dangerous whispers. Nightmares of the soul.

And just ahead of them all was the shadow of a girl crying, mockingly, "Give me my blue cardigan. Give me my blue cardigan." She turned her empty face. The dark child looked at them directly, pushed her sullied dark into Kat's eyes and said, "NOW."

The whispers rose through the ground like tattered leaves. They wisped around Kat's feet until Kat looked down and found that her ankles were no longer visible. She looked across at the vampire and discovered it had taken its female form. It was looking across at her, satisfied.

"Stupid," she said. "We were stupid."

"Speak for yourself," said Mabel. She and Jackey-Jackey had their whips and they lashed at the vampire cat. The woman's form yowled to the hushed world, but the dark child didn't move to help. "I don't need you anymore,"

247

the child said. The vampire snarled and hissed. The whips snaked again. She turned back into a cat and fled.

"There once were two cats of Kilkenny," said Mabel.

"Give me my blue cardigan," mocked the shadow child. Kat looked down and the darkness welled up her calves.

"Do you know what I can give you?" asked Kat. She had no idea what she was saying, but she had to say something. She didn't like the feeling of being trapped in a sea of evil whispers.

The dark child turned its empty face at her. "You? What have you to give?"

"Can't show you if you don't let me close," Kat said.

The shadow wavered uncertainly. "Why would you give me anything?"

"Why did my friends give you a raincoat and a jumper and a blue cardigan?"

"Because it's a charm." The evil voice was on certain ground here. "Because it banishes ghosts."

"Except you're not a ghost, are you? The blue cardigan couldn't banish you. Even when you got your own shadow back, no-one could get rid of you. You can tell all the evil whispers in the world who to talk to and how to behave." said Kat. "You're special. Very, very special."

"I'm special."

"And I know what to give special children. My parents taught me that."

"I don't know the rules for this." The voice was suddenly plaintive.

"It's easy. I give you the special things that my father gave me and you do what I did. Those rules worked for me. They must be right."

"You're sure I'm special?"

"I am certain-sure. You're more special than anyone."

"Do you need to come close for this?"

"I can't give you things from this far away, can I?"

"You can come close," the child said. "But not the others. They can keep on dying."

Kat looked and saw shadows swarming around everyone, like a rising tide. Their faces were already hidden, their mouths silenced. In a few minutes all her friends would be drowned in darkness. *What if it doesn't work? No time to think about that. Just gotta do it.* She stepped forward. Wisps of dark trailed after each step Kat took, but she ignored it and stepped forward stubbornly.

Up close, the dark child was a well of emptiness and sorrow. Kat hated herself for what she was about to do. She hated herself but she did not say badkat. She hated herself but she opened her bag anyway. She hated herself, but she loved Lil and Mabel and even Ann more than she hated herself and if she could save them from the shadows, she would. Even if it meant she was cursed forever.

The first thing she took from the bag was a sheet of stickers.

"It was the last thing Dad bought me," Kat said, confidingly. "The very last thing, ever. He said he'd never give me anything else. But I'm giving it to you because you're special."

The sheet of stickers faded into the darkness of the child.

"There is a second thing," Kat said. "I need to give you a big hug. Special people give big hugs. My mother taught me this. It was the last thing she did for me. She didn't give me stickers." She leaned into the black and wrapped her arms around it as if it was a real child and she thought of how much she loved her mother and how much she missed her. She shared that love with all her might.

"Interesting," said the child. "But not so special."

"But that's not all," Kat said. She was stung. But that was good. She built the hurt up inside. "I need to tell you what my father told me and give you one thing he gave me that I will never, ever forget."

The child smiled. You never want to see a dark child smile. There is no mirth. No happiness. No face.

"Give me what your father gave you."

"You accept it freely?"

"Oh, yes." The evil voice expressed nothing but pleasure.

"Fine."

Kat took one very small step back, swung her arm back and landed the heaviest blow she could on the child's face. The face coiled back in shock, then composed itself again, waiting. "He said, 'You will obey me, always, or you will leave and never, ever come back.' He gave me the stickers two days later."

"You obeyed him?" The child's voice was suddenly small. A whisper of a whisper.

"No. Why should I obey him? He hurt me. I left. I've never seen him since. Not once. I never went back."

"You hurt me. I shall leave. I don't like your bargain." A whisper of dark and it was as if the shadows and rustles and fear had never been.

Lil was lying down. Mabel was making tea. Ann had gone home. Jackey-Jackey and Kat were looking over Sebastian's shoulder and making whatever comments they thought suitable. It was as if that time with the dark child had never happened. Yet it had, and they were all changed by it.

Seb was trying to work out if the banishing was forever, or could be made to be forever. He had refused Lil's help because he was worried about her (and said so) and refused Mabel's help because, as Mabel had said, he was "a stubborn git." Eventually his pencil and paper calculations caused him to look up.

"Well, this is a surprise," he said. "Not quite as I had calculated it earlier."

"Jack can stay?" Mabel was jubilant.

"No," said Seb. "They've not gone very far. If Westwood travels a sufficient distance, the child won't be able to come back and the cat will lose its power, and if he stays, this will be to do all over again. He should leave as soon as possible." Sebastian gave Westwood a shrug of apology.

"Let's give Mabel and Jack some time alone," suggested Ann. They all moved off a respectable distance. Kat kept sneaking looks at the couple, until Lil firmly took her hand and pulled her around the corner, out of sight.

"Time to go." Jackey-Jackey looked as if he didn't care.

"You'll still be round, though." Mabel didn't try to hide the fact that she did.

"An echo, that's all." Westwood sounded bitter. He looked at his shoes. "Not me anymore," he said to those shoes.

"Kat thinks we should have a romantic farewell."

"Stuff Kat. We do things our way."

"Yes," said Mabel. She suddenly wished that the flirting and the romance had lasted into that sudden discovery of love. It would have made the moment easier.

"If I don't go, that cat woman will come back. And the shadow."

"I know. You've got to go. It's just . . ."

"I've got a present for you. Seb reckons he's done something to it. It'll stay here after I'm faded." Mabel's eyes started brimming. "Don't do that, woman!"

"A hug then."

"A hug and a kiss and a faretheewell and then I'm gone. Take this first."

'This' turned out to be his stockwhip. "That Adam's still around and you need two stockwhips to deal with his kind." There was a silence, and then, "I wanted to give you some jewellery. All mine went when Lil's appeared. It's gone."

"It was stolen anyway."

"The stockwhip wasn't. I bought it in Goulburn. Good bit of stuff, there."

And they hugged. And they kissed. And then it was fare thee well. He was gone.

Ann rang Kat. "I need you to help me pack," she said. "I'm going to the South Coast and there are just too many possessions and too many boxes and I want you to just shove everything in and get it ready for the removalist."

"I can do that." Kat wore her obedient voice. It was the safest of all voices with Ann. Kat had no idea what Ann was thinking, though she wasn't surprised that she had finally made the decision to leave Canberra.

The work went quickly, largely because Ann was more organised than she had sounded. Kat didn't like it when some of the things she was supposed to be packing ended up in a pile that was for herself. Ann insisted on giving and Kat didn't know how to refuse. It made this last day together uncomfortable, and Kat didn't know what to say to that, either. She wished she could just shrug and accept the goodies.

At the very end of the tiring day, Ann brought out a wrapped present. She brought it out cautiously. Kat opened it then and there. Underneath the elegant silver paper, she discovered a big soft beautiful leather-bound book.

"I thought you could use it for your Book of Shadows," Ann said, almost diffidently.

Kat thanked her profusely and inwardly cringed. Ann still thought that Kat was the same person as she had been last January. And she wasn't. Kat would use the book and love it, but she didn't need a Book of Shadows. She was going to get her great-whichever grandparents to teach her their magic. Jewish magic. Or fairy magic. Maybe both. And besides, besides . . . she thought of her little diary in the room, hiding the golden haze. She thought of the Melusine stories. It was too dangerous to write things down. Except maybe poetry. She could fill her book with glorious poetry.

A few days later she was given the inspiration for her very first poem.

They were difficult days. Mabel was being brave and pretending nothing hurt. Lil spent most of her time resting. Seb was busy with his papers and his diagrams, trying to save his beloved. That morning, Lil had told Kat she needed to go for a walk.

"I want to try something," she said. "Just one more thing."

"Can't I help?" Kat hated sounding plaintive.

"I must do this thing, even though it is a thing I've never done before."

"But it'll work?" Kat hated sounding so worried.

"I don't know, my love, but I want to do it, and I need space and time."

"I will take Sebastian with me," Kat declared, "and get him out of your way."

"I wouldn't do that." Lil smiled and Kat felt squicky.

"It's not what you're thinking of," reassured Lil. "He may not like what I will do."

"But if it even has a chance of working," Kat said, the words pushing out of her mouth in hurry, in hope, "then you've gotta try."

"And try I will. Go for your walk."

So Kat went for a walk, alone. Her brave new world was falling to pieces. They'd saved everyone except themselves. She didn't want to walk. She wanted to cry. Kat didn't believe in Lil's solution. Lil's eyes showed that she didn't believe in it, either. How could something work when everyone had given up?

So Kat was walking in the park, forlorn. She heard Lil's voice. Then she realised she hadn't heard Lil's voice at all. She looked around, and the only adult nearby was a young mother, chasing after her children, laughing. Lil called again. Kat realised at that moment that Lil's voice was in her mind. What was Lil's voice doing in her mind? Was Lil dead? Is this what happened when fairies died? Inside her, something snapped.

Then Lil's voice took on words. "Look up," it said and so she did.

A golden winged creature filled the air with its glory, with its shining scales, and with its lashing serpent's tail.

"Me," said the voice in her mind, young and powerful and oblivious to everything that had gone before. "Watch me fly." And so Kat watched Lil in all her melusine splendour cavort in the crystal air. Golden and bronze and full of grace and light. The rest of Canberra was oblivious. The young mother still chased her children around the trees. Only Kat saw the dream and the beauty.

Then Lil flicked her tail one last time and was gone into the heavens.

❖ ◆ ❖

Kat went back to the house, smiling. No-one was there. It didn't matter. Lil had found her creature-self. She wasn't dying any longer.

A few days later she had not yet returned home. Kat was worried. She rang Mabel. "I mean, she changed shape and flew and they just went and I haven't seen either of them."

"She'll be back," said Mabel, sanguinely. "They're having a romantic getaway."

"But when? Do I do the shopping for all three of us or just for me? And do I use Lil's money and pay her back if she doesn't come, or what?"

"Keep all the receipts," Mabel advised. "Buy just enough fresh food for one meal for all three of you and a few days' worth for yourself. Then wait."

"Easy for you to say," grumbled Kat, but she put the phone down before she said it. She went in search of Lil's purse, feeling desperately guilty. Before she got further than the hall, she heard a fumble at the door. It was locked and all the keys were inside. Kat raced to see who it was.

It was Sebastian.

"You shoulda knocked," Kat said, "or rung the bell."

"I didn't think of that," he confessed.

"Where's Lil?"

"She's fixing our papers. Be here right away."

"Our papers?" Kat was suspicious, but she still put the kettle on.

"We married," said Sebastian with dignity. "Again."

His eyes looked shifty. "What was wrong?" Kat was imperious.

"She proposed to me. Women do not propose!"

Kat thought how very good for Sebastian that was, and smiled, then she realised the obvious. "Without me?"

"It was easier outside the country. We . . . er . . . bought our papers."

"And now?"

"Lil wanted to get started on applying for citizenship. She's claiming Australian parents and I'm claiming marriage to her."

"That takes forever."

"Normally, yes." Sebastian sat down. "She has some odd abilities, you know."

"If I missed the wedding, can we at least have a party or something?"

253

"Maybe."

They argued about suitable celebrations until someone came in the door. "Didn't you close it?" Kat accused Sebastian. He was hopeless.

A delicately beautiful young lady with rich dark hair and supple olive skin walked through to the kitchen and sat down with them.

"All done?" asked Sebastian and put his arm around her.

"Lil?" Kat couldn't believe it. She blinked and rubbed her eyes.

The woman laughed a warm laugh and suddenly Kat knew this young woman was Lil. "I have decided that I am Melusine," she told them both. "My own granddaughter. Your cousin who you ran to when you needed help. My parents, alas, are dead."

"I thought you decided on Elizabeth," Sebastian complained. "I really liked the thought of Elizabeth."

"Melusine," said Lil, firmly. "All the papers say this: it must be so."

"Are you going to tell Mabel, or am I?" Kat demanded.

"We shall let Mabel think it through for herself."

"And Ann?"

"Where is she?"

"She went to the South Coast. She's buying a small place there. She says she never wants to see any ghosts or magic ever again."

"If she finds us, then we shall see," Lil said.

Kat thought it through. "So you've inherited your own stuff?"

"Yes."

"Then you have to tell Mabel. She won't believe you're your own granddaughter. Not Mabel. And you have to be buried. I mean, we need a funeral. They do it in all the best movies. A fake funeral."

"All the best movies?" Sebastian teased her.

"Yes." Kat lifted her chin to show she was going to stand firm on this.

"Why a funeral, really?" asked Lil.

"Mabel. Can't find Jackey-Jackey — she needs to say goodbye."

"She needs closure." Lil nodded.

"He can't come back without a bridge between worlds, and I reckoned that with you two there and a funeral, there ought to be one."

"I like the thought," said Sebastian, his free hand drawing circles on the tablecloth. "It should work."

"Let us bury my grandmother, then," said Lil, gently.

A few days later they were at the cemetery, pretending sadness.

"Is it strange being at your own funeral and inheriting your own possessions?"

"I never quite get used to it," Lil/Melusine said.

"I do," said her husband. "You might too." This last was directed at the teenager.

"What do you mean?" Kat rounded on him, her eyes snapping a demand to know.

"Who knows what your bloodline gives you?"

"My family is human, you know. You two are just strange." Kat loved giving Seb cheek. It brightened her world more than almost anything else.

"My little great-great granddaughter, your human family didn't spend enough time with their fairy kin to be anything but ordinary."

"Kat has never been ordinary," said Mabel, returned from her rather sadder farewell, putting an arm round the teenager's shoulder.

"I'm going to assume I'm human. Sorry if that upsets you. But if I turn out to be and have wasted my life because I think there's going to be more, well . . ."

"You'll feel damned silly when you die," said Mabel.

"That's it," Kat said.

"Have you finished farewelling yourself?" the love of her life asked Lil.

"I need coffee."

"I need something stronger. Burials are thirsty business."

Epilogue

TIME PASSES, EVEN IN Canberra when it has its fairy tale moment. All fairy tale moments end: this is inextricably linked to time passing. This particular fairy tale moment ended with dying days of the year. It ended as it had begun, with a dinner party.

It was a dinner party for four. Lil used it as an excuse to teach Kat just a few more of her favourite dishes. They made almond biscuits to go with the coffee, and eggplant and cheese pastries, and various fried snacks for Chanukah. There was bread and olives and there were round fried pastries that Lil insisted on calling rosquillas even though the others couldn't pronounce the word. There were far too many chocolates. Lil took especial joy in bringing out roast eggs (served in halves with red vinegar and parsley dressing).

Everything was brought out at once and everyone nibbled their way through. Kat noticed that Sebastian avoided quite a few of the dishes. When she found herself in the kitchen with Lil (both trying to replenish supplies) she asked her, "Does he have dietary restrictions?"

"No, dear, it's his background. He is wonderful in all other respects, but he has no tastebuds. I was going to educate him, but he ran away."

"He says he got lost."

"He did, but that doesn't mean I shall be nice to him about it."

"Why doesn't he have tastebuds?"

"That's a good question. If he had been born a hundred years later, in London, he would have an excuse. He was born near Chepstow, however, in Wales, at the end of the seventeenth century. Maybe the food wasn't as good as the rest of Britain."

"Or maybe his mother couldn't cook?"

"His mother's chef, dear. He was born into a rather nice family. His father was very human."

"So his mother is like you and his father was Welsh."

"English. It's complicated."

"I bet you can't change his eating habits."

Lil laughed. "I bet I can."

"What do we bet?"

"I teach you if you lose."

"And if I win?"

"I still teach you."

"So either way I win?"

"Or lose — it depends on how you handle that side of yourself. It's not always a blessing."

"Better to understand it, though."

"Always."

On the smallest side table was Ann's farewell card, open for everyone to read. From time to time one of the women would pick it up or glance at it or nod in its direction, including Ann in everything in the only way they could.

In one corner of the lounge room there was a small Christmas tree. An elegant Christmas tree. Decorated in silver and white, with just a touch of Goth. It was Kat's corner and it was Kat's tree. Lil had created it as a surprise present. As a second surprise, she had put a Christmas pudding and custard under wraps there, for Kat to "open." Kat shared it with everyone, but insisted they sit in her Christmas corner to eat it. "Everywhere else is Jewish," she explained.

After they had eaten, they couldn't move. Kat dragged herself from her nice bit of floor and made coffee. When everyone had a cup, she asked the question that had been fretting at her. "What will happen when I get older?"

"I'll stay as long as I can," said Lil. "Both of us will. Then you can visit us, for as long as you live."

"I'm scared it'll be like Peter Pan," confessed Kat.

"How is this?"

"You'll forget."

"I will never forget you. I know you as well as I know your own name."

"You don't actually know my name," Kat confessed.

"How is this?"

"I called myself Kat when I left home. I needed to tell you. That's why I wanted to talk. I rang my parents again and we talked again. I'm going back home and finishing school. I don't like it, but I need to face my father. He needs to learn. And I need to stop being scared. If he won't stop, Mum says she'll help. But if it doesn't work out, can I stay in your granny flat? And if it does work out and if I come to uni in Canberra, can I stay in your granny flat? And will you still teach me stuff?"

"We will keep everything safe for you. I shall teach you."

There was a pleasant silence.

"I'm using my own name from now on," Kat said, into the silence. "You can still call me Kat, but I thought I should be all of myself now. After all, I've changed so much."

"You have grown up."

"Yes. Gwendolyn wasn't right for an unhappy child, but it's right for me."

"Gwendolyn: it suits you." Lil's face showed that she was thinking of another Gwendolyn, long dead.

"My middle name is Justina — it suits me too, now, I think. They're both family names. And 'Melusine' suits you. I like it that your name is also what you are."

Melusine laughed with the same warm laugh she had always had, as Lil.

Life was worth living, when one had friends, a lover and a great-great-granddaughter.

Acknowledgements

Karen Herkes, for the gift of Canberra's ghosts

Clarrie Burgmeister, for his knowledge of stockwhips.

Lesley Rose, Sonya Oberman and Elyse Buchhorn — for helping me sort out sufficient background so that each generation was not embarrassingly wrong in what they knew. Lesley is guilty of introducing me to Crash Craddock.

Ros Trasker — for Mabel's garden.

Rachel McGrath Kerr — for helping me with various aspects of the book, especially Weston Park and for introducing me to that coffee machine.

Canberra Speculative Fiction Guild for maybe one of the oddest beta reads I've ever experienced. I hope you've all recovered.

All my friends — for sanity during a very tough year.

The members of Book View Café, but especially Vonda N. McIntyre, Marissa Doyle, and Maya Kaathryn Bohnhoff.

About the Author

Gillian Polack is an Australian novelist, editor and historian. Her hobbies include reading, cooking and making bad jokes.

.

About Book View Café

Book View Café Publishing Cooperative is an author-owned cooperative of over fifty professional writers, publishing in a variety of genres such as fantasy, romance, mystery, and science fiction.

BVC authors include *New York Times* and *USA Today* bestsellers; Nebula, Hugo, and Philip K. Dick Award winners; World Fantasy Award, Campbell Award, and RITA Award nominees; and winners and nominees of many other publishing awards.

Since its debut in 2008, BVC has gained a reputation for producing high-quality e-books, and is now bringing that same quality to its print editions.

Printed in Great Britain
by Amazon

36168134R00158